Satan's Shadow

Satans Shadow

KENNETH J MUNKENS

ISBN 978-0-966-3951-5-0

 Published by:
Minther & Sklar
P.O. Box 2903
Matthews, North Carolina 28106

Printed in the U.S.A.

Writing is a lonely task. You must step into your mind to discover vast worlds, unique characters, and uncommon situations. That very act separates you from the real world. Indeed, while one can get lost among the visions and shadows, it is there where the writer finds fertile fields from which to harvest. Satan's Shadow is dedicated to Michael Faletti a unique character who resides in the real world. For years I have valued his knowledge, insights, and sense-of-humor. A simple conversation with him often sets the creative wheels turning. Mike is a friend, thinker, philosopher, and inspiration.

CHAPTER 1

"I crawled through a river of shit to save your life and that's what you got?" Adam "Watch Dog" Hayes spat.

"Sorry, I couldn't do better!" Michael "Owl" O'Neal replied.

"Hell, I bleed more than that after shaving."

"You shave your legs?" Owl asked while holding a pressure bandage on a leg wound to his left calf.

"Doesn't everybody?"

The firefight began when a foreign government patrol they were with was ambushed by insurgents. Adam "Watch Dog" Hayes and Michael "Owl" O'Neal, two mercenaries, were assisting the ruling regime troops. When the first government soldier dropped the two seasoned combatants dove for cover. Owl caught one in the leg. At the same time the remaining members of the government patrol fled, leaving the two Americans to fend for themselves.

Watch Dog looked around. They were in a ravine through which ran a small muddy stream. The insurgents held the high ground which gave them a distinct advantage. It was an advantage they would likely improve upon quickly.

Small arms fire emanating from the direction that the government troops had run told the colleagues that their fair-weather friends didn't get very far.

"You have any grenades?" Adam asked Michael.

"Yeah—two."

"OK, I also have two." A bullet whizzed by kicking up a small dirt cloud.

"What's your plan?" Michael O'Neal asked.

"I'm going to take the four grenades, leave you here, and escape."

"How fast can you run with a bullet up your ass?" Owl asked, not liking the idea of being left behind.

"I'd say that's pretty good incentive to run really fast," Adam deadpanned. "OK, here's what I got. These guys aren't very good shots."

"They hit me, for chrissakes!"

"A lucky shot."

"Not lucky for me."

"Oh, quit cryin' like a little girl. It's not like you got hit in the nuts," Adam snickered and added, "Of course, then you would cry like a little girl."

Adam "Watch Dog" Hayes and Michael "Owl" O'Neal devised their plan. Another two or five bullets hit objects around them.

Owl arched his neck, raised his M-16 and took out the shooter.

"Nice shot."

"I would do a lot better with my M110." He referred to his semi-automatic sniper rifle manufactured by the Knights Armament Company used by U.S. Army snipers.

Another insurgent showed himself and Michael eliminated him.

"You keep that up and we won't have to escape."

"That's the idea. Let them know there is a price to pay if they want to kill Americans."

Adam Hayes looked at his partner. A retired Army sniper, Michael "Owl" O'Neal, had the ruddy complexion and curly red hair of a good Irishman. His red mustache was a source of pride for the man whose facial hair grew relatively slowly. At five feet ten inches in height he wasn't the biggest man in their unit, but he did have the largest heart. Many a drunken brute who knocked Owl down with a sucker punch found himself going one-on-one with a mad man. Michael was fast, powerful, and resilient. If an opponent was lucky enough to knock him down again—he didn't stay down. Owl would come back again and again until he wore his opponent down. As a sniper, he not only was extremely accurate at great distances he also had quick reflexes in close order situations, which was what they were in at present.

"Run over there and when they show themselves to shoot you I'll pick them off," Owl instructed Adam.

"Are you nuts? What if five of them take aim?"

"I'll shoot fast."

"I have a better idea." The two longtime friends discussed their escape plan.

Part of the plan was for Adam "Watch Dog" Hayes to carry Michael O'Neal out of their fix. Michael knew his six foot two, two hundred pound, in-perfect-condition cohort was capable of carrying him. It was a matter of at what speed he could do it. Watch Dog was an ex-Green Beret who didn't have the capacity for fear. He simply followed orders, or executed his own plans without considering the risk. That was not to say that he didn't think about the odds or consider potential unpleasant outcomes, they were always there so why dwell upon them. At one time, he had been married and had a daughter. Too much war and too many firefights made him undomesticatable. He never did anything aggressive toward his family, but he was keenly aware that strangers had to "beware of dog." Split-second reactions that kept you alive in the bush made you dangerous on civilized pavement. Owl witnessed, more than once, what could happen and understood his friend's decision to distance himself from innocent, good, kind, unsuspecting souls.

"You feeling strong?" Owl asked Watch Dog.

"I'm feeling a little off. I might drop you."

"So, that's a yes?"

"You ready to kick up some dust?" Adam Hayes asked as a bullet pinged off a rock.

"Roger that!"

Adam pulled the pin on a grenade, counted one, two, and tossed it onto the bank of the stream in the direction they planned to run. When it exploded a cloud of dust and debris rose into the air. The two soldiers jumped up, Adam flung his friend over his shoulders, and proceeded along the stream. Shots rang out but the retreating mercenaries were slightly obscured therefore more difficult to hit. Adam tossed a second grenade onto the bank ahead and after it did its job ran under the cover of another cloud of dust. A third grenade got them to a stand of trees where they had a far better chance of defending themselves. They located a good defensive position and dropped behind a fallen log.

Insurgents attempted to follow the two men, but after Michael dropped the third one they withdrew.

Both mercenaries knew their future did not lie back at the ruling government installation, so they made their way in the direction of the border with a friendly nation.

"By my reckoning, it's two or three clicks to the border," Adam stated.

"A walk in the park," was Michael O'Neal's reply.

A day and a half later, two tired Americans crossed the border and found refuge in a small village. A local ersatz doctor cleaned Owl's wound.

After a little negotiating, they procured a ride in a fifties vintage Chevrolet station wagon. A few hours later, they were in a large city at an American consulate. As mercenaries, their status was tenuous, at best.

They were questioned by consulate personnel, local police, national police, U.S. military, and U.N. representatives.

"It seems our previous employers want us back in their country to stand trial for killing their soldiers," Adam told Michael after a conversation with the consulate liaison.

"Right, we killed them while being shot at by insurgents."

"I told them you did it."

"Thanks."

Adam "Watch Dog" Hayes sat next to his friend. He fumbled with a challenge coin that had been given to him by General Maxwell Hughes after a successful, high risk, clandestine rescue mission. When they shook hands, the General slipped the coin into, then Master Sergeant, Hayes' hand.

Challenge coins originated during World War I. In 1917, American volunteers traveled to Europe and joined flying squadrons in support of the French. The United States had not yet entered the war. A particular squadron had bronze medallions forged that were given to members of the unit. One pilot wore his medallion in a small leather pouch around his neck. During one battle when his plane became damaged and he crash landed he was captured by German soldiers. They took away all his identification but overlooked the leather pouch around his neck. At a later date, he escaped and made it through the German lines wearing civilian clothes. Unfortunately, he was captured by the French who accused him of being a saboteur. Had it not been for the challenge coin he carried in a small leather pouch displaying his flying unit insignia he might have been executed. After that event, all pilots carried medallions. It became a social game to ask to see the medallion. When challenged if a coin was not produced the unit member was required to buy the challenger a drink of his choice. Conversely, if a coin was shown the challenger paid for the drinks.

Over the years challenge coins were used by different military units in various conflicts. In 1969, Army Colonel Verne Green, Commander of the 10th Special Forces Group-A, gave his men coins with the unit's crest and motto on them. By the 1980s more and more military units embraced the idea.

The challenge coin carried by Adam "Watch Dog" Hayes was unique in that it was not for a designated military unit. Nor was it ever asked for in a social setting. Indeed, if one did see it, they would have no idea what it was or represented. On the front was a dragon, sword, and a circle of thirteen stars. The reverse had the words inscribed; Est ultra de tenebris et in umbra satanas. He had no idea how many of those coins were in existence or who carried them.

"I just found out that we have transport back to the States," Adam told Michael.

"Great, I'm ready to get back home and retire. There's just too much nonsense going on anymore for my taste," the ex-sniper admitted.

"Yeah, it's getting harder and harder to know who are the good guys and who are the bad guys."

"It's pretty clear that we aren't making a tinker's damn of difference."

"The world, my friend, has become a very confusing and mixed-up place," Watch Dog concluded as he raised his glass of what the locals called beer.

"I have a small farm in the western part of Virginia," Owl replied, "Think I'll raise horses, sit on the porch, and let someone else figure it out."

Adam Hayes nodded his head in agreement. It was time to fold the tents. He didn't have any place to go or anyone waiting to greet him. In essence, when he stepped off the aircraft, he could go in any direction and get to his undefined destination. One positive fact that was true was that a good mercenaries' compensation often was considerable. Of course, one has to live long enough to enjoy it. Anyway, money was not an issue. However, Adam Hayes, at forty-two years old, was starting over.

"It's been quite a ride," Owl continued, "I've kinda grown accustomed to your ugly puss."

"Ah, now don't go getting all sentimental on me," Watch Dog countered.

"Shut the fuck up! I'm trying to tell you if you ever need a safe LZ in the world you're welcome at FFP anytime."

"FFP? Final Firing Position? Nice name for a horse ranch."

"I thought so."

Two brothers-in-arms who faced death numerous times, watched each other's back, and developed a level of trust most never realize parted company at Kennedy Airport late on a spring evening. The expectation was that they might never see one another again. How far wrong that prediction was neither could have imagined.

CHAPTER 2

His given name was Darius Holiday, but he went by his self-adopted Muslim name Ihtsham Azlan which translates to "strong lion." Born in Wilkes-Barre, Pennsylvania, Darius grew up in a coal town. He played basketball relatively well in high school and hoped for an athletic scholarship to college—any college. Unfortunately, his academic performance held him back. And, who scouts high schools in Wilkes-Barre, anyway? No offer was forthcoming leaving Darius, aka Ihtsham Azlan, no alternative but to join the shadowy figures that trudge to coal mines before dawn only to return home filthy and exhausted after a long grueling shift.

Something, even he couldn't define, made Darius feel out-of-place and alone. He had no direction, sense-of-self, or clearly defined value system. Life had deteriorated to a long, torturous, boring, routine. His only escape was the used computer purchased a few years earlier that allowed him to surf the world wide web. It began with simple searches, which led to checking sports scores, watching video highlights, and finally pornography. Then late on a Saturday night he came upon a video that seemed to speak directly to him.

An Imam spoke of Islam as being the one true answer to all the world's problems. Without clearly defined rules and strict adherence to them there would always be chaos and corruption in the world. Hedonists had captured power and were taking advantage of others for their own personal gain. The answer was Islam which literally means submission to the will of God. It was possible for one to bring meaning and order to their life. Darius Holiday became a regular viewer of the Imam's videos, visited mosques, read the Quran, and eventually converted to Islam in his mind. He found a level of peace in this new life.

As his web surfing widened Ihtsham Azlan found more and more radical Islamic videos and websites. After a while they began to make sense. Capitalism was keeping the poor down. Western nations were perverting human morals. Jews were persecuting innocent Muslims. It was clearer than ever that Sharia law was the only answer. But, misguided infidels ignored the answer. They turned their backs on Allah and were beneath contempt condemned to the depths of hell. Violence was not only needed but warranted by the Quran. Pictures of innocent babies killed by American bombers angered him. Military convoys in the Middle East where they didn't belong angered him. Women walking down Main Street in Wilkes-Barre wearing skimpy outfits angered him. Gay men holding hands angered him. Television programs angered him. Rich businessmen angered him. Everything he was exposed to angered him. Ihtsham Azlan's feeling of peace boiled into militaristic outrage.

Over the next three months, Ihtsham Azlan built two pressure cooker bombs. This was accomplished using detailed plans from one of the radical websites. He wanted, no needed, to make a dramatic statement to awaken the United States to the error of its policies and way of life. If they would not live a moral life under Sharia, they would die for their sins. Only, Wilkes-Barre, Pennsylvania was not the appropriate venue for such a lesson.

Slowly and methodically, Ihtsham Azlan devised a plan to deliver an unambiguous message. On a Saturday morning, he loaded his barely running used car and headed south on U.S. Highway 476. He passed Allentown, then drove west on U.S. 276, U.S. 202, and U.S. 30 which became the main street of his ultimate destination the city of Thorndale. Rather than a city Thorndale was a small 1.8-mile business district with less than two-thousand households. It was most famous for the fact that it is where President James Buchanan had his summer home. However, over the years the structure had been converted into a restaurant and surrounded by a golf course. None of this was of interest to Ihtsham Azlan. What was of interest to him was the fact that it is the last stop on SEPTA's Paoli/Thorndale Line which carries passengers to downtown Philadelphia. In addition, there were plenty of places for him to inconspicuously park his car.

At 11:39 a.m. Ihtsham Azlan boarded the train and rode to the Jefferson Station at 11th and 12th Streets in downtown Philadelphia. The ride took an hour and ten minutes. Above the rail station was the Gallery at Market East Mall. It was the largest of all indoor malls in center city. The retail facility stretched out over three blocks and had 120 stores on four levels, as well as a food court, gym, and a fish market. There was where the lesson would be taught.

To Ihtsham Azlan's surprise the once magnificent and flourishing mall had deteriorated to a more than half-empty edifice with discount and low-quality/low-price stores. Homeless people congregated in empty stores, teenagers roamed about and fought with each other, the food court was unhygienic, and dark corridors hid activities better kept unknown. At first, he was disappointed. Then he realized it would allow him to execute his plan at a much lower level of risk. Neither were there any guards to contend with nor many employees who might be too observant. He returned home to make final preparations.

A week later Ihtsham Azlan returned to Thorndale. He had two pressure cooker bombs inside two gym bags in a suitcase with a handle and wheels. The combination of explosives and nails made the suitcase heavy. However, the plastic wheels on the suitcase hid that fact. By all appearances he was innocently traveling. Once again, he boarded SEPTA's Paoli/Thorndale Line at 11:39 a.m. During the hour and ten-minute ride Ihtsham Azlan found he was excited, mentally, physically, and sexually. It struck him as strange. The thought of doing Allah's work brought him to new heights. He Darius Holiday, nae Ihtsham Azlan, was a strong lion sent to rid the world of infidels and aggressors. His life would then have meaning. His name would be remembered and feared.

"Those who believe, fight in the Cause of Allah, and those who disbelieve, fight in the cause of Satan. So, fight you against the friends of Satan; Ever feeble indeed is the plot of Satan."

His act would be just and necessary as those who fight for Allah are required to do so. Holy Quran (9:5) "And when the forbidden months have passed, kill the idolaters wherever you find them and take them prisoners, and beleaguer them, and lie in wait for them at every place of ambush. But if they repent and observe Prayer and pay the Zakat, then leave their way free. Surely, Allah is Most Forgiving, Merciful."

The train rolled to a stop in the Jefferson Station. Ihtsham Azlan exited onto the platform pulling his suitcase behind him. As he did he looked around for any sign of police or other authorities who might thwart his plan. The station was relatively empty. As he recalled, it was not well kept with garbage strewn about, overflowing trash baskets, and the ever-pungent odor of urine. He made his way into the lower level of the Gallery at Market East Mall.

Immediately, a panhandler approached him. The grimy man with few teeth walked toward Ihtsham Azlan with his hand out mumbling. He was rewarded with a dollar bill. Charity was one of the five pillars of Islam. When he handed the man the money, Ihtsham Azlan thought, "Your troubles will end soon."

Slowly and very carefully, the strong lion walked down a dark corridor to the restrooms. Filth and garbage reflected a long-neglected facility. Two men were in the men's room sharing a needle. They neither acknowledged his arrival nor attempted to hide what they were doing. In addition, they ignored the fact that he had opened his suitcase and removed one of the gym bags. Silently, Ihtsham Azlan made his way back to the food court. The lunchtime crowd caused the area to be half full. Teenagers sat around at various tables smoking, cursing, fighting, and carrying out different sexual acts. The few eateries that were operating seemed dark and dirty. Odors, foul and putrid, filled the air. To his delight he found one of the center tables empty. Darius Holiday, aka Ihtsham Azlan, sat.

While trying to remain inconspicuous Ihtsham Azlan glanced around to determine if anyone was looking in his direction. Due to burned out bulbs the lighting was subdued. This worked in his favor. With his foot, he pushed the gym bag to under the center of the table. He believed it would go undiscovered long enough for his plan to work. After a few moments, he rose and left the food court.

After a second trip to the men's room he departed the mall carrying a gym bag and dragging an empty suitcase. As planned, he arrived at the Jefferson Station in time to catch the 1:38 p.m. train. When he boarded he was dragging an empty suitcase.

Two young people carried their tacos to a table in the center of the food court. A girl sixteen and her boyfriend, who was seventeen, were hanging out in the mall. As they ate they clowned around. At one point the boy moved his leg and kicked something under the table. He looked under and said, "Someone left their bag here."

Ihtsham Azlan pressed the last number on his cell phone. A flash of light filled the air in the food court, followed by a loud boom that two young people never heard. Others were struck by flying nails as shrapnel filled the entire area. Acrid smoke rose among the screams. Torn bodies were left in contorted positions around the food court. A fire started at one of the restaurants as grease from a punctured vat hit the flames of the griddle. A fire alarm sounded high above the carnage. Those victims who were ambulatory walked, crawled, or otherwise dragged themselves toward the doors. Those employees who had been spared tried to help the injured.

Police arrived approximately, eight minutes after the blast. Though horrified by the scene they attempted to identify victims who were still alive and render assistance. A sergeant made the decision to evacuate the train platform. At ten minutes after the first bomb was detonated Ihtsham Azlan pressed the last number of the second phone. The gym bag that was hidden under a pile of newspapers at the entrance to Jefferson Station detonated just as the police sergeant passed by. He and seven others in the immediate area were killed instantly by the blast.

Philadelphia became a new ground zero. First responders, even though aware of the risk of there being additional bombs, entered the mall and train station to evacuate the injured. The carnage they encountered was beyond belief. Even seasoned veterans found themselves sickened. Blood, body parts, clothing, food, broken furniture, and unidentifiable debris were strewn everywhere. Police and bomb squad teams moved carefully through the area searching for any additional threats. Sirens were heard outside and streets were cordoned off. A quiet Saturday afternoon had erupted into a cacophony of suffering.

Ihtsham Azlan sat back in his seat to enjoy the ride back to Thorndale. While he had no way of confirming that the bombs did indeed detonate, in his heart he knew that they had brought the wrath of Allah down on the non-believers. In less than an hour he would be back in his car and would then hear the news reports on his radio. When the news was good he would begin his plans for lesson number two.

As adrenaline dissipated, Ihtsham Azlan became fatigued. He whispered, "Allahu Akbar," and fell asleep.

CHAPTER 3

"How do you stand it?" Adam Hayes asked.

Michael O'Neal puffed on his cigar, leaned back in a wooden chair on the spacious porch and replied, "I tell myself every day that I don't have to watch for what is behind every tree, or listen for any out-of-the-ordinary sounds, or plan my next move, or put up with a pain-in-the-ass like you." He smiled, "Makes it real relaxing."

Adam sipped his Scotch. As he looked out over the plush green grass of FFP Ranch he wondered if he could ever find that kind of peace once more. He glanced over at his friend, "How's the leg?"

"Good. I get to enjoy a twinge from time to time, but nothing too bad."

"I really thought you were going to lose that leg," Adam joked.

"My ass!"

"Yeah, that too."

Alice, Michael's wife, walked out onto the porch. Immediately, there was tension in the air. She didn't care for Adam Hayes and had trouble hiding her feelings. Adam was aware of her antipathy and wanted to punch her in the face. Of course, that was simply a passing thought. Why she held him in such disfavor he wasn't sure. The most likely reason, he surmised, was the fact that it was he who convinced Michael "Owl" O'Neal to participate in so many private missions as mercenaries. Was it her fear for her husband's safety or abhorrence of the fact that they were killing people that bothered her? That, Adam couldn't determine and she never gave any clue.

"Good meal, Alice," Adam said as pleasantly as he could muster.

"Thank you."

He then added, "Now, I have a mission I want to discuss with Mike."

Alice stormed off the porch.

"Why do you do that?" Michael asked.

"I don't know. She hates me. Brings out the worst in me."

"Everything brings out the worst in you. Now, I'm going to spend the rest of the night telling her you were joking and that I'm retired."

"Well, in truth," Adam began, "I'm headed to Virginia Beach. There's a meeting. No details. Just a meeting with an unnamed individual. It may require someone with your particular skills."

"If you mean raising horses that's one thing."

"No, asshole, I mean the other thing."

"I'm retired," Michael insisted.

Adam changed the subject. "Last week I was talking to this lady—fine looking lass. We were getting along really well. When the fact that I was ex-military came up suddenly she got all indignant and judgmental. Without knowing a thing about me she told me that she thought I was a horrible individual. At one point she spouts, 'I could never kill another human being.' So, I asked her if her life was at stake wouldn't she fight to defend herself? Her reply was unbelievable." Adam sipped his Scotch then said, "She told me she couldn't kill someone so would probably end up being a victim."

"That's really sad," Michael O'Neal shook his head.

"There's more. I asked if her children were at risk and the only way to save them was to kill the person threatening them would she do it?"

"What did she say?" Michael inquired.

"She gave me an icy stare that caused frostbite on my nose and walked away."

"You struck a nerve."

"I struck the truth." Adam Hayes rose from his chair and walked to the edge of the porch. He looked out at the beauty of nature. There were rare times when he truly appreciated the miracle of Mother Nature and all she offered. He turned to face his friend. "A hunter kills to eat. A police officer kills to protect the public. We kill to defend our way of life. I don't expect everyone to understand. I, also, do not regret what I've done nor feel guilty in any manner, shape, or form. Without us the world's population would live under the yoke of ruthless dictators who have no concern about life."

"That bitch got to you."

"No, a newspaper article got to me," Adam confessed.

"How so?"

"You know that bombing in the Philadelphia mall?"

"I read about it."

"Those bastards killed twenty-three and wounded forty-one. It has all the earmarks of middle eastern terrorism. Ten-minute delay before the second detonation to involve first-responders. Innocent civilians blown to pieces, many with limbs blown off, shrapnel torn bodies, families facing years of suffering and some son-of-a-bitch reporter writes a fucking article wondering what drove the bombers to do it. He could give a shit about innocent people shopping at a mall being murdered. According to him we are at fault. We have to be more understanding of the views of others."

"Sounds to me like surrender," Michael concluded.

"Political correctness is leading to political suicide." Adam "Watch Dog" Hayes walked over to where Michael "Owl" O'Neal sat and stood over his colleague, "Correctness is the wrong word. It's political censorship—if you ask me. Those sick bastards in the government and media condemn any reference to the truth for fear of offending someone somewhere. It's even gotten into our schools. A kid calls another kid a name and it's hate speech. You point out that illegal aliens walking across the border are a threat and you're a racist." Adam sat down and asked his friend, "It's a one-sided sword. I point out something and they cut me up with vile labels and there is no repercussion for their insults."

Michael O'Neal stood, took Adam's glass, entered the house to return shortly with refilled drinks. He handed a glass to Adam, "The world has always been a dangerous place. More dangerous than the average everyday citizen realizes. That's because we and the police are doing our jobs. If we simply went away they would come face-to-face with a truth that they are not prepared to handle."

"Roger that," Adam raised his glass.

"Listen, Adam, I am retired. I don't regret what I've done. In fact, I'm proud to have fought on the right side," he paused, "most of the time."

Adam smiled, "You remember that mission in the Philippines? I still don't know what we were guarding."

"It's probably better that way."

"Yeah. It got a bit hairy."

"With you it always gets hairy," Michael concluded.

"Just lucky, I guess."

The two combatants reminisced for a short time and then Adam decided it was time to leave. He told Michael to tell Alice thanks again for the meal and that she didn't have to worry about another mission. Four hours later, Adam "Watch Dog" Hayes pulled into the parking lot at the Blue Tree Pub in Virginia Beach, Virginia. Per instructions, he sat at the bar and nursed a beer. A combination of anticipation and vigilance kept him alert. Time passed. In the mirror behind the bar he kept his eye on the door and the patrons in the establishment. He thought about the fact that there were times in the past when he was on a clandestine mission when things went astray and only his watchfulness and quick action kept him from harm. Awareness of his surroundings and remaining alert became a habit.

After twenty minutes Adam decided the meeting had been cancelled. It was time to leave. Just as he began to rise from the barstool a middle-aged man with grey hair and dark rimmed glasses sat beside him. Adam remained seated. The man ordered an Irish whiskey neat. From his initial examination, Adam determined that under his blue pin-striped suit jacket the man had a pistol in a shoulder holster and a backup gun on his right ankle. He was obviously right handed. A mark on his right ear indicated that he had worn a communication device for a lengthy period of time. Finally, he sat upright and moved in slow steady motions so as to not draw attention to himself. Adam concluded that he was Secret Service. What he didn't know was whether or not he was active or retired.

Nothing was said. Then ever so slowly the visitor reached into his pocket and withdrew a bronze coin. At first, he turned it over and over in his hand. Then he placed it on the bar next to his glass. Adam recognized the dragon, sword, and circle of thirteen stars that matched the coin in his pocket. This was his contact. Watch Dog waited. After taking a sip of his beer he reached into his pocket, retrieved his challenge coin, and placed it on the bar next to his glass. The stranger immediately picked up his coin, stood, and headed toward the door. Adam followed. Outside the man nodded and said, "Follow me." He entered his dark blue Ford Expedition and started the engine. Adam Hayes got behind the wheel of his Jeep Grand Cherokee and proceeded to follow the leader.

They drove west on Highway 60. After a short distance, his guide made a right turn onto Helicopter Road followed by a left onto Gator Boulevard. On the left was a large parking lot and commercial dock area. It was well lit and busy for that time of night—10:30 p.m. They parked and left their vehicles. Adam looked around. A number of Navy boats were moored at four long piers that stretched straight out into a cove. One boat anchored at the left-most pier didn't have a Navy appearance. Instead of being painted battleship grey, the hull was a lighter grey and the cabin portion was white. It was a large craft of approximately 80 feet and had a distinct military design.

"This way," the guide of few words indicated as they headed toward the boat Adam had been examining.

There was light inside the vessel, however, no movement was visible.

Midships there was a wooden four step box on the dock and a three-step ladder hung on the side of the craft. When they got to the steps the guide stopped, turned to face Adam and said, "Clear your weapon."

Adam took his 9mm Skye CPX-1 semi-automatic pistol out of its holster and dropped the magazine into his hand. He placed it in his pocket and cleared the chamber by pulling back on the slide. A cartridge popped out and dropped into the water.

They climbed aboard the boat.

CHAPTER 4

Adam Hayes and his guide climbed aboard a converted Navy patrol boat. On the tarpaulin-covered fantail was a glass top oblong table with four wooden slat chairs. Nothing was on the table. An air-conditioner hummed in the rear window of the cabin and a light glowed next to the open door. Upon entry they went down four steps into a living room complete with couch, chairs, desk, computer, bookshelves, and flat-screen television. A full kitchen was also visible on the left.

In the room were four individuals. One sat on the couch and one in each of the armchairs. Adam immediately recognized the man who stood holding a drink in his hand and staring directly at the new arrivals. Retired Marine General Maxwell Hughes walked over to Adam, extended his hand, and said, "Welcome aboard Ismenios."

Adam remembered the man who had given him his challenge coin a number of years earlier. "General, it's good to see you. You look fit. A little older but still a force to be reckoned with."

"Help yourself to a drink," the General waved his hand in the direction of a fully stocked bar. "Now that we are all here, I'll make the introductions." He walked over to the armchair on the left of the couch and put his hand on the shoulder of a man with grey-hair and a well-cropped grey beard. He wore a tailored blue suit with white shirt and red tie. "This is retired Navy Captain Jarvis Demoye. He's in command of this vessel. His last command in the Navy was as Captain of the guided missile destroyer Hopper." The General addressed Demoye, "Tell us a little about your ship."

Captain Demoye nodded and spoke, "The USS Hopper (DDG 70) is an Arleigh Burke-class Guided Missile Destroyer with the most advanced Aegis combat weapons system available. She's 505 feet in length—about six times the length of this craft. Fully-loaded she displaces 8,500 tons and can achieve speeds in excess of 30 knots. Without going into details, she is one lethal gal against enemies in the air, on the sea, below the sea, and on land. An interesting fact about her name. The USS Hopper was named for Rear Admiral Grace Murray Hopper, better known as 'Amazing Grace,' or 'Grand Lady of Software,' or 'Grandma Cobol.' It seems she co-invented

COBOL which stands for 'common business-oriented language' which made it possible for computers to respond to words instead of just numbers. Admiral Hopper was one impressive lady. It was a good name for my ship and a good assignment."

General Hughes moved over to the other armchair and stood beside a tanned man in his late thirties with sandy hair and blue eyes. He puffed on a cigar and had an air of confidence or arrogance, depending on one's point-of-view. His manner of dress was casual with black chinos and short sleeve light blue polo shirt. One outstanding feature was a pair of black Laredo cowboy boots. "This young man is retired Air Force Major Ken Farmingdale. His nickname is cannibal. He was a test-pilot in the Air Force and can fly anything from a fixed wing propeller plane to a jet to a helicopter to a kite. Tell us what you're doing these days, Ken."

"Staying in the air as much as possible. I freelance as a test pilot, fill-in pilot, and private pilot. On the side, I repo aircraft from rich bastards that don't pay their bills."

On the couch sat retired Navy Seal Master Chief Petty Officer Ronald Clew. The General nodded in his direction and introduced him. He then asked the well-built, clean-cut, African-American to give a rundown of his experience and skills. Ronald Clew wore a brown sportscoat over a black tee-shirt and jeans. He held a bottle of spring water. When he stood from the couch his true size became unmistakable. "As you all know most of my missions are classified. I've been in some tight spots and lost some brave friends. I love this country and everything it stands for. I'm not sure why I'm here but if my skills are needed by General Hughes I'm ready to serve."

"Master Sergeant Hayes," the General spoke to Adam, "have a seat. Relax. It's going to be a long evening. There's food over on the counter and plenty to drink. Why don't you tell the others who the hell you are?" There was a friendliness to the General's voice as he had history with Adam Hayes and both trusted as well as liked the man.

Adam introduced himself, "I spent my military time in the Army Special Forces." A glance at Ronald Clew revealed the natural competition between the services. "After retiring, an Army sniper and I filled our days as mercenaries and special ops for the US government. I guess the fact that I, uh, was on General Hughes' team at one time and got that coin gained me entrance to this unique group."

The last man in the room remained in the shadows. It was Adam's contact and guide. The General called to him, "Manny, let me tell the group about you." The man moved quietly into the light. "This is Secret

Service Agent Emanuel Vegas. At this time, the less you know about him the better. He is an essential part of our group, however, also the one who needs to remain in the background."

The men took some time to meet and greet as they made sandwiches and refilled their drinks. There was inter-service ribbing and also displays of respect for fellow warriors. Finally, General Hughes addressed the group. "The name of this vessel is Ismenios. There is a Greek legend that goes along with that name. The Drakon Ismenios (Ismenian dragon) was a giant serpent which guarded the sacred spring of Ares near Thebes. Cadmus arrived seeking to found a city and sent some of his men to fetch water from the spring of Ares. But, Drakon Ismenios guarded the spring and destroyed most of those who had been sent. This angered Cadmus who slew the dragon with a large stone. The gods were not pleased for it was Mars' dragon. To appease the gods the goddess Athena instructed Cadmus to sow the dragon's teeth in the earth. Cadmus followed the instructions and out of the furrows grew armed men—the Spartoi, Race of Mars, Children of the Serpent. Ultimate warriors who fell upon each other until only five remained Echion, Udaeus, Chthonius, Hyperenor, and Pelor who became the ancestral lords of Thebes." General Hughes sipped his Scotch and water. Then continued, "Dragon comes from the Greek 'drakeîn' meaning 'to see clearly.' Although it is a myth, we, my friends, are going to be the teeth of the serpent."

Silence hung in the room. It was a strange way to begin a discussion of a mission which each man had come expecting to hear about. No mention was made of a mission. A few glances among the team revealed their slight confusion. It also revealed their sense of anticipation.

"Did you ever wonder what went through Colonel Paul Tibbets mind as he flew the Enola Gay toward Japan carrying the nuclear bomb, code-named Little Boy?" It was a rhetorical question. "There's a backstory that answers that question." General Hughes paused. "We all know he named his aircraft Enola Gay after his mother. In fact, it was painted on the nose of the plane the day before the mission. At a later time, he recalled, 'my thoughts turned at this point to my courageous red-haired mother, whose quiet confidence had been a source of strength to me since boyhood, and particularly during the soul-searching period when I decided to give up a medical career to become a military pilot. At a time when dad had thought I had lost my marbles, she had taken my side and said, 'I know you will be all right son.'"

"Ah, the love of a good mother," Adam remarked.

“Don’t you wish you had one?” was General Hughes dry response. He walked over to the bar retrieved a bottle of Scotch, poured a reasonable amount in Adam’s glass, and then continued, “Paul Warfield Tibbets Jr. enlisted in the Army in 1937 and qualified as a pilot in 1938. He flew the B-17 Bomber. Initially, after Pearl Harbor, he flew anti-submarine patrols over the Atlantic. Then he went to England and flew the lead plane in the first American daylight heavy bomber mission against Occupied Europe on 17 August 1942. He also led the first raid over Europe that included more than 100 aircraft.” The General looked at Ken Farmingdale, the retired Air Force test pilot, and remarked, “He was a pilot’s pilot.”

Farmingdale nodded and raised his glass.

“Tibbets flew 43 combat missions and was selected to fly the plane that carried Major General Mark W. Clark and Lieutenant General Dwight D. Eisenhower to Gibraltar. He then returned to the United States to assist with the development of the Boeing B-29 Superfortress which, of course, one was to be the Enola Gay. He was a test pilot on the B-29 and eventually logged more flight time than any other pilot after the Chief Test Pilot, Edmund T. Allen, had been killed in a crash.” He again glanced at Ken Farmingdale.

“This may seem like a lot of info, but I want you to understand the man—get in his head.”

Retired Marine General Maxwell Hughes stood before his team wearing a tan shirt and green pants which appeared much like a military uniform while not actually being one. His short-cropped grey hair, weathered face, and strong jaw showed age and strength at the same time. His voice was steady and clear with a command element still present.

“The mission actually began on 1 September 1944 when Colonel Paul Tibbets reported to Colorado Springs Army Airfield, where he met with Major General Uzal Ent and three representatives of the Manhattan Project, Lieutenant Colonel John Lansdale Jr., Captain William S. Parsons, and Norman F. Ramsey Jr., who briefed him on the project. This was the beginning of his understanding of the sheer enormity and consequence of the project.

At 2:45 a.m. on 6 August 45 The Enola Gay took off from the Mariana Islands along with two other B-29s, The Great Artiste and Necessary Evil. Those two craft carried instrumentation and were to take photographs of the event. It was a six-hour flight to Hiroshima. Six hours to contemplate what was about to happen.”

“The bomb was dropped at 8:15 a.m. and took 43 seconds to fall from 31,000 feet to 1,968 feet where it detonated. The area of total destruction was approximately one mile with secondary damage ranging to about 4.7 miles. It was estimated that 69% of the buildings of the city were destroyed and 70,000-80,000 people killed. Of those it is believed 20,000 were soldiers."

General Maxwell Hughes looked around the room. What he saw were expressionless faces. This was a reaction he welcomed.

"Colonel Paul Tibbets was quoted as saying after the mission, 'I'm proud that I was able to start with nothing, plan it and have it work as perfectly as it did . . . I sleep clearly every night.' Sixty years later, when interviewed by a reporter he said, 'I knew when I got the assignment it was going to be an emotional thing. We had feelings, but we had to put them in the background. We knew it was going to kill people right and left. But my one driving interest was to do the best job I could so that we could end the killing as quickly as possible.' The Enola Gay was exhibited at the Smithsonian Institution on the 50th anniversary of the event and Tibbets called it, 'a damn big insult,' because it focused on the Japanese casualties rather than the brutality of the Japanese government during the war."

As an aside the General pointed out, "During just two campaigns in the Pacific, Iwo Jima and Okinawa, there were 88,000 U.S. casualties of which 18,800 died. Just imagine the numbers if mainland Japan had to be taken by ground troops."

"Brigadier General Paul Tibbets died 1 November 07 at the age of 92. He requested no funeral or headstone to deny protestors any opportunity to use him as a prop. Per his wishes, he was cremated and his ashes were scattered over the English Channel."

Retired Navy Captain Jarvis Demoye stood, raised his glass and stated, "In war, while everything is simple, even the simplest thing is difficult. Difficulties accumulate and produce frictions which no one can comprehend who has not seen war. I give you Brigadier General Paul Tibbets Jr."

All in the room stood, raised their glass, and drank a toast to a brave man.

CHAPTER 5

Six men sat in silence. It was a normal lull in the conversation or, more accurately, the presentation. They were all military, therefore, it wasn't difficult to understand the mindset of Paul Tibbets and the logic of dropping the first atomic bomb. However, when applied to each man's experience they each had a different hue.

Adam Hayes entered the Army right out of high school. He became a Green Beret and saw combat on the ground up close and personal. He killed hand-to-hand, saw comrades die, saved others, earned a silver star, and fought as a mercenary. In a violent world you had to choose sides or be washed away in the swirling waters of indifference.

Navy Captain Jarvis Demoye saw combat from a distance. From the bridge of a Guided Missile Destroyer, he launched Tomahawk Land Attack Missiles carrying high explosives or cluster munitions on enemy targets. While he didn't witness the carnage, he did receive reports of the effectiveness of the strikes. Significant body counts were common. In a numbers game they often lose significance.

Navy Seal Master Chief Petty Officer Ronald Clew had the most unique experiences. He often found himself behind enemy lines alone, in the dark, hidden for days, eaten by insects, filthy and tired, when his prey finally made itself accessible. Like a dark cloud RC would silently drain the life from his quarry. He then had to find his own way back to safety. The one kill he would always remember was a female drug lord in South America. She had orchestrated the deaths of dozens and had no conscience what's-so-ever. Yet, when he finally caught her in an alley behind the home of her mother for one instant her gaze was that of an innocent little girl. He hesitated and she put a knife into his side. It was a minor wound and he completed his mission. Master Chief Clew never made the same mistake again—innocence doesn't exist.

Secret Service Agent Emanuel Vegas was a Marine before joining the government service. He saw combat much as thousands of other Marines. Nothing special. He did his job, served with honor and moved on. In his new job with the Secret Service he was in a position to see the human toll of political decisions.

Air Force Major Ken Farmingdale never saw combat. As a test pilot, he was busy risking his life perfecting the weapons of war. His courage was one of facing the unknown alone and vulnerable. When you push an aircraft to its limits the potential for something unexpected to occur that tests your skills is always there. A cool head is the best means of survival. He took pride in the aircraft he helped develop when they were put to the test in combat.

Marine General Maxwell Hughes was a general's general. He had extensive combat experience, command experience, and understood the political side of the military establishment. Thrice wounded he carried shrapnel in his hip, had a long scar on his back, and endured pain on humid days. Maxwell Hughes also had charisma. His men trusted him, fellow officers respected him, and political leaders sought his advice. Finally, there was one personality trait that defined him—he was a pragmatist.

The marine clock on the wall chimed twelve times. It was midnight. General Hughes looked at the group he had assembled and asked, "Anyone tired?" When no one indicated that they were fatigued he continued, "Good." He walked over to the counter and picked up a newspaper, unfolded it, and pointed at a headline, "Terror In Philadelphia." "It's come to our shores," he stated. "More accurately, it's been here and ignored for too long." He ran his right hand through his short-cropped hair. "Shootings at nightclubs, on military bases, on campuses, bombs at marathons and elsewhere have been called the actions of unbalanced lone wolves or persons with a grudge. Our government has its head up its ass. Look at Europe, Great Britain, the Netherlands and you see the future of America." He paced about the small cabin as though lost in thought. Then he stopped turned to face his team and asked, "Do you know what the weapon is that the terrorists use?"

"Fear," Jarvis Demoye offered.

"That's their objective."

"Bombs, guns, knives," Ken Farmingdale said.

"Tools, but not the weapon."

"Psychological effect," Secret Service Agent Emanuel Vegas concluded.

"Side effect."

Neither Adam Hayes nor Ronald Clew spoke. They knew the General had something in mind and didn't wish to join in a guessing game.

Finally, General Hughes answered his own question, "Death." He said it in such a manner that it hung in the air. Death. Simple, maybe too simple, but not to the man who just spoke the word. Maxwell Hughes looked each of his guests in the eye. These were men who understood death, faced death, and conquered death. But, did they see it only as something to be avoided or thrust upon an enemy? Or, did they see it as a weapon.

Hughes continued his statement, "Terrorists use death as a weapon to instill fear, promote their message of hate, force their will upon others, and gain a strategic advantage. Unfortunately, it's a strategic advantage that is difficult to overcome because in most cases they don't fear death themselves. Many welcome it."

"I'd be more than happy to give them a helping hand," Watch Dog Adam Hayes offered.

"We can kill them all, after the fact," General Hughes replied, "But, that won't stem the tide." He walked over to the counter and poured another drink. "What we have to do is find a way to constrain them from taking action in the first place."

"Are you talking about better intelligence?" Jarvis Demoye asked.

General Hughes glanced in the direction of Secret Service Agent Emanuel Vegas then replied, "That's neither practical nor actionable." He changed the subject, "What keeps you from walking down the street and killing the first person you come upon?"

"No motive," Air Force Major Ken Farmingdale stated.

"Don't wish to spend my golden years in jail," Adam said.

"Exactly," Hughes declared, "the price is too high."

"Yes, but terrorists couldn't care less about jail. It's probably a luxury to them," Adam concluded.

"True. What I'm referring to is a deterrent. Jail is enough for you to not kill someone indiscriminately. That's because you value your freedom. Loss of freedom is not going to thwart the actions of a terrorist hell-bent on promoting an extremist ideology."

Once again silence hung over the room.

"The way you influence individual's actions is to identify what they fear, want, or value. When you get into their head and cause them to second guess or rethink their actions you stand a good chance of inhibiting those actions," after a pause he added, "At least reducing the number who are willing to perpetrate their crime."

The ticking of the clock on the wall accompanied each man's consideration of what had been said. There didn't seem to be any obvious deterrents for the wide range of terrorists supporting various ideologies and points-of-view. And, what about the lone wolf all twisted out of shape about something only he understands? They all fear different things and value different things. It's not like during the cold war where you can threaten that if you drop a nuke on us we will eradicate your country. The power of assured mutual destruction could not be underestimated. Still the General brought them together, so he must have something in mind. All eyes focused on the old man.

General Maxwell Hughes looked into each man's eyes, one by one, with the exception of Emanuel Vegas. It was as if he were gazing into their soul. Then in a somber probing voice he said, "I have to touch on this one carefully. What I am about to describe is a strategic deterrent program that will test your basic sensibilities, belief systems, intellect, sense of duty, and possibly faith. Upfront, you can leave at any time. I only ask that what is said here tonight remains confidential to the highest degree. Each of you were selected because of your skills, proven loyalty, honesty, and dedication." He reached into his pocket, withdrew his challenge coin, and held it up. "Take out your coin and look at it."

Each member of the team followed instructions and examined their coin.

"The dragon is Ismenios. I told you the myth of it guarding the sacred spring of Ares and its teeth giving rise to the Spartoi, Race of Mars, Children of the Serpent. The circle of thirteen stars represents the United States of America. However, it represents the purity of the founding father's vision, rather than the bloated, socialist, nanny state, that she has become. Finally, the sword represents the strength of the warrior that has throughout history proven to be the difference between tyranny and liberty. On the reverse side, in Latin, are the words, 'est ultra de tenebris et in umbra satanas.' The translation is, 'it is beyond dark in Satan's shadow.' These are not empty words. They are precise in their meaning. Accurate down to the rending of your humanity."

In the comfortable living quarters of a converted patrol boat on a dark moonless night six warriors prepared to go beyond the dark.

CHAPTER 6

The Ismenios steamed slowly out of Little Creek Cove, turned north, and headed toward Bay Breeze Point. On the bridge was Jarvis Demoye. It was a far cry from a guided missile destroyer, but she was a solid, seaworthy craft. The four Detroit Diesel engines, each putting out 225 horsepower, moved the boat along at eight knots. After four months with a hired crew of craftsmen they had fully reconditioned the 1958 Converted 80-foot Navy Patrol Boat. With a beam of 18 feet 9 inches, refurbishing the wooden hull in drydock was the greatest challenge. Jarvis put in long hours laboring on that worn hull. The physical exercise felt good. In the end, the Ismenios now boasted two double berths, a cabin, two heads, depth sounder, GPS, radar, plotter, navigation center, autopilot, and a full galley. Not only did they have all the comforts of home but they were fully capable of sailing anywhere in the world. His mind drifted to the hidden compartment cunningly built into the structure to evade detection. A cache of weapons for defense and offense were stowed for future use. This dragon can breathe fire when provoked. He ran his hand along the highly polished wooden wheel and looked around the bridge with pride. Every captain eventually falls in love with his craft. It's in their DNA.

Surprisingly, test pilot Ken Farmingdale volunteered to man the engine room. It might not have been that much of a surprise as he wanted to be alone. Now that he understood Satan's Shadow his mind raced at a speed that matched the four big engines he tended. The truth of the matter was that it made sense—logical, practical, strategic sense. Yet, it ripped at his sensibility. Indeed, he had been torn and tempted to leave. There would have been no questions asked and no admonitions. However, he chose to stay. Why? Was it that General Hughes made such a compelling argument? Or, was it so clearly a solution that it couldn't be ignored? The hum of the engines began to echo in his head. He simply wanted to be high above the clouds flying alone in solitude. Diesel fumes smelled of brimstone and he knew things would never be the same.

General Maxwell Hughes, Adam Hayes, and Ronald Clew sat around the table on the fantail. A breeze off the Bay was refreshing. Secret

Service Agent Emanuel Vegas had left the boat—not because he declined to participate. Quite the opposite. Satan's Shadow was the joint creation of he and General Hughes. His involvement required that he be on shore and at his post as a Secret Service Agent.

"General," Adam began.

"Call me Max."

"General."

"Asshole."

"Max, remember that leather skirted nymphet in, where was it, Naples. Whatever happened to her?" with the discussion over, decision made, and Adam onboard with Satan's Shadow there was no reason to dwell on it.

General Hughes smiled, "She was a Russian spy. Went back to Vladivostok, got decorated, later defected, said something about a Green Beret turning her, now living in Peoria."

"What part of that is true?"

"She did defect."

Adam turned to Navy Seal Ronald Clew, "Where are you from, Ron?"

"Lexington, Kentucky."

"The Kentucky Derby?"

"That would be Louisville. Lexington is called the 'Horse Capital of the World.'"

"Do you ride?"

"Like a jockey."

"Big fucking jockey, if you ask me—poor damn horse."

"Yeah."

"Any family?"

"In our line of work that's not advisable."

"Tell me about it."

Ronald Clew was a man of few words, but when he spoke it was straightforward and direct, "Given the direction we've chosen, I believe a family is out-of-the-question now and in the future."

"Yeah, I'd say your right on that one."

"I never gave it much thought before. It's like, maybe I'll get to it sometime. Now that I know it will be impossible, I kind of miss the idea."

"Sometimes the sacrifices we make are greater off the battlefield."

"Roger, that," Ron raised his bottle of spring water.

Maxwell Hughes observed the interaction of the two men he had chosen. He liked what he saw. They were capable, loyal, and tough. And, for what they had to do, they would need all the strength they could muster. It was the depth of that strength that he was counting on. No doubt they had courage, resilience, and physical stamina. However, every man has a breaking point—that moment in his life where things stop making sense and the fog of uncertainty causes him to question reality. General Hughes wrestled that demon early in his life. It was when his brother discovered the seduction of heroin in high school—a gift from a cheap tramp. For three years Max tried desperately to rescue Jerry. Even a beating from his big brother couldn't break the harness that pulled a lost soul deeper and deeper into an irretrievable pit. Petty theft, lying, lost days, and finally an overdose. Max Hughes found his brother behind the garage unconscious. He was an emaciated, filthy, empty hulk of a human being. Through his actions he destroyed a family and squandered a life. Max stood looking at his brother. His first instinct was to summon help. It was the proper thing to do. Then, he turned, walked away, and let him die.

On the bridge Captain Jarvis Demoye guided the Ismenios past Bay Breeze Point out into the Chesapeake Bay. At fifty-one years of age he had become discontented. His twin daughters were full-grown and his wife had more social engagements than the Queen of England. Add to that the fact that he never developed the art of sitting around, watching television, or puttering. Where the hell does puttering get you? He graduated from Annapolis at the age of twenty and after thirty years in the Navy was unable to simply turn it off. A chance meeting with General Maxwell Hughes brought him to this time and place. Alone, piloting the boat, he stared out over the black waters of Chesapeake Bay. Was Satan out there waiting to welcome him? In a strange way he was more curious than anything else. How was the strategy going to play out? What would they reap? Would their efforts be successful? A foghorn and lights on the starboard side caught his attention. He answered with two blasts of the airhorn. Ships in the night. One headed to its destination the other its destiny.

CHAPTER 7

Darius Holiday, aka Ihtsham Azlan, sat at his family's dinner table lost in thought. He was proud of what he had accomplished in Philadelphia. It was a wakeup call for the infidels who dared to ignore the laws of Allah. America would learn to accept Sharia over time and by the sword, if necessary. And, it was his destiny to lead the fight.

Darius' father looked at his son and wondered what had come over the boy. He was more and more withdrawn, grew a beard, and proclaimed that he had converted to Islam. That last point worried the older man. One didn't have to read many newspapers to know the dangers of home-grown radicals. Yet, Darius hadn't done anything his father considered unusual or of concern. He was just a lost soul looking for some kind of identification—it will pass. Sam Holiday recalled when he was a lad. His form of rebellion was to smoke grass and grow an afro. He decided that he had to give Darius time. If he objected to his son's conversion it would push him further in a direction that he didn't like.

"You need to wear more modest clothes," Ihtsham Azlan suddenly said to his fifteen-year-old sister.

"What?" the surprised girl replied. She then added, "What I wear is none of your business."

"You dress like a tramp. It's a sin. You're going to hell."

"Stop!" the senior Holiday said. He addressed Darius, "I know you decided to follow this new religion. That's your choice, but it isn't ours. So, leave your judgements and opinions outside this house."

"I'm trying to save you—don't you understand?"

Darius mother, Marcella, said to her son, "We don't need saving. Why don't you come to church with us on Sunday?"

"I don't worship false gods. There is no god but Allah."

"Enough!" Sam ordered. "Not at this table."

Ihtsham Azlan stood, threw down his napkin, and stormed out of the room.

"Darius," his mother called.

"Let him go," Sam said.

Once in his room Ihtsham Azlan knew his next "lesson" not only had to be impressive, no shocking, but it needed to carry a message, as well. He sat at his second-hand computer and began composing the words from "Strong Lion." They needed to be clear and powerful and frightening. He worked late into the night until he was finally satisfied. Then as he lay in bed he began planning his method of delivery.

In the next week an evil plan was formulated and all the requisite materials gathered. He experimented, tested, made adjustments, and finally had his new weapon he dubbed a "Flaming Sword."

On the following Saturday, Ihtsham Azlan drove his old car two and a half hours, 125 miles, to Manhattan Island, New York. It was late afternoon when he parked in the Port Authority Bus Terminal public parking garage on 42nd Street. Though fatigued from his drive he knew he had to work fast for his plan to come to fruition. He walked west on 42nd Street toward Grand Central Station. His left arm held a grocery bag with cereal, potato chips, and celery sticking out of the top. The bag was quite heavy. In Ihtsham Azlan's right hand was a 20-ounce Venti Starbucks cup of coffee. He didn't drink from the cup.

Inside the cup was a balloon filled with propane occupying a third of the available capacity. On top of the balloon was finely ground coal dust packed tightly and covered with plastic wrap and a lid. All coal miners are acutely aware of the dangers of coal dust explosions. Strong Lion was not only aware of the danger but also had access to all the coal dust he required for Flaming Sword. In addition, he had done his homework.

There were four conditions necessary for a dust explosion; combustible dust, dust suspended in the air at a sufficient concentration, an oxidant (air), and an ignition source. Coal dust was a perfect combustible dust. Through his research he found that the dust must consist of extremely small particles. With a solid or liquid, burning can only occur at the surface where it reacts with oxygen. For example, a 2.2-pound solid piece of combustible material would have a surface area of approximately .52 square feet. If that same material were ground into fine powder it would have a surface area of 1,300 square feet causing it to catch on fire with far less energy and to burn considerably more quickly. Ihtsham Azlan carefully ground the coal dust to a fine powder. He selected propane as both the ignition source and means of blasting the coal dust into the air where it would become an enormous fireball. He hoped the intense heat would ignite the surroundings, burn any infidels in the area, and possibly cause asphyxiation due to sudden depletion of oxygen. The final piece of the puzzle was to set off the ignition. For this he placed a 9-volt battery in the bottom of the cup under the balloon. A strip of metal was taped across the terminals. When it heated to a high enough temperature it would cause the balloon to tear open and the propane explode expelling the coal dust which instantaneously would ignite into a fireball. To keep all of this from happening prematurely he placed a strip of cardboard between the battery terminals and metal strip. One end of the cardboard stuck inconspicuously out of the bottom of the coffee cup.

Ihtsham Azlan arrived at Grand Central Station. He knew that venerable structure was guarded by police, private security, and video surveillance. It was not his target. He continued to Lexington Avenue and turned north. Darius Holiday, aka Ihtsham Azlan, then began the improvised part of his plan. There were no predetermined targets. Selection would be arbitrary. One block north he came upon a crowded bar. Silently, he entered. The music and conversations were loud. Laughter filled the air. Unnoticed, Ihtsham Azlan pulled the cardboard strip from the Starbucks cup. He then placed the cup on a counter next to a wastepaper basket. Quickly he exited the bar. From his experiments he knew the imprecise battery timer would take from three to ten minutes to heat the metal strip.

The lone terrorist proceeded to walk quickly north on Lexington Avenue and turned west on 45th Street. As he walked, he reached into his grocery bag and retrieved a second Starbucks cup. One block farther he came upon a crowded deli where people were ordering sandwiches for their dinner. Cup two was left on a shelf. A third cup was placed in another bar. After traveling north on Broadway at Times Square, Strong Lion entered a crowded McDonalds. He dropped his cup into a waste basket and left. Before he could place his next cup, he heard sirens in the distance. They sounded as if they were headed in the vicinity of his first target, but he couldn't be sure.

A large delicatessen/café on the corner of 7th Avenue and 50th Street next received Allah's calling card. An Irish pub on 50th Street was next. At 8th Avenue he turned south. More sirens were heard headed in the direction of where Ihtsham Azlan had traveled. His seventh and final cup-bomb was left in a Starbucks on 8th Avenue. He smiled at the irony.

The last step in Flaming Sword was for his message to be delivered. On a prepaid cellphone, he called the *New York Times.* He asked for the newsroom and was connected with a woman. From a secluded location he ordered, "Write this down. The hand of Allah is all powerful. He can bring you peace or he can punish you with flames. New York has tasted the fires of hell. Accept Islam, Sharia, and your destiny—or burn." Ihtsham

Azlan wiped the phone clean, removed the battery, and smashed it under his heel. The pieces were disposed of down a sewer.

As he entered the Port Authority Bus Terminal he heard a low boom and screams. The ride back to Wilkes-Barre, Pennsylvania was a glorious victory for Strong Lion. He listened to radio news reports of panic in the streets of Manhattan as seven firebombs killed an untold number of people and injured many more. Authorities tried to calm the situation but had to admit they didn't know if any additional bombs were waiting to go off.

When Ihtsham Azlan heard his message quoted over the radio, he knew he had earned his place in heaven.

CHAPTER 8

Ismenios steamed east across the Atlantic Ocean. Jarvis Demoye put the craft on autopilot and joined the others on the fantail. It was early evening and a cool breeze was refreshing. Only he and General Hughes knew their destination. The others didn't object or inquire. They knew they would be told at the appropriate time.

"You saw what took place in New York over the weekend," Maxwell Hughes stated rhetorically.

"Eighteen dead and hundreds burned and injured," Ken Farmingdale reminded the others.

"I'd like to get my hands on the scum that did that," Navy Seal Ron Clew stated with enough venom to scare the bravest of men.

"Maybe, you will someday," Maxwell Hughes said.

"Well, we know it was fundamentalist Muslim radicals based on their message," Adam Hayes said. "It could be a terrorist cell. No telling how many are involved."

"I believe both recent terrorist attacks were done by a lone wolf from Pennsylvania or New Jersey," Jarvis offered.

"Why Pennsylvania or New Jersey?" General Hughes inquired.

"He started in Philadelphia most likely because he was acquainted with that city. Someone from eastern Pennsylvania or central Jersey would be the most likely one to have knowledge of 'the city of brotherly love.' An amateur will always start with something familiar. They don't have the confidence or ability to scout an unfamiliar objective and develop a plan. The use of pressure cookers indicates a low-level of skill or training. We don't know what he used in New York yet, but I'll wager it's going to be some kind of homemade device."

"Whatever it is," Ron Clew spat, "I'd like to shove one up his ass and light it."

"Not until you apply butyl rubber sealant," Adam added, "this way the fire will come out of his mouth."

His remark brought about a round of laughter.

Jarvis Demoye continued, "New York was a logical second choice. He wanted to make as big a splash as possible to get his message out. Well, it worked."

"What do think will be his next target?" Ken Farmingdale asked with interest.

"I think he will realize that he runs a greater risk of being caught if he continues to operate in a limited geographic area. His next target will be a long distance away from where he lives. It will be his attempt to direct attention away from himself. I have a hunch he'll go north or south, rather than west. I also believe he will repeat his firebomb tactic. After all, he was able to plant seven bombs in busy establishments in a city with police and surveillance cameras everywhere and no one noticed."

"If you had to guess, what's his next target?" Adam asked.

Without hesitation Jarvis answered, "Atlanta."

"OK, let's go inside to discuss our target," General Hughes stated as he stood and headed for the door to the cabin. All followed. Once inside, a photograph was displayed on the flat screen monitor. "This is Fahmi Nabiil Nabiil, a Somali refugee who ran a truck into the crowded flea market of the Place du Jeu de Balle in the Marolles section of Brussels, Belgium. Eleven dead and eighty-three injured." As an aside he explained, "Somalis do not have surnames. In Somalia, three names are used: a given name followed by the father's given name and the grandfather's. There aren't any family names as we know them. In the past, parents chose their children's name after consulting a wise family member, astrologist, or religious leader. Today, they generally pick the name of a family member or friend. It's not uncommon for someone to have three similar names like Awaale Awaale Awaale."

"They shot and killed that pig," Jarvis reminded the group.

Two new photographs appeared on the flat screen monitor—an older man and woman. "He has a mother and father who are located in a small village in southern Greece named Vathia. There's a brother, Yasin Nabiil Nabiil, but we don't have a lot of info on him. He could be with them."

"Probably out renting a truck," Adam surmised.

"Birds of a feather," Navy Seal Clew offered.

"You three," General Hughes indicated Adam Hayes, Ron Clew, and Ken Farmingdale, "will go ashore when we get to our destination, locate the pollutants and remove them. Until then, use *Google Earth* to familiarize yourself with the surroundings around Vathia."

Three days later, Ismenios anchored in international waters off the coast of Greece. They remained on the far side of an uninhabited island in the Mediterranean Sea to avoid detection. This necessitated a long trip in the dark in a rubber raft. As Ron and Adam were in top physical condition, the two-hour eleven-minute journey was of no consequence. They landed on a secluded, rocky, unfriendly shoreline in the middle of the night, hid their raft, and made their way to the main paved road along the rim of a cliff.

As the sun rose three tourists stopped at a small café for breakfast. Fortunately, the waitress spoke some broken English. With little information and only grainy photographs they began their hunt. One factor was in their favor—there were only a handful of Somali refugees in the area and they had congregated along an unpaved road in an unpopulated part of the village. A makeshift tent city of twenty tents had popped up and became Little Somalia.

With a Bushnell 4.5-30x50mm XRS Elite Tactical Riflescope Adam scanned the village from a hidden observation vantage point. For over an hour surveillance turned up very little. A few women were observed, children ran about, young men congregated off by themselves, and some old men sat and chatted. Just before noon, while on his watch, Ron Clew said as he peered through the scope, "I have something. A woman. Looks like momma." He handed the matte black tube to Adam.

Through the lens, Adam saw a woman wearing a guntiino, a traditional plain white fabric tied over the shoulder and draped around the waist. She also had on a white head-scarf called a shash and a shawl known as a garbasaar common with married Somali women. In her arms she carried a large jug. He adjusted the scope to 20x magnification to gain a closer look. "Confirmed," he stated. He followed her through the lens until she entered a tent three in from the end. "We now have an address," he added.

Ken Farmingdale watched the two seasoned combatants with interest. They went about their business with precision and efficiency. No emotion was heard in their voices. In fact, they almost seemed to know each other's move before it was made. He knew why he was there but that didn't change the fact that he was uneasy with the program. Yes, he signed on board. Yes, he would do his job. Yes, he understood and supported the concept. No, he would not sleep soundly that night or, as a matter-of-fact, for a long time.

Adam Hayes dialed a number on the team's satellite telephone. When it was answered, a voice said, "Speak."

"Three blind mice in the cupboard. Tomorrow's a school day,"

Adam broke the connection.

They spent the remainder of the day taking turns sleeping and observing. By nightfall it was clear that Fahmi Nabiil Nabiil's mother, father, and brother were in tent number three. Tent city settled in for the night. A few young men wandered about the compound but there were no identifiable guards. Ken Farmingdale, holding an M-16 at the ready, remained in a blind near the camp. He was not to shoot unless absolutely necessary.

Two imposing men moved remarkably quietly for their size. In darkness, they glided off the dirt road, down a steep slope, past the outer boundaries of the compound, and stopped outside tent number three. For two minutes, they remained silent and listened. No voices, movement, or other sounds emanated from the shelter. Their plan was put into action using hand signals. Flimsy tent material was sliced open to allow entry. Night vision glasses provided a view of the interior of the tent. Yasin Nabiil Nabiil lay upon a straw mattress on the right. His parents slept on the far side of the tent. A large black hand over the brother's mouth kept him silent until he was silenced forever with a 5-inch black blade on a Zero Tolerance ZT0160 Combat Knife. Twenty seconds later the parents met the same fate.

A laminated card was left with the bodies. On it were the red eyes of Satan and a tattered wing creating a penumbra. In the blackness reverse type stated: When you serve Satan those in your family live in his shadow and share evil's fate.

Three figures moved silently to where a raft had been deftly hidden. Though tired, adrenaline provided the energy for them to begin to paddle their way back to Ismenios.

"So, Jarvis thinks Atlanta is the next target for the Jersey firefuck," Adam stated as they paddled.

"Wish we could stop him," Ron Clew remarked.

"Maybe they'll get enough info about him from Philadelphia and New York before he strikes."

"Just give the info to me. I'll take care of the rest."

Ken Farmingdale listened to Ron and Adam. As he did he wondered how they could be so blasé after killing three people. Three people who, for all intents and purposes, were innocent. Yet, while innocent, they were pawns in a global chess game. When terrorists begin to realize that their own family members will be the price paid for their malevolent acts, they might think twice before taking action. He understood General Hughes' argument that the only way to influence an individual is to determine what they value. Most terrorists aren't concerned about dying. They don't value life like we do in the United States. Certainly, they don't fear prison. It's probably a step up from what they are accustomed to, anyway. The key is their family. Wife, children, parents, siblings all are held dear by cold-hearted terrorists. In some cases, leaders of terrorist organizations agree to take care of martyr's families. Satan's Shadow is a cold, heartless, vicious tactic, yes. But aren't the lives of four, or five, or six, or more relatives of warped killers a small price to pay to save hundreds? In fact, they are not all that innocent. By association, knowledge, and shared beliefs they bear some of the responsibility for heinous acts committed.

No longer a virgin, Ken Farmingdale joined the conversation.

CHAPTER 9

The Ismenios steamed west in the Mediterranean Sea. It had been two days since the raid and there wasn't any news coverage that they could locate. Fahmi Nabiil Nabiil was dead, as was his father, mother, and brother. Yet, the world was unaware.

General Hughes had a late-night conversation with Secret Service Agent Emanuel Vegas on a Low Earth Orbit (LEO) satellite telephone with Milspec encryption and receiver-specific coding. No one but Hughes and Vegas could hear what was being said. It was agreed that through non-traceable sources Vegas would leak the story to the press. Both men further agreed it would probably remain a page eleven one-inch blurb about revenge.

The next morning, over breakfast, Maxwell Hughes shared the details of his conversation. "It is imperative that every potential terrorist knows the risk to their family and friends if they initiate a violent act. Simply eliminating them will not achieve this. We need to add another dimension to the story to raise the level of media interest—shock."

"What kind of shock?" Navy Seal Ronald Clew inquired as he buttered a piece of toast.

"It will depend on the situation, however must be dramatic enough to be disturbing. The world has to be horrified to take notice. We thought killing a terrorist's family was enough and it would be if they heard about it. Unfortunately, the media are the ones who need more motivation."

"You mean like leaving the bodies in the main square or some other public place?" Adam Hayes asked.

"If it were only that easy," Hughes lamented. "Think about those three in Vathia. If you left the bodies in the town square it would still only be a local issue. We need a high-profile demonstration that will get worldwide coverage."

"General Hughes," Adam began.

"Max."

"General Hughes."

"Still an asshole."

"We're on board with the program, as distasteful as it is to kill civilians, it's a tactic that promises long range success. You said we're going to get our hands dirty on this one. An undeniable fact is we're going to get our hearts, souls, and consciences dirty, as well. This is a suicide mission. None of us are coming back alive. The question is will we meet our objective? I'll kill men, women, and children and hang them from the Eifel Tower if it will stop these vermin from carrying out their evil acts. Terrorism is a cancer in the world. Sometimes you have to cut out healthy tissue to stop the spread."

"We're trained to take a bullet to protect our team. Keep our eyes on the objective. Leave the analysis for the debriefing," Ron Clew added, "Mental masturbation clouds the mind and slows the reflexes. I know why we're doing what we're doing—that's all I need."

Ken Farmingdale joined the conversation, "There is a risk." All at the table turned to hear his point-of-view. "If we do anything that is seen as brutal, inhuman, or sadistic the bleeding-heart press will focus on the act not the message. We want the headline to read, 'Terrorist's Family Killed' not 'Bodies Hung from Eifel Tower.'"

"That's a fair point," Captain Jarvis Demoye stated.

"I think our message was too subtle or vague," Farmingdale continued, "Tell it like it is. 'Terrorism has a price. If you commit a terrorist act your family is the price you pay. We will locate and kill every member of your family, your friends, associates, and any who offered you support. Through your actions you condemn them all to death. They can hide but we will find them. Satan's Shadow is everywhere.' Leave that with every body and it cannot be ignored."

"Dammit, I like it!" Maxwell Hughes bellowed. "Captain, we need to set a course for Belgium."

"Belgium?" Jarvis Demoye asked.

"Fahmi Nabiil Nabiil had friends and possibly allies who assisted him. If we can identify any, they need to be eliminated and Ken's message delivered."

In a small room 4,330.5 miles west of Ismenios, Ihtsham Azlan, aka Darius Holiday, sat at his computer examining a map of the eastern United States. His first thought was to repeat what he had done in New York City, only in another section of Manhattan. It would show the infidels that they could not stop the "strong lion." In addition, it would raise the level of fear and trepidation to extreme heights in America's largest city. The thought of putting so many in a state of near panic pleased him. Yet, he knew it would be a significant risk to return to the scene of the crime. While unreasonable, he had the feeling that if he walked down the streets of Manhattan someone would recognize him and point him out to the authorities. No, New York was out. He continued to study the map.

Captain Jarvis Demoye studied the map on the navigation table. He plotted a 6-day, 2,400-mile course to skirt the continent around Spain and Portugal, then across the Bay of Biscay to the English Channel, landing in Dover Harbor, Kent, England. There they would tie-up and refurbish the boat and lay-in for a few days. Their diplomatic passports with fictitious identifications would provide adequate cover. Adam Hayes, Ron Clew, and Ken Farmingdale would then take the regularly scheduled ferry to Dunkirk, France where they would disappear into the crowd.

Ihtsham Azlan needed another city where he could dissolve into the crowd to do his noble deed. Size offered both better hunting and human camouflage. He considered a city in New England but the traffic and roads inhibited unrestricted travel. His attention turned south. Washington, D.C. was definitely out. When the time came for the lion to visit that city it would be to deliver an unforgettable lesson that would leave an indelible mark. Richmond, Raleigh, Charlotte, and Greenville all offered only limited appeal. It was then he found his target.

During their six-day cruise the team gathered information on the terrorist attack in Brussels and the perpetrator of the crime. Back in the United States Emanuel Vegas used his many intelligence sources to gain information, as well. As a result of news releases and uncovered confidential data three individuals were identified as having helped or supported Fahmi Nabiil Nabiil. One was his roommate and friend. His body was found tied to a tree behind the small apartment where they lived. The second man, who was often called Fahmi's uncle, provided money and support to the Muslim extremist. His head was found on a sewer grate in the flea market of the Place du Jeu de Balle in the Marolles section of Brussels, Belgium where the terrorist act had taken place. A final victim, the woman who rented the truck used by the terrorist who denied knowing what he was going to do with it, was found under the wheels of a truck crushed to death. All three bodies had with them Ken Farmingdale's direct straightforward message.

Atlanta became the city of interest to Ihtsham Azlan. Yes, it would work perfectly as it would expand the web of fear while keeping his identity and location unknown. The challenge was that he had no knowledge of Atlanta, had never been there, therefore would have to study the city carefully before making his move. He went to work surfing the web.

This time the media took notice. The "Terrorism has a price" message could not be ignored. It was clear why the three persons had been executed. What wasn't clear was who had done it. And, the declaration, "Satan's Shadow is everywhere," gave it an ominous unsettling threatening attribute. International press services quickly spread the story. The world was on notice.

CHAPTER 10

FBI Special Agent Peggy Fox read the initial report on the New York City fire bombings. The incendiary substance was identified as coal dust. Metal strips, 9-volt batteries, and balloon fragments made it easy for technicians to reconstruct the crude fire bombs. Also found at multiple locations were charred pieces of Starbucks coffee cups. These were of great interest as there might be a latent finger print on one of the pieces. None had been found, to date. Only a few security cameras were operating and the images they provided were dark, grainy, and out-of-focus. One camera did show a young black male enter the store carrying what appeared to be a Starbucks coffee cup. He also carried a paper grocery bag with items sticking out of the top. It was quickly concluded that he had the additional fire bombs hidden in the grocery bag. Review of street security cameras turned up two instances where a young black man appeared carrying a paper grocery bag and Starbucks coffee cup. They were distant images but confirmed the general description of the perpetrator.

Cameras were being checked in the Port Authority Bus Terminal, Grand Central and Pennsylvania train stations, and all subway platforms in the midtown area. At that time, nothing had turned up. Peggy knew over time more clues to the identification of the perpetrator would be found. She only hoped that they would find a sufficient number for them to make an arrest before he struck again.

Ihtsham Azlan chose the section of Atlanta where he would unleash his swords of fire. It was called Buckhead. There were ample numbers of restaurants, night clubs, bars, and retail establishments within walking distance. He also found a gay bar which he decided had to be among his targets.

He would repeat the approach taken in New York City. That would require that he stockpile more coal dust.

Ken Farmingdale stood in the bow of Ismenios looking out over the vast Atlantic Ocean. They were his words that had been left with three bodies in Brussels. Terrorism has a price. Make it too expensive, psychologically, and the number of events would be dramatically reduced. If Ahmed knows his mother, or sister, or daughter, or brother, or wife, or all of them will be assassinated as a result of his actions, he has to think twice about it. It makes logical sense. But, these animals are emotion driven. Would logic even come into play? Could someone be so heartless as to let their family be sacrificed to advance their warped view of the world? Immediately, his mind asked, could someone be so heartless as to kill an entire family because of the actions of one member? He knew the answer to that question.

Of course, the news stories with Satan's Shadow message would be quashed in Muslim countries. No matter, let them kill each other and reduce the population of future terrorists. It will be enough if it stops the violence in Europe, Great Britain, and America.

The smell of salt water filled his nostrils. Once more he longed to be high above the ocean soaring in an uncertified aircraft testing its systems and aerodynamics. He would challenge the aircraft, push it to its limits, test its mettle, and determine if it could be counted on in a combat situation. A dark shadow slithered over his mind. Death is the weapon. It was his weapon, now. No longer the pristine high-tech jet capable of delivering a lethal blow from a distance. Blood was on his hands. Murder was on his conscience.

Inside the cabin that was the bridge Captain Jarvis Demoye and General Maxwell Hughes observed their colleague standing on the bow. Only his back was visible to them.

"Our boy is facing his demons," Hughes stated.

"He's the only one on the team who does not have combat experience," Demoye pointed out.

"Too bad his christening is with the blood of innocents. It's a double-barreled blast to the senses."

"He did his job," Jarvis Demoye stated.

"He didn't like it."

"None of us like it. We see the need for it, the strategy, the tactics, and the objective. After that we execute—pun intended—to the best of our ability. It's what we signed on for. Contrary to all the technical advances with smart weapons, war is neither clean nor humane."

"Ken has flown around the fringes—pun intended—now he's in the mud seeing it all face-to-face," General Hughes observed.

"Do you think he is a security risk?"

"I trust every man on the team. If Farmingdale can't handle the pressure he'll jump overboard or we'll find him bled out in his rack. He won't betray the team."

"He's looking into the faces of those innocent targets."

A photograph of a twenty-four-year-old woman with burns on sixty percent of her body appeared in a New York City newspaper. Her face was contorted in pain. In the story were numerous accounts of victims with horrendous injuries and families torn apart due to the loss of a loved-one. Ihtsham Azlan read the story with great interest. Pride swelled in his breast. He was a soldier. His noble hand had slain many infidels. It was his destiny to slay many more. Another story in the newspaper caught his eye—Terrorist's Family Slain. Upon reading about the murders in Brussels and the fact that Fahmi Nabiil Nabiil's mother, father, and brother had been slain in Greece anger erupted in Ihtsham Azlan. They were innocent people who did not deserve to die. He needed to exact vengeance on the unholy cowards for his fallen brother Fahmi Nabiil Nabiil and his family. Allah's hand will rain hell upon non-believers and his message will be in response to this Satan's Shadow. They will learn the meaning of fear and the price their actions demand. His family and those of all of Allah's soldiers will be left alone. Ihtsham Azlan knew his swords of fire would not be enough. A far greater lesson had to be delivered.

CHAPTER 11

Retired Army sniper, Michael "Owl" O'Neal, sat in his den reading the newspaper. Pressure cooker bombs in Philadelphia and fire bombs in New York made it undisputable that terrorism had come to America. Unconsciously, he exhaled slowly then held his breath in preparation to take his shot between heartbeats. A part of him wanted to hunt down the perpetrators of the attacks, but that was an emotional response. He knew he neither had the facilities to do an investigation nor the full list of clues the authorities had already gathered. It was up to a very capable law-enforcement system to find the fiends and bring them to justice.

His eye caught the headline of another story. As he read of the assassinations of the associates and family of Fahmi Nabiil Nabiil, the Brussels bomber, he concluded that the Europeans had finally decided to get tough. For too long they had handled terrorism as a criminal matter when it was, in fact, an act of war. In war, you don't follow due process, you eliminate the threat. In war, you are either an ally or an enemy, therefore, if you associate with the enemy you become a target.

Alice, Michael's wife, entered the room. She sat in one of the upholstered chairs and asked, "What are you reading?"

"An account of the Europeans killing the family of a terrorist. That's a new twist."

"I read it. It's immoral and inhumane. Those people were innocent. They didn't do anything to deserve to die."

Michael looked at his wife wondering if he should give his opinion or let it go and keep peace in the family. It would be easy. Simply, close the newspaper and change the subject. No need to stoke the fire. He smiled and said, "I don't know, it's a new tactic that might work."

As expected the response was immediate, "How can you say that! Innocent people being murdered is OK in your book?"

"I'm looking at it from a strategic perspective."

"There's no perspective that justifies killing innocent people."

The proper response would be to agree. Therefore, Michael said, "If eliminating three innocents prevents the murder of hundreds, there is a logic to it."

"Now, you sound like that mad dog Hayes."

"Watch Dog."

"He thinks nothing of killing. It's almost second nature. Heaven help the poor guy who cuts him off on the highway."

"Adam Hayes never killed anyone without justification."

"And, who decides the justification—Adam Hayes?"

"Why do you hate the man so much? He saved my life on numerous occasions."

"He ruined your life."

"How so?"

"Dragging you off to who knows where to kill who knows who?"

"Without those high-paying missions we wouldn't be sitting here financially and physically comfortable," Michael pointed out.

"Or, I could be sitting here alone mourning a lost husband who was never home."

"Adam and I looked out for each other. We had each other's back."

"He got into your head."

"And, under your skin."

"Yes, under my skin. I've watched an honorable caring man become hard and callous."

"What have I done to cause you to draw that conclusion?"

"You just said that you support killing innocent people. There was a time that you would never have uttered those words."

"I said that I can see the logic of the tactic."

"I feel like I'm talking to Adam when you say things like that."

"You're listening to me, your husband, an Army sniper who killed because it was necessary. Who understands the dynamics of the endless struggle for power, the aggressive nature of man, and the essential role of violence in our world."

"Violent men doing violent things in the name of peace. Talk about a lack of logic," Alice stated in a mocking tone.

Michael "Owl" O'Neal thought back to the point in their conversation where he could have agreed and let the whole thing drop. Maybe, he was like Adam Hayes. He just had to poke the bear. He decided to end the heated debate, "I'm not violent, now. I'm retired. I'm doing non-violent things, raising horses, and enjoying the quiet life."

"Until he shows up, again. Then you'll be off to some godforsaken place to do what you and your bff do best."

"My god, you're jealous of Adam," Michael concluded.

"Why not? He's had more of your time than I have."

"That's over. I'm retired."

"I can't believe you when you say that. Adam Hayes will be a factor in our lives, once more. You can count on that," Alice rose and left the room.

Adam Hayes and Ken Farmingdale sat at the table on the fantail of Ismenios. It was late afternoon and they were sailing west into a setting sun. General Hughes had informed the team that their destination was Virginia Beach. They were going to meet with Secret Service Agent Emanuel Vegas and another unnamed person at an undisclosed location.

"Who do you think the mystery guest is?" Ken asked.

"I gave up guessing a long time ago," Adam replied, "I found I was never right."

"I don't know. Curiosity isn't an easy thing to turn off."

"Is it raining in Virginia Beach?" Adam asked.

"What? I don't know."

"Exactly, we'll know when we get there."

Ron Clew joined the two men. He carried a bottle of spring water. Upon seeing the large Navy Seal, Ken Farmingdale asked, "Ron, you think it's raining in Virginia Beach?"

"I know it is. I just checked the weather. It's raining on the entire each coast as far west as Pittsburgh."

Ihtsham Azlan, aka Darius Holiday, walked in the rain out by the railroad yard in Wilkes-Barre, Pennsylvania. Droplets sprayed his face. It felt refreshing. He was deep in thought. The next lesson had to be big—so big they would fear retaliating against any family member of a fellow soldier of Allah. A drop hit him in the eye. He looked up getting hit by more rain and thanked Allah for the inspiration.

CHAPTER 12

After tying up at a pier in Little Creek Cove, five men climbed into General Hughes black Escalade and drove into the night. They still did not know their destination. A rendezvous had been set up with Secret Service Agent Emanuel Vegas. The team rode north on Ocean View Avenue past houses and hotels. At one-point Maxwell Hughes slowed their speed enough to miss a traffic signal. A bright red ball hung above the roadway. From the right, a dark colored Lincoln MKZ appeared from nowhere and turned onto Ocean View Avenue headed in the same direction as the team. The signal changed and the rendezvous was complete. They then played follow the leader.

The two-car caravan entered US Highway 64 which led to the Hampton Roads Bridge Tunnel. In the distance, they could see the red flashing light of Old Point Comfort Light, a lighthouse located at Fort Monroe in the Virginia portion of the Chesapeake Bay. Built in 1775, it is one of the first locations designated for a light by the new United States federal government. Appropriations were made starting in 1800. It is the oldest operating lighthouse in America.

They emerged from the Hampton Roads Tunnel in Newport News, Virginia. For the next twenty minutes, two vehicles wound through dark streets to a sparsely populated area. A private road led to a Spanish style stucco house nestled in the woods overlooking a lake. The Lincoln pulled into a parking area and Secret Service Agent Emanuel Vegas climbed out.

After quick pleasantries, Vegas said, "We are going to meet a gentleman who will remain anonymous. His name, for all intents and purposes, is Liam. He's French. I've done extensive vetting and through channels have determined that he is loosely associated with the French government. This meet is by his request." Vegas leaned closer and said in a low voice, "As far as he knows, you are a team of mercenaries."

Six men entered the house in silence. In the living room sat a white-haired gentleman in a dark grey suit. His years were obvious as he slowly rose to greet them. In his right hand he held a cane. His countenance was friendly and unthreatening. Small of stature it appeared that he would have a difficult time with any member of the team.

"Messieurs, c'est mon honneur. Gentlemen, it is my honor," Liam said in a cordial manner.

"Liam, I am Emanuel Vegas, I believe we spoke on the telephone."

"Oui," he replied, "I appreciate you arranging this meeting."

After introductions were made using only first names they settled into chairs and on the sofa. Silence ruled.

When he was comfortable, Liam began, "Terrorism has become a cancer in the world—a cancer that is destined to spread. En effet, in France, we have suffered more than our share of events." He shook his head as if resigned to the inevitable. "All civilized nations have become targets. And, like civilized countries, they—we—use the rule of law to investigate and punish the malfaiteur, uh, criminal. But it does not prevent their actions."

Once more, silence hung heavy in the room as Liam searched for the words to continue.

"In Brussels, a truck was driven into an open market. Many died and were injured. The terrorist was killed. Generally, that would be the end of it except for investigating whether or not others participated in the act. In this case there were three accomplices. All three, as well as the terrorist's mother, father, and brother have been assassinated." He read the words that were on notes left with the bodies in Brussels. Liam looked up and repeated, as if digesting, the final words, "Satan's Shadow is everywhere."

Secret Service Agent Emanuel Vegas spoke, "We are aware of the events in Brussels."

"To prevent future terrorist acts we must have better intelligence or a different approach," Liam admitted. Once again, he searched for the correct words. "The world's intelligence is severely lacking. Quite honestly, we do not believe it will keep our people safe. Unfortunately, terrorist acts will continue." The elder French gentleman looked at the others in the room and stated, "In no way can the French government condone the taking of innocent lives. However, the primary purpose of government is to protect the welfare of its people. Leaving us no choice but to . . ."

"Shake hands with the devil?" General Hughes finished the sentence.

"Who better to fight the devil?"

Emanuel Vegas added, "Liam, this Satan's Shadow is something we are unfamiliar with."

Liam smiled a sardonic smile, "What is unfortunate is the fact that our intelligence agency cannot identify terrorists before they act, but can provide the location of a certain converted military vessel on the dates when the, uh, military actions took place in Greece and Belgium."

"Strictly coincidence," Captain Jarvis Demoye offered.

"Please, understand, I have no official status and that information, shall we say, no longer exists." Liam waved his hand and added, "We made unofficial inquiries as to the owner of the craft and were directed to Mr. Vegas."

Emanuel Vegas spoke, "I explained that a corporation I represent owns the vessel and leases it to research and other entities. Why it was where it was, at the times indicated, we neither have any knowledge of nor interest in."

Again, a sardonic smile, as Liam said, "Oui, we understand." He rose from his seat and walked over to a wall and examined a painting. "The world is never what it seems. An artist sees beauty. A doctor, the miracle of life. A teacher, great possibilities. A priest, some master plan. A scientist, vast opportunities." He turned to face the room, "A soldier, harsh realities."

No one spoke. Each man was keenly aware that Liam and, by virtue of his comments, the French government suspected that Ismenios was connected to the aforementioned eliminations. How much they knew was unknown. But, why had Emanuel Vegas set up this meeting and exposed them personally to unnecessary risk? Once he learned that Ismenios had been compromised other arrangements could have been made. Satan's Shadow only worked if they remained in the shadows.

"J'étais autrefois soldat, I was once a soldier," Liam stated proudly. "Soldiers sometimes see reality too clearly. Difficult decisions must be made, but always with an objective in mind. We are not diplomats." He walked back to his chair and sat, "As I stated earlier, I have no official status with the French government. In fact, I am not here and neither are you." This time he presented a genuine smile.

"Why are you not here?" Maxwell Hughes asked.

Emanuel Vegas answered, "What Liam is about to say, I felt you needed to hear firsthand so that there are no misinterpretations or misgivings."

"When the next inevitable event occurs in France, we will do our investigations, as usual," Liam stated. "However, we will not be looking in shadows. Should information be illegally shared or assistance rendered it will be without the authority or knowledge of the French government. Any action taken in response to a terrorist act will officially be condemned by my government, even though it is understood that terrorism has a price."

All in the room understood. How much information would be shared or assistance rendered remained a question. However, it was not a question that would be answered in that room at that time.

"Do you mind me asking, your rank when you were a soldier?" Adam Hayes broke the silence.

"Not at all. I was chef de bataillon in the infantry, Commandant, what you call Major in your army."

Captain Jarvis Demoye spoke, "I hope there are no further events in your country. It is a beautiful place that I would like to visit in the near future. Although, I am not comfortable with my vessel being tracked."

"Let me assure you, that was an anomaly," Liam replied. "In the future, should you visit, there is a retired anchorage that is little used that you might find accommodating."

As the discussion continued and became more friendly, Emanuel Vegas invited them to join him in the dining room where he had set up food and refreshments earlier. A fine French wine was opened and Liam made a toast, "Dans l'ombre de Satan, la paix soit trouvée. In Satan's Shadow may peace be found."

CHAPTER 13

"We have a partial fingerprint from one of the Starbuck's cups," NYPD Detective Larry Bartholomew told FBI Special Agent Peggy Fox. "Unfortunately, no match was found in the national database."

Peggy Fox nodded as she listened to the police update.

"We searched all the garbage cans in and around the Port Authority to see if he disposed of his grocery bag. Nothing was found." Detective Bartholomew scratched his head and added, "If he took the bag with him, we should be able to identify him from one of the parking lot cameras as he walked to his car or one of the subway platform cameras. Yet, we looked at the footage of all the cameras during the time period right after the last firebomb ignited and didn't see a young black man with a grocery bag."

"If that bag contained all of the Starbucks cups it would be pretty empty after he made all of his deliveries. He probably discarded the few grocery items, folded the bag, and put it in his pocket," Special Agent Fox suggested.

"Could be," Detective Bartholomew agreed. He added, "Our labs are analyzing the coal dust residue to determine its origin. They pretty much believe it came from Pennsylvania. There are four main types of coal. They are rated by carbon content. Lignite is the lowest ranked. It is soft and ranges in color from black to shades of brown. Mainly it's used for power generation and accounts for 17 percent of the world's coal reserves. Sub-bituminous coal burns more cleanly than other type of coal due to its low sulfur content. It makes up 30 percent of the world's coal reserves. Bituminous coal is harder and blacker and is divided into two types: thermal and metallurgical. Thermal is used for power generation, cement manufacturing and other industrial purposes, while metallurgical is used for manufacturing iron and steel. And then we have Anthracite, the most mature coal with the highest carbon content of any type of coal. It generally is used for home heating and accounts for about 1 percent of the world's total coal reserves." He looked up from the paper he was reading and finished, "The coal region in Pennsylvania is home to the largest known deposits of Anthracite coal found in the Americas. And, that is the type of coal dust we appear to be looking at."

FBI Special Agent Peggy Fox nodded. What might seem like a small fact about a very big state could vastly narrow the origin of their evildoer. After all, one doesn't go into a hardware store and order a box of coal dust. Their firebomber most likely works, or worked, in a coal mine.

After her meeting with NYPD, Agent Fox investigated the coal industry in Pennsylvania. Bituminous coal was plentiful in western Pennsylvania, while anthracite coal was generally located in four principle fields in eastern Pennsylvania. Originally, it was found that anthracite coal would not burn. The difficulty lies in the fact that anthracite is almost pure carbon—it does not contain a sufficient number of hydrocarbons that become volatile at elevated temperatures. Actually, there was evidence that those living among the coal fields did learn how to burn anthracite in their blacksmith forges by adding grates that eased the process of igniting the coal and developing a sustainable fire. In a letter dated 1826, Jesse Fell noted that blacksmiths in the Wilkes-Barre area, located in the heart of the Northern Coal Field, had been using anthracite since about 1772. Special Agent Peggy Fox determined that more than 75% of anthracite production still came from underground mines with many small room-and-pillar operations still in existence. The enormous state just became smaller.

Ihtsham Azlan, aka Darius Holiday, continued to search information about Atlanta, Georgia. Given his change of plans the bars and restaurants in Buckhead would no longer suffice. His plan was simple. Those who refused to see the truth shall see no more. The divine sign from Allah was clear, delivered through a drop of rainwater. The tool he had chosen would also be clear in appearance but would have a nasty bite. In fact, it would burn as the fires of hell brought forth to serve a most honorable soldier. Concentrated sulfuric acid would be the new flaming sword in his jihad.

H2SO4, sulfuric acid, is corrosive to metals, living tissues, and even stones. At a high concentration it can cause very serious damage upon contact. Not only does it cause chemical burns via hydrolysis, but also secondary thermal burns through dehydration. It can also lead to permanent blindness if splashed into eyes and irreversible damage if swallowed.

All mining operations use sulfuric acid. In some cases, it is used to digest and remove organic constituents and release bound metals in an ore sample. Concentrated sulfuric acid, or 98% grade, is more stable therefore best for storage. As it turned out Darius had access to significant amounts of concentrated sulfuric acid at the coal mine where he worked. The acid sat in several quart-size glass containers in the mine's storage facility open to all employees. Only a red warning sign stood between him and his object of interest.

It was not uncommon for miners to enter the storage area for supplies. Darius, aka Ihtsham Azlan, brought a matching glass quart container filled with water to work in his lunch box. At an opportune time, he strolled into the storage facility switched jars and left with nobody the wiser. The theft would most likely remain undetected for an extended period of time as no ore samples were scheduled to be tested. Strong Lion had new teeth.

To deliver the bite, Ihtsham Azlan needed a device with which to spray the caustic liquid. Allah smiled on him when he located a Graco 20V Cordless Paint Sprayer on eBay. Using a 20-Volt MAX XR lithium-ion battery his sword could produce up to 2,000 psi and hold a quart of liquid. This was the exact amount of venom he possessed. The airless spray could be adjusted from narrow to wide and operate in any direction—even upside down. He had some concern about the 10-pound weight, but with some practice using water he knew he could master the sword. Allah frowned when he saw the price, $598.90. However, Darius decided to use his only credit card, after all, he had no intention of repaying the moneylenders.

Late on a Saturday night he found what he was looking for—an appropriate target.

CHAPTER 14

The world was relatively peaceful for three weeks. There were, of course, regional conflicts, crime, and other threats, but no terrorist attacks. Then on a Friday afternoon on an overcast day, Ralph Hillsman, a seventeen-year-old senior at Torrey Pines High School in the North County Coastal area of San Diego, California went out to his car and retrieved a Glock 19 Gen 3, 9mm Pistol and three 15 round magazines. He was angry. He'd been angry for a long time.

At six-feet, 210 pounds, and an offensive linesman on the Falcons, the varsity football team, Ralph was not a force to underestimate. He had a quick temper and got a degree of pleasure from intimidating those smaller than him. One character he specifically disliked was Walter Umbridge, a pipsqueak with a big mouth. Whenever they crossed paths there was friction. Ralph could spot Umbridge a mile away. The short, skinny, long-haired, blond twerp seemed to have a unique swagger that just pissed Ralph Hillsman off—even at a distance. And, when Walter opened his wiseass mouth, it was all Ralph could do not to knock him senseless.

Two weeks earlier the Falconer, the school's monthly newsletter, came out. An article applauded the award-winning debate team. They had done very well in regional and national competitions. On that team was Walter Umbridge who during an interview stated, "Words can move nations and change the course of history. I know an offensive linesman on our team who can't move defensemen out of the way. Maybe he should consider debate." Everyone in the school knew to whom Walter was referring. As a result, Ralph Hillsman received a lot of ribbing. This did not sit well as he was accustomed to dishing it out, therefore was not prepared to be the brunt of jokes. Verbal bullying, though supposedly good-natured, took its toll. Ralph's temper quickly got the best of him. In the end, he broke up with his girlfriend after shoving her against a wall and was suspended for two days following a confrontation with a teacher.

This was his first day back at school and Ralph Hillsman was going to settle all scores. He walked through a side door that he had propped open with a book, down the hall, and into the classroom of the teacher who had turned him in. Two students were standing at the teacher's desk discussing a homework assignment. Ellen Yee turned upon hearing the door burst open. A flash of light and loud deafening bang caused her to fall backwards. She was not hit by the bullet. Her teacher, Gordon Klein, a thirty-five-year-old father of two was hit in the throat. Instinctively, he tried to stand, but a second round pierced his skull and he dropped to the floor. The second student in the room, Sherell Johnson, screamed. A bullet at point blank range ended her outcry. Ralph Hillsman turned and left the classroom without acknowledging the existence of Ellen Yee.

In the hall a number of students were frozen in place not sure what they had heard. Two boys, freshmen Bobby Hill and Hector Rodriguez, were within ten feet of Ralph when he emerged from the classroom. Both dropped from bullet wounds as the angry 17-year-old fired two more times. Chaos erupted as students began to run in every direction. Ralph fired three more rounds but didn't hit any targets. Quickly he moved in the direction of the room where the debate team met and practiced. Upon entry he found one student sitting at a desk staring at him in shock and fear. A single shot to the head drove the lifeforce out of Jamal Hatch.

School alarm bells began sounding and slamming doors were heard up and down the hall. Ralph Hillsman proceeded to an open common area and found it empty. A noise to his right garnered his attention. He saw a shadow disappear down a hallway. At a sprint he followed. In the hall he saw an adult female attempt to open a locked classroom door. When she couldn't she turned to face her approaching assassin. In one last desperate act she said, "You don't want to do this. Put the gun down."

"I have to," Ralph replied.

"You can stop, now. Just put the . . ." Geraldine Pearl Mason felt two sharp impacts. In disbelief she stood looking at her assailant. He had blank eyes and an expressionless face. Slowly, that haunting face disappeared into a fog as she slid down the wall to the floor.

Other classroom doors that Ralph Hillsman tried refused to allow entry. Because he lost count of how many rounds he had fired, eleven, he pressed the magazine release and let it drop to the floor. It took but two seconds to insert a full magazine and pull back the slide to place a cartridge in the chamber.

Ralph became aware of sirens in the distance outside the school. Time was running out yet he had two primary targets that he still wished to find, the principal and Walter Umbridge. It wasn't as though he hadn't come unprepared. From previous observations he knew the little shit Walter Umbridge would be in the debate room. He wasn't. Somehow that didn't fit the pattern. He had to be there, unless . . .

Of all the bad breaks, the little twerp was probably in the boy's room. Ralph Hillsman turned and ran back toward the debate room. As he did he spotted a classroom door that was open. Inside stood a teacher in front of three students. Mrs. Harriet Gambrel threw a book at the gunman as he entered and yelled, "Get the hell out of my class!" Ralph ducked and fired four shots as he retreated. No one was hit.

Red hot anger drove the crazed student as he headed toward the boy's room closest to the debate room. Behind him he heard the sounds of heavy boot steps. The police had arrived. With one last stride he crashed through the boy's room door. Inside stood a lone boy staring wide-eyed at the larger boy.

"Where's Umbridge?" Ralph Hillsman bellowed.

"Who?"

Two shots rang out creating a deafening echo in the enclosed bathroom. Freddie Jordan died instantly. Ralph Hillsman kicked open the stall doors but no one else was in the bathroom. Reality suddenly set in. He was not going to kill Walter Umbridge on that day. It was the time for reckoning. He had to choose to go down fighting, take his own life, or surrender.

Noises outside the door told Ralph that the authorities had arrived. A loud voice ordered, "Drop your weapon and come out with your hands up."

Indecision ruled the moment.

Outside the bathroom a SWAT team prepared to enter. Other police teams were in the process of clearing the building. The threat was contained.

Ralph Hillsman stared at the muzzle of the Glock 19, 9mm pistol. Four pounds of pressure was all that was needed to end his suffering. He wondered if he would hear the report or see the flash. A loud boom and blinding flash ended his speculation.

CHAPTER 15

"Five dead, three wounded," Adam "Watch Dog" Hayes stated as they watched a news report.

The team had assembled at the Spanish style stucco house in Newport News upon being recalled by General Hughes. He switched the monitor from broadcast television to his computer-driven PowerPoint presentation. The face of Ralph Hillsman appeared. "The SWAT team tossed a flashbang grenade into the lavatory. Knocked him on his ass. They entered and found him deaf and blind and non-resistant."

"Magnesium oxide and ammonium perchlorate has that effect," Adam offered.

"He's now in custody in the San Diego Central Jail, Downtown," Maxwell Hughes continued unbothered by Adam Hayes aside. The next slide showed a man and a woman. "His father is a doctor and mother a teacher." Slide three presented the visage of a twenty-year-old boy. "His brother is in college in Alabama—Auburn."

"What's his major?" Ken Farmingdale asked.

"Does it matter?" Navy Seal Ron Clew responded.

After an awkward moment of silence Ken replied, "Guess not."

"There is an aunt. His mother's sister, Michelle Gillespie. She lives in San Francisco with her husband and two children."

"This just keeps getting better and better," Ken Farmingdale concluded.

"When that young man fired the first round he essentially signed the death certificate on all these individuals," Maxwell Hughes declared. He forwarded the presentation. A man in his thirties appeared. "Gordon Klein, teacher, thirty-five-years-old, father of two." A young black girl replaced the teacher, "Sherell Johnson, sixteen, cheerleader, wanted to be a pharmacist." A blond haired fourteen-year-old boy appeared next, "Bobby Hill, freshman, not a lot of info on him." Before the group stood a young Indian boy holding a fishing rod. His smile was enchanting. Here was someone full of life and getting pleasure out of every moment. "Jamal Hatch, cancer survivor, class clown, philosopher, well-liked kid destined to be successful at whatever he chose to do." The final photo was of a fifteen-year-old boy sitting in an orchestra playing a violin. "Freddie Jordan, 15, musician, adopted." Three pictures were displayed side-by-side. "All three wounded are expected to survive but will need rehabilitation." General Maxwell Hughes paused for effect.

Silence ruled.

When he proceeded, Hughes looked in the direction of Ken Farmingdale, "The path we have chosen will save countless other innocent lives like these. What we have to do stinks. There is no doubt about it. The only way we can function is by depersonalizing it. We are the A-Bomb over Hiroshima. The objective is to ultimately save innocent lives. It's a high cost but will be worth the price paid."

From the shadows, Secret Service Agent Emanuel Vegas stated, "The very fact that no one is immune will be a telling message. From a strictly strategic perspective this is an outstanding opportunity to emphasize our point. Add to it the fact that the perpetrator survived and the impact will be tenfold. The press will show his reaction to the repercussions of his actions. If he cries or is distraught or commits suicide it will deliver a clear unmistakable message. This situation offers more communications value than ten camel farmers with nondescript families."

Navy Captain Jarvis Demoye spoke, "Eventually, we are all going to have to get our hands dirty."

"Out damned spot! Out, I say!—One; two: why, then 'tis time to do't.—Hell is murky." Adam Hayes quoted Lady Macbeth.

Jarvis continued, "We understand the strategy and have accepted the tactics. For sure, we did not choose these targets. Instead, we chose to be the instruments by which terrorism will be defeated. I'm prepared to pull my weight." He looked at the Navy Seal and Green Beret in the room. "I believe Ken should sit this one out."

"Wait . . ." Ken Farmingdale began.

"I agree," General Hughes made the decision.

Two days after that meeting Michael Hillsman, brother of the school shooter, returned to his single room in South Donahue Residence Hall at Auburn University. The Veterinarian major finished a long day and was looking forward to just chilling out. He unlocked the door and reached in for the light switch. Abruptly pulled inside by the arm he never saw the assailant who snapped his neck killing him instantly.

Two-thousand-sixty miles away Arlene Hillsman dialed her son's telephone number. As there was a two-hour difference in time zones, she made it a habit to call early in the evening. Outside in the garage her husband, Daniel, lay dead from a slit throat. Then, after failing to get an answer multiple times Arlene went to the garage to express her concern to her husband. She never saw his body only to join it on the cement floor.

A shot rang out in a quiet San Francisco suburb causing all the dogs to begin barking. Michelle Gillespie, who had been walking her dog, lay on a gravel path that went through the woods with a bullet hole in the back of her head.

At all three crime scenes a message was left. "Terrorism has a price. If you commit a terrorist act your family is the price you pay. We will locate and kill every member of your family, your friends, associates, and any who offered you support. Through your actions you condemn them all to death. They can hide but we will find them. Satan's Shadow is everywhere."

Initially, police at each crime scene were baffled. They were unaware of the other slayings. It was when the Auburn police attempted to contact the parents of Michael Hillsman only to find they too had been murdered did the pieces fit together. Once the press carried the story, San Francisco police connected the dots. At that point the story took on a life of its own.

"The family of Ralph Hillsman, the San Diego school shooter, have been murdered. His mother, father, brother, and aunt have been slain." A network news anchor announced. He read the message found with the bodies. "It appears that a vigilante group of sorts has been organized to wreak revenge upon the family of terrorists. This is a new phenomenon that leaves us all feeling very vulnerable and uncomfortable." He turned his attention to a guest on the program, an NYPD detective.

In response to questions, the detective stated, "We are a nation of laws. No individual or group can take the law into their own hands. The killer or killers of these innocent people are as guilty as the young man who shot those people in the school. They will be brought to justice."

When asked if he thought the killing of a terrorist's family might reduce the number of terrorists the detective hesitated before he replied, "That is not the issue. Whether it would or would not does not justify the taking of innocent lives."

Ron Clew said, "I said a prayer for the young man."

The other members of the team looked at the Navy Seal.

"I felt it was the least I could do. His life was buying the lives of hundreds, maybe thousands, who will not fall prey to future terrorists."

CHAPTER 16

Darius Holiday, aka Ihtsham Azlan, read an account of the assassinations of Ralph Hillsman's family. He also read the message that had been left with the bodies. As he did, anger welled up inside. These infidels think they can stop the forces of Allah? That student was a demented madman with no moral authority. He was not leading the fight to rid the world of non-believers. He was a barbarian. There was no honor in what he did.

When Darius heard his sister's voice in the other room it made him wonder whether or not his family was at risk? Were these unholy servants of Satan going to come for them? Should he warn them? Or, should he let them become martyrs and enjoy the rewards of paradise? In the end, he decided the solution was to not get caught.

A children's festival in a park in downtown Atlanta had been selected by Strong Lion as the site of the next lesson. Liquid fire would wash away the evil images of America and leave them in the dark to ponder their heresy. Ihtsham Azlan's mind reflected on the Satanic message left with the family of Ralph Hillsman. He decided that he needed to remold his message.

Maxwell Hughes poured two-fingers worth of Scotch into Ken Farmingdale's glass. He also added the golden liquid to his own glass and sat next to his colleague. "I asked you to join me because I want you to have an opportunity to say and do what you wish without the pressure of the other team members.

"You think I'm a weak link?" Ken asked.

"What I think at this moment doesn't matter. It's what you think that counts."

Ken Farmingdale sipped the Scotch, placed his glass on the table, and said, "Contrary to appearances, I understand what we are doing, support what we are doing, see the logic of what we are doing—but it doesn't mean I have to like what we are doing."

"Agreed," Hughes nodded. He then explained, "There are police officers who go their entire career without ever firing their sidearm. And, there are those who do. Some of those who shoot and kill someone never come to terms with it. They heap so much guilt upon themselves that they no longer are effective as police officers. In combat, I've seen soldiers do their job and move on. I've seen others who can't get the image of a human being dropping lifelessly to the ground out of their mind. It's difficult to predict." General Hughes leaned back in his chair, "What we are doing is not taking out a combatant or stopping a criminal. A rational person can come to terms with that. What we are doing is counter-intuitive to all of our moral learning, sense of right and wrong, and idea of justice. It creates a philosophical conflict that cannot really be resolved." Maxwell Hughes stood and paced for a moment, "None of us can celebrate a kill. Because it wasn't a righteous kill. None of us can be proud of what we have done. It was not an honorable act. None of us can predict the future. So, we fear that it will be in vain and innocents were unnecessarily sacrificed. None of us can live with what we are doing. To a man, we will only find peace in death." He looked directly into Ken Farmingdale's blue eyes.

Ken downed the remainder of the liquid in his glass. "In the movie *Patton*, George C. Scott states, 'No one ever won a war by giving his life for his country. He made the other son-of-a-bitch give his life for his country.' In a way, we are giving our lives for our country. The stench of what we are doing can never be removed from our souls. Yet, we do it because we believe it will have long-term positive results. That's not much comfort when doubt rears its ugly head. It doesn't make our mirror any more friendly. Captain Demoye put a bullet in the back of an innocent woman's head. He will never forgive himself for that."

"Captain Demoye fired cruise missiles into distant villages killing hundreds of innocent men, women, and children. He neither seeks forgiveness nor has to forgive himself. In war tactics always include collateral damage. And, we are in a constant never-ending war. Man's inhumanity to man is everywhere. Drug dealers take thousands of lives every year. Murders occur every hour. Children are abused and neglected. Mass killings are not new."

The General continued, "On 10 April 1891 an old man walked up to St. Mary's Parochial School in Newburgh, N.Y. brought a shotgun up to his shoulder and fired on a group of children playing in front of the school. There was neither warning nor provocation. The good news was that none of the children died."

"A South African farmer named Stephanus Swart shot dead at least eight people and injured three others in Charlestown, South Africa, before committing suicide."

"In 1966, Charles Whitman went on top of the clock tower on the campus of the University of Texas and shot dead 14 persons while wounding 31 more."

"Port Arthur, Australia, in 1996, 28-year-old Martin Bryant killed 35 and wounded 21 before being captured by police."

"Stephen Craig Paddock on 1 October 17 opened fire from a hotel room window into a crowd at a country music festival in Las Vegas. There were 58 fatalities and 851 injuries before he committed suicide. No one knows the motive for this mass murder."

"Today, it is not always the unbalanced who are committing mass murder although they are still a factor. Most often, it is a group of religious zealots hellbent on promoting their ideology through terror. They have no remorse about killing innocent people and are not afraid to die. However, we believe they have enough humanity left to care about their family. You see it in news stories where they are wailing when their wife, parent, or children are killed. And so, we fight terror with terror."

"Captain Demoye, Ron Clew, Emanuel Vegas, Adam Hayes, and I have accepted our role in the effort to combat terrorism."

"And, me," Ken declared.

"That's why we are talking. If you no longer can rationalize what we are doing you are free to leave the team."

"I know too much," Ken warned.

General Hughes smiled, "This isn't the Mafia. We don't tell you that you are free to go only to have Clemenza waiting in the back seat of your car. Any member of this team can choose to leave at any time with no repercussions. Should they betray our trust that would be unfortunate, however, Emanuel and I accepted that risk from the beginning. To leave, a team member simply has to leave his challenge coin on the table."

Ken Farmingdale reached into his pocket a retrieved his coin. He turned it over and over with his fingers. The dragon, ring of stars, and sword became the words est ultra de tenebris et in umbra satanas. He stated the translation, "It is beyond dark in Satan's shadow." He looked at Maxwell Hughes and asked, "Will the sun ever rise over a peaceful meadow?"

"Not for us," the General admitted.

FBI Special Agent Peggy Fox read a map of the Wilkes-Barre/

Scranton area that indicated all active underground anthracite coal mines. There were sixteen. She and an FBI lab technician planned to go to the area to collect coal dust samples. From what she had been told there would be subtle differences based on the depth of the coal vein and content of trace minerals such as; mercury, arsenic, and selenium. With a little luck they would be able to identify the mine from which the firebomb coal dust had been gathered. Once they identified the specific mine they would then examine all of the employee records. She was beginning to feel hopeful, after all they had grainy distant photographs of a young black male and a partial fingerprint. Her only hope was that time was on their side.

CHAPTER 17

Three men sat in a dark basement room in an old apartment building in Jersey City, New Jersey. They spoke in Arabic. A plan that had taken three years to develop was ready to be executed. It would be the beginning of the end of the Great Satan—America.

"The fools look where we are not and guard what is of no interest to us," Haji Ejder Jahandar stated with a wry smile. The prefix "Haji" meant he was one who had made the Muslim pilgrimage to Mecca.

A Hajj is a pilgrimage to the holy city of Mecca that occurs during the Islamic month of Dhu al-Hijjah. Pilgrims travel to within 6 miles of Mecca. There they don Ihram clothing, which consists of two white sheets. The main rituals include walking seven times around the Kaaba (Tawaf), touching the Black Stone (Istilam), traveling seven times between Mount Safa and Mount Marwah (Sa'yee), and symbolically stoning the Devil in Mina (Ramee). Every able-bodied Muslim is expected to make a pilgrimage to Mecca at least once in their life.

"They cannot predict the unpredictable, or prepare for that which cannot be anticipated," Rashid Teymouri pointed out with great confidence and enthusiasm.

The third member of the group, Toufan Ghorbani Mashti, remained silent. The suffix "Mashti" indicated that he was one who had made a pilgrimage to Mashhad.

"The past infidel leader used the term 'shock and awe' when their boots defiled our sacred ground," Haji Ejder Jahandar reminded the others. "They shall see the true meaning of 'shock and awe' very soon."

"I wait with the greatest anticipation," Rashid declared.

Haji Ejder Jahandar turned to the third man, "And you, Toufan, does not your heart soar at the dawn of a new califate?"

Toufan Ghorbani Mashti was a man in his late twenties. Small of stature, he stood only five foot two inches tall. While he had a slight build, his muscles were like strands of steel. A light chin beard adorned his face and a gold tooth was obvious when he smiled which was only on rare occasions. He had a wife and young daughter. Together, they lived in a small apartment a few blocks away from the location of the meeting.

Toufan was considered a refugee, had a green card, and worked in a commercial print shop in Jersey City. Ink stained fingers ran across his chin as he said contemplatively, "I worry."

"Of what do you worry, my friend? This plan is flawless."

"Not about the plan—it is good. Allah will be pleased," Toufan stated. "Instead, I worry about these slayers of families of righteous fighters for Allah. These shadows of Satan would kill my family if my identity became known."

"Were that to happen they would be martyred and enjoy eternal happiness." Haji Ejder proclaimed, then added, "But, that will not happen. We shall find them and with the light of Allah dispense of this shadow of Satan."

"I am prepared to die as a servant of Allah. What I fear is retribution against my innocent family."

Haji Ejder Jahandar stood and walked over to his confederate and stated with pride, "They shall be the hunted and their families will die as a demonstration of the will of Allah. There are many loyal Muslims who watch within the American government. One, who shall be referred to as euyun allah—Allah's eyes—is following a path he believes will lead to those who must die."

"Still I worry if we do not kill them first, they will kill my family."

"And, if that happens it is Allah's will," Haji Ejder Jahandar stated firmly. "Did you not declare shahada and do you not accept what Allah wishes?"

Shahada is a declaration of faith and trust. Recited in Arabic, "lā 'ilāha 'illā-llāhu muhammadun rasūlu-llāh," it confirms, "There is no god but God (and) Muhammad is the messenger of God." To become a Muslim and to convert to Islam one must proclaim this fact.

"You know I am faithful. Have I not made the pilgrimage to Mashhad? Have I not killed infidels? Am I not loyal?"

"Yes, you are," Haji Ejder Jahandar replied. He stated in a consoling voice, "You need not worry about your family. Allah will deliver Satan's Shadow to us and we will slay them like rabid dogs in the street."

Darius Holiday arrived at the Reeds Fork coal mine in Wilkes-Barre, Pennsylvania at 7:00 a.m. He didn't look forward to another tedious, filthy, backbreaking, eight-hour morning shift. In addition, it was becoming more and more difficult for Ihtsham Azlan to do manual labor amongst the ignorant blasphemers. They weren't interested in learning and laughed at his attempts to enlighten them.

As he walked toward the coal-breaker building he witnessed a black Chevrolet Suburban pull up in front of the management office. The shiny, clean, massive, black vehicle was distinctly out-of-place at Reeds Fork. Darius Holiday, aka Ihtsham Azlan, stopped and observed three people exit the vehicle. Two men and a woman. Both men wore dark blue suits. The woman wore a black skirt, white blouse, and low-heel black shoes. They might as well have worn jackets with big letters stating FBI. Ihtsham Azlan moved to the side behind an excavator so as to not be seen observing them. Sweat appeared on his forehead. His first thought was that they were looking for him. However, slowly logic dispelled that idea as they would have come to his home and made a pre-dawn raid. He concluded that they had discovered that the firebombs in New York City contained coal dust. How much they actually had determined or whether or not they could tell from which mine the coal dust had come, he didn't know. What he did know was that the authorities were closing in. For the first time he felt true fear.

The children's festival in a park in downtown Atlanta was still more than two weeks away. And, one fact was blatantly clear, he had to leave home as quickly as possible—no immediately. The clock was ticking. How many ticks did he have? Most likely fewer than he'd like. Darius Holiday did not clock in that morning. Instead, he headed home with great haste.

Darius' mother was surprised when he arrived unexpectedly home. She was washing dishes and upon hearing the door close grabbed a towel and went to investigate. "Darius, what are you doing home? Are you ill?"

"Uh, no," he muttered, "I decided not to go to work today. I have something that I have to do that can't wait."

"What is it? What do you have to do that would cause you to miss work?"

"Nothing. It's personal. I'll tell you later," he blurted out as he ran upstairs to his room.

Marcella Holiday watched her son disappear upstairs. She wanted to know what Darius was up to, but lately he had become withdrawn, noncommunicable, and moody. She decided to wait and returned to her dishes.

Darius cursed as he waited for his far-too-slow laptop computer to boot. When the clock is ticking it is like the heartbeat of a dying man. Finally, he was able to get on the World Wide Web. Quickly, he went to one of the more radical Muslim websites he had discovered during his regular searches. He scanned the articles written by various clerics. Some of the articles gave the name of the Imam and the mosque with which they were affiliated. New York, Chicago, Boston, Los Angeles, then he found what he was looking for; a mosque not in a major city that was within driving distance. A particular Imam wrote about the need for Shari'a Law to spread throughout the world for a century of peace to come to pass. Imam Rajavi made such a strong and beautiful case with erudite and flowing words. He was a cleric at a mosque in Jersey City, New Jersey.

Betty Ann Myers practiced her dance steps. The eight-year-old, third grade student at Cliftondale Elementary School was one of the many chosen to perform at the upcoming children's festival in Atlanta. She would never know how close she had come to becoming a victim of Darius Holiday, aka Ihtsham Azlan.

CHAPTER 18

"So, what have you been up to?" Michael "Owl" O'Neal asked his friend Adam Hayes. The two men sat in the den of O'Neal's house. A fire in the fireplace warmed the room.

"Now, you know, I can't talk about classified activities," was the response with a half-smile.

"You don't look any worse for wear. Any new scars?"

"Not a one," Adam stated holding his arms up as if showing an untouched body.

"I'd tell you to be careful out there among those no-goods, but then, I know you all too well."

"That's when you get hurt—when you're careful," Adam retorted.

Owl smiled widely, "Yeah, you're right." He looked directly at Adam "Watch Dog" Hayes and said in a serious voice, "You look tired."

"No more than usual," was Adam's not fully believable reply.

"Without me looking after you, you're probably not taking care of yourself."

"Yes mother. Don't worry, I'm eating my vegetables."

"Are you playing nice with others?"

"Absolutely, not!" this brought forth a wide grin. Adam then observed, "You look well-rested and fit. Is retirement what you thought it would be?"

"I wake up in a comfortable bed with a beautiful woman by my side. Don't have to reach for my sidearm or listen for intruders. I wear clean clothes and have warm meals and don't answer to anybody."

"So, the answer is, it sucks."

"Only to an adrenaline junkie."

"Come'on, you miss that comfortable hillside in some exotic location with fleas, snakes, rodents, and scalding sun."

"Not one bit."

Adam changed the subject, "Did you read about that family in California that was assassinated after their son shot up a school?"

"I saw it," Michael said. "They left some kind of message about retribution against any terrorist's family."

"You think that will make a difference?"

"That strategy has been bandied about as a logical means of stopping terrorism for years," Michael O'Neal said thoughtfully. "However, it is so far afield from our moral values that it could never be seriously considered."

"Well, apparently someone is not only considering it they have implemented a program," Adam stated as he stared at Owl to see if he could read any reaction. As usual, Michael O'Neal was impossible to read. Adam wanted to punch him in the face. That steady unflappable sniper personality brought forth confidence in and trust of the man. It also was a pain-in-the-ass. Yet, there was one thing Watch Dog knew for sure and that was Michael could be a valuable asset to Satan's Shadow. Not only as a highly skilled sniper, the man was a combat veteran who could kill using a wide range of weapons, including bare hands. Adam also had to admit to himself that it would feel good to have Owl on the team. Unfortunately, he also knew it was a dark malevolent team. It was not something he wished on a friend.

"When I read about the family and associates of the terrorist who ran a truck through a crowd in Brussels being killed, I wondered if it would have an effect. My first thought was it just might," Michael said.

Adam Hayes saw a glimmer of hope for recruiting Michael O'Neal.

Owl continued, "But, I'm really torn about the logic of killing the family of a deranged student. He wasn't a terrorist in the political sense of the word."

"Religious zealot, political extremist, communist, racist, or deranged student—it's essentially all the same. Someone who kills a group of innocent people to make a statement is a terrorist," Adam concluded.

"Satan's Shadow?" Michael O'Neal asked.

"What?"

"Satan's Shadow. That group is making a statement by killing innocent people."

Adam sat and thought for a moment. Owl always had a keen sense about him. In this case he was correct. Satan's Shadow was a terrorist organization. That could not be denied. Every member of the team knew there was an evil element to what they were doing. No one sugarcoated it. In essence, they had made a pact with the devil. They killed and would again kill innocent people as a form of counter-terrorism. Fight fire with fire. Maybe the numbers would someday prove it to be a valid strategy, but there would be no way to really know. If the killing of four innocent persons caused one, two, five, or more would-be mass murderers to think twice or not act at all and it saved hundreds of lives wasn't that a good tradeoff?

Michael O'Neal continued, "North Korea is obsessed with secrecy. They also have very little respect for citizen's rights. Political prisoners are sent to the Kwan-li-so concentration camps along with their relatives without any fair trial. Citizens convicted of more serious political crimes are sentenced to life imprisonment, as well as the next two generations of their family. Their children and grandchildren will be born in the camps as part of the '3 generations of punishment' policy established by state founder Kim Il-Sung in 1948. Defectors are considered political prisoners. Originally, if an individual escaped from the North his or her family would disappear and never be heard from again. Many family members were sent to the Kwan-li-so concentration camps. This tactic kept a major portion of the population in line. However, there were still those who chose to leave even knowing that their families would pay the price and be sent away to remote rural towns or prison camps. These defectors sought freedom in spite of the cost. How that compares to hellbent, driven radical terrorists I don't know."

"You have to wonder how someone could defect knowing their family will be sent off to a concentration camp or executed," Adam said, thinking out loud.

"There is a philosophy that each individual is responsible solely for their own actions. If those actions impact on another individual it is not their fault. It is the result of that other individual taking some action on their part which places them where they would be affected."

"Huh, what the fuck are you talking about?"

Michael O'Neal explained, "Say you are driving down the road, get distracted, and run down a man in the dark. It was his decision to walk on that road at that time which placed him where he could be hit."

"So, I'm innocent because he chose to be there and was wearing black by the way."

"No, you're still guilty as shit."

"Then why are you telling me this?"

"Our lives are made up of constantly encountering others due to the decisions that we each have made."

"Great. What does that have to do with defectors from North Korea?"

"The defector is only responsible for his or her own action. They could have been captured or killed. They could have remained and been a good citizen and their parents still get sent off to a prison for some other reason. Or, their parents may have supported the idea of their son or daughter having a better life and were willing to pay the price."

"So, this kid in California chooses to shoot up a school but bears no responsibility for what happened to his parents?"

"In essence, yes. The ones responsible are these Satan's Shadow characters. They chose to kill the family." Michael sat back for a moment, then added, "However . . ."

"There's always a 'however' with you."

"However, when the risk of one's family being executed if they proceed with plans to do a mass murder becomes more well-known then the perpetrator will bear some of the responsibility. Maybe . . ."

"Oh, now you throw in a 'maybe.'"

"Maybe, responsibility isn't the correct term. They are a catalyst which set the wheels in motion. The responsibility remains with those who do the actual killing."

"Back to that, what is your opinion of that strategy to thwart terrorism?" Adam asked his fellow combatant.

"Logically, it makes a degree of sense. If this kid in California was aware of the risk his family would face, he might have decided the price was too high."

"Bingo!"

"A sensible person might think that way. But, are religiously driven terrorists sensible people?" Michael asked.

"My take on the whole thing is that until now these terrorists have had nothing to lose except their life and they don't give a shit about that. Then you hear that the leaders guarantee that the terrorists' families will be taken care of. That adds a whole new dimension to the thing," Adam smiled and added, "but then again, how would they know if the leaders lived up to their promise or reneged? Obviously, they do care about their family, but how much?"

"The only way to know if this approach is a deterrent is to do it," Michael O'Neal admitted. "No government entity would ever consider such a step so this vigilante group is made up of unaffiliated scoundrels."

Adam looked at his friend and fellow warrior and wondered if the ex-sniper would ever endorse the actions of Satan's Shadow. He also wondered if Owl would ever participate. Adam knew his friend extremely well, however, this was an area that tested one's faith and threatened their values. If he ever approached Michael O'Neal it would have to be for some important reason because, without a doubt, it would be a life-changing decision.

Alice, Michael's wife, entered the room. She peered at Adam with her standard "I wish you weren't here" look. "Dinner will be ready soon. You are staying, aren't you, Adam?"

There was no love or affection between Alice and Adam. There was between Alice and Michael. It was clear Owl had found his nest and was content. Adam Hayes stood and answered, "As good as your cooking is Alice, I have to be pushing on. I have to see to Michael's travel arrangements," Adam turned toward Michael with an mischievous grin.

"You son-of-a-bitch," Michael swore, "Why do you do that?"

CHAPTER 19

"Saif al-Haqq—Sword of Truth—will be our tool," Haji Ejder Jahandar stated with pride as he examined the scimitar he held in his hand. "One hundred heads will deliver a greater message than any single bloody event."

Rashid Teymouri gazed at the gleaming metal and saw the bright reflection of the awesome power of Allah, "And, in the end it shall be Saif al-Islam—Sword of submission to Allah."

"When the beheadings begin, we must be sure to videotape the sacrifice's protestations and pleas for mercy. While the American broadcast media will not show the blessed event, they will describe it and the internet will make it available in all its glory."

"The fools, in their arrogance, they protect their airports, and power plants, and shopping malls, and sports arenas all the while failing to protect their people," Rashid Teymouri said as he laughed.

"Once we conquer their people we shall have their airports, power plants, shopping malls, sports arenas, and all they possess."

Toufan Ghorbani once more remained silent. He fully supported the jihad yet could not reconcile the risk to his family.

"One hundred heads in one hundred days," Haji Ejder Jahandar smiled. "And, they have no way of knowing or predicting where we might strike next." He looked accusingly at Toufan Ghorbani and added, "And, they have no way of knowing who we are. We are as the wind blowing across this cursed land leaving our unmistakable message."

Once complete, our cell goes back to sleep to dream of a global caliphate."

"A magnificent plan," Toufan Ghorbani admitted.

Haji Ejder Jahandar pointed out, "Thirty-two percent of murders are never solved. When it is a random murder with no connection between the perpetrator and the victim the unsolved percentage rises to over eighty percent."

Rashid Teymouri, said with reverence, "Allah has guided us with a divine plan and will protect us."

"Remember, our pattern is a non-pattern. Targets will be anywhere and everywhere," Haji Ejder Jahandar said. "It could be a truck driver in Alabama, then a school teacher in Indiana, a police officer in Missouri, nun in Kentucky, housewife in a small town in Texas, or a store keeper in California. Every police officer, homeland security official, FBI agent, and citizen will be desperately looking—but for what? They will not know. A beautiful, overwhelming sense of fear and panic will shroud the Great Satan."

"Where do you hide?" Rashid Teymouri asked a rhetorical question.

Haji Ejder Jahandar looked at his friend and smiled.

Blood ran down the gutter of a Paris street. Twelve victims lay dead or dying from gunshot wounds. The attack happened quickly and ended with the death of two terrorists Rashid Sassani and Nebez Pahlavi. Their identities were kept from the press.

Aboard Ismenios, four solemn warriors sat in the living area. Rain and waves caused them to seek refuge. Captain Jarvis Demoye was on the bridge. The converted Navy patrol boat was sailing east across the Atlantic Ocean.

"I hear that Ralph Hillsman, the kid who shot up the school, has not been told about the fate of his family," Ken Farmingdale offered.

"And, the press is downplaying the Satan's Shadow angle," Adam Hayes observed.

General Hughes responded, "That's the good thing about the internet. The rest of the world is aware of the price he paid for his act."

"You ever get the feeling that America is the least informed nation on Earth?" Navy Seal Ronald Clew asked. He looked at his cohorts and explained, "I mean, the foreign press seems to deliver the facts while the American press picks and chooses what to cover and then always puts a spin on it. It's like *Pravda* for chrissake."

"I don't think they even know they are doing it," Ken stated.

Adam Hayes remarked, "Yeah, and for my money, they've been so conditioned to want to be seen as open-minded the exact opposite is what happens. They close their eyes to the truth. In their vain attempt to be seen as not attacking a religion, they ignore the fact that a religion is attacking us."

"A history lesson," General Hughes announced. He placed a disc into the computer and narrated a slide show on the large monitor. "Four North African states, Tripoli, Algiers, Tunis, and Morocco were collectively known as the Barbary States. For centuries their Corsairs captured merchant ships in the Mediterranean enslaving or ransoming their crews. As a result, Muslim rulers of these nations gained wealth and built their naval power. Between the 16th and 19th centuries the Roman Catholic church under the order of "Mathurins" collected and disbursed funds for ransom of captive sailors."

"Appeasement. It has never worked in history," Adam Hayes pointed out.

"American ships had been protected by France until the end of the Revolutionary War. Then on 11 October 1784, Moroccan pirates captured the brigantine Betsey. Spain negotiated the return of the captured ship and crew. The Spanish government at the time recommended that the United States offer tribute to prevent further attacks against merchant ships. Algeria captured the schooner Maria on 25 July 1785 and a week later the Dauphin. Thomas Jefferson, the U.S. Minister to France, tried to purchase treaties and the freedom of the captured sailors held by Algeria. Morocco signed a treaty on 23 June 1786. Unfortunately, the other Barbary states continued their piracy. In the end, all four Barbary Coast states demanded $660,000 each ransom for the crews. Negotiations quickly broke down and the crews remained enslaved for over a decade. Finally, in 1795 at a cost of over one million dollars Algeria released 115 American sailors. Back in those days this was no small sum. It represented about one-sixth of the entire U.S. budget."

"We didn't learn then and we're not learning now," concluded Ron Clew.

"In March 1786, Thomas Jefferson and John Adams went to London to negotiate with Tripoli's envoy, ambassador Sidi Haji Abdul Rahman Adja. They inquired how a group of states could make war upon nations who had done them no injury. The ambassador replied, 'Islam was founded on the Laws of their Prophet, that it was written in their Quran, that all nations who should not have acknowledged their authority were sinners, that it was their right and duty to make war upon them wherever they could be found, and to make slaves of all they could take as Prisoners, and that every Musselman (Muslim) who should be slain in Battle was sure to go to Paradise.'"

"There you have it," Adam Hayes stated, as he stood, "they are authorized by their religion to make war on all who do not accept their religion. Why can't our government simply accept that fact?"

"The U.S. continued to pay Algiers as much as one million dollars ransom per year over the next 15 years. In 1798, after growing tired of the demands for extremely large tributes from the Barbary States, the United States Department of the Navy was founded." General Hughes added as an aside, "And, on 11 July 1798 President John Adams signed into law the creation of the United States Marines."

The history lesson continued, "On Thomas Jefferson's inauguration as President in 1801, Yusuf Karamanli, the Pasha of Tripoli, demanded $225,000 from the new administration. Jefferson refused. Consequently, on 10 May 1801, the Pasha had the flagpole in front of the U.S. Consulate cut down as a declaration of war. Subsequently, Jefferson sent a small squadron, consisting of three frigates and one schooner, under the command of Commodore Richard Dale to the Mediterranean to protect American ships and citizens against potential aggression. On 1 August 1801 the schooner Enterprise, commanded by Lieutenant Andrew Sterret, defeated the 14-gun corsair Tripoli after a one-sided battle."

"Don't fuck with America," Adam Hayes said as he raised his glass.

"The turning point in the war was the Battle of Derna, April–May 1805. Eight U.S. Marines and five hundred mercenaries crossed the desert from Alexandria, Egypt to capture the Tripolitan city of Derna. This was the first time the United States flag was raised in victory on foreign soil. Yusuf Karamanli signed a treaty ending hostilities on 10 June 1805. Here's where it got sticky. The two sides agreed to swap prisoners, however there were 300 more Americans than Tripolino subjects. As a result, the United States agreed to pay $60,000 for the difference essentially paying a ransom."

"Yeah, that's going to end well," Ron Clew said as he shook his head.

"Two years later Barbary pirates again began seizing American ships."

"There's a surprise," Adam said as he glanced at Ron Clew.

"Unfortunately, the War of 1812 kept the United States from responding until 1815. At that time, naval victories by Commodores William Bainbridge and Stephen Decatur led to treaties ending all tribute payments by the U.S."

"You can't reason with a rat," Adam said.

Immediately, Ken Farmingdale said, "Rooster Cogburn—*True Grit*."

General Hughes finished the lesson, "Thomas Jefferson read the Quran and concluded fundamentalist Islam was like no other religion the world had ever seen. A religion based on supremacism, whose holy book not only condoned but mandated violence against unbelievers. This was unacceptable to him. His fear was that someday this brand of Islam would return and pose an even greater threat to the United States."

Jarvis Demoye summed it up perfectly, "And, now here we are with the same threat on a global basis rather than contained in the Mediterranean Sea."

CHAPTER 20

FBI Special Agent Peggy Fox had read the report with interest. The lab identified the mine from which the coal dust in the New York City firebomb attacks had come. Reeds Fork was an older mine. Its anthracite coal had a distinct chemical composition due to the depth of the vein. With that information in hand she and three other agents returned to Wilkes-Barre, Pennsylvania. A subsequent discussion with Reeds Fork management turned up three potential suspects. The first two had iron-clad alibis for the weekend of the attacks. The third suspect, Darius Holiday, Reeds Fork management told the FBI agents had recently converted to Islam. He was not at home. His mother explained that he had come home after failing to report to work three days earlier, packed a few things, and left. She had not seen or heard from him since.

A search of Darius' room convinced the agents that he was, indeed, the perpetrator of not only the New York City attack, but also the Philadelphia mall attack. An additional forensic team showed up with a van and began removing all evidence.

Sam and Marcella Holiday, Darius' parents, stood in shock as they watched the FBI agents work.

"Do you really think my son did these terrible things?" Marcella asked desperately wanting for it to be untrue.

"I'm afraid so," Agent Peggy Fox answered. Once again, she inquired, "Do you have any idea where Darius might have gone?" She emphasized, "It's important. If he has another attack planned many lives may be at risk."

"He didn't say anything when he left," Darius' mother stated sadly.

"That boy chose wrong," Sam Holiday lamented as he shook his head.

"I have something," one of the forensic agents said as he entered the room. In his hand he held a piece of paper on which was written the details of the children's festival scheduled in Atlanta.

Agent Peggy Fox immediately dialed her smart phone. "Connect me with the Director of the Critical Incident Response Group (CIRG)." After a few seconds she spoke once more, "This is Special Agent Peggy Fox, give me the CIED Unit immediately." The Counter-Improvised Explosive Devices Unit shares critical information among federal, state, and local law enforcement agencies concerning bombs, hazardous materials, and weapons of mass destruction. Agent Fox alerted the agency as to a possible planned attack on Atlanta's children's festival. She also provided information pertaining to the person of interest. He was to be detained for questioning.

After three days, Darius Holiday hung slumped over tied to a wooden chair in the basement of an old apartment building in Jersey City, New Jersey. When he first arrived, he proceeded directly to the masque where Imam Rajavi was a leader. Rajavi listened politely as the young man explained how he had converted to Islam and wanted to join in the struggle. When further questioned about his knowledge of the faith, Darius' answers revealed many gaps and misunderstandings. The Imam grew impatient and suspicious. It was clear that the young man was not a government agent. They were far better trained and convincing. This one could be telling the truth or he could be out to do harm to their efforts. It was then he told Darius that he had some others for him to meet.

The unsuspecting "lone wolf" was fallen upon, captured, and tortured. Through tears he insisted that he wanted to join them. With a finger smashed under the hardened steal head of a hammer Darius confessed in detail his attacks in Philadelphia and New York.

Haji Ejder Jahandar, his face uncomfortably close and breath filling Darius' nose with stale wretched aromas of meat and spices, said menacingly, "You lie! We know who performed so nobly in Philadelphia and New York."

Darius insisted he was the one. In a weak pleading voice, he asked, "Why do you not believe me?"

With a changed tone, Haji Ejder Jahandar asked, "Why did you come here?"

"The FBI were at the coal mine where I got the coal dust that I used in my fire bombs. I don't know how they found out. I told no one. I saw them and immediately left. A speech by Imam Rajavi told me he believed as I do that the only way to spread Shari'a is through violence." Darius' breathing was labored.

"You fool, you could have brought the FBI here."

"They were at the mine when I left. They didn't follow me."

“If they identify you, they know your car. In no time at all, every police officer in the country will be on the lookout for it.” Haji Ejder Jahandar paced for a moment than asked, “Where is your car, now?”

“I parked it on the street a block from here.”

The interrogator walked over to Darius and searched his pockets until he found a set of keys. “What kind of car is it?”

After Darius described his old car, Haji Ejder Jahandar spoke to another man in the room in Arabic. The man took the keys and left.

“You come at an inconvenient time,” Haji Ejder Jahandar said. “We don’t have time to investigate your story so we cannot open our doors to you.”

“Please, I just want to be a mujahid.”

“And, what do you know of jihad?”

“I know jihad is to continue until all mankind either embraces Islam or submits to the authority of the Muslim state.”

Haji Ejder Jahandar left the room.

For two days Darius Holiday was locked in a storage room with little food or water and a pail. He slept on a cement floor with some old tattered filthy rags to keep warm. On the third day he was dragged out and tied to the wooden chair, once more.

Haji Ejder Jahandar entered the room. He raised Darius’ head by pushing his forehead. “Our source confirmed your story. You have done well. Unfortunately, you put us at great risk when you came here.”

“I didn’t mean to,” Darius whispered. Ihtsham Azlan, strong lion, did not feel very strong at that moment.

“We may have use for you, little brother,” Haji Ejder Jahandar continued with a smile.

Darius returned a weak smile.

“You must trust us. Until we are ready to move, you must stay locked up in the cell for security reasons. You will receive plenty of food and water and be given bathroom breaks. Later, we will bring you clean clothes and allow you to shower. When the time is right you will join us.”

Through his overwhelming feeling of relief all Darius could do was utter, “Thank you.”

Haji Ejder Jahandar smiled and said, “You will be number one.”

Ismenios was on autopilot.

General Hughes spoke with the four members of the team seated around on the fantail, "Manny received information from the man who wasn't there."

"How does he know?" Adam Hayes asked in jest.

"The two Paris terrorists, Rashid Sassani and Nebez Pahlavi, have immediate family and known associates who provided material support. Their families are located in different parts of France. The known associates are in Paris." General Hughes spoke to Captain Jarvis Demoye, "I have the coordinates of a safe harborage." He then returned his attention to the three other members of the team, "We'll start with the associates, then move on to the families. Sassani has a wife and two children. Pahlavi just a wife and sister."

Ex-Navy Seal Ron Clew asked, "With the news of Satan's Shadow spreading the word, do we have any information on increased security around any of these people?"

"I wasn't informed of any, however, we have to assume that each operation will get progressively more risky," General Hughes replied.

"That means more reconnoitering before execution," Adam Hayes concluded.

"Like it or not, that's a good thing," Max Hughes stated. "When we remove the package even when it is being guarded it will cause others to better understand the risk they are taking and the price to be paid."

"One thing," Ron Clew stated with conviction, "No police or other non-target casualties."

General Hughes gazed long at the large man, nodded, and said, "If the target is not accessible without non-target damage—abort. There will be another opportunity. Whether we take them out immediately after an attack or two months later the effect remains the same."

Ken Farmingdale, who had sat silently taking in the discussion, finally spoke, "Carry the battle to them. Don't let them bring it to you. Put them on the defensive and don't ever apologize for anything—Harry S. Truman."

CHAPTER 21

Special Agent Peggy Fox sat in her office considering the situation. They were close to 100% sure the perp was one Darius Holiday from Wilkes-Barre, Pennsylvania. Evidence from the crime scenes, Reeds Fork coal mine, and the suspect's home provided more than enough circumstantial evidence—probably enough to convict. Unfortunately, they did not have the man in custody, therefore, neither had a confession nor the results of an interview. His fingerprints had been confirmed by samples collected from his room. And, a positive comparison was made with the fragment collected in New York City.

In frustration, she threw the file down onto her desk. This arrest would be a career-maker. Yet, she had nothing that would indicate where the young Holiday might have gone. A nationwide alert had turned up nothing. No car, no credit card usage, no contact with friends or relatives, no sightings, no body, and no other leads. In the back of her mind, she thought, some small-town sheriff who never did any more than check locked doors and issue traffic summons would probably stumble upon Darius Holiday and gain national recognition.

It was critical for many reasons that she, Special Agent Peggy Fox, find and arrest the culprit. First, they had to prevent his next attack. Next, the arrest had to be pure leaving no avenue for a slimy lawyer to get him off on a technicality. Finally, an opportunity like this rarely falls into an agent's hands and should not be squandered. She picked up the phone and dialed a number. When it was answered she stated with authority, "Put the team together. We're going back to Pennsylvania. There's got to be something we overlooked that will point us in the right direction."

Ismenios steamed past the jetty and up the L'Herault River in Southern France. Although there were resorts along the Mediterranean the river quickly became less commercial surrounded by forests and farm land. Captain DeMoye cut the engines and allowed the craft to drift alongside a small indistinguishable wooden dock. They were in the vicinity of the village of Agde.

A few curious fishermen observed the unmarked boat for a few moments and then went back to their nets. It was not uncommon for a research vessel, yacht, or government craft to stop at that location.

No one met the Ismenios. That was to be expected as they were not there. While on the trip across the Atlantic the team had received information concerning assets available to them in France. These were unofficial—therefore non-existent.

General Hughes reviewed his notes. High speed Rail Europe trains left Agda every 36 minutes headed to Paris. The trip averaged 4 hours 42 minutes. Fake passports were adroitly hidden in a safe location under the dock. Other credentials were included giving them diplomatic immunity. A map of Paris was also provided, as well as a French/English dictionary.

A list of targets had been compiled during their trip. In addition, they had been informed that the families of both terrorists were under police surveillance. This was as a precaution while not actually being full-fledged protection. Without question, they could be reached. There were four known associates of Rashid Sassani and Nebez Pahlavi in Paris. Others obviously existed but remained unidentified.

Adam Hayes, Ronald Clew, and Ken Farmingdale boarded the train to Paris. They made sure that there was no discussion of the terrorist attacks or their military backgrounds. The role of tourists was played perfectly. Ken Farmingdale read a brochure about sights to see in and around Paris. While at the same time Ron and Adam tried to teach each other French using the dictionary.

Before they left Ismenios a plan had been developed. Because it was believed the four associates of Sassani and Pahlavi lived near or with each other it would require a coordinated effort by all three men.

Two days of surveillance provided a clear picture of the situation. Paris police were watching the men but only on occasion and they made no secret about it. Once an hour a marked patrol car would slow in front of the apartment building where the targets resided. In addition, two foot-patrolmen passed periodically. Nothing else was observed. Ken Farmingdale wandered inside the building and identified two apartments where the targets lived. There were two men in each apartment. This fact vastly improved the logistics of the operation.

On the third day, after a patrol car did its pass by, three men entered the building at carefully timed intervals—Ken Farmingdale, followed by Ron Clew, and then Adam Hayes. Their first stop was an apartment on the third floor. The test pilot knocked on the door. A voice from inside inquired in French, "Qu'est-ce?" As planned, Ken responded, "La police." The door opened slowly and a face peered through the crack. Before he could say anything, a huge figure kicked open the door. Ron Clew and Adam Hayes were upon the man and he was killed instantly. In a back room they found the other target reading a book. He too was dispatched quickly.

The other apartment was on the fourth floor. This time the tactic was for Ken to bang on the door and yell in anger. As expected, the window on the rear of the apartment opened and one of the men scurried out. Before he knew what had happened a large hand grabbed him and tossed him off the fire escape. The other resident of the apartment heard the screams and headed for the bedroom. Two bullets from a 1911 45 caliber pistol stopped him. As residents of the building began to open their doors to investigate the disturbance they never saw the three men who fled down the fire escape and disappeared into the darkness.

When police arrived, they found the note with Satan Shadow's message. No one in the building saw or knew anything. Immediately, word was transmitted to the police in the two villages where the families of the terrorists lived and protection was intensified.

Darius Holiday, aka Ihtsham Azlan, felt much better after taking a shower and putting on clean clothes. His captors had become friendly and he felt as though he belonged. When he told them his adopted Muslim name, they laughed.

"You are strong lion?" Haji Ejder Jahandar said mockingly. "You are lion cub."

"Would a lion cub achieve what I did in Philadelphia and New York?"

"You are an assassin—not mujahid."

Darius became angry and asked in a raised voice, "Why do you treat me this way. I only wish to join you and fight for Allah."

"What do you know about Islam? You are a pretender. Have you declared shahada, do you not recite the salat five times a day, are you even aware of the five pillars of Islam?"

"I have learned what I can on the internet," Darius stated in a more subdued voice.

"Toufan, teach Shabal the proper way to pray," Haji Ejder Jahandar ordered.

Toufan Ghorbani led Darius Holiday into another room in the basement. He was not as brash or high-handed as Ejder when he instructed the young captive, "Salat is the Islamic prayer. It is recited five times a day; Fajr dawn, Dhuhr noon, Asr afternoon, Maghrib evening, and Ishā night. Salat is the second pillar of Islam."

Darius tried to take it all in and remember what he was being told. The different language, Arabic, made it impossible.

Toufan continued, "The prayer ritual is over 1,400 years old and is repeated five times a day by hundreds of millions of people all round the world. It is how you come in direct contact with Allah."

The man before Darius reflected one who was highly spiritual. He was driven by his faith and loyal to its tenets. This was a man Strong Lion could respect and learn from.

"Shabal, prayer is always done in the direction of the Ka'ba shrine in Mecca."

"Why do you call me Shabal?" Darius asked after hearing it twice.

Toufan smiled, "Haji Ejder Jahandar has dubbed you Shabal which means 'little lion.' It is not an insult."

Darius, aka Shabal, nodded.

"Salat must be preceded by ablutions of ritually washing the face, hands, and feet. This can be done with sand when water is not available." Toufan rose, "It begins in a standing position with hands raised. At this time you say, 'Allahu Akbar' meaning 'God is most great.'"

Darius stood and mimicked Toufan.

"You then fold your hands over your chest and recite the first chapter of the Qur'an in Arabic. This you can learn later. Now, raise your hands while saying, 'Allahu Akbar.' Then bow and repeat three times, 'Subhana rabbiyal adheem meaning 'Glory be to my Lord Almighty.'"

Toufan smiled as Darius vainly attempted to say the Arabic words. He offered, "You will get it in time, Shabal."

This time Darius smiled growing accustomed to his new name.

"Stand once more while reciting, 'Sam'i Allahu liman hamidah,' God hears those who call upon Him and, 'Rabbana wa lakal hamd,' Our Lord, praise be to You." Upon seeing the lost look on Shabal's face Toufan stated, "I will write it down for you to memorize."

"Thank you."

"Next, raise your hands up and say, 'Allahu Akbar.' Then while prostrate on the ground say three times, 'Subhana Rabbiyal A'ala,' Glory be to my Lord, the Most High. Rise to a sitting position, saying 'Allahu

Akbar.' Prostrate again as before. Rise to a standing position and declare, 'Allahu Akbar.' This concludes one cycle of prayer called rak'a. Generally, there are two rak'as and additional recitations, but this is enough for you for today." Toufan nodded as he concluded, "You have a lot to learn. As you do a beautiful world will be opened to you. Inner peace and a uniting of mind, body, and soul. Islam is the only true religion and you have been blessed to have found it and embraced it, Shabal."

"Thank you. I will learn as much as I can. I am ready to die for Allah. I wish to fight to destroy the Great Satan."

Toufan rubbed his chin. He appeared lost in thought. Slowly, he shook his head and said in a subdued voice, "We are not trying to destroy the world. We are trying to save it. When all become believers, there will be peace and harmony and prosperity. It is Allah's wish." He looked directly at Darius Holiday and asked, "Do you not fear for your family?"

CHAPTER 22

The golden color of a fine Scotch Whiskey reflected the lights in the cabin on the Ismenios. Around the room five men sat in silence. All, with the exception of ex-Navy Seal Ron Clew, held their drinks as they pondered what had been said. Clew held his standard bottled water.

Retired Air Force Major Ken Farmingdale had requested that he be the one to kill the children of terrorist Rashid Sassani. After observing the surprised looks on the faces of the other men he explained, "Adam, Ron, you two are soldiers, brave men, and powerful forces in this, uh, ignominious endeavor. We all see the logic and the need for it and pray, maybe not appropriate any more, for it to make a real and lasting difference. When you cut out cancer you always end up taking healthy living tissue with it." Ken realized he was rambling and returned to his original point, "You two have and will face formidable adversaries. It is obvious that you are more capable than me in this area. To be effective you have to have clear heads. My concern is that if you come face-to-face with a child and take it's life it will leave a psychological scar that will compromise your future actions. That is dangerous and cannot be allowed to happen."

Ken Farmingdale had the room's full attention.

"I, on the other hand, am the weak link in the combative arena. My reflexes are tuned to regaining control of an unpredictable experimental aircraft. I'm trained to stay calm in such situations, to consider the facts, and remember procedures. But, there is one unmistakable reality—only my life is on the line. What I do is about as individualized as it gets. It's me against the elements. Quite frankly, I'm not a team player. Never have been. Don't know how to take into account those around me."

"You did fine in Paris," Adam Hayes offered.

"Thanks. But, I was a small part of that operation and will continue to facilitate future efforts. However, let me ask, how comfortable would you have been if it was me who was waiting on that fire escape?"

"Don't underestimate yourself," General Hughes stated with authority.

"Please, understand, I'm neither feeling sorry for myself nor making excuses. I am facing two realities. First, there are limits to what I can do.

And second, this is something that I must do for the team. None of us in this room can take the life of a child and not have it leave a mark. Adam, you're a seasoned veteran with many battles under your belt. You are tough and resourceful and someone I wouldn't want to meet in a dark alley," Ken smiled, "Or a lit alley for that matter."

Adam Hayes smiled and nodded.

"Ron, you are one tough motherfucker. Can't handle booze, but I won't hold that against you."

Ron Clew snickered and raised his bottle of water.

"When you killed that college kid you said a prayer for him. That's what got me thinking. We all accept killing adults, male and female, to end this plague of terrorists that is hurting so many innocent people. Those four men in Paris—good riddance. The families in California—collateral damage. If what we are doing reduces or eliminates terrorist activities, we will all sleep well at night." Ken hesitated, then continued, "Back to the children. It has to be done because that sends a powerful message that cannot be ignored. Even the most cold-hearted terrorist has to have some feelings about his family and children. So, we have to do it and I have to be the one."

"What about the effect on you?" General Hughes asked. "You don't think it will bother you? In my opinion, you have the most compassion in this room."

"In the movie *African Queen*, Humphry Bogart has to get in the water to pull his boat out of the doldrums," Ken responded. "When he climbs back aboard he is covered with leaches. He almost panics as he can't stand leaches. After getting them off he realizes that the boat is still stuck and he has to go back into the water." Ken Farmingdale looked off into an unseen distance, "I'll always remember that scene because at the time I wondered if I would have the courage to do such a thing. Now, in this place at this time I find I have the opportunity to do something for the team even as repulsive as it is."

"Listen, Ken . . ." Adam started.

"Adam, I'm not being noble. There's nothing noble in this. I very well may be sacrificing myself, but isn't that a part of war? If my doing this allows you and Ron to remain highly effective it is a good strategy and you know it."

"Are you sure?" Ron Clew asked.

"The only thing that I am sure of is the fact that we are not trying to destroy families—we are trying to save the world."

The silence in the room continued. Each man pondered the words of Ken Farmingdale. Each man gained an elevated level of respect for the man who had been seen as incidental. Each man came face-to-face with his own river of leaches. Each man thought about what they were doing and the effect it was having on them. Each man understood the argument. In the end, each man concluded that he was right.

Back at the Holiday household in Wilkes-Barre, Pennsylvania Special Agent Peggy Fox and her team once more scoured the bedroom of their suspect. The kid took his laptop computer with him so there were no electronic tracks to follow. From all appearances, he lived a relatively Spartan life.

Darius' mother waited in the kitchen. She was experiencing a feeling of mourning. Her son was not dead, but if he did what they accused him of he was lost to her forever. A parent sees the good in their child while unconsciously overlooking their suspicious behavior. How many parents are blindsided when their child is arrested or dies from use of drugs?

Agent Fox entered the kitchen. Both women looked at each other trying to anticipate what was to come next. Agent Fox wanted answers and Marcella Holiday wanted her son to be innocent. Neither was going to get their wish that day.

"Mrs. Holiday, are you sure that Darius never mentioned any other friend or relative where he might find a place to hide?"

"My son, Darius, never said much. He was a quiet child. When he got that computer, he got even quieter." Marcella brushed crumbs off her apron, "Then he found that religion and seemed to change. I tried to get him to come to church but he wouldn't."

"Did he receive anything in the mail?"

"Not a thing."

"How about telephone calls?"

"He has his own phone, but I don't remember seeing him ever talking on it."

"Any visitors?"

"No."

Agent Fox asked the next question in an official voice, "Has he contacted you in any way since he disappeared?"

Marcella Holiday looked at the FBI agent and with tears in her eyes replied, "My Darius is gone. He left. I know I won't see him again and my heart wants to stop beating."

CHAPTER 23

"Rashid Sassani's wife and two children live in Orleans and Nebez Pahlavi's wife is in Dijon. His sister's whereabouts is unknown at this time," General Hughes stated as a map of France was displayed on the large flat screen monitor.

"Any info on exact locations?" Ron Clew asked.

"We're hoping to get that from the man who wasn't there," Hughes answered. "Nothing yet."

"Police protection goes without saying," Adam Hayes remarked.

"That's good and bad," Hughes replied. "Good that it will lead us to them, bad that once we do find them they will be difficult to get to."

"A diversion will have to be employed," Clew stated.

"Or, nontraditional approach," Hayes added.

"Once we have more information we will develop plans. If it seems too hot we will postpone any action. Put their names in the corral for future execution," the General declared.

Ralph Hillsman, the San Diego school shooter, sat in court in silence barely moving. Even though the authorities tried extremely hard to keep the news from him, he was aware of the murders of his father, mother, brother, and aunt. He also had seen and read a copy of the Satan's Shadow note.

When he was taking the lives of innocent students and teachers the impact on their families never crossed his mind. Then, a cold savage slap of reality taught him a lesson he would never forget. Remorse for a senseless act that cannot be undone is relentless. It refuses to yield. It remains a powerful image. It is impervious to the effects of time. It destroys the spirit.

Charges against Ralph Hillsman were read, as well as the names of the dead and wounded. He neither spoke nor heard his court-appointed lawyer enter a plea of guilty. A deal had been struck to avoid the death penalty. Ralph Hillsman would spend the rest of his life in jail with no opportunity for parole.

After the procedure he was led in shackles from the courtroom. As he departed, he couldn't help but see the skinny, long-haired, blond student, Walter Umbridge, sitting in the gallery. The young man was looking directly at him as if he knew the murdering thug had missed his primary target.

Imam Rajavi and Haji Ejder Jahandar sat in a parlor in an old brownstone on the south side of Jersey City. They had eaten dinner together, discussed masque business, and now were about to finalize plans for the upcoming demonstration of the power of Allah.

"This child, is he of any value?" Imam Rajavi inquired of his friend.

"He is a pretender. But, can be useful. He has proven to be resourceful in Philadelphia and New York. Originally, I had stated he would be number one in the lesson. Now, I find he is easily manipulated and led. We can use that to facilitate our efforts." Haji Ejder Jahandar leaned back and smiled revealing brown teeth, "I believe a fitting honor for Shabal is to be number 100."

"And, he can be trusted?"

"Yes, but I shall keep him under the supervision of Toufan Ghorbani."

This time Imam Rajavi leaned back and looked off at a distant point. The room hung silent as a tapestry. Finally, the older man spoke, "Toufan is a concern to me."

"He worries about his family because of these vigilantes—these Satans."

"Yes, I can see that." Imam Rajavi looked directly at Haji Ejder, "Yet, his loyalty must be to Allah and the jihad. He must be ready to sacrifice how and when necessary. His devotion to his family may cloud his judgment. You must observe and act should he become unreliable."

"It shall be done."

"Reassure him. We have brethren in the Great Satan's government. They are gathering information as to who these assassins are," Imam Rajavi revealed.

"I have heard. Have you met them?"

"No. That would be too dangerous." Rajavi added, "In fact, I do not know who they are. I only know they exist. I have also been told that they are close to identifying our enemy."

"That is good. We are ready to proceed."

"Ah, then, the final preparations can be made."

Haji Ejder Jahandar handed Imam Rajavi a piece of paper on which was a list in Arabic, "These are the 100 locations we will visit to leave our message. We will need assistance at the ones indicated for alternate transportation, shelter, and clothes. There are far too many surveillance cameras in this accursed country. Eventually, the authorities will identify a similar vehicle where we have been. By that time, we will have changed to a different one. We shall come as a breeze off the desert and leave as the moon surrenders to dawn."

Secret Service Agent Emanuel Vegas ran a computer file on Rashid Sassani and Nebez Pahlavi. Little new information had been added. He reread the same data he had reviewed before. What he saw was already in the hands of General Maxwell Hughes. His cellphone rang.

"Manny, comment vas-tu mon ami?"

"Liam, this is a surprise. I am well. Are you in the States, my friend?"

"Yes, I am here on holiday. I remember your invitation to take me to dinner should I ever make the trip."

Emanuel Vegas understood immediately and knew he had to keep the conversation as general as possible with it being on an unsecured telephone. "That was a long time ago. How many years has it been?"

"Too many. The children have grown and have their own children."

"Yes, we can't stop that from happening."

"We had some good times when we were younger. I look forward to catching up on the years."

"Ah, a different time, younger men, pretty ladies," Manny offered.

"And, too much wine. Ah, ma tête."

"Why don't we meet at six at the Capital Brewing Company pub on the corner of 11th and H Street NW? Do you think you can find it?"

"Better than you found the Les Deux Magots in Paris."

"Yes, that was an adventure."

At five minutes after six Emanuel Vegas walked into the Capital Brewing Company pub. He looked around for his friend, Liam. When he didn't see him, he left. After approximately five minutes, a white-haired gentleman in a blue suit rose from a corner table. With the aid of a cane he departed the pub. Outside he walked along H Street. Pedestrians filled the area to near capacity. Slowly, he made his way along the thoroughfare in an arbitrary direction. One block later a man came up behind the older man and said softly, "Indeed, Les Deux Magots?"

Without stopping or turning around Liam replied, "It was the first thing I could think of."

Emanuel Vegas passed Liam and led the way.

From a discreet distance the Frenchman who wasn't there followed. Separately, they entered a small grocery store, walked through, and out the back door. Together friends left an alley and hailed a taxicab.

"Precautions. They are necessary," Liam concluded.

"I can't be sure, but I get the feeling that there are eyes watching. It is not my wish that you be exposed."

"Merci mon ami."

The two men spoke no more until the taxi dropped them off on a side street. Manny opened the trunk of his dark blue Lincoln MKZ and both men placed their cellphones in a lead lined box. Once inside the vehicle the conversation flowed with abandon.

"So, what is so important that you had to come here without notice at great risk?"

"This war, it is not a simple thing."

"Nor, will it be won in our lifetime."

"Oui c'est vrai, that is true. Si triste," the old man shook his head.

Secret Service Agent Emanuel Vegas drove along a number of secluded routes to determine if they had been followed. When he was satisfied they were not in jeopardy he headed for their destination.

"When I was a young man it was easy being French. We shared a taste for good food and fine wine and the young girls. In being French we shared pride in our achievements, resilience, art, and culture." Silence followed. Then, Liam continued, "The socialists drained the can-do spirit from the people. The EU erased our identity. And, now we are being pushed out of our own country by Muslim interlopers who wish to take what we built over centuries. Now, it is no longer easy being French—it is a crime."

CHAPTER 24

"There is a mole in your government and we believe a counterpart in ours." Liam sipped the wine he had been given by Emanuel Vegas when they arrived at a safe house. "I am afraid that your friends might be at risk."

Manny reacted only slightly with a raising of his chin.

"The location given you on the whereabouts of Nebez Pahlavi's wife. It was stated that she is in Dijon. This is untrue." Raised eyebrows were the only overt sign from the Frenchman. "The source of this information is unknown to me. It was provided to me from a secondary source and believed to be correct. If a trusted friend hadn't come forth to provide contradictory information we would not have been aware of the inconsistency. She is, indeed, in Toulon with his sister."

"Information is always mercurial."

"Yes, but in this case, we have indications that this misinformation was purposeful." Liam nodded, "There has been movement by a number of subjects that have been under surveillance. And, chatter on suspect websites has increased. From all indications we suspect a trap is being set."

"I will inform those who are not there," Manny stated.

"Before you do, there is more." Liam rubbed his chin as he organized his thoughts, "We cannot be sure. However, transmissions were intercepted on official encrypted lines that provided unusual wording and numbers. When such a thing occurs, we attempt to determine its meaning. In this case, the only thing we have been able to uncover is that part of the encoded message is in Arabic and we believe the name Dijon was hidden in it."

"Do you know where the transmission originated and to whom it was sent?"

"We only know that it came from the Ministry of Immigration, Integration, National Identity and Co-development which is a relatively new agency. Of importance is the fact that it has absolutely no reason to contact the United States government."

"And, to whom was it sent?"

"The American State Department. Unfortunately, there are so many transmissions to unnamed general numbered addresses we do not have a name."

"Leads us to a dead end," Emanuel Vegas concluded.

Liam stood with the aid of his cane and walked over to Vegas. In a low voice that seemed to be a whisper he said, "I would not come here if this was the extent of our concern."

"What is it my friend?"

"On a return message that was uninterpretable there was a name—Vegas."

Ron Clew walked over to where Adam Hayes was sitting. Adam nodded in welcome. Clew sat and said, "You think he can do it?"

"How many members of your team have let you down over the years?"

Slightly surprised the ex-Navy Seal thought for a moment and replied, "One."

"Did you suspect that he might be ineffective at any time beforehand?"

"Not at the time. Afterward, there might have been signs that we missed. He had a habit of jogging before a mission. On that night he didn't, but no one noticed. What changed, why he froze, he took to his grave.

"I keep trying to read Farmingdale," Adam admitted. "So far he has performed well."

"He doesn't have any blood on his hands."

"And, he has an empathetic heart."

"I'm not sure we are doing him a favor putting him in such a position. Especially, as it will be his first time seeing life run out of a human being."

"He's putting himself in such a position."

Ron Clew nodded but didn't answer.

"You two talking about me?" Ken Farmingdale asked as he entered the room.

"You know it," was Adam Hayes response.

"Concerned I won't be able to kill two children."

"Man," Ron said, "I don't know how I feel about killing children close up."

"That's the difference," Ken stated, "This thing we are doing is filthy dirty. It stinks! It goes against everything we have been taught about fair play, justice, morality, and God knows what else. No rational person can see it as a good thing. Only, the one thing that makes it right is that doing nothing at all will lead to more innocent lives senselessly being taken by the monsters who move among us. These children are the spawn of those monsters. They are not innocent, happy, little urchins wanting to grow up to be teachers, or doctors, or bus drivers. I saw a television program a few years ago. It was a documentary about the Palestinians. When the children of this one family were interviewed, they said they hated Jews and wanted to kill them all. From the time they were infants they were told over and over that Jews were evil and deserved to die. For all I know these two children have been taught the same thing. They might be five or ten years away from following in daddy's footsteps for all we know. We are in the sewer swimming among the offal and waste. I signed on because we have to burn out the hatred even if it takes hell's fire."

"Look, don't hold back, man. Tell us what you really think," Adam Hayes said with a broad grin.

"You sure as shit put things in perspective," Ron Clew concluded.

"I will do this thing," Ken Farmingdale stated.

Darius Holiday, aka Shabal, swept the floor of the basement where he was residing. He wore a white thobe, a long robe that is tailored like a shirt which is ankle-length and loose. On his head was a kufi or prayer cap. As he did his work he thought about the last lesson Toufan Ghorbani had given him on the five pillars of Islam. Over and over, he tried to memorize the Arabic words along with their meaning; Shahada: Faith, Salat: Prayer, Zakāt: Charity, Sawm: Fasting, and Hajj: Pilgrimage to Mecca. These are considered mandatory by believers and are the foundation of Muslim life. In the back of the young black man's mind was a thought that kept attempting to be acknowledged. Islam was far more restricting than he had realized.

He liked Toufan. The man seemed too gentle to be a terrorist, but was a devout believer. He had a green card and worked in a commercial print shop in Jersey City. A few blocks from where Darius was being kept Toufan lived with his wife and young daughter in a small apartment. The five foot two inches tall Toufan was significantly shorter than Darius, yet he looked up to him. He had a way of making everything about Islam seem clean and beautiful and right. Even the taking of infidel's lives were for a noble reason.

A door opened and Haji Ejder Jahandar entered. This man Darius did not like all that much. He was stern, arrogant, condescending, and distant. Darius almost wished he was an infidel so he could deal with him. Ejder walked around examining the sweeping job the young pretender was doing. Finally, he stopped. "In a short time, we will have use for you."

"I'm ready to serve Allah."

"Yes, and you will." The older man with a slightly greying beard and receding hairline leaned against a post. "Keep learning from Toufan."

"I will. Some of the words are difficult."

The first smile Darius had seen on Haji Ejder Jahandar presented itself, "Yes, it will take practice. Make sure you know the meaning of those words. 'Woe to those who pray, but are unmindful of their prayer, or who pray only to be seen by people,' Qur'an 107:4-6. Allah does not need human prayers because he has no needs at all. You pray because Allah has told you that to do this and because you believe that you obtain great benefit in doing so."

"Sam'i Allahu liman hamidah,' God hears those who call upon Him," Darius stated.

"Good. You will be given a copy of the Qur'an to further your studies." Ejder then said in a subdued voice, "Toufan is a good man. He loves Allah and is a trusted friend. There are times that he worries about his family because of these Satans. Watch him for me. If you think he is unable to cope, let me know so that I might help a friend. After all, we are all brothers."

"I will do that."

"Good."

Special Agent Peggy Fox stood before the desk of the Executive Assistant Director for National Security Branch. She knew this meeting was coming and didn't look forward to it. He shuffled papers on his desk. She waited. Finally, he removed his reading glasses and stated, "If this individual is able to execute another attack it will negatively reflect upon this agency."

"I am aware of that."

"Has there been any progress in locating the suspect, his vehicle, or tracking credit card activity, computer activity, or even possible sightings?"

"He hasn't used any credit cards, his car has not been found, and our technology people haven't turned up anything."

"In other words, we are dead in the water."

"We have countless agents searching for the suspect, have eyes on the more radical mosques, are tracking chatter, have been in touch with confidential informants, are watching his home and place of business, tried pinging his phone, and have his photo in the hands of law enforcement nationwide. He's dropped off the face of the Earth."

"Agent Fox, do I need to assign this highly volatile investigation to a more senior staff member?"

"No, sir."

"Then what do you plan to do."

"Find the bastard and bring him to justice."

"You have two days. That will be all."

CHAPTER 25

A map of Dijon, France appeared on the flat screen monitor aboard Ismenios.

"Without a location we may have to reconnoiter the town and ID where there is increased police activity. At least, we do have a photograph of the target," General Hughes stated as the face of a woman appeared. He continued providing information about the city, "Throughout history, Dijon was a place of wealth and power. It was a center of European education, art, and science. The city has a population of 151,576, about the size of Kansas City, Kansas or Hollywood, Florida. The architecture is distinguished by Burgundian polychrome roofs."

"Polyunsaturated what?" Adam Hayes asked.

Ken Farmingdale spoke up, "It's glazed tiles in terracotta, black, yellow, and green that are arranged in geometric patterns. You should see it from the air."

"Adam looked at the test pilot and replied, "Thanks."

"Dijon is 193 miles southeast of Paris, 118 miles northwest of Geneva, and 118 miles north of Lyon. I think we better get our hands on a car."

"That could take a while," Captain Jarvis Demoye observed, "Maybe, we should shift our attention to the other target."

"The wife and kids?" Ron Clew asked as he glanced at Ken Farmingdale.

"Low hanging fruit."

General Hughes changed the image on the screen and a map appeared, "Orleans is larger than Dijon with a population of 250,000. About the size of Scottsdale, Arizona or Lubbock, Texas."

"Or, Reno," Adam added.

"It's less than an hour from Paris. During World War II the Germans made the Orléans Fleury-les-Aubrais railway station one of their central logistical rail hubs. The allies bombed the shit out of it. In the end, Orleans was one of the first cities to be rebuilt after the war."

"Do we have any info on location of the targets?" Ken Farmingdale asked.

General Hughes did not immediately answer which left the room shrouded in silence. The screen went black. Each man watched their leader and waited. It was out-of-character for the Marine, therefore, to be taken seriously.

"Communications have gone dark," General Hughes stated unemotionally. He picked up the satellite phone from the bar, "Vegas has neither contacted us nor responded to contact."

"Compromised?" Demoye inquired.

"At this point, it could be no more than a dead battery," Hughes replied. "I don't think it should hold up our operation. However, we are on our own."

"Three needles in a haystack, in a foreign country, where we don't speak the language, in a town none of us have ever seen, with police everywhere, and the possibility of being exposed. I like it!" Adam stated.

Others in the room couldn't help but snicker.

"So, the same situation exists in both cases," Demoye observed. "One is as unknown as the other."

"Although," Ron Clew offered, "One is smaller than the other."

"Dijon," Ken Farmingdale stated.

"Then, if we are agreed, we continue with the Dijon operation," General Hughes concluded.

Special Agent Peggy Fox stared at a map on her computer screen. She was trying to visualize what a desperate young black man might see and decide to do if he were on the run. He had been to and initiated terrorist attacks in Philadelphia and New York City. She just couldn't see him taking the risk of revisiting either crime scene. For him they would not be comfortable places to which to return. Given this reasoning, she felt that he could have decided to go in the opposite direction and head north, south, or west. North of Wilkes-Barre there was nothing except mountains. To the south was Philadelphia. And then something in her empathetic mindset made her decide that he would want to get out of the state of Pennsylvania as quickly as possible thus eliminating going west. That meant traveling east. The map seemed to grow before her eyes. There it was—New Jersey. Even more clearly, northern Jersey. Of course, she thought, there were more terrorist cells than pizza parlors in that area. It became clear that it was in that unique area where she would concentrate the efforts of the agency. It was there where a cold-blooded killer was most likely hiding. It was there where this investigation would be brought to a successful conclusion. In fact, she would stake her reputation on it. And, she was.

Darius Holiday, aka Shabal, was getting tired of hanging out in a basement. He read the Qur'an, prayed, and was bored beyond belief. There was talk of an upcoming terrorist plot, but he was not given any information. He wanted to belong but couldn't shake the feeling of being an outsider. Only Toufan Ghorbani made him feel welcome. He enjoyed their talks and hearing about the older man's family. It struck Darius that if they weren't so driven to destroy the Great Satan he could like this man as a friend.

"I remember my father, who ran a small restaurant, telling me that there was no more beautiful sound than the call to prayer in the morning," Toufan reminisced. "He was a quiet man. Always seemed to be thinking deep thoughts. It was a different time. Jihad was a distant concept not spoken of. The restaurant was his main focus." After a moment of silence, Toufan added, "And, his family."

Darius watched a change flow over the face of his teacher. The man had reached back and discovered something from the past that would undoubtedly influence his decisions about the future. Toufan Ghorbani Mashti seemed lost. It was as though someone turned on a light in a dark room and nothing was as expected. Things were out-of-place and peculiar. He woke up from a dream and was lost. The man whispered, "Allah, would not wish me to sacrifice my family."

Ron, Adam, and Ken rode north on Highway A7 in a rented car. By American standards the Renault Clio 4 RS 200 was a sub-compact. It was, however, the best-selling car in France. It was also a tight fit for the huge frame of Ron Clew. Behind the rear seat, under a blanket, were a number of weapons they believed might be needed.

"We're working completely in the dark," Ken Farmingdale stated the obvious.

"Not really," Adam replied, "We just have to be logical. People tend to stick with their own kind—especially when threatened. We'll start wherever there are Muslims congregating. How many mosques could there be in Dijon?"

Ron Clew added as he bounced in the back seat of the small car,

"Then we have to consider habits. It amazes me that even when trying to be inconspicuous people follow the same routine."

"Unfortunately, we don't have any info on the target so we don't know anything about any routine," Ken said.

"We have a photo," Adam stated, "She's wearing a crimson hijab. She won't give that up. That color is rather unique—stands out in a crowd. How considerate of her."

Countryside slid by as the three travelers fell into their own thoughts. It would be approximately another hour before they reached Dijon.

Unknown to Ron, Adam, and Ken there were an increased number of mujahid in the city of Dijon. Men waited in strategic positions to alert the others of the arrival of suspicious strangers in the relatively quiet town. In addition, they observed the two police stations, various mosques, halal markets, and public parks. Fighters were also waiting in nearby areas ready for quick deployment.

"When we get there I want a breakfast," Ken stated. "I'm accustomed to early morning starts on an empty stomach when testing an aircraft, but I'm not doing that today. I'm hungry."

"Maybe we'll get you some French pastries," Adam said as he drove the Renault. He added mischievously, "Or, maybe some French pastries—if you know what I mean."

"Roger that," Ron said from the back seat.

Special Agent Peggy Fox stood outside a mosque on Elizabeth Avenue in Jersey City, New Jersey. It was the fifth such structure she and her team had visited that day. Without probable cause or other evidence they did not have a search warrant. As a result, they could only observe. Yet, sometimes observation is enough. A trained eye can pick up subtle things that to most mean nothing. The other four mosques were quiet as they were between the morning and noon prayer times. Few entered. This particular mosque was known to the FBI and had significantly more activity. Young men arrived and left in high enough numbers to raise an FBI eyebrow.

Agent Fox stood across the street from the object of attention. She made a mental note to have a team assigned to randomly follow some of the men who leave the mosque to see where they go and who they meet with. It was a long-shot but long-shots have paid off in the past. One of those young men might lead them to something important.

What Agent Peggy Fox was unaware of was that in the basement of the tenement building she stood in front of was the fugitive she sought—Darius Holiday.

CHAPTER 26

"Abort, abort, abort," General Hughes voice came through the satellite phone loud and clear.

The team was approximately two clicks from Dijon when the call was received. Due to the direct and very clear message they did not try to call back after the General abruptly ended the phone call. Given the order, Adam turned the Renault around and headed south back toward Ismenios.

"Maybe he heard from Vegas," Ken Farmingdale surmised.

"Whatever the reason Dijon is not the place we want to be. That's for damn sure," Adam stated.

"There goes my damn breakfast," Ken snorted.

Ron Clew sat silently in the back seat pondering the turn of events. General Hughes obviously had new information. The only place that information could come from was Secret Service Agent Emanuel Vegas. If that information indicated that the team was at risk he had to get it from the man who wasn't there—Liam. It was the abrupt nature of the call that was disconcerting. If there were too many police involved, or the target had moved, or they discovered she was the wrong person, or some other bit of information came to light the mission would be cancelled—not abruptly aborted. He finally spoke, "I believe we may be in trouble. They may know who we are. Or, at the very least, suspect us. We need to get back to Ismenios ASAP."

"What makes you think that?" Adam asked as he increased their speed.

"Simple, abort with no explanation, means there are potential ears on our communications. The General wouldn't have any reason to abort the mission unless he was given new info that indicated we were about to step on a claymore. That information had to come from our friend who wasn't there. There's been a breach in security."

"I buy that," Ken said.

Adam added, "When we get back to Ismenios, we better approach it as a possible unfriendly." He turned to Ken and ordered, "Turn off the satellite phone."

"You think we are being tracked?" Ken asked.

"We're on the Iridium Satellite Network—the same one used by the Department of Defense. That's an Iridium Extreme 9575. Damn thing is near indestructible. But, it has built in GPS and tracking. Good if you're wandering around in the wilderness. Not so good if you don't want to be found."

Ken examined the handset. He found the Tracking Button which looked like an arrowhead on the right side of the phone. "Here, I can turn off tracking."

"Not good enough," Adam said. "Government authorities and the military have equipment that can locate time check and other radio emissions for whatever IMEI they want."

"IMEI?"

"International Mobile Equipment Identity."

From the backseat Ron Clew ordered, "Give it to me. I'll take care of it."

Ken handed Ron the telephone. The retired Navy Seal proceeded to remove the battery and SIM card. "OK, now it's safe."

"So, if they could find us, they could find Ismenios," Ken concluded.

"I'm sure Ismenios has gone dark, as well," Adam stated with conviction.

"We might as well settle in for a long ride," Ron said.

"I wasn't hungry, anyway," Ken Farmingdale reluctantly stated.

Darius Holiday couldn't believe his ears. The three men he was with were planning to cut off the heads of one-hundred random infidels in one-hundred days. It was an ingenious bit of terrorism. Every city, every town, every street would be afraid throughout the nation. Police would be on high alert and at the same time feel powerless. And, even after 100 days they wouldn't know if there would be more. It was delicious. He was pleased that they had taken him into their confidence. Yet, a part of him was terrified by their cold-blooded discussion. Although, he couldn't overlook the fact or not be acutely aware of the callous terror activities that he had devised, as well as the acid-rain attack he had planned. These men were no different. In the end, they were in agreement—non-believers didn't have a right to live.

Haji Ejder Jahandar handed Darius a camcorder and ordered him to practice with it until he was proficient. During their operation he was to film the victims begging for their lives and ultimately being executed. If they could get them to condemn America, all the better. They were still going to die.

Haji Ejder Jahandar, Rashid Teymouri, and Toufan Ghorbani Mashti would wear black masks and make statements during each event. The video would then be uploaded to the internet to be distributed throughout the Middle East, to all media outlets, radical websites, and wherever else it could be displayed to show the world the consequences of not accepting Allah as the only true God. They also would call on others to begin their own beheadings.

"If we can convince one-hundred believers to each vanquish one-hundred non-believers a wave of terror will cross this accursed land and bring them to their knees," Haji Ejder Jahandar concluded with a malevolent smile.

"Subhana Rabbiyal A'ala, Glory be to my Lord, the Most High," Rashid Teymouri stated with enthusiasm.

Toufan Ghorbani remained silent.

The Satan's Shadow team arrived back at Agde, France, which wasn't far from where Ismenios was anchored on the L'Herault River. They parked the Renault mini-car and made their way to the river on foot. Ismenios was dark, silent, and lifeless. Ron, Ken, and Adam observed it from a distance. General Maxwell Hughes and Captain Jarvis Demoye had either hunkered down, abandoned the craft, or been neutralized.

"I'll board her and check it out," Adam Hayes stated with authority.

"Why you?" Ron Clew inquired.

"Because I'm stealthier than you."

"My ass!"

Exactly, that's what I'm talking about. Your big fat ass couldn't sneak aboard that boat at midnight in a hurricane."

"At least I wouldn't trip over every loose object laying around on the deck like some clumsy, gung-ho, special forces, here I come, bull in a candy shop incompetent oaf."

"That's China shop—ya dink."

Ken Farmingdale observed the debate. Military humor is unique, disrespectful, uncivil, creative, and unbelievably funny. Test pilots were the same. Only there were so many superstitions among flyboys it was often difficult to come up with something witty to say. Finally, Ken said, "Why don't you both go. This way if you get shot and killed, I'll get some peace and quiet."

"Now, man, that's cold," Ron Clew said. He looked at Adam Hayes and asked, "Isn't that cold?"

"Like a well-digger's lunch."

It was decided that Adam would reconnoiter the Ismenios. He grabbed a Colt 1911 45 caliber pistol pulled back the slide to make sure there was a cartridge in the chamber and slipped it into his belt. After a quick glance around he disappeared into the undergrowth. Ron Clew covered him with an M-16 fully-automatic rifle equipped with a Trijicon TA31RCO-M4 4x32 USMC M4 Rifle Scope.

Slowly, Adam Hayes approached the boat from the upriver side. There was more foliage and rock cover in that direction. At a distance of approximately twenty yards away he stopped and observed the craft. The only sound heard was that of water lapping against the bow. No movement of any kind was seen onboard. The sun had begun to set causing long shadows to creep across the wooden dock. Local citizens were not to be found. Adam proceeded to approach the boat. It was then he saw movement, not on the Ismenios, but below the dock. He pulled his trench knife from his belt and proceeded silently toward the shadowy figure. In the fading light he approached cautiously. At a wooden piling he paused. His eyes adjusted to the darkened surroundings and he recognized Captain Jarvis Demoye. A quick glance around failed to reveal any other individuals in the vicinity. He drew near Demoye from behind and put his hand over the Navy officer's mouth.

"It's me Adam Hayes," he whispered.

Jarvis Demoye nodded.

Adam removed his hand and whispered, "What are you doing here. Where's General Hughes?"

A voice in the shadows answered as General Hughes stepped out, "He's on guard duty."

Slightly surprised, Adam Hayes turned to face the senior officer, "I see an old Marine doesn't forget his training."

"That's how he gets to be an old Marine."

Once the entire team was on board the conversation was kept to a minimum. In many cases hand signals were used. Weapons were stowed, all lines were released, and Ismenios turned downstream as she steamed out toward the Mediterranean Sea. In less than a half hour they were safely away from France.

"We're heading back to America," General Hughes stated. "While you were on your way to Dijon, I received a call from Emanuel Vegas—only it wasn't Vegas. They tried to sound like they were French which was an instant giveaway. In addition, they asked too many questions. I played along, but knew I couldn't for too long at the risk of being tracked. Given the proprietary encryption on our two phones, it was definitely Vegas' phone. The fake Vegas insisted that Dijon was where our target was located and that it was safe. They even provided an address. When they asked where I was located, I told them at the private airport near the English Channel where we had been given clearance to land. At that point I broke the connection and aborted the mission."

"Why did you abandon ship?" Ken Farmingdale asked.

"To observe," General Hughes answered.

Ron Clew explained, "If their position was discovered it would be easier to determine who was approaching and from where from an observation post."

"They knew we were coming and didn't want to mistake us for enemy combatants," Adam Hayes added.

"It also gave me a chance to practice taking out a careless Army green beret," Hughes quipped.

"That would have been difficult with a .556 in your skull," Ron Clew pointed out.

General Hughes turned toward the Navy Seal and nodded as he acknowledged the fact that he had been in the sights of the other team member.

"We need to refuel before crossing the Atlantic," Captain Demoye pointed out. He added, "We'll stop at Ceuta on the north coast of Africa. It's a busy port across from Gibraltar. Lots of private vessels pass through there."

Michael O'Neal, retired Army sniper, and his wife Alice were in a paddock with a mare and a recently born foal. They began by grooming the mother to allow the young horse to get comfortable with them and develop trust. As the foal remained at a distance, Mike crouched down, began opening and closing his mouth like he was chewing without looking directly at the foal. It's called "snapping" and is what foals do when around older horses to show that they are not a threat and to seek not to be hurt. Within a few minutes the new addition walked over to Michael. Slowly, they gently touched the foal to get him accustomed to it.

Abruptly, Michael stopped and looked up and in the direction of the road.

"What is it?" Alice asked.

"It may be nothing, but you should go inside."

In the distance Michael watched a black SUV turn into the long drive of FFP Ranch.

CHAPTER 27

Ten FBI agents were assigned to follow random young men leaving the Elizabeth Avenue mosque and report where they went. After the first day nothing suspicious turned up. Most of the men went to their various jobs or to their homes. A second day was also fruitless. It was on the third day that FBI Agent Arnold Mandesto followed a young man three blocks to a rundown tenement building that had been condemned. It was clear that there was no valid reason to enter the structure. From a distance Mandesto watched the building. After ten minutes the young Muslim appeared carrying a box and headed toward Journal Square. Agent Mandesto made a decision to not follow the young man. Rather, he crossed the street and entered the condemned building. As it was not a residence or business he did not require a search warrant.

Inside the crumbling tenement there was garbage, old furniture, parts of the building that had fallen off, rat droppings, puddles of stagnant water, broken glass, and a stench that would be difficult to get out of his clothes. Mandesto explored the first-floor walking carefully in the dull light that was streaming in from outside. He fully expected to find some kind of weapons or contraband stored in the recesses of the structure. There were none so far. Slowly, he made his way up to the second-floor on rickety stairs that lacked a stair rail. At one point a tread shifted causing him to almost fall. The second floor yielded a number of cardboard boxes in which were a variety of knives, a 22-caliber pistol, and cartridges of various calibers. That told him there were more firearms to be found.

After finding a few more boxes with weapons or unidentified materials—perhaps for bomb making, FBI Agent Arnold Mandesto made his way to the basement. The old coal-burner furnace had been dismantled. More garbage and debris were strewn everywhere. At one point, the law enforcement agent came upon a major stash of Firearms. The motherlode, he thought, as he congratulated himself. He made the decision to call in a team.

In less than twenty minutes a team of FBI agents began examining every inch of the condemned building. Special Agent Peggy Fox was in attendance. Two black Chevrolet Suburbans stood at the curb with their rear gates open. Box after box of suspect materials were loaded. A crowd of local residents swelled as they watched. Derogatory comments could be heard.

Then an agent dialed Peggy Fox's phone and when it was answered stated, "You have to see this. Come into the rear where there is a storage building."

Inside a wooden structure that was filled with debris there was a car hidden beneath all the garbage. The license plate was from Pennsylvania and matched that of Darius Holiday.

Peggy Fox stood motionless staring at the find.

Another agent who stood beside her said, "You made the right call Fox—well done."

Special Agent Fox turned to face him. She looked right through the man at Jersey City behind him. In a monotone she said, "He's here. That son-of-a-bitch is here. And, I'm going to find him and bring him to justice."

In the background they heard the call for Salat al-'asr, the late afternoon prayer.

Ismenios entered Chesapeake Bay as the sun set. After receiving clearance from harbor control, they turned south, passed Bay Breeze Point, and continued into Little Creek Cove. Permission had been given to moor at the third dock. In a little over an hour all required papers were signed, inspections executed, and questions answered. Five men left the boat and climbed into General Hughes black Ford Expedition. Nothing had been said.

Once out on the open road General Hughes spoke first, "I believe we can speak freely."

"You sure the car isn't bugged?" Ken Farmingdale asked.

"If they suspected us, we wouldn't have gotten off Ismenios. I'm certain that telephone call was a fishing expedition. They had what they suspected was one half of the communications devices. Who or what was on the other end they still don't know."

"The question is how did they get Vegas' telephone and how did they know he was involved?" Ron Clew stated the obvious.

"And, is he still with us?" Adam Hayes added.

"These are all questions that are going to be answered, shortly. If we are lucky," General Hughes admitted.

They drove north on Highway 60, through the Hampton Roads tunnel, onto U.S. 64, and on into Richmond, Virginia. There they stopped to get fuel and General Hughes wandered off, made a telephone call on his smartphone, and returned. They left Richmond heading west.

"Where we going, chief?" Adam Hayes asked.

"Chief? What am I—a fireman? General, Sir, Your Highness will all do—not chief."

"Where are we going General, Sir?"

"We're going to Lynchburg to meet up with Secret Service Agent Emanuel Vegas."

News spread quickly about the discovery of the fugitive Darius Holiday's car by the FBI. A flood of agents streamed into the area and subsequent searches raised tensions. As a result, the young terrorist was hurriedly shepherded to an apartment a few blocks away.

"That discovery is unfortunate, but it will not interfere with our plans," Haji Ejder Jahandar stated as he poured black tea into a saucer, placed a lump of rock sugar in his mouth, and sipped the hot liquid.

Darius sat quietly listening to the three men.

"We can leave in the morning," Rashid Teymouri offered.

"Good," Haji Ejder turned to the other man and asked, "Toufan, my friend, are you ready to serve Allah in this most holy lesson?"

Toufan Ghorbani Mashti nodded sadly.

"You worry me—Toufan," Haji Ejder stated, "What now is bothering you?"

"You know what I fear," Toufan admitted, "I do not fear for myself—I fear for my family. If we are identified, those Satanists will kill my family."

Haji Ejder Jahandar shook his head in displeasure, "Have you no faith?"

"I have faith," the smaller man declared. "I also have fear."

"You must conquer fear," Haji Ejder ordered. "We will not be identified." He stood and walked over to a window and looked out. "These Americans, they are children. They will chase their own tails at each location. We will be back in our beds as they try to connect the dots in vain." He turned back to face his reluctant cohort, "If it is Allah's will that we become known and your family becomes at risk that should be accepted by you." With a raised eyebrow he asked, "Who are you to question the wisdom or perfection of Allah?"

Toufan Ghorbani did not speak.

"If your wife and daughter are to play a role in our jihad, you should welcome the opportunity."

Darius Holiday watched the exchange. He felt sympathy for Toufan, his teacher, his friend, and wanted to jump to his defense. He knew better as these were dangerous men.

The other man in the room, Rashid Teymouri, was busy reviewing their plans and checking the GPS in his phone.

Haji Ejder Jahandar stated flatly, "Tomorrow, we proceed to our first destination and begin to unleash Saif al-Haqq—Sword of Truth."

The Satan's Shadow team rolled into Lynchburg, Virginia. General Hughes stated as they entered the downtown, "We have to find a restaurant named Bootleggers on 13th Street. It's supposed to be about a block from the James River. We'll probably get there before Manny. It took us a little over 2 hours to go 114 miles from Richmond compared with 180 miles he has to travel from DC. It will take an hour or so longer."

Bootleggers was in a large stone front building high upon a hill. It required climbing numerous flights of stairs to get to the front door. Under the sign above the door were the words, Burgers, Bourbon, Beer. Five men entered and found a large table in a corner.

"Burgers and sandwiches, my kind of place," Adam Hayes said with enthusiasm.

"There are more kinds of bourbons than I knew existed," Jarvis Demoye observed.

"Ah, here is an interesting item on the menu," Ken Farmingdale stated. "A beer named Satan's Pony. Says here it is brewed by South Street Brewery, Charlottesville, Virginia. A medium bodied amber ale with a 5.3% ABV. Worth a try."

Maxwell Hughes spoke in a serious voice, "We still don't know the details on what happened with communications. Stay alert. When Vegas gets here let him do the talking. Also watch for any prolonged gazes from later arrivals."

"Don't give them the time of day unless they offer to buy you a Satan's Pony," Ron Clew quipped.

"Or, make you Satan's pony," Adam Hayes added which brought laughter from the gathering.

"Hayes, how often do you visit Earth?" General Hughes asked rhetorically.

Before Adam could answer, the General looked past him at the door. Emanuel Vegas had entered Bootleggers. To everyone's surprise, with him was Liam. After a short reunion, seven men sat around the large table in the corner.

"Did you pick this location to torture me?" the Frenchman with a cane asked with a smile.

"Quite honestly, I didn't know you were coming?" was the General's response.

"Liam is central to our present situation," Emanuel Vegas pointed out.

The conversation became an exercise in code talking.

"Our friend came to me when he became aware that there were impurities in the product. The address of your delivery was intentionally wrong. Competitors were waiting. He and I went to one of our favorite restaurants to discuss the situation. It was clear that they knew him but not me. And, unfortunately, we did not know the identity of any of them. So, we decided to change the formula. Let me STATE this very clearly, my DEPARTMENT received the information in question from our friends. Who we don't know. I gave Liam my watch with time check."

Liam spoke up, "I am afraid I was very careless and left it on the bureau in my hotel room. When I returned from taking a walk it was vole, how you say, stolen."

"So now, in a manner of speaking, time is on our side," Vegas concluded.

All present now knew the satellite phone had been purposely allowed to fall into the hands of their adversaries as a means of finding that needle in a haystack. They also had a good idea that it was someone in the State Department. How high up and whether or not it was sanctioned they didn't know.

"It stands to reason that there would be a negative reaction," General Hughes admitted.

"I have the equipment to excavate the jobsite," Vegas said, "It will require that you keep track of time."

"We can coordinate that. Anything else we can do?"

"My side of the river remains a concern," Liam stated. "I will return and take a few days off to go fishing."

CHAPTER 28

In London, at the very time when seven men discussed their next steps in Lynchburg, Virginia, Shahin Pouran walked into the offices of a watchdog website news operation. He smiled at the receptionist and told her he had inside information they would be interested in hearing. She took his name and invited him to have a seat. After a few minutes one of the news staff, Ellen Fontaine, came out and introduced herself. Shahin stood, smiled, and said he was a member of a mosque where he overheard three men making plans for a terrorist attack.

The reporter was immediately interested and asked if he could provide details of the planned event. After a quick glance around he asked if there was somewhere more private where they could talk. As a precaution, the reporter asked him to wait while she arranged for a conference room. Shahin amiably agreed and sat once more.

After ten minutes Ellen Fontaine reappeared and told Shahin Pouran, "I've asked some other members of our staff to join us." With a smile she explained, "This will insure that we get all the facts straight."

"I understand," Shahin said agreeably.

They entered a small conference room with a rectangular table in the middle that sat eight. Two male staff members rose to greet the visitor. After all the introductions were completed Shahin and Ellen sat on one side of the table opposite the two male staff members.

"I do not feel comfortable telling what I heard to the bobbies," Shahin began. "These are dangerous men and if they learned that I revealed their plans I would be killed."

"I assure you we will not use your name," Ellen stated.

"Thank you. I am not a brave man. I simply wish to live in peace. These terrorists make it more and more difficult. When I walk down the street people stare watching to see if I am a threat." He shook his head, "I am no more of a threat than you. Yet, people don't know this."

Ellen repeated, "We will not reveal who told us about the plot. Can you provide details about what you heard?"

"It was after evening prayer. I stopped to pick up a new calendar of events that had been put out. The table was next to an alcove. On the other side of a curtain I heard a voice say they could maximize the death toll if all three events happened at the same time. This, of course, got my attention. I pretended to look at the other printed materials on the table and continued to listen." Shahin looked at the other three persons in the room for a reaction.

One of the male staff members asked, "Did they give any details about how they were going to do this and when?"

"I'm sorry they didn't. They did mention three of the deep-level tube lines. Let's see, there was the Central Red Line, the Northern Black Line, and the Piccadilly Dark Blue Line. Morning commute hours were discussed." He stopped and looked down at the table. "I couldn't stay any longer but wanted to get a look at the men involved. As I walked toward the door I glanced into the alcove and recognized the men. I will give you their names."

All three reporters picked up their pens to write down the would-be terrorist's names. That was all the time needed for Shahin Pouran to pull a TA035GSC Tac Assault Bowie Knife from beneath his shirt. In a flash he was over the table and the 10" black finish stainless saw back blade cut the throat of one of the male staff members. The other man was caught by surprise and could only stare in disbelief and a second later his throat was cut. Ellen Fontaine's scream was cut short by a hand over her mouth and knife blade held under her chin.

"Make another sound and you will join them," Shahin hissed. He proceeded to push the terrified woman against the wall. With the blade across her neck he told her, "Silence is your only path to salvation." He uncovered her mouth. No sound was made. While holding her against the wall the false informant raped his victim and when finished slit her throat. Shahin left the conference room and proceeded down a corridor to where a number of offices were located. He entered each office so quickly and unexpectedly that none of the three additional fatally wounded individuals uttered a sound. Three other offices were empty. The assassin headed to the reception area. As he was covered with blood he ran toward the girl at the desk and yelled, "There's been a terrible accident. Call the police." She never pressed a single number on the telephone.

Shahin Pouran left the office and carnage and walked through the door to the stairwell. There he retrieved a change of clothes that he had hidden earlier. Baby wipes allowed him to remove blood spatters from his hands and face. With his blood-soaked clothes and knife in a messenger bag he casually left the building knowing the cursed website would no longer carry any disparaging news about Islam.

Michael O'Neal sat with his wife, Alice, in their kitchen. They had just finished dinner in relative silence. Each was left to their own thoughts concerning a request that had been made a few days earlier. Two men from the government, one from homeland security and the other from the State Department, had visited FFP Ranch to recruit Michael O'Neal for a special assignment. He explained that he was retired, but they appealed to his patriotism.

The topic of discussion was a clandestine group known as Satan's Shadow. Little was known about them. However, it was the government's position that what they were doing was not only illegal and immoral, but was a threat to national security. If they were Americans, they were perpetrating crimes in foreign countries. If they weren't Americans, they were foreign nationals who had committed murder in the United States. Either way it was essential that they be stopped.

"What are you going to do?" Alice O'Neal asked her husband.

"For the moment, I'm not going to make a commitment," Michael said thoughtfully, "However, I can't definitively refuse. It will depend on the situation."

"At least it's not that Dog taking you to some foreign country to put your life on the line for some unnamed government entity."

"He'll probably show up tomorrow."

Alice didn't laugh. Instead, she rose from the table and began clearing the dishes. Adam, Watch Dog, Hayes gnawed at her emotions even when he wasn't there.

FBI Special Agent Peggy Fox was able to get a judge to issue a search warrant for the mosque on Elizabeth Avenue in Jersey Cty, New Jersey. Greeted with protests, hateful stares, and muttered insults, a five-member team examined every inch of the premises, reviewed written materials, pulled fingerprints, and asked questions. At the same time another team of agents canvassed the area around the mosque, as well as where the car had been found with a photograph of Darius Holiday. No one had seen him.

Time was not on Agent Fox's side. There was the growing potential for Darius Holiday to strike once again. In addition, the time limit given her by the Executive Assistant Director for National Security Branch had expired. Fortunately, when they located the suspect's car the clock stopped ticking for the moment but that wouldn't last long. They were hunting for a needle in a haystack and she was almost out of ideas.

"How do you find a needle in a haystack?" Adam Hayes asked.

"With a magnet," was General Hughes reply.

Adam nodded and smiled.

Rashid Sassani and Nebez Pahlavi had shot and killed twelve innocent people in Paris before being cut down by police. The Satan's Shadow team subsequently took out four known associates of the terrorists in Paris but had been unable to get to the families of the killers.

"We know, or assume, the wife of Nebez Pahlavi and his sister are hiding in Toulon. Obviously, we can't go door-to-door looking for them. We need to get them to come to us," General Hughes stated.

"That'd be a neat trick," Ron Clew admitted.

General Hughes continued, "It may be a long shot, but I have an idea. We send a letter from a law firm to Pahlavi's wife care of the local mosque. It states that there has been a cash settlement from an anonymous source for the family of an honored martyr. It further states that due to the substantial amount involved the recipient must show proper identification and sign for the payment. She has to come to us if she wants the money." He looked around the room, "Greed, my friends, the universal language."

"Yes, but how many mosques are there in Toulon and how do we know which is the correct one?" Ken Farmingdale inquired.

"I've been able to identify four; Mosquée ligue des musulmans du var, Mosquée an nour, Mosquée, and Salle de prière. We send a duplicate letter to all four."

"Won't they be suspicious and tell each other?" Ron Clew asked.

"If the Catholic church down the street gets a letter for someone they don't know do they ask the minister of the Methodist Church or Episcopal Church?"

"I see what you mean."

"We will have to have a believable letter prepared written in French. In it we provide an address for a nonexistent law firm in Marseille—it's about forty miles from Toulon. It would take about an hour by car and trains run between the two cities about every half hour. Then we wait."

CHAPTER 29

Secret Service Agent Emanuel Vegas made it clear when the team met at Bootleggers in Lynchburg, Virginia that he might have been identified as being somehow involved with Satan's Shadow. There was little other explanation for his name to be in the intercepted message. For this reason, communications between him and the team would be on a different encrypted satellite phone that he would keep in a secure place.

The original satellite phone that Liam carelessly allowed to be stolen from his hotel room would be used for misdirection and as a means of identifying the mole at the State Department, if possible.

The first attempt to use the purloined satellite phone for their purposes was when General Hughes made a call on the tainted phone line. A stranger's voice answered. Hughes used a pseudonym when he said, "This is Lang, we have information that a payment for the terrorists' attack in Paris is being made to the families. Not much is known. Some letter from a law firm. We need to identify who is making the payment so that we can put them on our list. Find out what you can." He ended the conversation, shut off the satellite phone, and removed the battery.

"If that gets transmitted to those involved it will add credibility to our letter ruse," General Hughes told the others in the room aboard Ismenios.

"Lang?" Adam Hayes asked out of curiosity about the false name.

General Hughes filled his glass with orange juice, walked over to one of the upholstered chairs, sat, and replied, "Just a little private joke. Hermann W. Lang was a Nazi spy who worked at the Carl L. Norden Corp., which manufactured top secret U.S. military equipment and materials. They developed the incredibly accurate Norden bombsight. It was kept so secret that we didn't even share its existence with our allies before entering the war. Lang had moved to New York City in 1927 and was above reproach. He was a draftsman and worked at Norden. In time, he became a factory inspector, therefore, had access to the blueprints of the bombsight. The little traitor snuck a set of blueprints home, copied them, and gave them to a German agent. The agent smuggled the copy to the fatherland in an umbrella aboard a passenger liner. Lang continued his espionage efforts until he got arrested along with other spies. After pleading guilty he got twenty-years." Maxwell Hughes put down his glass, "I'd have shot him."

"What happens if, instead of the wife going to Marseilles to visit the law firm, some other associate goes to check it out?" Captain Jarvis Demoye asked.

"They'll find a locked door with a corporate logo," Hughes answered. "This is why we will keep the location under surveillance and follow anyone who knocks on that door. They become the thread that leads to the needle—the ladies."

"A mighty thin thread," Ron Clew pointed out.

"Won't they be suspicious?" Adam asked.

"They will. However, think about it. Here is a firm purported to represent a group that sponsors terrorism. It stands to reason that they are not going to be an above-board, run-of-the-mill law firm. They will be a front. As such, they will be cautious and remain in the shadows. The very fact that they are hard to contact will enhance their dark image."

"But, if they don't answer the door how would the wife get her money?" Ken Farmingdale chimed in.

"Hidden, not too well, above the door will be a simulated video camera. The visitor will assume that the observer can be located anywhere. Hopefully, it will give the impression that someone is watching that door waiting for the real Mrs. Pahlavi to arrive."

"Hell, they have to make a lot of assumptions and buy into a lot of questionable things to fall for all this," Adam said.

"That thread is getting really thin," Ron Clew remarked.

"Twenty bucks says it leads us to the ladies."

Sword of Truth had been delayed due to all the FBI activity in the area. Nothing was done to bring attention to their plot. Even though Darius Holiday was hidden safely in an apartment he was considered a distinct problem.

"As I feared, you have brought them to us," Haji Ejder Jahandar spat in anger.

Darius Holiday, aka Shabal, didn't know how to answer, therefore he remained silent.

"These shurtat kariha are like the roaches in a dark room—everywhere. They are watching. Now, it is essential that we delay." Ejder

Jahandar paced in the room thinking out loud, "What cursed wind brought you here?"

Darius remained silent.

Ejder considered the young Shabal, "We could give you to them, but then they would focus on us and whether or not we had any involvement with your previous acts. No, that will not do." He stopped, turned, and with his face inches from Darius face said contemptuously, "We could kill you, leave your body to be discovered, and go quietly on with our original plan." Ejder Jahandar then stood straight up, "No, that would solve nothing. They would eventually connect us to this location." The older man ran his hand through his beard, "There is one thing that cannot be overlooked. It is the fact that you know our plans. That is the most critical consideration." He looked questioning at the young man, "But, you wish to be one of us and to be mujahid?"

Darius nodded.

"We must be wise at a time like this," Haji Ejder Jahandar paced in thought. "We are embarking on a glorious journey to demonstrate the power and scope of Allah. Each day they will wake to another example of what awaits them if they continue to ignore the truth. Each day the level of apprehension and fear will rise among the infidels. Each day Allah will grow stronger in their minds. We will touch them as no one has before." Suddenly, he stopped. As if in a trance he stood motionless. The others in the room could only stare in bewilderment. They waited. Noises outside the apartment down on the street were ignored. Time passed slowly. When Ejder Jahandar spoke once more the impact was dramatic, "I have a vision." Snapped back to reality all present listened. "One-hundred heads in one-hundred days will receive far greater attention if the first is of great consequence." With eyes of fire he scanned the room, "The first example of our power shall be that almar'a, evil woman, who stalks us. That woman of the FBI. Her head will be the initial sacrifice. Yes, it is a gift from Allah. She is here at our disposal for us to use as an example that cannot be ignored. That ill-wind that brought our young friend here was indeed a gift."

"But, she is with the police and impossible to reach," Rashid Teymouri cautioned.

"You surprise me," Ejder replied, "We know all too well that anyone can be touched." A wicked smile punctuated his next remark, "Especially, when they do not expect it."

Rashid also smiled, "It is a delicious thought." He couldn't keep from sharing an additional desire, "Maybe, before the actual event we could enjoy our little fox."

Haji Ejder Jahandar nodded. "We need to observe and determine where she is staying, what are her habits, who else is around, and when she will be most accessible."

"It will be very dangerous," Toufan Ghorbani warned.

"The rewards exceed the danger," Ejder stated with the wave of his hand. "Besides, it is the will of Allah."

After Haji Ejder Jahandar and Rashid Teymouri left the apartment, Darius Holiday and Toufan Ghorbani Mashti sat in silence. Each man was left with his own thoughts and feelings about what had happened and what was planned. It was indeed bold and unexpected, as well as guaranteed to generate a media frenzy and long-term coverage. If successful, America would learn a new level of fear.

Darius was impressed by Ejder Jahandar's plan. He wouldn't have had such inspiration or courage. These were ruthless men. However, they were true believers and destined to be rewarded by Allah. He felt fortunate to have been found by them and accepted by them. In Darius' mind Allah had led him to them. "Lā ilāha illā-llāhu muhammadun rasūlu-llāh, there is no god but God and Muhammad is the messenger of God."

Across the room Toufan sat in silence rubbing his hands together. His mind was venturing down a different path. Visions of his wife and daughter refused to diminish or release their grip upon him.

Finally, Darius spoke to his teacher and friend, "Toufan, how does one prepare for the fight?"

"Shahada, a declaration of faith, salat, and reading of the Qur'an. It is important to live as a Muslim at all times because you do not know when death might come. Make sure that all your thoughts concentrate exclusively on God. Allah created you to worship him, not worldly possessions or relationships . . ." his voice trailed off.

"What is wrong, my friend?"

Toufan picked up a Qur'an, opened it and read, "O you who believe! Choose not your fathers nor your brethren for protectors if they love disbelief over belief; whoever of you takes them for protectors, such are wrong-doers. Say: if your fathers, and your children, and your brethren, and your spouses, and your tribe, and the wealth you have acquired, and business for which you fear shrinkage, and houses you are pleased with are dearer to you than Allah and His Messenger and STRIVING in His way: then wait till Allah brings His command to pass. Allah does not guide disobedient folk. Qur'an 9:23, 24."

After a few moments of inactivity, Toufan rose and said, "Shabal, I will not be going with you. I hope you understand. My family should not have to pay at the hands of Satan's Shadow as a result of my deeds."

"Your faith should give you comfort and confidence that Allah will protect your family," Darius pointed out.

"And, your family, are you certain that when you are identified that they will not fall victim to this evil shadow?"

Darius pictured his father, mother, and sister. It was funny that in a way that he did not consider them in danger. Of course, his acts of terrorism took place before he ever heard of Satan's Shadow. Therefore, the die was cast and he could do nothing to change what comes next. Out of curiosity Darius asked, "What about Haji Ejder Jahandar and Rashid Teymouri, do they have families?"

"Ejder Jahandar is dedicated to jihad to such a degree he would sacrifice anything. His goal is paradise. Rashid Teymouri has a wife, but from what he has expressed he would not miss her or her family."

The two fell into silence, once more. After a few minutes, Toufan spoke, "Before the threat to my family arose, it was not difficult to commit myself to jihad. I would willingly die in service to Allah. Then this shadow appeared and everything changed."

CHAPTER 30

Special Agent Peggy Fox entered the Holland Tunnel Hotel and headed to her room. They were planning to wrap up the investigation in the next two days and had not made any progress in finding the suspect. Methodically, over and over, she searched her mind for any other approach they could take to ferret out Darius Holiday. He was there—she knew it. She could feel his presence in the area. What she didn't feel was the presence of an observer who had followed her into the two-story hotel and run up the stairs when she took the elevator. Alone she walked down the hall and entered her room while lost in thought. From his vantage point the observer determined that FBI Special Agent Peggy Fox was located in room 224.

Inside the room Agent Fox sat on the bed and examined her notes on her tablet. Agents found a number of questionable documents at the mosque which were turned over to another team. They didn't, however, relate to her case in any manner. Canvassing the area by FBI and Jersey City police, roadblocks, and observation posts turned up nothing. Even deep-rooted undercover agents had heard nothing.

Peggy Fox was restless. For years she worked exceedingly hard to prove herself and gain a reputation of being highly effective. It had been a long and arduous journey. For some reason, other agents seemed to get unexpectedly lucky at some point in their investigation which allowed them to solve a crime or apprehend a suspect. She couldn't help but wonder, where was her flash of good fortune. She was the one who deduced that Holiday would go to Jersey City—a stroke of genius. Her orders for agents to follow visitors leaving the mosque resulted in locating the car. Another brilliant decision. Then nothing. They hit a brick wall. Short of standing on a street corner and calling his name she was out of ideas as to how to find the son-of-a-bitch. Fatigue brought with it a dulling of the senses.

The Muslim observer who had followed FBI Special Agent Peggy Fox reported to Haji Ejder Jahandar where she was staying. His information was well-received. It allowed for a plan to be quickly developed for the kidnapping, raping, and execution of this high-profile victim. A venomous smile crossed Haji Ejder Jahandar's face. It would be a dramatic unleashing of the Sword of Truth. Media coverage would be extensive and hysterical.

This was the ultimate goal of a terrorist. Maybe—yes, it was a good thing this pretender, Shabal, had come among them. Together, they would wash the continent with blood and spread a new level of fear. And, in the end, he shall slay the "little lion" as a final act that would send him to paradise.

Liam continued to scan through message logs looking for any contact between the Ministry of Immigration, Integration, National Identity and Co-development and the United States State Department. There would be very few, if any, as these two entities had no reason to deal with each other. However, with the large volume of correspondents between the two governments it was a long and fatiguing search. With tired eyes he focused on each day's log on his intelligence-cleared laptop computer.

A call on his cellphone interrupted his search. It was one of his trusted sources out in the field. "My friend, there is word of a letter—from a law firm—to one of interest," a voice stated in French.

"Carrier pigeons have been active, I see," Liam responded in the same language.

"And, they are flying in many directions."

"Let me know where they land." The call ended.

The stolen satellite telephone had done its job. Now, all he had to do was find the transmission—if one existed—between the moles in their respective governments. Of course, something as innocent as this could have been passed through casual conversation on a commercial telephone line. It did confirm that the lost satellite telephone was in the hands of the traitors. Time, effort, luck was all that was needed. There really wasn't a great deal of hope as he continued his search.

"Well, I'll be damned," Ron Clew said as he watched Nebez Pahlavi's wife and sister enter the building where the fictitious law firm was located. The terrorist's wife was wearing her distinctive crimson hijab. The ex-Navy Seal tracked the two women through a Leupold Mark 6 rifle scope he held in his left hand. Without looking he dialed his cellphone with his right hand.

"Speak," General Hughes' voice stated.

"I owe you twenty bucks. Crimson bird and sister entering the nest alone."

"Over," the call was ended.

The two women entered the building and looked around. It was empty except for a guard who stood near the stairwell. They neither spoke to nor acknowledged him as they proceeded up the stairs to the third floor. Ken Farmingdale, the guard, waited a few moments before following.

When they reached the third floor, the two women looked for the door of the law firm that promised them riches. In her hand was the letter that had been passed on to Pahlavi's wife from one of the mosques in Toulon. Because she didn't share the contents of that letter with anyone other than Pahlavi's sister, no one warned of a possible trap or offered to investigate. Greed had clouded logic.

When the door lever wouldn't open it Pahlavi's wife knocked. With her attention focused on the door she didn't see Adam Hayes arrive behind Pahlavi's sister, place his hand over her mouth, and thrust a six-inch blade into her back exactly where it would reach the heart. The sound of her body dropping to the floor got the other woman's attention. She turned and was pushed backward against the wall and suffered the same fate.

Ken Farmingdale arrived as the second woman slid to the floor. He placed the Satan's Shadow letter on the body of Pahlavi's wife. Nothing was said as both men worked in silence. Once cleaned-up they left the building and joined Ron Clew who was waiting across the street.

Back on Ismenios, General Hughes informed the team of the terrorist attack in London where seven members of a news organization were slain. The assailant was unknown.

"You ever get the feeling that what we are doing isn't having the effect that we desire," Adam Hayes asked while shaking his head.

"The problem is we become aware of the acts of terrorism that occur while having no idea of any that have been thwarted," Captain Jarvis Demoye pointed out.

"I guess all we can do is compare the numbers over time," Ken Farmingdale suggested.

"This campaign is still young," General Hughes pointed out. The older man looked at some notes he had made and added, "Also, while you were away I received news of a car bomb attack in Turkey that killed and injured numerous people. The identity of the bomber was known. Members of his family and other associates have been arrested and their condition unknown."

Captain Demoye observed, "That is interesting. Even if they throw them in some hell-hole prison with a long sentence, rather than execute them, that could also have a deterrent effect."

"Or, did they do it to protect the family from us?" Adam Hayes asked.

"Cynic," Demoye responded.

"Regardless of which, we have made it clear that terrorists no longer operate in a vacuum. As our letter states, 'Terrorism has a price. If you commit a terrorist act your family is the price you pay.' It may not stop the most radical hardline assholes, but I believe it will make others think twice," Ron Clew stated.

Jerry Young was tired of being bullied and humiliated. The last straw was when Irene Dunne not only laughed at him for suggesting that they could be boyfriend/girlfriend, but when she shared his proposal with the boys who regularly harassed him. Once again, he was stopped in the schoolyard by four young hoods who pushed him this way and that, knocked him down, laughed at his professed affection for Irene, made crude remarks about his mother, and spat on him. In addition, they reminded him to remember to have his "freak tax" the next day.

A desperate young man, Jerry sat in his room holding his father's Glock 17 9mm pistol. Even loaded with 17 rounds the polymer-framed semi-automatic pistol felt light in his hand. Indeed, the look and feel of the weapon instilled a feeling of power in the teenager. No one could push him around if he had this remarkable instrument in his hands. No one would laugh at him ever again. If they did, it would be the last sound that they made. Jerry Young envisioned his four tormentors lying in the mud holding their bullet ridden stomachs. He then saw Irene Dunne holding her hands up in front of her face as he fired round after round into that insipid smile.

The plan was to bring the gun to school the next day wrapped in a plastic bag. Hide it in the bushes near the schoolyard. Then after school he would tell Irene he had a gift for her to get her to follow him into the yard. Without question, the four others would be there waiting. Jerry smiled as he pictured making a big deal out of retrieving his love gift for Irene. The pistol would then be quickly uncovered and four creeps would be shot two times each. Then Irene would meet her fate.

In his mind he had nothing to lose. Constant harassment and condemnation did its work by lowering a human being's self-image to the point of feeling valueless. What was there to live for? He would be doing the world a favor by removing the evil that so tortured him. In a way he was protecting future victims. He aimed the gun at a poster on the wall.

The sound of his little sister's voice entered the room from downstairs. Her distinctive giggle was most likely caused by something dad was doing. They were always roughhousing and playing. It was a sound of unbridled happiness. Jerry Young listened. Slowly, a smile formed on his downcast face. It was then that he remembered hearing about the family of the school shooter in California being killed as a result of his actions. Jerry Young slid the firearm under his bed. He would return it to its rightful place. Life would go back to how it was and he would remain in his personal hell.

Reality was punctuated by the laugh of a little girl.

CHAPTER 31

Special Agent Peggy Fox sipped coffee from a Styrofoam cup as she stood in Journal Square with Jersey City Police Detective Mario Grasso. Over night she had decided the only way to shake Darius Holiday loose would be to give the impression that they had wrapped up their investigation and left the area. The detective indicated that he had a carefully selected team who would not be conspicuous in place to observe streets, mosques, and transportation hubs. Once word of the FBI packing up and leaving the hope was that the fugitive might appear. Realistically, they didn't expect him to walk down Kennedy Boulevard. What they did expect was that he might change locations or attempt to leave Jersey City. While a long shot, it was the only thing left to try.

Orders were issued and two FBI teams left the city. An effort was made to be as obvious as possible. Without question, anyone who was concerned with or aware of the FBI presence knew they were leaving. This included Haji Ejder Jahandar, Rashid Teymouri, Toufan Ghorbani Mashti, and Darius Holiday.

"Events have raised the need for us to act quickly," Haji Ejder Jahandar stated with authority.

"It also has opened the door, as many have left," Rashid Teymouri pointed out.

"Yes, it is a delicate balance."

"With the help of Allah, we shall have our bright shining example."

Neither Toufan Ghorbani Mashti nor Darius Holiday spoke.

At mid-morning FBI Special Agent Peggy Fox returned to her hotel in order to pack her bag. Her mind raced as it continued to search for some other tactic that might bring forth her nemesis. Even though she developed the plan, a part of her felt like it was retreat or defeat. This was not comfortable for her. Throughout her career she always proceeded with an intensity and zeal others couldn't muster. This was also a reflection of her life. As a child she never walked—she ran. In school, anything less than 100 was failure. Even on the soccer field both opponents and teammates learned she was a force to be reckoned with or avoided. Even though never stated, her long-term goal was Director of the Federal Bureau of Investigation.

Peggy Fox entered the Holland Tunnel Hotel. With her attention focused only on the apprehension of Darius Holiday, she was lost in thought. She walked through the lobby of the hotel and past the small restaurant without paying any attention to her surroundings. Over and over she reconstructed the facts and findings they had. Was there something they missed? Something she missed? One moment of inspiration was all that was needed. It didn't come. Agent Fox entered the elevator. A man, who had been a few steps behind her, also entered. As the elevator doors closed Agent Fox looked at the other passenger and her eyes grew wide.

Liam sat in silence. Before him was a name on the screen of his laptop computer. Kareem Reza was a trusted friend, government official, member of an anti-terrorist taskforce, and French patriot. He worked at the Ministry of Immigration, Integration, National Identity and Co-development and was well-respected. Yet, the computer that sent two questionable messages and received three from the United States State Department had been logged onto by Kareem Reza.

It was not a smoking gun, but indeed was smoke that needed to be investigated. What concerned Liam most was the fact that the man might not be alone in his treasonous efforts. If he turned over the wrong stone he might reveal more than he could handle. It was clear that he had to proceed with caution.

After leaving the government facility, Liam walked about Paris. He stopped at a small café and ordered un café—a tiny cup of espresso. As he sipped the strong liquid he smiled while watching Americans make such an order expecting a large cup of coffee. Then they ask for milk which brings forth sneers. After he paused long enough to observe his surroundings Liam took a taxi to a busy market and disappeared into the crowd. From past experience he knew the location of an old flight of stone stairs hidden in the back of a store that led to an underground tunnel. It had been used by the resistance during World War II. Dark and musty, with the sound of dripping water, the old man stepped carefully with the aid of a flashlight and his cane. Fifteen minutes later he emerged in the basement of an old church.

Confident that he had not been followed, Liam went to a nearby station and boarded a train. After making two transfers he rode the high-speed Rail Europe train to Agde, France. The trip took 4 hours 42 minutes.

It took another hour for him to reach Ismenios that was anchored on the L'Herault River.

A motion alarm sounded and Captain Jarvis Demoye stated, "We have company."

Almost instantly, all members of the team were armed and at their respective posts.

"Does that man look familiar?" Ken Farmingdale asked.

"What's he doing here?" Adam Hayes added.

"Let's ask him," General Hughes said as he walked out onto the fantail.

Inside the cabin, following all the greetings, Liam explained his presence, "Some things it is better to not place in the public domain. At this time, I am led to believe that I have identified the agents in our governments who have been in contact with each other. All I have are names and the fact that they have been in contact—no more. For all we know, they were planning a vacation together or are les amoureux—lovers." He paused, shook his head, and added, "Unfortunately, unless they are going with Emanuel Vegas, that is not the case."

"Is there anything else you could get from the messages?" Maxwell Hughes asked.

"Unfortunately, a combination of Arabic in code and limited translation resources we can trust at this time, it only leaves us with the names Vegas and mine."

"What if they are lovers who simply want to go to Las Vegas?" Adam asked in jest. Cold stares were the response.

"Do you believe that you or Emanuel are in danger?" Captain Demoye inquired.

"As long as they don't suspect that we know anything about them there is no need for concern," Liam offered with the wave of his hand. "The question must be, what do they know about Satan's Shadow and how did they come to identify Vegas and me?"

"There are more traitors, that's a given," Ron Clew chimed in.

"What are the names of those we know are dirty?" General Hughes asked.

"In my government the salaud is named Kareem Reza. On your side of the pond, in your State Department, the person I identified is named Nadia Noorani."

"Through proven trusted resources we will prepare a dossier on our little rat," Hughes stated.

"We need to keep them in sight, use them, eventually take care of them, but right now make sure they don't interfere with our operation," Liam concluded.

"Roger that," Ron Clew added.

"With that in mind, I have some information for you concerning Rashid Sassani's wife and two children." Liam looked around the room as he changed the subject. "Given the untimely demise of Nebez Pahlavi's wife and sister in Marseilles, government authorities have moved the mother and two children to an undisclosed location on a military base. A camarade de regiment provided the undisclosed location. They are counting on secrecy, rather than security." Liam's eyebrows raised slightly as if to signal that their strategy failed. "Fifty miles north of Marseilles is French Military Base 200-Apt-Saint-Christol on the Plateau d'Albion. Between 1971 and 1996, this base was home to 18 S3D ultra-secret land-based nuclear missile launching silos housing intermediate range ballistic missiles aimed at the Soviet Union. Following President Chirac's decision to close down land-based nuclear missile launching sites, the Defense Ministry stationed 1,000 legionnaires, who were part of a new combat engineers unit, at the base. These numbers have since dwindled to less than one hundred. This is a non-operational base."

"They moved the mother and children to a non-operational base?" Ron Clew asked not sure of the logic of such a move.

Liam responded, "As I indicated, the authorities chose secrecy. Hidden on a decommissioned military base near the Alps in an area known for its lavender farms probably seemed like an ideal solution. There are a handful of soldiers there, and maintenance personnel, along with some civilians. It is very much like your country's witness protection program."

"What can you tell us about the base?" General Hughes asked.

"A great deal." Liam explained, "You will have to travel there by automobile. No trains go to that area. It is very rural with few roads. This is both good and bad. Good that there is little traffic and few witnesses. Bad in that strangers will stand out. If the authorities have observers posted your vehicle will be scrutinized, possibly stopped."

"Looks like we're in for a five-mile hike," Adam Hayes stated in recognition of approaching the target on foot at night.

"There is an unused runway down the center of the base, 34N/16S magnetic heading. East of the runway has been all but abandoned. It is where the missile silos had been located. This is the best point of entry. Just watch out for jackrabbits and debris. On the west side of the runway is where all the activity takes place. The few legionnaires stationed there are billeted in the northwest corner. Maintenance and other personnel work and reside in the southwest corner of the base. There are numerous low buildings located there. Most are empty and falling apart. The main building, a four-story structure, is located on the southeast side of the complex facing south. That, I believe, is where the Sassanis will be kept."

"What are the chances of this being a trap?" Jarvis Demoye inquired.

"I would say, very good," was Liam's surprise response. "I trust my source, but that doesn't mean that those in command aren't going to exercise due diligence and not make an effort to be prepared for any attempt on their charge's lives. If it were me, I would develop a plan of attack and then put in place defenses against it."

"Anybody can be gotten to," Adam remarked.

"Quite right," Liam agreed, "They may attempt to be prepared but given previous situations I've witnessed, both the resources and experience may be limited."

CHAPTER 32

Three Muslim men waited in dark recesses on the second floor of the Holland Tunnel Hotel. They were strategically placed to intercept Special Agent Peggy Fox on her way to her room. A few moments earlier when she entered the hotel an observer across the street sent a text message to one of the abductors. As a result, they knew their quarry was on the way. Metallic sounds indicated that the elevator had begun its climb and all of their attention was on the two sets of tan doors.

Haji Ejder Jahandar had developed a wickedly simple plan that would have dramatic effect. The abductors would capture her and take her into her own room—224. There they would rape and defile her, over and over. Haji Ejder Jahandar, Rashid Teymouri, Toufan Ghorbani Mashti, and Darius Holiday would arrive as quickly as possible. Once the FBI agent was reduced to a state of shock and submission she would be forced to make a videotaped statement about the illegal and immoral actions of the United States government in the Middle East, treatment of Muslims worldwide, and offensive support of the State of Israel. She would be told if she proclaimed Allah as the one and only true God they would free her. After that, she would be beheaded on videotape.

The elevator clunked to a stop on the second floor and the doors slowly opened. Three sets of eyes strained to see inside. When the doors were completely open they saw—nothing. The elevator was empty. Their first thought was that Agent Fox had stopped in the lobby or the restaurant. She was in the hotel, that they knew. Where, was the question.

When FBI Special Agent Peggy Fox entered the elevator, a man had followed her in. As the doors closed, she recognized him. Immediately, she slipped her hand into her purse to retrieve her Glock 9mm pistol.

The man hit the emergency stop button and said in a frantic voice, "They are waiting to kill you upstairs!"

"You're under arrest," Agent Fox said as she pointed the gun at Darius Holiday.

"I will go peacefully, but we need to go out the back. They want to kill you. It's part of a huge terrorist plot. Please, believe me." He pushed the "Open Door" button and the first floor of the hotel appeared. "Shoot me, if you have to, but don't go upstairs." After a pause, "They're watching the front of the hotel from across the street."

What the young man said began to sink in. Here he was giving himself up. Why? To warn her? Or, was he a decoy sent to lure her out back where she would be abducted? That seemed highly unlikely as she could sit him down in the lobby and call for backup—which wasn't a bad idea. Yet, if she did that, he might fall silent and not tell her more about the supposed terrorist plot. Agent Fox made a bold decision. She led Darius toward the back door of the hotel.

Outside he stopped and said in a low voice, "I came here through that alley."

Agent Fox produced a pair of handcuffs and placed them on Darius Holiday's wrists. He did not resist. "Tell me about that terrorist plot," she ordered.

"I have one condition."

"No, conditions."

"One."

"No."

"Then, I have nothing to say."

Agent Fox relented, "What is the condition?"

"One of the men I am going to tell you about is a reluctant participant. I want him let go."

"I can't promise that."

"You have to."

"Why?"

"He doesn't want to be a terrorist, but is afraid. He cares about his family."

"The best I can do is tell you I will try to help him."

Darius Holiday thought for a moment. He decided this was the best he was going to get. He went on to describe how he came to Jersey City, ended up with the terrorists, and their plot to behead one-hundred random people, in one-hundred random locations, in one-hundred days.

Special Agent Fox didn't show an outward reaction while horrified inside. Her mind pictured beheaded bodies being found by local police who have no idea it is a larger crime until the videos are released. At that point, law enforcement would have no way of knowing where the next victim would be found until it is. It would be a race against time to find any clue of who the perpetrators were or where they were headed. Memory of how difficult it had been to find Darius Holiday crept in. They knew the city he was in and still could not locate him. If he hadn't turned himself in he would still be at large and possibly participating in this gruesome scheme. It's a big country, she thought. What became frighteningly clear was the fact that without this incredible stroke of luck they might not have been able to stop the carnage. Her attention turned to Darius Holiday. He was guilty of terrorism—a murderer—yet sacrificed himself for one man and his family. It doesn't make sense. He did not express any remorse for his own acts or for those innocent people he killed and injured. In addition, he did not ask for any leniency on his part, as if any could be given. He would be prosecuted to the full extent of the law. Yet, here he was. Why?

"Tell me who the perpetrators are and where we can find them," Agent Fox ordered.

"I'll give you their names and location, but if they discovered that I had escaped they might have already gone into hiding or begun their rampage," Darius warned. "The leader is Haji Ejder Jahandar, he is ruthless and dangerous. Rashid Teymouri is mujahid—a soldier. The man who is not a willing part of this is Toufan Ghorbani Mashti. He does not want to do it. He simply wants to take care of his family. He fears this Satan's Shadow gang will kill his family."

"Why did you come here and not just call in an anonymous tip?" Fox asked.

"If I didn't stop you, you would have been number one."

Darius' words echoed in Peggy Fox's ears, "You would have been number one." She had been about to fall into a trap that would conclude with her beheading. A cold chill ran down her spine. In truth, she would have walked right into it. She walked into the elevator and, had Darius Holiday wished, he could have caught her off-guard. With all her training she had allowed herself to be a sitting duck. And, a cold-blooded murderer had saved her. A cold-blooded murderer she hunted and hated and wanted to capture was the one who she now owed her life to. The incongruity was palpable. The impact on her ego was dramatic. Confusion replaced confidence. What was the next step?

Darius Holiday gave Agent Fox the location of the three conspirators. He described as much of the interior of the apartment as he could. In addition, he told her there were three men waiting on the second floor of the hotel. When she failed to act, he said, "If you don't do something fast, they'll all get away."

FBI Special Agent Peggy Fox called the field office and relayed all of the information that she had been given. She indicated that she would remain where she was with her prisoner while other agents and local police made the arrests.

Two hours later, they were in the Jersey City Police East District offices at 207 7th Street. The three would-be abductors that had been arrested on the second floor of the Holland Tunnel Hotel were transferred to the Hudson County jail on Erie Street. The observer from across the street of the hotel vanished when the first police car showed up. Haji Ejder Jahandar, Rashid Teymouri, and Toufan Ghorbani Mashti remained at the police department offices for questioning by the FBI. While it was not revealed that Darius Holiday was the one who informed on them, it was obvious to all three.

"That's correct, he turned himself in and implicated the three suspects of planning a terrorist attack on the United States," Peggy Fox told the Executive Assistant Director for National Security Branch of the FBI over the telephone. "Me? Yes, he indicated that I was a target." She felt sweat run down her back as the narrowness of her escape once more presented itself. "My team will bring Holiday to the Federal District Court in Newark for arraignment." She listened to a brief, less-than-glowing, congratulatory comment from the Director and responded, "Thank you, I was just doing my job and got lucky." Very lucky, she thought. She caught a wanted fugitive terrorist and broke up a major terrorist plot. Those two facts could not be ignored by those who controlled her future at the Bureau. Her eye caught the shining metal of a scimitar that lay on a desk marked with an evidence tag. All, without losing her head, she thought, and smiled. Beneath her professional façade a frightened girl cried.

CHAPTER 33

Retired Navy Seal Master Chief Petty Officer Ronald Clew stood on the fantail of Ismenios with Air Force test pilot Major Ken Farmingdale. Both men looked out at the L'Herault River.

Ron Clew answered an inquiry, "It is possible to kill a man," he turned to look directly at Ken Farmingdale, "or a child, with bare hands, but very few are skillful enough to do it well." He sized up his cohort. Ken Farmingdale was solid, brave, trustworthy, and intelligent. However, he was not a combat soldier, pugilist, martial artist, or street fighter. Ron added, "There is no humane method of killing a person—man, woman, or child."

"I realize that. What I want to know is if there are quick—less painful, less frightening methods that I may employ."

"Shit, man, you're killing them," Ron said in a stern no-nonsense voice. "Get that straight in your head."

Ken Farmingdale nodded.

"How quickly, painfully, or violently depends on the situation. If the target fights back it gets ugly. If you screw up it gets ugly. If someone interferes it gets ugly." Ron Clew studied the test pilot, "If you think for even a moment that you're not up to this—now is the time to speak up."

"I will do this," Ken stated emphatically. "I just want to do it . . ." His voice trailed off.

Ron Clew shook his head, "I don't know, man, indecision and hesitation have gotten many good men killed. You fail to act with authority and falter in any way and you're dead."

"I can do this."

"There are many reasons why someone may think twice. Too many to go over. I will tell you one thing though. The moment you start identifying with the package you become ineffective and vulnerable. You have to stay distant to stay alive."

"I can do this."

"I'm not getting my ass captured or killed because you looked into the eyes of a child and froze. No thanks."

"I can do this."

"You trying to convince me or yourself?" Ron slipped a small snap-open knife from his pocket. In one smooth rapid move he was upon Ken Farmingdale. The bigger man spun the test pilot around, placed one hand over his mouth, snapped open the three-inch black blade, and dragged the back non-sharp edge across his victim's throat. "You're dead."

Ken got the point. Caught by surprise there was no time to react. In fact, by the time he could have reacted—it was over—literally over.

"If you are on my team, you will be prepared for the expected, the unexpected, and any breakdown in the plan. You have to have your head in the mission. The package is the package. They are dead the moment you enter the theater."

"Got it."

Ron Clew just stared at his would-be partner. He didn't like the set-up. There were so many variables that it would be a challenge for a seasoned veteran. Adam Hayes would be a better choice on this one. Farmingdale was an unproven asset. Not only that, he was exhibiting all the signs of someone who cannot depersonalize planned actions. This was a significant problem. They were not shooting the targets from two-hundred yards away. They were getting up close and personal. Victim's blood was literally going to get on their hands.

"I'm going to do this," Ken Farmingdale stated, once more.

"I fuckin' hope so," Ron replied.

In a dark room with only a grey metal table and two metal chairs, Darius Holiday sat with his wrists shackled to his sides. After he surrendered to FBI Special Agent Peggy Fox, he had been taken to police headquarters and then to the Hudson County jail on Erie Street. He was stripped searched, fingerprinted, photographed, examined by a nurse, and booked into custody. A note was attached to his file indicating that he was being held as a federal prisoner. In spite of all the events, he was acutely aware of all that was happening.

Agent Fox entered the room and sat in the chair opposite Holiday. They remained in silence as each considered the other.

Peggy Fox spoke, "I want to thank you for warning me about the planned abduction."

Darius nodded.

"I have to ask, why did you warn me?"

Darius shook his head, "I didn't do it to warn you. I could care less about whether or not they behead a government infidel."

Agent Fox did a poor job of covering her surprise at his comment, "Then why?"

"Toufan Ghorbani Mashti is a good man—a good Muslim. He taught me. I am a better Muslim because of him. He did not wish to be a part of Sword of Truth. The only way I could save him was to stop it before it began. You just happened to be chosen to be number one."

A cold shudder passed through Peggy Fox, "Is that what it was being called—Sword of Truth?"

"That's what Haji Ejder Jahandar called his scimitar."

"The sword he was going to use to behead one-hundred innocent people?"

"One-hundred infidels."

"And, what role were you going to play?"

"I was going to videotape each sacrifice."

"Did they have a list of locations?"

"I don't know."

"What about other collaborators?"

"I don't know."

Somewhat frustrated, Agent Peggy Fox stated, "All three men are being held on conspiracy to commit terrorism charges."

"Let Toufan go."

"That's out of the question."

"He goes free or I have nothing to say."

"We have you on two acts of terrorism, multiple murders, conspiracy to commit terrorism, unlawful possession of weapons of mass destruction . . ."

Darius interrupted Agent Fox, "You have me, but you do not have them. Without my testimony they were three men in an apartment minding their own business when the FBI invaded their residence without a warrant."

"We have the men who were waiting on the second floor of the Holland Tunnel Hotel."

"Again, without my testimony they were simply waiting for a friend."

"We have ways of making perps turn," Agent Fox tried.

"Not these guys."

Silence engulfed the room. Darius knew, if he didn't testify Haji Ejder Jahandar, Rashid Teymouri, and Toufan Ghorbani Mashti would go free. He would be cast as the rat. This was not an ideal situation as they would most likely begin developing other plans which would include Toufan. The best outcome would be for Haji Ejder Jahandar and Rashid Teymouri to be convicted and Toufan set free. This would require his testimony and an agreement from the FBI and Attorney General. Darius' sole objective was to get Toufan Ghorbani Mashti back with his family. After that, what happens to him he really didn't care about.

"An overdose of morphine will cause death and is difficult to detect. About two grains will suffice," Navy Seal Ron Clew indicated. "However, you first have to render the subject incapacitated. By the time you do that you could have finished the job. That's best for someone who does drugs or is an alcoholic."

"So, what is the plan?"

"Don't know?"

"What the hell does that mean?"

"It means, from what we have gathered about the location, terrain, personnel, and the main building where they are purported to be housed, it isn't going to be easy to scout." The big man looked out at the river, "There aren't any high vantage points from which to observe. All around the base the terrain is flat farmland. It's a patchwork of fields of blue lavender and wheat. We have to enter the base under the cover of darkness. Good news is that the chain link, barbed wire topped, fence has not been maintained. It should be easy to negotiate." He walked over to the table on the fantail and activated his laptop. A Google map of the base appeared, "On either side of the main building there are empty barracks buildings."

"I saw that," Ken said.

Ron turned back to face Ken, "Our best vantage point will be from one of those empty barracks. The good news is there are four buildings on right angles to each other that are all interconnected. We can gain access to the barracks farthest from the main building and make our way to the one that is closest." He tapped the table and cautioned, "That is if nobody is sleeping in those barracks."

"How will we know?"

"When you hear a voice that isn't mine or Adam's. Or worse, fifty voices, you'll know."

"Then what do we do?"

"Me, I disappear into a wheat field just as fast as my legs will get me there. You cover my six."

"That'll be a little difficult to do from in front of you."

"That's the way to think." Ron returned to the display and explained, "Problem is that we will only be able to observe the front of the main building. If they never come out the front or don't reside in a front room, we may come up dry."

"What then?"

"In the dark of night, we enter the main building."

CHAPTER 34

Secret Service Agent Emanuel Vegas read the file on Nadia Noorani. She was an assistant to an Under Secretary for Political Affairs in the office of East Asian And Pacific Affairs (EAP) in the United States Department of State. He noted there was not much reason for her to be contacting someone in the French government. Born in Pakistan, she went to college in the United States, worked for a number of government officials, and eventually entered the State Department. She became a citizen of the United States and had "Confidential" security clearance, not "Secret" or "Top Secret."

Emanuel Vegas, on the other hand, had Department of Defense (DoD) Top Secret/Sensitive Compartmented Information (SCI) clearance and completed a counterintelligence (CI) or full-scope polygraph (FSP). In addition, as a Secret Service Agent who worked with the President and Vice-President of the United States, he had passed the "Yankee White" investigation.

What became clear to Emanuel Vegas was the fact that Nadia Noorani most likely did not have access to information which in any way might link his name to the satellite telephone, any of the members of the team, terrorist information, or Satan's Shadow. Information that might cause one to suspect anything had to come from higher up. She was for all intents and purposes an information mule—nothing more. But, which side of the pond was the source?

On the other side of the pond, Liam walked along a tree-lined path in a Paris park. It was a warm and pleasant day. His pace was relaxed and steady. The empty path stretched on before him. Lost in thought, he kept reviewing a list of names. It was a short list. He could count on one hand those who knew of his connection with the government of France and the group known as Satan's Shadow. Five people and one or more were traitors.

In a secluded portion of the tree-lined path a rustling sound caused a bird to take flight. Liam immediately observed his surroundings. From behind a tree a young thug casually walked out to block Liam from proceeding. In his hand he held a six-inch knife. In French, he demanded Liam's money.

Liam stared directly into the hoodlum's eyes.

The man repeated his statement and motioned with the knife to punctuate his demand.

Without warning, Liam's cane spun through the air striking the perpetrator's wrist knocking the knife out of his hand. Before he could act, the would-be thief was struck in the neck by the lethal cane. He fell backward hitting his head on the ground rolled over and made a desperate escape into the bushes. Liam did not follow.

On the ground lay the weapon the thug had threatened to use. The old man, while leaning on his cane, bent down a retrieved the knife. When he examined it, a cold chill ran down his spine. It was military issue.

"Lā 'ilāha 'illā-llāhu muhammadun rasūlu-llāh, there is no god but God and Muhammad is the messenger of God," Darius Holiday repeated over and over in the small interview room.

Special Agent Peggy Fox entered. In her hand she held a piece of paper. "Mr. Holiday, we have agreement. The federal prosecutor will waive any charges against Toufan Ghorbani Mashti in exchange for his and your testimony against Haji Ejder Jahandar and Rashid Teymouri."

As if in a daze Darius stared blankly at the FBI agent. Following a few seconds of silence, he said uncharacteristically softly, "He won't do it."

"Isn't that his choice?"

"If he doesn't agree to testify, he will not get immunity?"

"That is the offer."

"And, if he doesn't get immunity, I will not testify," Darius stated with finality.

"You do realize that you are facing the death penalty?" Agent Fox looked at the paper in her hand.

"What happens to me, happens to me."

What became clear to Agent Fox was that convincing Toufan Ghorbani Mashti to testify was the lynchpin of the investigation. While the little murderer, Darius Holiday, might believe his friend wouldn't turn state's evidence, there was plenty of precedence that indicated otherwise. The key to Toufan Ghorbani Mashti's cooperation was his family. Experience had taught her when you know where a suspect is vulnerable it becomes far easier to convince them to do what you want. She would paint a dire picture of his family suffering while he rots at Gitmo under suspicion. There might be leaks that indicate that he is cooperating with authorities making his family outcasts in the Muslim community. Finally, a threat to tie him to the Philadelphia and New York City terrorist attacks would surely put his family in the crosshairs of Satan's Shadow. Her mind smiled. Yes, this case was coming together and she was the agent that located and arrested Darius Holiday while also braking up a planned monstrous terrorism plot on the verge of implementation. Careers are made by events like this. She looked at Darius who was mumbling his gibberish and thought, this can be done and I am the one who can do it. "Let us assume that Toufan agrees to testify. Will you then agree to testify, as well?" Fox asked.

"Yes."

"Then we have a deal?"

"One more thing," Darius surprised Agent Fox.

"No more conditions," she said in frustration.

"Not a condition—a request."

"What is your request?"

"Can you protect my family from those Satanists? My family had no idea about what I did. They are dumb, stupid, coal town, common folk just trying to live their lives."

Agent Fox remembered her conversation with Darius' mother, Marcella Holiday, who lamented, "My Darius is gone. He left. I know I won't see him again and my heart wants to stop beating." Not for the killer before her, but for the despairing mother bent under a burden of guilt and torn by emotions unable to justify their existence, she said, "I'll see what I can do."

Three members of the Satan's Shadow team rode north in a rented Renault Clio 4 RS 200. Their destination lay 50 miles north of Marseilles at the decommissioned French Military Base 200-Apt-Saint-Christol on the Plateau d'Albion. The plan was for all three to enter the base under cover of darkness, reconnoiter the area where they believed the mother and children to be living, and then devise a plan for a quick elimination.

"Blows should be directed to the temple, or the area just below and behind the ear, or the lower, rear part of the skull," Ron Clew continued to tutor Ken Farmingdale in the fine art of assassination. "Stay away from the lower frontal portion of the head, from the eyes to the throat. Contrary to what you see on TV, these areas can withstand enormous blows."

"Got it."

The Navy Seal glanced at his friend and wasn't so sure that he did, indeed, get it. He continued, "In the hands of an expert, the knife is a silent and deadly weapon. There is no sure defense against it other than a gun or running like hell." He smiled, "Good news is that most knifers will not throw their weapon."

"I can see that," Ken commented.

"When the time comes, don't look into their eyes. If you do, you will freeze. Come up from behind, grab them around the mouth and slice their throat as quickly as possible. The most reliable method is severing both the jugular and carotid blood vessels on both sides of the windpipe."

This time Farmingdale didn't answer. When Ron Clew glanced over he saw the test pilot looking straight out the windshield of the car. He was not looking at the road ahead, he was looking at a dark and uncertain future.

CHAPTER 35

Retired Marine General Maxwell Hughes sat in his stateroom on Ismenios. In his hand he held a glass of Scotch on the rocks. The only other member of the team onboard, Navy Captain Jarvis Demoye, was on the bridge attending to craft maintenance. In the quiet of his cabin General Hughes reminisced about the formation of Satan's Shadow.

As a retired senior military personality, he was often called upon for consultation by various branches of government. Most often it was the Department of Defense, followed by the State Department. There were questions about military capabilities and procedures, tactical recommendations, threat evaluations, security technique, international situational analysis, and more. Given this role he often took meetings with strangers to discuss consulting opportunities.

On a Friday night after ten o'clock his telephone rang. When he answered a voice asked softly, "General Hughes?"

"This is Hughes, with whom am I speaking?"

"For now, you can simply refer to me as Dave, I represent an organization that might have need for your services. If you have time I'd like to talk with you."

It was not uncommon for some private companies and even government organizations to wish to remain anonymous, therefore, Dave being mysterious was not a problem or a reason for concern. "When would you like to meet?"

"Now."

"A little short notice, wouldn't you say?"

"Very short—my apologies."

"I require a few minutes to get ready. Where would you like to meet?"

"I'm at the end of your driveway in a dark green Cadillac Escalade."

"I see," General Hughes decided to carry his Colt 1911 45 caliber pistol with him.

When he entered the Escalade he found a middle-aged, slightly overweight, clean-cut, driver wearing a brown suit and glasses. The man didn't offer his hand but welcomed the General with a friendly, "I appreciate your being flexible and accommodating. You could have told me to go to hell."

"That was my first thought."

"I suspect so."

General Hughes understood the dynamics of clandestine meetings, therefore didn't ask any questions. He knew he would get the answers he needed in due time. In addition, he didn't try to guess with what organization Dave worked. There simply were too many to consider and it was late at night. They drove into the darkness.

After five minutes of silence Dave spoke, "I've read a great deal about you, General. You are quite an impressive individual with an outstanding military record." Before Hughes could make a remark, Dave added, "No, I'm not laying it on thick. I just want you to know that you are not a stranger to me. However, I will remain a stranger to you."

"You do realize that unless I have sufficient information and feel comfortable with whatever your organization wishes my assistance with that I won't make any commitments."

"Understood."

More silence. On a long straight empty highway, the huge SUV floated along.

"I am associated with the Central Intelligence Agency, however have come to you as an individual."

"Interesting."

"A little history. The CIA is actually a civilian foreign intelligence service. We gather, process, and analyze national security information from around the world, primarily from the use of human intelligence (HUMINT). The agency has no official law enforcement function. However, we are the only agency authorized by law to carry out covert action through tactical divisions, such as the Special Activities Division."

"I've had dealings with the CIA," General Hughes remarked.

"Operation Gold Hook, the Alexander affair, take down of Colonel Hartif, and the arrest of Sanchez."

The last event listed surprised General Hughes as he was deep undercover on that one. "You've done your homework."

"Always do. It's how you stay alive." Dave pulled off the highway and stopped at a gas station. "You want anything to drink or eat?" he asked as he exited the vehicle. In the lights of the gas station General Hughes got a better look at the man. He had a pleasant appearance—almost innocence. His movements were smooth and relaxed. One might take him for a lawyer or doctor. While there was no sign of a firearm, Hughes knew there were one or more on his person.

When they were back on the road Dave returned to the subject. "In 1949 the Central Intelligence Agency Act (Public law 81-110) authorized the agency to use confidential fiscal and administrative procedures and exempted it from limitations on the use of Federal funds. It also exempted the CIA from having to disclose its organization, functions, officials, titles, salaries, or number of employees. We pretty much are as secret an organization as you can get."

"And, you plan to stay that way," Hughes commented.

"Precisely. Remember, though, I come to you as an individual."

General Hughes did not respond.

"Within the agency there are agents who report to nobody, have no designation, no assigned duties, are not on any lists," Dave explained. "In essence, do not exist."

"And, have no oversight, supervision, or responsibility."

Undaunted, Dave continued, "When you send a special operations team into a hot zone where there are many unknowns you expect them to adapt, improvise, and operate independently—if necessary."

"As long as they remain focused on their mission."

"Given the right circumstances, even their mission becomes fluid." Dave's voice took on a friendly, "I know," tone, "You know that fact General, you've been there."

"Accepted."

"The world has become one enormous hot zone. The need for independent operators to act immediately is increasing. Oversight, is now a hinderance with indecision causing catastrophic outcomes. You've seen it with ridiculous rules of engagement. The bad guy is in your sights with his finger on the button and you have to wait for clearance. By the time you get it, a village, dozens of innocents, and the bad guy are gone."

"Point taken," Hughes said in the darkness of the SUV. "However, it significantly raises the potential for an agent to go rogue and forget the objective."

"Absolutely. Can't say that it doesn't happen. But when it does, we deal with it appropriately."

"Let's put our cards on the table. Why am I here?"

"I'm going rogue," was Dave's monotone response.

Caught off guard, General Hughes did not respond.

"What I am about to say is my opinion. Albeit, it is based on many years of experience and an enhanced understanding of human nature." They pulled off the highway onto a secondary road. "Technology has changed the dynamics of world politics. Some tactics, such as worldwide warfare, have become less feasible. While advanced communications capabilities raised the effectiveness of other tactics. Propaganda has become a powerful weapon. On November 18, 1956, while addressing Western ambassadors at a reception at the Polish embassy in Moscow, Soviet premier Nikita Khrushchev said, 'About the capitalist states, it doesn't depend on you whether or not we exist. If you don't like us, don't accept our invitations, and don't invite us to come to see you. Whether you like it or not, history is on our side. We will bury you!' The American press interpreted it as a nuclear threat. Years later he explained, 'I once said, we will bury you, and I got into trouble with it. Of course, we will not bury you with a shovel. Your own working class will bury you,' he referred to the Marxist saying, 'The proletariat is the undertaker of capitalism.' It was the concluding statement in Chapter 1 of the *Communist Manifesto*: What the bourgeoisie therefore produces, above all, are its own grave-diggers. Its fall and the victory of the proletariat are equally inevitable. Sadly, he was correct. Our schools and media have become indoctrination tools of socialist ideology. Propaganda has proven a frightening weapon."

General Hughes noted that Dave's statement was without emotion. He was simply presenting facts. They continued to ride on back roads in dark wooded terrain.

"There is another weapon, while not exactly new, that has gained effectiveness due to advanced worldwide communications—terrorism." After a pause Dave added, "Terrorism is psychological warfare. They kill innocents to send a message that no one is safe. Yet, they know the same tactics are not going to be used on them. The goal is to place their cause top-of-mind and make the masses fear opposing it. Unfortunately, it works all too well in the modern world. Think of how many millions are afraid to draw a picture of Muhammad."

They turned onto a dirt road and disappeared into the forest.

"One time I was interrogating a prisoner," Dave stated, "He was a cold bastard who had killed many innocent people, beheaded men, women, and children, and wasn't giving up anything. After hours of fruitless efforts, he had a smug smile when I left the room. When I reentered the room with his ten-year-old son and put a knife to the brat's neck everything changed. The stone became putty and he gave up everything."

The Cadillac Escalade stopped.

Dave turned to General Hughes and asked, "Do you think I would have really slit the kid's throat in front of his father?"

"In fact, I do," was the General's response.

"Good. Because I would. Evil men only understand evil things. If he held my son at knifepoint he would have executed him without a second thought. In a brutal world, brutality wins. Yet, we keep trying to be civilized when the opposition is not. That is a no-win scenario."

"What do you have in mind?"

"We need to change the rules of the game. Terrorists have to understand that they literally have skin in the game. No longer are they immune to personal loss. Whether they kill or injure one or one thousand the price they pay will be something they understand and value. It may not work with every depraved fanatic, but it will cause some to reconsider their plans. This I believe."

"I'm sure with your training that you don't need any pointers from me," General Hughes concluded.

"Pointers? No. I require your leadership." In the darkness Dave handed General Maxwell Hughes a coin. The retired military leader didn't have to see the challenge coin to know what it was. He could feel the dragon, sword, and stars. "Est ultra de tenebris et in umbra satanas," Dave stated which was the inscription on the back meaning, it is beyond dark in Satan's shadow.

At first, General Hughes was confused. There were so few of those coins he knew all who possessed one. Dave was not one he recognized. He was compelled to ask, "Where did you get this?"

"I wasn't always a non-existent entity in a sea of secrecy. At one time my partner and I were assigned the task of gathering human intel in Iraq. We posed as businessmen interested in helping revitalize the failing agricultural industry. A combination of wars, government influence, the oil for food program, mismanagement, and loss of labor all contributed to declining yields in every sector. Of course, that was our cover. Under that cover story we did a great deal of intel gathering at the time. Then, one night my partner was lured to a meeting in an unfamiliar place where he was to be introduced to a key contact. He left me a note but failed to return. I went to where he indicated and found him in a back alley. He was cut up and dying. They had tortured him. I held him as he died. Before he did, he gave me this coin and told me if I ever needed a man who was 100% trustworthy, honorable, and strong I should contact General Maxwell Hughes—you."

General Hughes held the coin in the dark and asked the question that had to be asked, "What was his name?"

"Troy Benson."

"Troy, I remember him. Damn good man. Sorry to hear about his loss. When I knew him he was with special operations. Outstanding Marine."

"He told me that coin was my ticket. That you would give me an audience and take what I say seriously."

General Hughes handed the coin back to Dave and replied, "He was correct."

"As I stated, I'm going rogue. I am not here representing the CIA. I'm here planting a seed and offering to help it grow."

The two men ended up talking the entire night. Dave indicated that America had lost its stomach to take the necessary actions required to influence activities of terrorists. He concluded, "While trying desperately to demonstrate to the world that we are a just and humane nation, we are actually signaling that we are a passive and timid entity not to be feared." Only once he showed any emotion, "I fear we have come too far and have permanently abdicated our positive role in the world. There is no doubt whatsoever that in Washington, our grave diggers are sealing our fate."

From that "night of the revelation" came the concept of Satan's Shadow.

CHAPTER 36

Under cover of darkness three figures dressed in all black entered the decommissioned French Military Base 200-Apt-Saint-Christol on the Plateau d'Albion. The facility was surprisingly quiet and still. No personnel of any kind were seen. A rusted security fence had been easily cut and breached followed by entry into the empty barracks building closest to the perimeter of the base. Once inside, the intruders moved silently to the innermost wall of the building. It smelled of dust and mold. Water was heard dripping in another part of the building. The barracks building was relatively wide open in the center with latrines and a few private rooms at each end.

To avoid detection each member of the team wore an ATN PS15 compact, lightweight, dual Night Vision Goggle System. The military-grade equipment provided remarkably clear and crisp images under the darkest conditions. Built-in infrared technology added to their capability by making it easy to read a map or function in a total darkness environment.

Adam "Watch Dog" Hayes led the way. There were four abandoned barracks buildings butted against each other to form a stair-step configuration. He was to take them to the end of the last building and then remain as, for lack of a better description, a watch dog. Ron Clew and Ken Farmingdale would cross the small parking lot in front of the main building and enter.

When they arrived at the end of the last barracks building they paused to observe the surroundings. It was eerily quiet. No movement, sounds, or light gave the impression of impending doom. Could a team of French soldiers be waiting in the shadows? Was the entire area abandoned? Was their intel faulty? The unknown weighed heavy on the team.

All communication was through hand signals. After a reasonable amount of observation Ron Clew motioned for Ken Farmingdale to follow. They silently left the cover of the barracks building and crossed the parking lot. A low moon on the horizon created dark shadows in which the two hunters could remain concealed. In but a minute they reached the front of the main building.

All of a sudden, the sound of a motor brought all three trespassers to full attention. Adam Hayes scanned the area to determine the source of the sound. When Ron and Ken saw the reflection of headlights on the right side of the main building they drifted into an overgrown area on the left side of the structure.

A jeep occupied by two soldiers arrived in front of the building. Headlights lit the front doors. For a few minutes the two men sat and chatted in French. One lit a cigarette. Team Satan remained hidden in complete silence. Finally, one of the soldiers left the jeep and, holding a flashlight, walked up to the doors. He tested them and confirmed that they were locked. Then, he sprayed the area surrounding the building with light. He walked first to one side and then the other. The two Satan's Shadow commandoes froze. Ken Farmingdale was not aware of the fact that visual acuity is often enhanced as a result of the perception of movement. Ron Clew, on the other hand, had direct experience with the phenomenon. More than once he became aware of a threat due to some barely perceptible movement. The human brain naturally seeks various stimuli in order to develop as accurate a picture of its surroundings as possible. After seeing nothing out of the ordinary the French guard returned to the jeep and they left.

Locked front doors were actually a potentially good thing. It could indicate that the rooms inside the building did not have locks on the doors. Or, that there weren't any military personnel inside. If there were, most likely, the soldier would have made contact with them to confirm everything was alright. The only concern Ron Clew had was whether or not any type of alarm was attached to those doors.

Ron tapped Ken on the shoulder and the two men proceeded to the front doors of the main building. After close examination, the retired Navy Seal used his trench knife to pry open the lock. As the door was slowly opened he held his breath waiting to hear an alarm. None sounded. They entered the building. Inside they found a large open reception area. Directly ahead was a large unmanned counter. On either side of the room were two couches and various chairs. Lamps on tables and coffee tables with magazines rounded out the scene. A flight of stairs leading to the upper floors was located to the right of the counter. Yellow ribbon and a sign indicated that the stairs were closed. Another good sign as it appeared only the first floor of the building was being used. Corridors opened on either side of the reception area leading to the building's left and right wings. Ron examined the floor and saw undisturbed dust on the left and relatively clean floors to the right. He proceeded to the right.

What struck Ron Clew first was the total ineptness of the security technique. Most of the doors to the various offices and rooms were left open. Like neon "open" arrows pointing at a diner they showed the way to the location of the targets. Midway down the corridor on the front side of the building a lone door was closed. He signaled Ken Farmingdale and examined the door. It was locked.

Back on Ismenios Maxwell Hughes and Jarvis Demoye waited. This was never easy as time crawled when no activity was taking place. Small talk was also something that just didn't seem appropriate, so silence dominated the room.

General Hughes thought about Dave and the CIA and the fact that the man in the brown suit who had gone rogue remained a specter. He had no way of identifying the man or contacting him. Yet, he did get contacted by the agent from time to time. Conversations were short and innocuous. Every once in a while, Dave would direct Hughes to a place where he would find information, some new piece of equipment, or financial resources. Satan's Shadow never had to face the limitations that come from a lack of funds.

Jarvis Demoye thought of his twin adult daughters. For some odd reason his mind made a leap from what he was doing with Satan's Shadow to the possibility of some revenge killing if he was ever identified as being a part of the organization. After all, they were raining down terrorism on the terrorists. Circuitous logic justified more killing and more killing. Would there ever be an end to it? He knew it was impossible. He pictured a young woman, maybe named Mary, with her baby walking in a park enjoying a spring day without a care. An innocent mother somewhere in America unaware of the evil forces that are constantly kept at bay by those who maybe know too much.

Ron Clew picked the inferior lock and turned the doorknob. The door opened slightly but was stopped by a security chain lock. He indicated the chain to Ken Farmingdale and motioned for him to have his knife ready. With one powerful stroke of his trench knife the chain was ripped from the doorjamb and the door opened.

A small living quarters was found inside with a single room off to the left. Without hesitation the two men crossed the room and entered the bedroom. A woman, who had been startled from sleep, sat in the bed in the dark. She saw a shadow and screamed but was silenced immediately.

Ken Farmingdale went directly to the other bed. With one swift move he cut the throat of a young boy. When the girl stirred and turned to face him, he looked into her eyes through his night vision goggles. He didn't see fear. What he saw was confusion, inability to comprehend what was happening, and innocence. A hand on his back triggered action. The girl dropped onto the bed losing the remaining few moments of her life.

The next day the authorities would find Rashid Sassani's family and the proclamation, "Terrorism has a price. If you commit a terrorist act your family is the price you pay. We will locate and kill every member of your family, your friends, associates, and any who offered you support. Through your actions you condemn them all to death. They can hide but we will find them. Satan's Shadow is everywhere."

CHAPTER 37

FBI Special Agent Peggy Fox read the agreement that she had gotten from the federal prosecutor's office. It stated that Toufan Ghorbani Mashti and his family would be placed in the federal witness protection program in exchange for his testimony against Haji Ejder Jahandar and Rashid Teymouri. At first, Toufan flatly refused. Agent Fox then went to work. She painted scenario after scenario of how his family would suffer. It was when she threatened to tie him to the Philadelphia and New York City bombings that he cursed her, but knew he was trapped. She gave him only one way out and he had to take it. Reluctantly, he signed the agreement.

Fox wasn't as lucky with the Darius Holiday's family. The prosecutor turned down her request for them to also enter the witness protection program. She was told that was not what the program was for. The best they could do was provide increased surveillance and protection for a period of time. In her heart she knew it was far too little.

Darius Holiday shook his head when he was told of the situation. However, he surprised Agent Fox when he told her he would still testify if she would agree to look into other means of protecting his family. She agreed but had just finished reading an international report about the assassination of Rashid Sassani's wife and two children at a French military base. It was clear the group known as Satan's Shadow were good at what they do. She was fairly certain they were military and suspected that they were American. The latter opinion was based on their ability to operate freely in the United States. A glance at Darius Holiday brought his mother's visage to her mind. The woman was innocent. She simply was trying to take care of her family and live the best life possible. Now, due to the actions of her son, her life and that of her husband and daughter hung in the balance. Agent Fox wanted to appeal to the Satan's Shadow angels of death for mercy. Yet, of course, that was impossible. Another thought fought its way into her mind. What mercy did the murderer before her show his victims? He created the present situation. If he had stayed in Wilkes-Barre and worked in the coal mine numerous individuals would still be alive or not suffered hideous injuries or not been maimed for life.

He alone condemned his family and unleashed the demon upon them. She repeated herself, "I'll do the best I can to protect your family."

Three men sat in the rear of a local restaurant outside of London. Their names were not important. A fourth man, Shahin Pouran, arrived. He was known to the others as the one who killed seven members of a watchdog website that had been critical of Islam. They both respected and feared him.

"My friends, we must act if we are to keep the idolaters off balance."

None of the others spoke.

"There are those who are opposed to our cause that must be taught a lasting lesson."

Silence endured.

Shahin looked at each of the men and inquired, "Why are you not moved?"

The middle-aged man with a greying beard and glasses replied in a low voice, "I fear now is not a suitable time."

"Why do you hesitate? There are numerous targets open to us that are as ripe figs to be picked."

A second man spoke, "Should the light of recognition shine upon us there is danger."

"There is always danger," he scanned the three cohorts, "Are you women?"

The third younger man spoke, "I do not fear for myself. I am ready to die for Allah. It is others who might be caught in the same net for whom I fear."

"Others? What others?"

The man with glasses said, "It is common knowledge that the infidels have begun killing those who know or help mujahid."

Shahin Pouran sat for a moment pondering what had been said. The three others at the table waited. They had agreed to meet with him, but shared a concern fostered by the latest news from France. A woman and two children had been slain in retaliation for a terrorist act. This was in addition to others who paid the price. The man with glasses had a copy of a newspaper article in his pocket which included the Satan's Shadow proclamation. He considered sharing the article with Pouran but rejected the idea.

The younger man stated, "I have a mother and sister who might be killed if I am identified."

"Then don't be identified," Shahin said coldly.

The younger man did not answer.

"It might be prudent to wait," the man with glasses offered.

A cold glare was Shahin Pouran's response.

"Maybe the authorities will catch the murderous heathen. Then we do not have to be concerned," the younger man said, hopefully.

"You disappoint me," Shahin said to the group. "You would be deterred by an unknown band of marauders." He stood from the table for emphasis, "The answer is not fearing them but defying them. We should increase our efforts, draw them out, and put them under our knives."

"They are nowhere and everywhere," one of the men pointed out.

"They are infidels! Allah will guide us. We shall make an example of them."

"I still believe we should wait," the man with glasses stated.

Shahin Pouran looked at the others and saw agreement in their eyes. It became clear that whatever he planned or did it would have to be alone. He sat heavily in a chair. With the wave of his hand he spat, "Leave me. You who are afraid of shadows are of no use to me."

Ismenios sailed west across the Atlantic toward the United States. Ron Clew, Adam Hayes, and General Hughes sat in the main cabin. Ken Farmingdale had joined Jarvis Demoye on the bridge. The sun was high in the sky, while a steady stiff breeze made the waters choppy. The eighty-foot craft negotiated most of the white caps but every once in a while, would rise or drop on a larger wave.

"You think the weather will improve?" Ken Farmingdale asked the Captain.

"From all indications it will get worse," Jarvis replied as he adjusted the engines.

"Figures. It's a good thing I don't get seasick."

"We may all have a touch of motion sickness before we reach the Continental United States," Jarvis Demoye predicted.

Inside the main cabin after one particular bounce over a wave, Adam Hayes observed, "I think we hit a whale."

"Was he white," Ron Clew asked.

"Yeah, and he had a peg-legged guy tied to his side."

"Was he beckoning?" Ron moved his arm mimicking Captain

Ahab from *Moby Dick*.

"It was more like this," Adam said as he slapped his bicep while giving Ron Clew the finger.

"That son-of-a-bitch, where is he?" Ron said as he rose. He walked over to the refrigerator a retrieved a bottle of spring water.

General Hughes changed the subject to something more serious, "Farmingdale, how's he doing?"

"Denial," Ron stated flatly.

"He'll get through it," Adam concluded.

"After he beats himself up for a good long while," Hughes predicted.

"It'll take time and he'll never get completely over it, but he'll learn to live with it," Adam Hayes spoke from experience.

"I think we all can use a break," General Hughes said. "I have information on the homegrown terrorist who attacked Philadelphia and New York City."

Both Ron and Adam gave General Hughes their full attention.

"The FBI have him in custody. He's a recent convert from Wilkes-Barre Pennsylvania. Pretty much a loner—acted alone. They're keeping his name from the press. It's Darius Holiday."

"A loner, what about family?"

"Mother, father, and sister."

"I'll wager they're in protective custody or heavily guarded," Ron stated.

"I don't have a lot on that. When we get back to the States we'll take a break—a little R and R. After that we should know more about the Holiday family."

CHAPTER 38

Ken Farmingdale walked onto the tarmac. The aroma of jet fuel and aviation gas were as spring flowers to the pilot who had been too long tied to the ground. After the events in the Plateau d'Albion, France, he needed to find refuge alone far from terra firma. Up there, clouds wrap around him and seem to protect him from forces he can't control. Above the clouds, the sky is deeper blue than is ever observed from the surface of the Earth. Quiet, with the exception of the aircraft's engine, offers a perfect oasis for meditation. And welcome solitude, alone, unreachable, distant, and without any human contact.

After providing his credentials and pilot's license, Ken was able to rent a Cessna 350 single-engine, turboprop, airplane. Unlike more common Cessna aircraft with the wing over the top of the cabin, this plane had wings under a streamlined cabin. In addition, it was fast with its 310-horsepower engine providing enough power to cruise at 220 miles-per-hour. While not a jet, it would allow him to touch the infinite blue once more.

Ken Farmingdale did not file a flight plan as his only goal was to take off and break the chains that bound him to Earth for the afternoon. It was a clear day with just a hint of altocumulus clouds at approximately 18,000 feet, the service ceiling of the Cessna 350. The test pilot was determined to fly above those white mists. Winds were calm and the temperature a comfortable 62 degrees. It was a perfect day for flying.

He taxied the Cessna 350 to the end of the private airport runway. Air traffic was light, therefore, he received immediate clearance to take off. He moved the throttle forward and the propeller increased rpms allowing the featherless bird to begin her run for the sky. A feeling of elation flowed over him as he felt the wheels lift off the ground. The Earth dropped away.

Almost as if purified air had been pumped into the cockpit Ken Farmingdale felt refreshed. He was where he was always most comfortable. The plane's wings became his wings as he soared higher and higher, a weary spirit breaking free.

The Cessna 350 with its side-mounted stick was like driving a sports car. He headed northeast at 030° and climbed to 5,500 feet. Using

Visual Flight Rules (VFR) aircraft heading 000° to 179° must fly at odd thousand plus 500 feet altitudes. Those flying in the opposite direction 180° to 359° fly at even thousand plus 500 feet. In this way aircraft will always be separated by a minimum of 1,000 feet.

After an hour of flying he approached New York City. Its glistening skyline was like no other. He crossed above the New York airports' glidepaths as he continued up the Hudson River. The first landmark he noted was the new Freedom Tower with its odd angles and pseudo modern design. It wasn't to his taste. By juxtaposition he passed the old section that was Greenwich Village with its hundred-year-old buildings. Then lower Manhattan where Hudson Yards had rows and rows of subway cars. Some older cars showing the rust of age. Midtown presented an endless forest of skyscrapers. At the George Washington Bridge, Ken banked right and proceeded due east. He crossed the Bronx and then observed the bedroom towns on Long Island. He was glad to be above all the hustle and bustle that was taking place below. Another ten-minutes and he was over the Atlantic Ocean. Directly ahead, in the distance, the deep blue sky blended with green ocean waters.

Ken increased his speed and took the aircraft to 13,500 feet. At that altitude he could play a little. A few barrel rolls, stall, long steep dive, play chicken with the water, and just seeing what the blue and white Cessna 350 could do. It did not disappoint. This was a fine aircraft. Once back at 13,500 feet he entered a cloud bank. Within the liquid curtain he saw a dragon flying with him. It coiled and turned and danced in the air teasing him. Moisture spread on the windshield. His playmate turned and hung in the air before him.

"I knew you would be here," Ken Farmingdale stated as he flew directly at the creature.

Ismenios rose above the small airplane towering higher and higher. Its wings seemed to reach from horizon to horizon. A flash of lightning struck at the ocean surface below.

"It is a terrible thing we have chosen to do," Farmingdale whispered, "terrible, but a sign of the times. Terror versus terror, hate versus hate, no, hate versus love. We have to use what they love to drive home our point. If only there was an alternative." Innocent eyes etched in his conscience stared at him from the clouds. A child beckoned. Tears filled his eyes. He had come here to run the aircraft dry and plunge into the ocean.

Another flash of lightning filled the sky followed by an immediate clap of thunder. Ismenios spoke and would not release the tortured soul.

The test-pilot's instinct engaged and he turned the Cessna south, then due west. He climbed to 14,500 feet. By his estimation he had just enough fuel to make it back to the airport where he rented the plane. A quick end—long planned—was impossible. There was more to be done. Ken Farmingdale spoke to the windshield as he told himself, "I'll have to bear the burden of guilt a little longer."

Michael O'Neal recognized Adam Hayes' green Jeep Grand Cherokee as it traveled up the long driveway of FFP Ranch. He finished putting away the tack gear and walked toward the house. By the time he arrived Adam was out of his car and walking toward him.

"You look like shit!" Adam observed. "All healthy, relaxed, tan, and not limping."

"How the hell are you?" Michael "Owl" O'Neal asked his friend.

"I'm unhealthy, stressed, pasty, but I'm also not limping."

"That's good to hear—no new wounds or injuries?"

"Not a one."

The two comrades shook hands and held the grip long enough to express their affection and concern for one another. They walked up onto the porch and sat.

"You want something to drink? You are staying for dinner? What have you been up to, or is it all top secret?" Michael asked and asked.

"Yeah, yeah, oh yeah," Adam smiled and added, "I've had a few gigs, met some great guys, and saved the world from tyranny."

"Some great guys? You cheating on me?"

"You cast me aside," he wrinkled his nose and waved his arm to encompass the ranch, "for this."

"Well, it isn't a filthy, muddy river bottom with bullets flying overhead, but I call it home."

"How is the horse business?"

"Actually, very good. I've got two thoroughbred mares about to foal. Probably have to sit up all night foal watching."

"Sounds like fun."

"You should try it. There's something rejuvenating and energizing about watching the emergence of life. It's good for the soul." Michael looked critically at Adam, "That is if you had one."

"I have a soul," Adam protested. "I just left it in my other pants."

The two men sat in silence.

After years together, conversation was unnecessary. Watch Dog and Owl were well-known in certain circles. Often in great demand when a team of mercenaries was being put together. Chemistry is a strange and unpredictable thing when it comes to human beings. On rare occasions, they are as one.

Adam then looked at Michael and said, “I think I'll try it—foal watching.”

A lone black man standing on the corner late at night in a bad part of town will always get the attention of local police. Ron Clew expected as much when the patrol car slowed to a stop. From inside the car, the Lexington, Kentucky patrolman asked, “You look like someone who is looking for trouble.”

“And, you look like someone who runs away from trouble like some candy ass little girl,” Ron Clew responded.

The police officer got out of the car and walked over to the larger man, “OK, put your hands on the car.”

“How about I put my hands around your dumb-ass throat?”

“You son-of-a-bitch, what are you doing here? Why didn't you call?”

“This is more fun—getting hassled by my little brother.”

“How did you know I'd be riding by here?”

“I called police headquarters and found out you were on duty tonight. I knew you'd come by this corner sooner or later.” Ron smiled, “I got propositioned by three hookers while I waited. You need to clean up these streets.”

Ron joined his brother in the patrol car and they reminisced as he did a ride-along. It was a quiet night. At the end of the shift, the two brothers stopped at a Waffle House for breakfast.

“I still think you should join the force, here, and make Lexington safe for its citizens,” Ron's brother, Felix, stated over a piece of toast.

“You know me, I'm a more worldly type. Lexington is just too small. I'd get claustrophobia.”

“You'd get used to it.”

“God knows with such questionable talent like you on the force, I could vastly improve the department,” Ron deadpanned.

“Come'on prove it. We're hiring.”

“I can't right now, I've got a contract.”

"For how long?"

"I can't really say."

"I guess you prefer traipsing all over the world and risking your life to settling down."

Ron Clew faced reality and stated a fact that was all too true, "Settling down isn't in my future."

Retired Navy Captain Jarvis Demoye sat in the kitchen of his home in Chesapeake, Virginia. The house was empty as his wife was out at some gala, committee meeting, reception, or funeral. He looked in the refrigerator for a beer but found none. The kitchen was foreign to him, however, that was always the case when he came home from a deployment. It was his house, but not his home. Too many years at sea and now the Ismenios kept him from truly putting down roots.

He went out into the garage. There, covered with dust, was his classic 1964 red Corvette Stingray convertible. With the keys he retrieved from a hook in the kitchen he attempted to start the neglected automobile. A few weak turns of the starter drained what was left of energy in the battery. He decided to buy a new battery the next day. In the meantime, he began wiping down the vehicle with a wet rag. After he made the car finish shine, he could see his visage as a reflection. His grey hair and well-cropped grey beard appeared a little lighter. New wrinkles and shadows added to the general appearance of aging.

Back in the house in the den Jarvis Demoye settled in a comfortable chair to read the local newspaper. On the front page in the lower right corner he found an article that quoted an FBI agent as saying they were closing in on the terrorist group known as Satan's Shadow.

Maxwell Hughes drove his black Escalade north on Ocean View Avenue. He entered US Highway 64 which led to the Hampton Roads Bridge Tunnel. In Newport News he followed winding roads in sparsely populated areas until he found a private road. At the end of the road in the woods overlooking a lake was the Spanish style stucco house where the team had met once before. A Lincoln MKZ was in the parking area.

Inside the house, General Maxwell Hughes found Secret Service Agent Emanuel Vegas and Liam. The two men sat in the living room looking at sheets of paper. They acknowledged the arrival of the retired

Marine. Hughes fixed himself a Scotch on the rocks and joined the other two men.

"There has been an attempt made on Liam's life," Vegas stated flatly.

"Terrorists?" General Hughes inquired.

Liam spoke in a calm calculating voice, "Military. I fear there are entities within the government that do not wish that I find whom is the traitor. With such a limited list of individuals who know of me or my charge its source must be of the highest level."

"Terrorism and infiltration make a formidable foe," Secret Service Agent Emanuel Vegas concluded.

CHAPTER 39

"As you are aware the Holiday family cannot be considered for the witness protection program," the FBI Executive Assistant Director for National Security Branch stated with finality.

Special Agent Peggy Fox nodded knowing that fact and expecting there was more.

"Of course, this offers us an opportunity," he added.

Once more she waited.

"As you know we have numerous teams investigating the vigilante group that call themselves Satan's Shadow. To date, we have very little to go on. Our friends in England and France have not been very helpful. They always seem to trip all over themselves at the crime scene and come up empty." He paused for a minute and then admitted, "Of course, we haven't been much better with the Torrey Pines High School in San Diego shooter's family's execution." He leaned forward, "But, this time we know they're coming."

Special Agent Fox finally spoke in disbelief, "You want to use the Holiday family as bait?"

"Bait? No. They are already on the menu. We simply want to catch the killers when they attempt to fulfill their proclamation."

"And, if we fail—what then?"

"Then you have to explain to me why that happened."

"Me? You want me to protect the Holiday family?" Peggy Fox asked not exactly pleased with the assignment.

"I want you to identify, capture, or neutralize the assassins known as Satan's Shadow. It's not every day we know who the target is before a crime is committed. Put together a team, get out to Wilkes-Barre, and put an end to these criminal acts."

"Do you have any information on Satan's Shadow that might be helpful?" Agent Fox asked not hiding her displeasure.

A folder that contained very little information was tossed on the desk in front of Agent Peggy Fox. She picked it up and left the office. As she walked down the hall anger welled up inside. This assignment was a career buster. If the assassins were successful it would be an indelible blot on her record. The fact that she found, arrested, and got a confession from the Philadelphia and New York terrorist would be forgotten. The identification of a wide-reaching terrorist plot that was thwarted would be forgotten. Yet, the fact that she allowed an innocent family to be murdered right under her nose would be long remembered. Obviously, it was a setup. She resented it. Therefore, it was essential that she succeed.

An anonymous tip was received by Scotland Yard. It came as a telephone call from a young man who outlined a terrorist plot and gave the name and location of the perpetrator. The caller explained that the would-be terrorist planned to rent a truck and run pedestrians down on a busy London street. He went on to say that he was revealing the plot because if it was carried out he might be identified as a friend or associate of the terrorist. Even though he would have nothing to do with the crime he might become a target. When told he had nothing to fear from the authorities he replied, "Not you—it's Satan's Shadow I fear."

Nadia Noorani, an assistant to an Under Secretary for Political Affairs in the office of East Asian And Pacific Affairs in the United States Department of State, had visited Pakistan her native country two years prior. Nothing out of the ordinary about that. She most likely visited friends and relatives. However, on a hunch Secret Service Agent Emanuel Vegas transmitted the dates she had been in Pakistan to Liam. He requested that the Frenchman investigate whether or not Kareem Reza, the suspected mole in the French government, had visited Pakistan and if so when. The answer he received was not a surprise, both parties had been in Pakistan at the same time. However, there was one surprise.

Emanuel Vegas sat alone considering what Liam had told him. What he heard was totally unexpected. It was disturbing and yet believable. It raised red flags while also obscuring the view. What he had thought might be an IED was turning out to be a mine field. Without question, he had to proceed cautiously. Manny also knew while the Secret Service is supposed to be nonpartisan, politics do come into play. He personally always tried to remain objective and remain in the middle by not taking any sides. Unfortunately, life in Washington DC had become chaotic, at best. Growth of extreme politics forced people to take a stand along a great ideological divide. The middle dissolved into the inevitable "if you're not with us, you're against us" mentality making one an outcast in both sectors. When you're not sure who can be trusted, your sphere of friends dwindles rapidly. Emanuel Vegas found himself wondering about all who were around him. Of course, he knew if they were aware of the path he had chosen it would pretty much eliminate every sane and reasonable person from his collection of allies. Luckily, that was not the case, however, someone had attached the name Vegas with Satan's Shadow no matter how remotely. In addition, the fact that in the last census there were fewer than 2,000 Vegas in the United States it put him high on the suspect list.

Manny made his way to the safe house and called General Maxwell Hughes on their new encrypted Iridium Extreme 9575 satellite telephone. When the General answered Manny stated, "New information has just come to my attention."

"Go ahead."

"Two years ago, Nadia Noorani visited Pakistan. During the same period, Kareem Reza from France also was in Pakistan. There are indications that they were in the city of Nawabshah at the same time. It's an agricultural area known for sugarcane, mango, and cotton. It is also the largest producer of bananas in Pakistan."

"It appears that they are in fact working together," General Hughes concluded.

"That's not the half of it."

"What else?"

"Our friend who wasn't there discovered that another American was in that dusty, hot, southeast Pakistan town at the same time as Nadia Noorani and Kareem Reza." There was a pause, then Manny Vegas said, "United States Congressman Blake Kane from Connecticut."

"Repeat."

"Congressman Blake Kane from Connecticut."

"Why was a U.S. Congressman in the banana capital of Pakistan?"

"It was two years ago. The best I can gather is he went to see the opening of a natural gas line China built that ran from Asaluyeh, Iran to Nawabshah, Pakistan."

"Not much of a cover."

"It was cover enough."

"You're right on that one."

"And, it places him in the middle of a possible foreign radical infiltration of our government."

"We need to find out who he is dealing with and what he's getting out of it—the traitor!"

"I know we don't want to jump to conclusions . . ." Vegas offered.

"When a man comes out of a whorehouse zipping his pants, you don't need an eye witness to have a pretty accurate idea of what he was up to," General Hughes pointed out.

"I might need part of your team for surveillance as I'm not sure who I can trust at this point."

"You have all five of us."

CHAPTER 40

There was little reason to track the whereabouts or interactions of Congressman Blake Kane as most were public knowledge anyhow. The target of their surveillance was Nadia Noorani of the State Department. Of course, with over 8,000 employees working in The Harry S Truman Building located in the Foggy Bottom neighborhood at 2201 C Street, NW, Washington DC the decision was made to surveil her at night and on weekends. After all, she would most likely avoid making contact with any suspicious characters on the job. She also would avoid any questionable activities at work, with the exception of those coded emails.

"The little lady, uh, Mata Hari lives in an apartment in McLean, Virginia. The address is 8421 Broad Street, apartment 21C. It's a 26-story building built a few years ago right at the Metro Silver Line Spring Hill train station," Secret Service Agent Emanuel Vegas told the five other members of Satan's Shadow.

They had decided to meet at a safe house so that plans could be openly discussed. This way they knew there weren't any listening devices or wire taps to be concerned with.

Vegas continued, "She drives a silver 2015 Nissan Altima, but takes the Metro to work. I don't have any info on acquaintances, friends, or lovers. She does have a cat—named Kashmir. Hobbies and activities—unknown. Her job is relatively structured working 9 to 5 with little overtime or off-hour requirements. The train runs every 6 minutes during rush hour and it takes approximately 28 minutes to get to the Spring Hill station. That means we need to observe from 5:30 p.m. until lights out. Weekends, 6:00 a.m. until lights out."

General Hughes declared, "It looks like all of us are going to have some long nights."

"The Metro is an elevated train that runs down the center of Leesburg Parkway. There's an Embassy Suites on the westside of Leesburg facing the apartment building. If we can get an upper story front room we can observe the front entrance of Miss Noorani's building. Obviously, we'll need a man in the window and one on the ground."

"Let's get an inconspicuous car," General Hughes ordered.

"A Porsche would work well," Adam Hayes pointed out.

After a prolonged look at Adam, Manny Vegas smiled and continued, "There's a McDonalds and Starbucks in the immediate vicinity of the building. While there are a wide variety of banks, stores, and restaurants in the area most would require a car for access." He took out a photograph of the building and stated, "We did have one stroke of good fortune, apartment 21C is a studio located on the Leesburg Parkway side of the building."

"How nice, a view of the highway and railroad tracks," Adam stated.

"It's to our advantage that we can see her apartment from the Embassy Suites," Jarvis Demoye observed.

"That increases our options," retired Navy Seal Master Chief Petty Officer Ronald Clew said which got the attention of all in the room. With experience in electronic surveillance devices and approaches, he was the resident expert. They listened as he discussed what was available to them, "In the past you had to enter the premises to plant a bug if you wanted to eavesdrop on conversations. This was risky and there are many counter-surveillance devices that can be used to locate bugs. A new non-detectable tool has been developed called a passive resonant cavity bug. Because it has no power source or transmitter, it is practically impossible to detect. It has a thin metallic diaphragm that moves in unison with sound waves from any conversation in the room. When struck by a radio beam from a remote location it returns a frequency modulated signal or sound. But you still have to plant the bug."

"OK, without entering her apartment, what are our best tools?" General Hughes asked.

"There is a long-range laser listening device only available to law enforcement, the military, and intelligence organizations. It uses an invisible infrared laser beam that bounces off a target window. Vibrations on the window glass caused by sound waves inside the room are transmitted back to a receiver which converts it into an electronic signal and you hear what is going on with a speaker or headphones."

"Have you used one of these?"

"I have. They are very impressive but hard to come by."

"Do you have one at home in a closet?" Adam asked in jest.

"No, but I do know where a system can be appropriated."

"Is that what you recommend?" Hughes asked.

"It's an option, but I'd start with something far simpler. I suggest that we get our hands on a StingRay," Clew began.

"A fish?" Adam asked. "What are you going to do hold it up like a parabolic antenna?"

"A cellular site simulator. The StingRay is an IMSI-catcher with both passive and active capabilities."

"What the hell is ISMI?" Adam asked.

Ron replied, "IMSI, International Mobile Subscriber Identity. Every phone has one, as well as an Electronic Serial Number (ESN). I could go into all kinds of technical facts, but it all comes down to the fact that cellular telephones are radio transmitters and receivers much like a walkie-talkie. Inside the telephone is a SIM card which is a Subscriber Identification Module. It's actually an integrated circuit that stores all the identification data, security authentication and ciphering information, network info, list of services and apps, two passwords, a Personal Identification Number (PIN), and a Personal Unblocking Code (PUC) for PIN unlocking." Ron Clew looked at Adam Hayes and asked, "Are you getting this?"

"MBJS—My brain just shut down."

"That would be MBJSD," Ron corrected. He stood as he continued, "It's important that you know what's going on as you will be operating the equipment. Cellphone towers generally operate at low power levels. The StingRay device mimics a cellphone tower only at a higher level of power. Because cellphones are designed to seek the strongest signal, they will most likely connect with the StingRay." He got a serious look upon his face and stated, "Now, this is important. When the StingRay is first operated it will attract every cellphone in use in the vicinity. And, when that happens, they will not connect to a real, active, network tower. Their call or message will not go through. There cannot be a prolonged outage while identification data is gathered. The quickest way to achieve our goal is to use the device when we have visual confirmation that she is using her cellphone. At that point we gather all necessary information to execute a "man-in-the-middle" approach."

"The Secret Service uses this tactic," Manny Vegas told the group.

Ron explained, "StingRay allows us to target a specific device based on IMSI. When a call is made by that device the StingRay cell site intercepts the connection and while simulating the target device, establishes a connection with a legitimate cell tower that provides service to the target device. It then forwards signals between the target device and the legitimate cell site while decrypting and recording communications content."

"So, this device gives us the capability of listening to her cellphone calls when she is at home or in the general vicinity?" Jarvis Demoye asked.

"Correct."

"What about when she leaves the area?" General Hughes asked.

"There is a handheld IMSI-catcher that will allow us to intercept calls if we are within range—500 feet." Ron Clew looked at Adam and added, "The handheld device is called a Kingfish."

"That helps with monitoring telephone calls but doesn't give us access to conversations in her apartment or car," retired test pilot Ken Farmingdale pointed out.

"Once we have all the identification, encryption, password, pin, and other data the software on the StingRay can alter the baseband chip that controls the phone. We can tell the phone to fake any shutdown and stay on. It's a neat hack. She presses the button. The phone buzzes, she sees the usual power-off animation, and the screen goes black. What she doesn't know is the phone secretly remains on with the microphone active. It's called a roving bug," Ron Clew explained.

"Technology—ya gotta love it," Adam Hayes exclaimed.

"The only way you can tell something is going on is if your phone feels warm when it's turned off. That means the baseband processor is still running."

"OK, let's get the necessary equipment and set this thing up," General Hughes ordered.

"One more thing," Ron Clew said, "I think we need to bug her car with a standalone device that has an unlimited range. Just like a cellphone it has a SIM card and transmits through cell towers. There's a company named Silent Circle that developed the Blackphone which uses PrivatOS that keeps conversations private and reduces the potential for tracking. We'll have our car bug use that as a contact."

"One night we'll need to get into her car," Manny Vegas concluded.

"This promises to be a long and tedious mission," Ken Farmingdale concluded.

An FBI surveillance team sat in the Wilkes-Barre Inn hotel room and reviewed all preparations with Special Agent Peggy Fox. They had spent two days setting up various pieces of equipment designed to alert them of any activity in or around the home of Sam and Marcella Holiday.

Motion sensors, infrared lasers, cameras with night vision, sound detecting devices, pressure change indicators, break beam silent alerts, heat sensors, and more had all been installed as inconspicuously as possible. These would all be monitored 24/7 in a van parked in an unused driveway across the street. By all appearances it belonged to the homeowners. Three teams consisting of two agents would alternate 8 hours on 16 off. In addition, a team of weapons experts would be stationed in the area on 24-hour call. The initial plan was for the surveillance to last two weeks.

"This could be a long and tedious undertaking," one agent observed.

CHAPTER 41

Nadia Noorani's smartphone had been compromised and was being controlled by Satan's Shadow StingRay device, her silver 2015 Nissan Altima was fitted with a remote-controlled bug, and a long-range viewing scope was directed at her apartment window from the eighth floor of the Embassy Suites.

After two days the team had gathered very little information that was of use. They knew her favorite restaurant for pick-up meals, name of her vet, and dress size. Everything reflected an average lifestyle. Unless her cat, named Kashmir, was an agent nothing useful had surfaced.

On the third day, her smartphone rang while retired Navy Captain Jarvis Demoye was on duty. He began recording.

"Peaches, my friend needs to use the phone to send a message," a male voice stated.

Unemotionally, Nadia replied, "When do you want me to send it?"

"Tomorrow."

"Time?"

"At 2:00 p.m. the text will be provided. As usual, send it immediately."

"I'll be waiting."

"Good." The voice changed to a friendlier tone, "By the way, the FBI are staking out the home of Darius Holiday with the hope of catching the Satan's Shadow vigilantes."

"I hope they are successful."

"I don't believe they will be."

"Why not?"

"There are too many leaks in this government. No secret is safe. There's always somebody who wants people to be impressed by what they know."

It was Nadia Noorani's turn to have a change in tone, "These Americans are such ignorant children. No wonder they can be manipulated so easily." She realized what she had said and quickly added, "I do not mean you, of course."

"Of course. In truth, I don't care about ideology or who runs what, as long as I have enough cash to remain above the fray. We both know I am in this for the power and money."

Jarvis Demoye shared the recording with General Hughes.

"Does that voice sound familiar?" Hughes asked.

"It sounds very much like our friend Congressman Blake Kane from Connecticut."

"That was my impression. Of course, he used a prepaid throw-away cell phone so the source cannot be identified," General Hughes stated. He added, "I need to inform the man who wasn't there to be alert to an incoming message."

"It sounds like the Holiday family is out-of-reach at this time," Jarvis concluded.

"Not exactly. There are ways, but we don't want collateral damage. I'll ask Clew and Hayes what they think."

Shahin Pouran was angry. After he executed those web journalists who spoke despairingly about Islam, he could not find mujahid brave enough to join him. One by one they found countless reasons to decline. Anger is the heat that ignites the flames of desperate acts. Shahin did not fear this shadow group. Indeed, he would challenge them and defeat them. All those cowards need to be shown the power of Allah. He would devise a plan to draw them to a place where he would slay them and display their heads for all to see.

A disassembled M110 Sniper rifle lay on a black cloth on a workbench. Michael "Owl" O'Neal was cleaning the weapon when his wife, Alice, entered the room. She watched her husband for a few minutes thinking about the man she married. When they met, she knew he was a sniper in the United States Army. At the time she didn't give it much thought. He was handsome, confident, strong, mysterious, and made her laugh. When she was with him he took care of her—she liked that. She felt safe when she was with Michael O'Neal. Over time, she found there was a depth of character and integrity that defined her soldier. During those times when he was deployed she worried about him. The few letters he sent were upbeat, positive, and funny. He gave no impression that there was any danger in what he was doing. Yet, she knew better. After all, being an Army sniper meant spending long hours or days alone in dangerous surroundings waiting for the right opportunity. Then after taking the decisive shot he had to escape. What was frustrating was the fact that when this was taking place she had no idea what was going on. On a particular day she might be worried that he was laying in the dirt in a ghillie suit when he was shooting pool with his buddies. Or, she might hope he was in a safe barracks when he was actually in hiding in a precarious position waiting for his prey. The only solution was to worry all the time.

"Are you getting ready for something," Alice asked not wanting to hear the answer.

"I received a phone call from homeland security." Michael looked at his wife, "They want me to spend a couple days in Wilkes-Barre, Pennsylvania to help the FBI."

Alice surprised her husband, "I understand. At least it's safer than going to some foreign country. When are you going?"

"They want me to get there yesterday, or sooner."

"When did you plan on telling me?"

"Tomorrow or later," his smile made his red mustache tilt outward.

Alice laughed. "You go play with your FBI pals."

No suspicious activity had taken place around the home of Sam and Marcella Holiday in the past three days. No threats were identified when Sam went to work, Marcella did the marketing, or when their daughter, Tara, went to school. In addition, local police didn't observe any strangers in Wilkes-Barre who seemed interested in the Holiday family.

Special Agent Peggy Fox had gotten over her anger. She decided that it was going to have to be she who captures or destroys the Satan's Shadow vigilante group. She also decided that she would use the fame that came with it to promote her career and possibly a future book. The agent who broke the back on terrorism would be of great interest to the reading public. A title that struck her was *Outfoxed—One Woman's Triumph Over Terrorism.* Peggy Fox smiled thinking how she would rub her superior's noses in it.

There's a time to be a good soldier and team player. Sharing of credit can go a long way in an organization like the Federal Bureau of Investigation. Without question, those in power would appreciate such a selfless gesture. Unfortunately, Special Agent Peggy Fox had a different gesture in mind. After successfully capturing Darius Holiday and breaking up a devious terror plot, she barely got a nod from those higher up. Releases to the media mentioned her name in passing. In truth, recognition for a job well-done was conspicuously missing.

She looked out of her hotel room window at the center of town. In her opinion, nothing was going to come of the stakeout. These vigilantes, no revengers, were too smart to walk into an obvious trap. They probably are familiar with all the surveillance equipment and alarms that had been installed in and around the Holiday home. It is exactly what one would expect law enforcement to do, given the situation. Most likely, they would pick a time and place away from the home. A sniper from a long distance could do the job without being detected. This was why she sent for a retired sniper—Michael O'Neal. He would be able to determine the most strategically advantageous positions from which to make an assassination shot. With his input they would be able to watch those locations for any questionable activity. She would then have him identify the best shooting site and position himself where he could take out anyone considered a threat in that location. Peggy mentally patted herself on the back for devising such a logical plan.

Ron Clew and Adam Hayes sat with General Hughes in the Embassy Suites hotel room in McLean, Virginia. They had come to discuss whether or not the Holiday family could be reached while protected by the FBI.

"A direct approach is out of the question," Adam stated the obvious.

"There are opportunities, but it would put the identity of the team at risk," Ron Clew stated.

"What kind of opportunities?" General Hughes asked.

Ron explained, "The FBI wants to catch us so their 'protection' is from a distance. You won't find agents walking alongside any of the family members like they do the president. That would make them vulnerable to a long-range sniper shot." He looked at Adam and continued, "It is risky. You could miss or be seen or captured after taking the shot. It also would not allow us to get to the other two targets."

"I can tell you have something in mind," General Hughes observed.

"Poison."

"What kind of poison?"

"Batrachotoxin, an amount equal to 2 grains of salt can kill an adult human. It comes from the skin of tiny brightly colored Central and South American Dendrobatidae frogs. You know, that's what the natives used on their darts in the Amazon jungle."

"I haven't qualified in blowguns," Adam Hayes admitted with a smile.

"The poison causes paralysis and affects the heart muscle. Death occurs within minutes." Ron Clew looked out the window as he pondered, "All we have to do is devise a way to prick each one with a needle, pin, or dart." He turned back to face the other two, "That won't be easy."

"Can we get our hands on this poison?" Adam asked.

"I believe I have a source," General Hughes answered. He thought about Dave the rogue CIA agent and wondered how he could get in touch with him.

Ron Clew stated matter-of-factly, "An interesting fact; Dendrobatidae frogs raised in captivity aren't poisonous. It is believed that the poison actually comes from the beetles they eat."

Maybe, if you eat some of those beetles you could become poisonous," Adam quipped.

Ron stared directly at his friend and after a long-enough period of feigned anger replied, "I am poisonous."

CHAPTER 42

A familiar voice was on the telephone when General Hughes answered. "I'd like to meet with you." It was Dave the rogue CIA agent.

A call from Dave was a complete surprise while also not being a surprise. "Dave, how did you know I was interested in talking with you?"

"Let me put your mind at ease. I do not have your phone, home, car, or body bugged. For now, let's just say I have good intel. Can we meet?"

"Absolutely, when do you want to meet?"

"Now?"

"And, you're at the end of my driveway?"

"Roger that."

Once inside Dave's dark green Cadillac Escalade General Hughes asked, "Do you know why I wanted to speak with you?"

"What do you think?"

"I think you know what I had for dinner, how many rounds I have in my sidearm, and the color of my underwear."

"Sounds a little paranoid."

"Am I wrong?"

"A steak sandwich, 7 plus 1 in the chamber, and I don't give a shit."

General Hughes laughed. Over time, he had grown to like Dave. After their initial meeting they spoke on the telephone a number of times. It was always cryptic, non-incriminating small talk of which they understood the real meaning. Dave was a ghost—he was there but he wasn't there. Money was funneled into an account that General Hughes had access to that funded Satan's Shadow, materials were left for retrieval, and information was provided to assist their efforts.

Dave continued, "In that bag in the back seat is the item you are looking for. Be very careful, its lethal and unforgiving."

"I won't ask how you got it."

"You can ask. I'll tell you a lie. You won't buy it," Dave replied. He added, "I could have left the package for you to pick up, but we need to talk."

"I'm a captive audience."

"You are surveilling a young lady with the State Department."

"We are."

"May I ask why?"

"What happened to your good intel?"

"Fuck you!"

"We have information that the young lady, Nadia Noorani, is transmitting secret messages to a counterpart in France named Kareem Reza." General Hughes concluded that there was no reason to hold back information because Dave knew all there was about Satan's Shadow. "The messages are encoded Arabic which can't be accurately translated. The only word in English was 'Vegas' which we are concerned may refer to Manny."

"And, you have someone on the other side of the ocean surveilling Reza?"

"I can't be positive. Our contact is not certain who can be trusted so he is moving cautiously."

"I see."

Impulsively, General Hughes asked, "You know Congressman Blake Kane from Connecticut?"

"He's a putz," Dave spat. "Self-centered, arrogant, useless con man who keeps getting elected by promising everything and delivering nothing. He relies on lies and charm. Why do you ask?"

"Because we have information that he was with Nadia Noorani and Kareem Reza in Pakistan a few years ago."

"Now, that is something I didn't know," Dave admitted.

"That good intel claim is getting less and less believable," Maxwell Hughes remarked.

"Can't argue with you on that one." Dave pulled into the same gas station as he did during their first meeting.

"You really like this place, don't you?"

"Do you think you can find it on your own?"

"Absolutely."

"Come with me," Dave ordered.

The two men entered the remote gas station. Inside everything was as would be expected. The cashier glanced at the two men as they passed. Dave led and Maxwell Hughes followed. They walked down a hall past the restrooms and entered through a door with a sign stating Employees Only. Inside was a storeroom typically cluttered and dusty. Dave proceeded to a metal shelf filled with various old pieces of equipment. Most of it should have been discarded years ago. On the top shelf was an old broken cash register. Dave took the apparatus down and placed it on the floor. General Hughes watched with interest.

As he opened the back and pulled out a device, Dave said, "This tablet will connect you to the deep web through a proprietary browser. Some call it the dark web and use the browser TOR which stands for The Onion Router."

"I'm familiar with the dark web," General Hughes stated.

Dave continued undaunted, "Only about 4% of the information on the world wide web is accessed through the surface web that most people use. Of the other 96% approximately 60% of the data is available through the dark web that you are familiar with." Dave fiddled with the tablet, "20% is peer-to-peer information that is relatively difficult to find. The remaining 20% is so encrypted and hidden it is only available to those given the appropriate key, password, and countersign." Dave looked directly at the General, "How's your memory?"

"It's still pretty good. Just don't ask me the name of my first-grade teacher."

"Mrs. Shelton."

"Son-of-a-bitch."

"This device automatically connects to our proprietary browser. That in itself is reason it must remain hidden here. You connect by clicking one inch in from the top and one inch in from the right edge. There is an invisible link."

General Hughes watched as the screen went black. Dave typed in a number of letters and numbers that did not appear on the screen. He pressed enter and the screen opened like two doors being pushed inward. Displayed was a reception area of an office. A young woman sat behind a large wooden desk. She looked up and asked, "May I help you?"

"Green Giant, open the door."

Immediately the screen dissolved to a menu. He chose Register User. The first slot was for the user name. Dave looked up from the tablet and said, "I need to give you a pseudonym." He paused, smiled, and said, "I've got it—Mrs. Shelton."

"Come on, have a heart," General Hughes protested.

"OK, you pick one."

Without hesitation General Hughes offered, "Ismenios."

"I like it. When the tone sounds simply say Ismenios for the voice recognition app."

After twenty minutes the registration was complete. Dave provided the code to open the doors of the reception area and the address to contact him. He instructed General Hughes to memorize them. "Now, you can reach me when necessary."

General Hughes nodded.

"There's one more thing," Dave said seriously. "Nadia Noorani works for us."

Michael O'Neal stood in front of the Holiday family home with Special Agent Peggy Fox. He had walked around the property, examined the interior of the two-story structure, and looked at what was around the home. Peggy Fox found that she was fascinated with this man. He was friendly and at ease, yet all business. And, he definitely knew his business. She found Michael O'Neal to be a contradiction—an easy-going likeable guy who was undeniably lethal.

"What do you think, Mr. O'Neal?"

"Michael. The location is actually better protected than you might think." Michael O'Neal looked across the street. He pointed and said, "A shot could be taken from any of those rooves, but that would be too close—far too risky." He then took a step to his right and pointed once more, "That is where I would be. See that hillside with high grass beyond those two houses?"

Agent Fox turned her attention to where Michael indicated. Between two houses across the street at least 200 yards away was a hillside. It would offer perfect cover and a narrow window of opportunity. She had been trained and was proficient with firearms but knew that would be a nearly impossible shot. Maybe impossible for her but for the man beside her just another day at the office. "I'll have someone monitor that location."

Together they turned their attention to other parts of Wilkes-Barre. The mine where Sam Holiday worked, school Tara attended, and stores where Marcella shopped were evaluated for potential vulnerabilities. Special Agent Fox was shocked at how many final firing positions existed. There was absolutely no way to watch all of them. "Mr. O'Neal, uh, Michael, if you were trying to assassinate these three people what would be your strategy?"

Michael thought for a moment and then concluded, "With all the activity and protection around I wouldn't try to take them out individually. Once the first one goes down the window of opportunity shuts on the other two. I'd definitely try to catch them in a group together."

"You could get all three in one location?"

Michael O'Neal's unthreatening but steady stare answered Fox's question. A cold chill ran down her spine. He spoke, "At a great enough distance, when the first one goes down the other two have no idea what happened. The tendency is to go to the aid of the fallen victim. Targets two and three are then easy to take out."

"What then do you suggest?"

"Don't let them go anywhere as a group."

"Good advice."

"Here's some free advice. I don't think a sniper will be the approach this group will take. From what I've read, they use more commando tactics—stealthy, at night, raids or ambush. These are military-trained men. I'd look for a diversion or outright attack. If they got their hands on a couple rocket propelled grenades (RPGs) and fired them simultaneously into the house they'd be gone when the first explosion occurred. It doesn't take a genius to determine which windows are the bedrooms. Replace the glass with bullet resistant panes."

Agent Fox realized how feeble their attempts were. She was compelled to ask, "If they were your targets, could you get them?"

"Yes."

Shahin Pouran had a plan. He would directly challenge Satan's Shadow. That evening he waited outside of a London pub. Couples came and went, as well as groups of partiers. Finally, a lone imbiber left the pub. He was an old man who had enjoyed a few pints of Guinness and was headed home. Everything was right in his world. Slowly, he strolled enjoying the night air. He had plans to visit his daughter in Canterbury in the next few days to see his granddaughter for the first time. When he turned down a dark empty street his plans were changed by a 10" black finish stainless saw back blade that pierced his back just below the shoulder blade on the left side of his spine penetrating his heart.

Later, a body was found by a passing pedestrian. When police arrived they found a note that read, "This person died as revenge for the acts of the criminal group known as Satan's Shadow. Find me before more die."

CHAPTER 43

Special Agent Peggy Fox instructed the surveillance team to never allow the Holiday family to travel in a group. In addition, she assigned an agent to each member of the family when they did travel. Michael O'Neal remained for a day and provided further evaluation of weak spots. All remained quiet.

On a sunny morning Sam Holiday left for work at the Reeds Fork coal mine. He arrived at 7:00 a.m. After placing his lunchbox in his cubbyhole and retrieving his hardhat with light and work gloves, he joined his coworkers at the elevator. The combination of burnt wood and kerosene aroma of coal dust wafted up from the mine. They waited. Right on time, as usual a whistle sounded and the crew boarded the old wooden elevator for a long slow journey into the depths of the Earth.

Tara Holiday stepped off the yellow bus and headed toward her school. Along the way she met two friends. Together they complimented each other's clothes and hair. Then the subject turned to boys and unsuspecting lads were judged hot or not. The banter went on until the first bell. When it sounded they entered the building.

Marcella Holiday checked her grocery list. As she did she stopped at one item—chocolate chip cookies. They were Darius' favorite treat. A mother, broken-hearted yet resigned to the fact that her son was a confessed murderer, saw a small boy smiling and playing in the yard. Filled with spirit and the picture of innocence, her Darius was a source of pride and anticipation of a bright future. What happened she just couldn't figure out. As is often the case, a mother wondered what she had done wrong. How had she failed that promising little boy? Guilt once more weighed heavy on her. Slowly she crossed chocolate chip cookies off the list.

When Tara reached her locker, she pulled the handle to open it. Something sharp caused her to pull her hand away. A small dot of blood appeared on the palm of her hand. She dabbed the wound with a tissue, gathered her books, and headed to class. By the time she reached her desk her lips were numb and she had trouble sitting. She stumbled and fell to the floor. A girl screamed and the teacher rushed over to Tara Holiday.

In the coal mine Sam Holiday walked with his crew to the far compartment. He handled a coal drill which bore holes into the vein allowing for it to be broken into manageable pieces. Upon arrival at his station he pulled on his work gloves. Something in his left glove stabbed his finger. He pulled off the glove to find a pin sticking out of his index finger. He removed the pin and inspected the glove for any others. There were none. Then, with his gloves on, he reached for the handle of the drill but blacked out.

Marcella walked down the aisle of the grocery store. She was thinking about what she would prepare for dinner. The store wasn't particularly crowded, however, every once in a while, there would be a congregation of shoppers at one particular place. This was the case in the produce area. Four other shoppers were making their selection where lettuce, spinach, and broccoli were displayed. Marcella joined the group. A man with a beard passed behind her. She felt a pinprick that she assumed was a sharp edge on one of the shopping carts. After choosing her vegetables she proceeded to the meat department. She didn't get there.

At noon on a sunny day Special Agent Peggy Fox sat in the Wilkes-Barre police department headquarters. Her face was drawn and voice gravely. Without question, she had failed. The Holiday family had been assassinated right under their noses. Poison was the suspected method. Which poison had not yet been determined and it would take a number of days to be identified. During the night, police patrols had not seen any suspicious characters at the school or coal mine and the patrons of the grocery store didn't see anyone in the produce section who seemed out-of-place. There were no clues what-so-ever. A Satan's Shadow note was found in the lobby of the Wilkes-Barre Times Leader.

Liam waited for the message that had been scheduled to be sent by Nadia Noorani to Kareem Reza at 2:00 p.m. Eastern Standard Time. He looked at his watch. It was 7:00 p.m. in France. The building was essentially empty as most government employees had gone home. With his security clearance he was able to monitor activity on most of the communications links. In this case he was tracking activity in and out of the Ministry of Immigration, Integration, National Identity and Co-development where Kareem Reza worked. Right on schedule a message was received from the United States Department of State. As expected, it was in Arabic and encrypted.

Impulsively, Liam rose from his chair and headed down the long corridor in the direction of the Ministry of Immigration, Integration, National Identity and Co-development. He didn't know what to expect or what he was going to do. What he did know was it was time for action. There was too much at risk to allow the illicit communications to continue. Given his slow pace, Liam hoped he could reach his destination before Kareem Reza departed. He got his wish.

As he passed the elevators in the center of the building, Liam saw the door of the Ministry at the end of the hall open. Kareem Reza appeared. When the 52-year-old, slim, dark skin and hair traitor turned he saw Liam.

"Liam, what are you doing here?" he said pleasantly covering his surprise.

"I wanted to be sure you received your message," the older man with a cane said.

"Message?"

"Ne mens pas, don't lie, it is beneath you."

A long silence followed as two men stood in the corridor trying to anticipate the next move or comment of the other.

Kareem asked, "How long have you known?" as he looked beyond Liam for any other guards that might be with him. Upon seeing none, he considered what his next step might be. Direct confrontation was a possibility. However, Liam was an ex-military officer who was fully capable of defending himself. He proved that fact in the park when he fended off an assailant with his cane. Another option was to simply deny any wrongdoing. His third choice was to come clean.

In a non-emotional straightforward voice Liam replied, "Long enough to know you are traitre."

"Yes, that is true."

"Why?" Liam asked in bewilderment.

"Why else—a woman." Kareem Reza shook his head slowly and resignedly.

"Nadia Noorani?"

Kareem moved to within five feet of Liam but made no aggressive gestures, "I met Nadia in Washington, D.C. three years ago. Or, should I say, she met me. At the time, I had no idea who she was or where she worked. She didn't work at the United States Department of State at the time." He looked off to the right as if looking for the memory. "I was there to provide to the American Homeland Security people anti-terrorist info that we had gathered. It was a three-day conference. On the second day—in the evening—I sat at the bar in my hotel when a young woman sat beside me. We struck up a conversation. She told me she had just moved to Washington and hadn't found a place to live yet. As it turned out, we were staying in the same hotel." Kareem stopped and stood in silence reliving the event. "I don't remember how it happened but we ended up having dinner together. We had dinner together the next evening, as well. Ultimately, I stayed a few extra days after the conference which we spent together." He looked directly at Liam, "Je suis tombé amoureux."

"So, you committed treason and betrayed you country for amoureux?"

"No!" Kareem took a step toward Liam who raised his cane. Kareem paused, stepped back, and explained, "Two years ago we met in Nawabshah, Pakistan. I assumed for a tryst. While we were there a United States Congressman, Blake Kane, joined us. He and Nadia Noorani knew each other. The two of them being there at the same time was not a coincidence. They convinced me to act as a courier for messages from America to unidentified recipients in France." He looked pained as he added, "He was a United States Congressman, putain tout! Why wouldn't I trust him?"

"L'amour embrouille la vision—love clouds one's vision," Liam observed.

"L'amour m'a mis en place—love set me up," Kareem admitted. "After I left the first few messages in a specified location and retrieved messages to transmit back, Miss Noorani informed me that I had been assisting an international terrorist organization called 'Hidden Cobra' that was targeting the United States."

"Why did you not alert the authorities?" Liam asked in disbelief.

"I told Nadia that I wouldn't carry any more messages for her. It was then that she showed her true self. She threatened to tell my wife of our affair, to expose me, to ruin my life."

"One life compared with hundreds, maybe thousands, did you not see that?"

"In time, I did. But then this Satan's Shadow emerged. Nadia contacted me and insisted that I help identify who these vigilantes are. I refused." Kareem Reza fell silent.

"However, you are helping," Liam pressed.

No response.

"I reiterate, why haven't you alerted the authorities?"

No response.

In anger, Liam spat, "Answer me!"

"They have my son," Kareem Reza whispered.

"Your son?"

"My twenty-five-year-old son, Faraz, is being held hostage in Afghanistan." Kareem shook his head, "I have no choice, but to cooperate."

"That option is no longer available," Liam pointed out.

Henrietta Washburn, a flight attendant for British Airways, walked up a side street toward her flat early in the morning. A weather delay had caused her flight that was supposed to arrive just before midnight to land at 3:40 a.m. She had been able to tag along with members of another flight crew that had a car in long-term parking. They dropped her off about three blocks from her flat. She assured them that no one would be out at that late hour. A slight chill in the air caused her to shiver. It was then she realized how quiet it was. The only sound was the clicking of her heels. Somehow it made her feel vulnerable as it brought attention to her. With no alternative she continued her journey toward home and safety. Her building was within sight when out of nowhere a dark figure grabbed the five-foot-four-inch, blond, 31-year-old from behind and plunged a 10" black finish stainless saw back blade knife into her back. She struggled but was held tight. Unable to make a sound she slowly dropped to the pavement where her final heartbeats were all she heard in her ears. The same note was left with Shahin Pouran's latest victim. "This person died as revenge for the acts of the criminal group known as Satan's Shadow. Find me before more die."

CHAPTER 44

Adam "Watch Dog" Hayes arrived at FFP Ranch as the sun dropped below the horizon. It was a calm cool evening. To his surprise, Michael "Owl" O'Neal met him at his car. The two comrades shook hands warmly and Michael said matter-of-factly, "Walk with me."

They proceeded along a gravel path that ran beside a pasture. Two young stallions trotted, spun, shook their heads, and frolicked with each other. It was obvious, the two equines didn't have a care in the world. Two warriors watched in silence. After a few moments of enjoying the purity of life, they continued on. It was Michael who had called Adam and asked him to drop by the ranch. For that reason, Adam knew his friend had something on his mind, therefore, he would let him begin the conversation. As dark surrounded them it became more and more difficult to discern fine details or facial expressions.

Unexpectedly, Michael O'Neal asked, "Did you enjoy Wilkes-Barre?"

Even though caught off-guard, Adam was able to quickly evaluate the situation. It was unclear what Michael did or didn't know about the operation. He could be on a fishing expedition based on hearsay. Most likely, he didn't have any direct evidence. The team had been very careful moving among the shadows to avoid being seen. They also worked independently so as to not raise any suspicion. From Adam's point-of-view it was up to Michael to reveal what he knew. Therefore, Adam's non-committal reply was, "Does anyone enjoy Wilkes-Barre?"

"I know three people who didn't."

"Yeah, I read about that. What's your take on the whole thing?"

"Three innocent people were murdered," Michael stopped, turned, and looked at his friend.

"That's true," Adam agreed. In the dark it was not clear what expression was on Michael's face.

"I was there," Michael offered.

Adam feigned surprise as he said, "You didn't do it—did you?"

"Poison is not my weapon of choice."

"Then why were you there?"

"The FBI asked for my input on how to protect the Holiday family."

"You fell short on that one," Adam said light-heartedly while shaking his head.

"They only wanted my opinion on where a sniper might find a final firing position. It was up to them to consider the use of poison or other potential threats."

"Why you?" Adam asked knowing there must be a few dozen active snipers who could have been called upon.

"I wondered that myself," was Michael's reply. He added, "It appears that I was recommended by a member of the Secret Service."

Adam thought about Emanuel Vegas. His position gave him access to his records and past association with Michael O'Neal. If he recommended O'Neal that was a tactical error. Adam returned to the original subject, "So, why are you asking me about Wilkes-Barre. In fact, I don't know anything about poison with the exception of some of the meals I've gotten from Alice."

Michael didn't laugh. A long silence hung in the air as two warriors began to walk once more. In the dark he commented, "I saw you in Wilkes-Barre."

Immediately, Adam responded, "You saw someone who looked like me."

"My eyes are still sharp enough to recognize your ugly puss," Michael said indicating that he was not being judgmental.

With less tension in his voice, Adam asked, "Where is it you believe you saw me in Wilkes-Barre?"

"It was quite by accident," Michael began. "I had finished consulting with the FBI and was headed out of town." He picked up a rock, examined it, and spoke to the rock, "Just outside of town on Route 81 there is a small gas station." Michael paused for effect. "You know the one I'm talking about?"

Adam didn't fall for the trick. He replied, "You'll have to ask my lookalike, because I don't know what gas station you are talking about."

"I could call your bluff," Michael countered, "you know that."

Adam Nodded.

Once more, unexpectedly, Michael asked, "Do you want to check me for wires?"

"That's not necessary," Adam replied, "I trust you." After what he learned from Ron Clew about electronic surveillance devices he knew if someone wanted to listen from afar, they could—without wires.

Michael O'Neal became serious, "Let's assume I'm wrong, which I'm not. The person I recognized as you came out of the convenience store, jumped in a car across the parking lot from me, and sped off in the direction of Wilkes-Barre before I could call out. My initial thought was that you were also acting as a consultant with the FBI."

"Or, that the mystery man was simply driving north on 81 and had no intention of stopping in Wilkes-Barre," Adam countered.

"When I first read about the actions of this Satan's Shadow group I could see the logic of making terrorists pay for their crimes with something they love. From a strictly strategic perspective it makes sense. On paper, it's a plan that might be effective. In reality, it's a plan that has to be difficult for seasoned military to execute. Killing innocent civilians doesn't come easy."

"In a war you bomb a village," Watch Dog explained, "innocent civilians die. Even though you don't see their faces, they're just as dead. If what these individuals are doing thwarts the actions of others who would kill innocent civilians, maybe these Satan's Shadow warriors see the big picture which validates the distasteful act they have to perform."

"In our time you and I have removed many combatants. In doing so, on occasion, there was collateral damage. So, our hands are not clean. However, my conscience is clear." Michael O'Neal said as he gazed at his friend in the dark.

"We did what had to be done for the better good," Adam offered.

"There were cases where the 'better good' was a matter of opinion," Michael admitted.

"Like you, I have a clear conscience."

"I don't doubt that," Michael responded. "As warriors we are nothing more than tools, but we are rational tools. We know the difference between right and wrong even when that difference is obscure."

"In your rational, I use the term loosely, mind is this Satan's Shadow right or wrong?"

"It's murder, there's no question about that," Michael stated in the darkness. "If they are caught they will be prosecuted and either executed or imprisoned for life. The law does not have a provision for PSYOP activities. In addition, United States PSYOP units of all branches of the military are prohibited from targeting U.S. citizens within the borders of the United States—Executive Order S-1233, DOD Directive S-3321.1, and National Security Decision Directive 130."

"You memorized that?" Adam Hayes said in disbelief.

"Didn't you?"

"Hell no," Adam stated. He added, "Terrorism is a PSYOP operation. Genghis Khan, the Mongol conqueror, used to send agents into cities he was trying to bring under his rule. They would tell of the horrible brutality the huge Mongol army would unleash against those who didn't surrender. Half the time he never had to go into battle." Adam looked into the darkness as if seeing his action of placing a poison needle in a workman's glove. He added, "Alexander the Great found he had stretched his armies too thin and needed to retreat. He feared his enemies would pursue his small force so he had large size breast plates and armor made that appeared to be for warriors who were over seven feet tall. They were left for the other forces to find. When they did come upon the ruse they were convinced that his army was comprised of giants. Alexander was left alone—PSYOPs."

Michael O'Neal concluded, "And now, Satan's Shadow is getting in the heads of those who contemplate using terrorism or perpetrating mass killing."

"It appears that way."

"During World War II the United States War Department took the position, 'Psychological warfare employs any weapon to influence the mind of the enemy. The weapons are psychological only in the effect they produce and not because of the weapons themselves.'"

"Let's get into the heads of our enemy," Adam suggested, "They want to instill fear in the population, silence those who oppose them, disrupt the daily life of honest citizens, and deliver their villainous message. They are zealots who do not fear death. If any humanity remains within them it is love of their family and friends." He paused. An owl hooted in the distance which caused Adam to smile as he told Owl O'Neal, "The only way to have a psychological effect on these animals is through what they value. Murder? Absolutely. However, the victims were defined by the terrorists. Keep in mind, it's not punishment—it's a deterrent on those who are considering the future use of terrorism."

"What about the school shootings? They're not zealots," Michael asked knowing the answer.

"Same thing, to give future shooters pause."

"You talk like someone who supports Satan's Shadow," Michael stated.

"Come'on, Owl, quit bullshitting me, you see the logic in what they are doing. Maybe, it's not what you would do, but it's one way to fight back. In fact, I'd wager you support Satan's Shadow, as well."

Michael didn't answer. In the dark both men knew what was the truth. It didn't have to be stated out loud. After inviting Adam to stay for dinner which he graciously turned down, Michael walked with his friend to his car. The sniper, turned rancher, said with sincere concern, "With every mission more clues become available. Eventually, Satan's Shadow will become the hunted rather than the hunter. There is no gracious way out. Much like those Russian sailors on the submarine K-19, the Widowmaker, who were exposed to high levels of radiation the only outcome is going to be death. I hope they will have given their lives for something that makes a real and positive difference."

As the two men once again shook hands warmly, Adam said, "If the loss of a few tired warriors saves countless lives it will be a welcome epitaph. I appreciate you allowing me to enjoy foal sitting with you. The miracle of life."

Michael "Owl" O'Neal had no intention of mentioning his sighting to the FBI. He looked at his former partner and knew they were saying goodbye. He stated, "I named that stallion Adam." As Adam closed the door, Michael added, "I won't focus on the dead, but on those who are free to live their lives because of your sacrifice. Just remember, in order to have a shadow there must be light."

Adam rolled down the window and said with a smile, "Tell Alice, she's right about me."

Special Agent Peggy Fox stood in the front of the room in the town hall of Wilkes-Barre, Pennsylvania. It had been two days since the Holiday family had been assassinated and the Satan's Shadow message had been published in the *Wilkes-Barre Times Leader*. She did not look forward to the press conference as it was clearly a failure of the Federal Bureau of Investigation and the agent in charge—Peggy Fox.

Right from the start she could see it was a setup. The protection of three people without taking them into protective custody or relocating them was essentially impossible. Her superiors offered no support, therefore, along with the demise of three innocent persons it was the death knell of her career.

Question after question inquired how the FBI couldn't protect a family when they knew the threat was there. While agent Fox outlined protocols, procedures, and the extraordinary steps they took to protect the family, she knew it all rang hollow. It left a bad taste in her mouth. The bureau knew they were targets, had information about Satan's Shadow, and still couldn't keep the Holiday family alive.

The question that finally struck a nerve that caused Special Agent Peggy Fox to end the press conference and leave the room was, "Don't you personally feel responsible for the deaths of this innocent family, including a 15-year-old girl?"

CHAPTER 45

Five men sat on the fantail of Ismenios. The craft was on autopilot as it steamed east across the Atlantic Ocean. They were headed to a rendezvous with Liam in France.

"We are to meet our friend who isn't there in Bayonne," Captain Jarvis Demoye stated.

"Bayonne?" Adam Hayes said, "we could have simply taken the Lincoln Tunnel."

Jarvis ignored Adam's joke and continued, "It's located at the confluence of the Nive and Adour rivers that flows into the Atlantic Ocean in Southwest France. Because it's close to the Spanish border it's part of the Basque cultural region." He leaned back in his chair and stated, "We'll be there tomorrow."

"We have a few things that need to be discussed," General Hughes began as he sipped his drink. "To begin, there has been a slight lull in the number and proportion of terrorist activities. How long this will last and whether or not it has anything to do with our efforts may never be known." Having made that statement, he turned to retired Air Force Major Ken Farmingdale and said, "There is a situation in London. What appears to be a lone wolf is murdering random people and taunting us to stop him. He obviously wants us to reveal ourselves. That's not going to happen. However, we need to set a trap for him. When we get to Bayonne, you will fly to London and gather what information you can about this mongrel." He cautioned, "Trust no one."

"Isn't that putting Ken in harm's way?" Adam asked.

"When two forces don't know where the other is or its strength—you send out a patrol."

"I'll see what I can find out," Ken Farmingdale said.

"Now, let's talk about your friend, the sniper," Hughes said to Adam Hayes.

"He saw me outside Wilkes-Barre."

"So, he suspects you are involved?"

"He knows."

"You're sure?"

"We've been friends long enough to read each other."

"Then he represents a security risk," the General concluded.

"Not at all."

"Are you certain?"

"Two things; if he was going to blow the whistle he would have already done it, second, he and I go back a long way. I've trusted him with my life too many times to have any doubts now," Adam stated definitively. "There's one thing I don't know what to make of, though."

"What's that?"

"He told me he was recommended to the FBI by a Secret Service agent. Didn't say who and I knew he wouldn't. Made me wonder if it was Vegas and, if so—why?"

"I'll ask him," was Max Hughes response.

The two men looked at each other, each man wondering if the other knew more than he was telling. They had no reason to doubt the other, but when the stakes are as high as they were any misjudgment could be fatal.

"Maybe he was trying to recruit your friend," retired Navy Seal Ron Clew observed.

"If he wanted to do that he would have asked me to try," Adam countered.

Jarvis Demoye chimed in, "As Max pointed out a while back, over time it is going to get more and more risky of us being discovered or identified. I wore a disguise in that Wilkes-Barre grocery store because my operation took place in daylight. We are at risk visually, when we communicate, when we follow patterns, or leave any kind of trail."

"I'm glad you brought that up," General Hughes interjected, "I've got an alert for you—Nadia Noorani, our lady at the State Department, works for the CIA or did, I'm not sure."

"How do you know?" a surprised Ron Clew asked.

"A source I deal with revealed the fact to me. This contact is why we are here, brought me and Manny together, is underwriting our operation, supplied the stingers we recently used, knows more about me than I am comfortable with, and yet is beyond reproach—I believe." The other four men aboard Ismenios showed increased interest. Ken Farmingdale let out a low whistle. "As to Miss Noorani, he was unaware that she had been in contact with Kareem Reza in France. He is the one who informed me that she works for the CIA. However, he did not know she had met with Congressman Blake Kane from Connecticut and Reza in Pakistan two years ago. As you know our surveillance of her apartment turned up nothing. He asked that we resume surveillance when we return and keep him informed."

"Sounds like little Miss Noorani left the reservation," Adam observed.

"Most likely. It's getting difficult to know who is playing on which team," General Hughes concluded.

"I guess we can assume your contact, the man who is our benefactor, can be trusted," Ken Farmingdale stated.

"And, Liam seems authentic," Ron Clew added.

"True on both fronts. however, it appears we have a very limited list of confidantes," General Maxwell Hughes admitted.

Emanuel Vegas was on assignment protecting the Vice President of the United States for the Secret Service. The entourage had traveled to Chicago for a conference on inner-city crime. Mayors from more than a dozen cities and various law enforcement professionals had gathered to discuss the growing problem. As Vegas had seniority he operated in a supervisory role directing the actions of the security team. He rode in the trailing SUV lost in thought about a conversation he had with the man who had introduced him to General Maxwell Hughes—Dave.

"Manny, the FBI are setting a trap for the Shadow in Wilkes-Barre. They're using the Holiday family as bait. The team is aware of this fact. It would be a good idea for you to contact the lead agent, Peggy Fox, to offer your assistance in devising a protection plan since that is what you specialize in," Dave's voice entered Manny's memory.

"Why would I do that?" Emanuel had asked.

"Two reasons; first your name has been mentioned in suspicious correspondence between Nadia Noorani and Kareem Reza. They have, it is believed, terrorist connections. How they got your name is unknown. But, it indicates that some might suspect you have a degree of involvement with Satan's Shadow. If you don't hide the fact that you are offering your assistance to the FBI in trapping Satan's Shadow it might cause them to wonder how accurate their information actually is. That may take some of the attention off of you."

"They might not even know I made the offer," Manny countered.

"They will know," Dave answered confidently.

"What's the second reason?"

"Recommend that they recruit a retired Army sniper to point out any areas where they might be vulnerable to long range attack."

"They probably already thought of that."

"It's the FBI, they investigate crimes. Protection is not their specialty. That's not their focus. Snipers are trained to identify the best firing position. A seasoned veteran can quickly identify from where they would take their shot. This might prove valuable to Special Agent Peggy Fox."

"I'll give it a try."

"One more thing. Recommend retired Army sniper Michael O'Neal. He owns a horse farm in Western Virginia."

"Why him?"

"To expand the circle slowly."

"I'll act as though I know what that means," Emanuel Vegas responded.

FBI Special Agent Peggy Fox sat in her office putting the final pieces of her "Event Report" together. It would be reviewed, she would be extensively questioned, accusations would be made, her superiors would remain annoyingly silent, her past successes would be forgotten, a deficiency notation would be placed in her folder, and she would be relegated to the records department. In essence, her career at the Federal Bureau of Investigation was over.

CHAPTER 46

Ismenios tied up at an industrial pier on the Adour River 3.7 miles west of the city of Bayonne, France. It was where Liam had indicated that they land. Five weary travelers locked down the craft and stepped onto the dock. Per instructions, they proceeded to a small parking area behind one of the warehouses. In space three was the vehicle that had been procured for the team. All five members stopped in their tracks and stared. Before them stood a full-size, brand new, dark green Peugeot 5008 SUV. What impressed them was, in a nation overrun with mini, micro, midget, and compact vehicles, this Goliath was a full-size welcome surprise. Inside the Peugeot they found seven comfortable individual seats, electronics galore, and a new car aroma.

Captain Jarvis Demoye climbed into the driver's seat with General Hughes on his right riding shotgun. The three other members of the team climbed into the second row of seats. The vehicle was spacious and luxurious. A high-tech dashboard added to the unexpected pleasant experience.

"Liam outdid himself," Captain Demoye commented.

"I wonder if it's stolen," Adam Hayes inquired from the back seat.

"Something tells me we're in for a longer road trip than expected," retired Navy Seal Ron Clew concluded as he fiddled with his seat.

Ken Farmingdale changed the subject as he finished his online transaction, "OK, I've booked a flight on the only airline that flies to London from here—Ryanair. It leaves from Biarritz-Anglet-Bayonne Airport in about two hours. I have to fly into London Stansted Airport which is 42 miles northeast of Central London. The flight will take approximately one hour and fifty minutes. From Stansted airport to Liverpool Street by express train it will take another 45 minutes. We're all set."

"All we have to do is find D810 south to get you to the airport," Jarvis Demoye stated as he looked at the GPS screen.

"What will be your cover?" General Hughes inquired.

"With my diplomat passport I'm going to pose as an under-secretary of international criminal investigation and research. I'm simply there to gather data on number and type of terrorist acts that have occurred in the past six months. Quite benign," Ken Farmingdale explained.

General Hughes nodded his approval.

They arrived at Biarritz-Anglet-Bayonne Airport after a short twenty-minute ride in luxury. The airport was comprised of a single terminal building that housed two gates. One was occupied with a Bombardier CRJ1000 with HOP! markings, a subsidiary of Air France. Two other aircraft were visible parked off to the side. One was a Ryanair Boeing 737. A single runway ran east and west. Very little activity was apparent.

"I can see parking is no problem," Adam Hayes observed.

After Ken left the group and entered the terminal, the four remaining team members continued their journey south on D810 and then on Rue Bassilour. They found themselves traveling through French countryside filled with small housing developments, fields, and forests.

Jarvis commented as he drove, "I still can't get used to these narrow roads with no lines."

After traveling 7.5 miles they arrived at a rustic ancient mill on a pond that was surrounded by trees. Le Moulin de Bassilour was a working authentic nineteenth century bakery with a bar and restaurant next to it. Outside were picnic tables with umbrellas in the woods. Everything was meticulously maintained, clean, and inviting.

A short older man leaned on his cane as he stood at the edge of the pond looking at the unused water wheel. Even from behind they knew it was Liam. As they approached he said without turning around, "Bienvenue au paradis, mes amis, Welcome to paradise, my friends."

"This is a beautiful and relaxing location," General Hughes stated.

"The aroma from the bakery brings me back to another time and another place," Ron Clew admitted.

Liam turned to face the four arrivals. He spoke to Ron when he suggested, "The cookies here are the best you will ever eat, the Basque cake is amazing, and the cherry biscuits . . ." he made a kissing sound as he drew his fingers away from his lips, "vraiment magnifique!"

"Do they have eclairs?" Adam asked with a smile.

"The éclair originated in nineteenth century France," Liam responded to Adam's joke. "It was called 'pain à la Duchesse' or 'petite duchesse.' The later name éclair is French meaning 'flash of lightning' because they are eaten so quickly. And, yes my friend, they have outstanding éclair here." Liam smiled and tapped Adam on the arm with his cane as he said, "You should try one."

Jarvis Demoye observed, "This is indeed a tranquil location. One could find solace here and forget all the strife that exists in the world."

"I grew up near here," Liam revealed. He led the group into the restaurant and ordered lunch for them as the menu was in French. As they ate, Liam provided a short history of Bayonne, France. "The name Bayonne is derived from the Basque word 'bai' meaning 'river' and 'ona' meaning 'good'—therefore, 'Good River.' The Nive River had a high mound on one side which offered natural protection and a usable port on the other side. It splits present day Bayonne in half before it joins the Adour River to flow out to the sea. The Romans saw the value of this port and built a wall around the city. For centuries the city was alternately dominated by the English and Vacones—ancestors of the Basque. Bayonne became a commercial port shipping Bordeaux wines, woad, resin, hams, and other products of south-western France. It also became an important military site."

"Shipbuilding was an important industry. It prospered because there was abundant wood available; oak, beech, and chestnut from the Pyrenees, as well as pine from Landes. My ancestors were master craftsmen in the shipbuilding trade and ship owners. My surname, Beauchêne, is derived from beau meaning 'beautiful' and chêne meaning 'oak.'"

"The Port of Bayonne also provided crews for whaling, merchant ships, and even the English Royal Navy. That was until conflict caused a loss of trade with England and the unfortunate natural movement of the Ardour to the north silting the port and making it unusable. However, the port was saved when the king had engineers divert the river to maintain the river bed in 1578. Fishing and whaling resumed which increased the wealth of shipowners."

Liam savored some wine as he enjoyed the atmosphere, the food, and the company of trusted compatriots. He addressed his next comment to Ron Clew and Adam Hayes, "In the mid-17th century there were many conflicts. During one of these skirmishes the Bayonne peasants ran short of powder and ball. In desperation, they attached long hunting knives to the end of their muskets making home-fashioned spears. These were later called bayonets."

He then spoke to General Hughes, "During World War II Bayonne was occupied by the 3rd SS Panzer Division Totenkopf from 27 June 1940 to 23 August 1944."

Finally, to the whole group Liam explained, "Today, Bayonne is an industrial port shipping steel and chemicals and many of the products that the region is famous for including chocolate, cured ham, and Izarra liqueur. Tourists come for the beaches while Bayonne has the oldest French bullfighting tradition dating back to 1283. Each year, during summer festivals, cows, oxen and bulls are released in the streets of Petit Bayonne. A dozen bullfights are held each year with the most famous torero participating. The arena, that was built in 1893, seats more than 10,000 and is the largest in south-west France." He raised his cane as he added, "Bayonne is also known for the manufacture of makilas—traditional Basque walking-sticks."

Over coffee Liam made an impassioned statement, "Why did I tell you all this?" He paused to compose himself, "My country is dying. It is being devoured from within. For centuries French citizens have died to protect our nation, our heritage, our culture, and our children's future. It meant something to be French. Now, they come to take and rape and force their evil ways upon us. They come, but they don't wish to be French, to foster French ideology, to continue centuries-old culture, to love her as I do. Authentic France lives in the shadows. She is a ghost. Here," he pointed at the table, "we are living in the past—a glorious proud noble past that is slowly sliding into the sea. I find that I am standing at the bedside watching her die and cannot stop the inevitable." Liam looked at the other men at the table and in a sad, dejected, resigned whisper said, "Vive la France—long live France!"

General Hughes spoke, "Liam, my friend, it is when things seem the most hopeless that a desperate irrational bold act sometimes changes the direction of history."

"Not far from here is the Chateau d'Aramitz, it is the home of my ancestors. They originally came from Aramits, a town in the Pyrenees. Today, it is maintained by a staff, but home to none. I am the last Beauchêne." He abruptly stood and leaned upon his walking stick, "We go!"

CHAPTER 47

A train rumbled into Liverpool Street station in the Bishopsgate ward of London. It was late afternoon when Ken Farmingdale gathered his things and left the white modern high-speed underground train. He entered the two-story terminal. It was his first time in this building. When he looked up at the glass panels that comprised the roof, he recalled that two terrorist incidents had occurred in London near this busy terminal.

The first happened on 24 April 93. In preparation for the attack, a month earlier, members of the Irish Republican Army (IRA) stole an Iveco tipper truck in Staffordshire. They repainted the white vehicle dark blue. Then a 1-ton ammonium nitrate/fuel oil (ANFO) bomb was placed in the bed of the truck and hidden under a layer of tar and small stones to appear like macadam.

It was on the morning of April 24, 1993 that two members of the IRA drove the truck into London and parked it outside 99 Bishopsgate that housed the Hong Kong and Shanghai Bank. They left the area in a waiting car. Two police officers came upon the truck and were investigating it when a phoned-in warning from Northern Ireland announcing there was a massive bomb in the area was received. The bobbies subsequently turned their attention to expediting evacuations. At the time, a *News of the World* photographer, Ed Henty, ignored police warnings and rushed to the scene. Exactly 10:27 a.m. the bomb exploded. The blast raised a mushroom cloud that could be seen by much of London and created a 15-foot wide crater in the street. Henty was the only death.

Damage extended as far north as Liverpool Street station, destroyed the nearby St Ethelburga's church, and blew most of the windows out of the fifty-two floors on the east side of NatWest Tower, the tallest building in London at the time. Casualties were low because it was a Saturday morning and the area had been evacuated. In the end, only 44 people were injured. However, property damage was extensive.

On Thursday, July 7, 2005 the United Kingdom experienced the country's first Islamist suicide attack. Commuters during the morning rush hour were targeted. At 8:49 a.m., three bombs were detonated onboard London Underground trains within 50 seconds of each other. The first bomb exploded on a six-car London Underground train that had just left Liverpool Street station travelling eastbound toward Aldgate. The second bomb exploded in the second car of a six-car London Underground train that had just left Edgware Road station travelling westbound toward Paddington. A third bomb was detonated on a 6-car deep-level London Underground train travelling southbound from King's Cross Street Pancras to Russell Square. Approximately, an hour later a fourth bomb was detonated on the top deck of a number 30 double-decker bus. In all, 56 innocent people were killed and 784 injured. The attack was perpetrated by sons of Pakistani immigrants born in Great Britain along with a convert born in Jamaica.

Ken Farmingdale exited the station onto the street and noted that there weren't any signs of past attacks. At the same time, he couldn't help but wonder when the next attack would occur. It seemed inevitable and made what he and the Satan's Shadow team were doing all the more logical in an illogical world. He took a London black taxi to the Curtis Green Building which was the new home of the Metropolitan Police Service known as New Scotland Yard. The original headquarters were at 4 Whitehall Place. Yet, generally the public used the rear entrance which was located on a street named Great Scotland Yard. As a result, Scotland Yard became the term used for police activities in London. Police headquarters moved from Great Scotland Yard to a newly completed building on the Victoria Embankment along the Thames River in 1890 and the name New Scotland Yard was adopted. Over the years two additional buildings were added to the complex. Then in 1967 the Metropolitan Police Service moved into a new 20-story building at 10 Broadway in Victoria. The building served their needs until in the summer of 2013, as an austerity move, 10 Broadway was sold to Yusuff Ali an Indian billionaire who was Chairman and Managing Director of LuLu Group International headquartered in Abu Dhabi. Metropolitan Police Services headquarters were moved back to one of the Victoria Embankment buildings—the Curtis Green Building. In addition to the sale of the 20-story building, the size of the staff was reduced from 3,500 to 600.

Ken Farmingdale found the Metropolitan Police Service officers to be quite friendly, open, and forthcoming. They were very busy, but cooperative. His diplomatic identification and cover story of simply doing unofficial fact-finding while he was in the country for other purposes was readily accepted. He was told the last major terrorist incident was at a watchdog website news organization where seven persons were murdered. In addition, there were a number of murders that were directly related to the actions of the Satan's Shadow revenge group. They showed him police reports and copies of the note found with each body. One of the more helpful facts revealed came from the medical examiner. He had determined the same weapon that was used at the news organization was used in the three apparently random murders. This allowed them to conclude that the attack on the news organization was Muslim terrorism. There was very little else they had to go on.

Farmingdale, the visiting diplomat, was offered the four police files and a quiet room in which to examine them. What Ken found were more questions than answers. The news organization was called *London Voice* and had ceased operations. Crime scene investigators found so many different fingerprints, threads, and hair samples that it was impossible to isolate any single one. Apparently, there regularly were many guests and interviews conducted on premises. From a visitor's log they had determined that six persons had been there that day—4 females and 2 males. Five of the six had been interviewed by police. The sixth and last name on the list could not be located. Omar Jahandar was an alias used by Shahin Pouran.

Ken Farmingdale decided that the best approach would be to investigate persons who had previous dealings with *London Voice* as this was indeed a planned event. He was given the name of the relative of one of the co-owners who claimed all of the property—Bridget Constantine. His first stop, however, was the crime scene. Through familiarity with the physical location he would better understand and visualize the situation and events. What he found were empty offices with no furniture. Most noticeable were the many blood stains on the carpets that had yet to be replaced. It was the frightening reminder of the carnage that had transpired. Unfortunately, none but the perpetrator or perpetrators knew what actually happened. The sight of blood was not foreign to Ken. He thought of the families of the innocent victims and then the families of the evil doers who would ultimately pay the price. It had to be done because it will make a difference.

The woman, Bridget Constantine, who had all of the *London Voice* property lived in Brighton. Ken Farmingdale rented a car and headed south on the 52-mile drive which he estimated would take approximately 2 hours.

The two-car caravan arrived at Chateau d'Aramitz. A long pea-gravel drive with stone walls on both sides led to a three-story limestone building with a two-story bowed bay entrance. Double doors and a single tall window on either side of the entrance greeted them. On the second floor the bowed bay had three windows. The main building boasted four tall windows on each of the two lower floors on both sides of the entrance. The symmetry was obvious. Small square windows ran the entire length of the house on the third floor. Steeply pitched blue-slate rooves topped the chateau with a Roman arch inset into the center roof. Five massive brick chimneys were visible as the Peugeot SUV entered the circular drive around a row of low hedges.

Jarvis Demoye stopped the automobile, turned to General Hughes, and said, "Me thinks there is more to our friend than we suspect."

"Well, he's not hiding it, is he?"

"I wonder if he could lend me a couple bucks," Adam Hayes speculated.

"I want to know if there is a head in this joint," Ron Clew stated revealing his growing need.

The four men climbed out of the car and were joined by their host. "Welcome to Chateau d'Aramitz," Liam said as he waved his walking stick in the direction of the structure.

"Quite impressive, 1890s?" General Hughes said.

"You have an eye for architecture, mon ami," Liam replied. "Actually, 1878 to be exact."

"Do you live here?" Jarvis asked.

"No, I live in Paris. I visit Chateau d'Aramitz on occasion. There is a small staff to maintain the chateau and grounds, as well as to keep away intrus, how you say, trespassers."

"Does it have a working head?" Ron Clew inquired.

"Les administrateur keeps things sous le contrôle."

"No head, you know, john."

"His name is Pierre."

"I mean bathroom," Ron stated with growing frustration and desperation.

"Ah, salle de bains. Oui, there are many, I believe eight."

"I only need one."

"I thought seals could go a week without relieving themselves," Adam observed enjoying his friend's dilemma.

"Up yours!"

They entered the impressive residence. In the foyer they were greeted by twelve-foot high ceilings, a huge crystal chandelier over a heavy wooden pedestal table upon which sat a three-foot bronze knight on a horse statue. The brown slate floor tiles were immaculate without a speck of dirt anywhere. Arched columns adorned with bas relief plaster sculptures led to the inner rooms.

They were met by the caretaker who upon instructions from Liam led Ron to the throne. The rest of the team entered a sitting room. Floor to ceiling wooden bookshelves lined one wall and were filled with leather-bound editions. A large tapestry hung on the opposite wall. It depicted various seafaring scenes with French schooners, waves, rocky shores, and more.

"Sit, gentlemen, we have much to discuss," Liam stated with authority.

Special Agent Peggy Fox reviewed the files on the Holiday murders, as well as the Hillsman murders. All were perpetrated by the Satan's Shadow gang. In addition to taking the lives of those innocent persons these criminals had essentially ruined her career. This she would neither forget nor forgive.

CHAPTER 48

A small two-story rowhouse on Dawson Terrace in Brighton, England was home to Bridget Constantine, sister of Patrick Constantine co-owner of *London Voice*. Ken Farmingdale stood at the purple front door wondering what he would say when it was opened. To his surprise a young woman in her mid-thirties appeared at the door.

"May I help you?" she inquired.

"Bridget Constantine?"

"Yes, who are you?"

"My name is Arthur Thompson. I am with the United States Department of State. Ken used his alias and cover that had been provided. I'm on a fact-finding tour gathering information on terrorist acts in the United Kingdom." He quickly added with sincerity, "I am very sorry for your loss."

"I see. How may I help you?" she asked somewhat formally.

"The London Metropolitan Police gave me your name. You are the person who claimed all of the property from *London Voice*?"

"My brother was co-owner. The other co-owner didn't have any family."

Bridget Constantine invited Ken into her home and they sat in the small parlor. She explained that while she didn't have any direct involvement with the organization she and her brother did have numerous and regular conversations.

"Please understand," Ken, alias Arthur, stated, "I am on a fact-finding mission and not doing a law-enforcement investigation."

Bridget nodded.

"However, if it turns out that I do uncover any helpful information, or even better, identify the perpetrator of this heinous crime I will share it with Scotland Yard."

For a moment, Bridget gazed at the American. She was torn between wanting to talk about the event and not wishing to feel the pain once more. After making a decision, she began, "It was all so horrible, but not completely unexpected."

"What do you mean?"

"Patrick often received threats as a result of stories or investigative reports."

Ken, aka Arthur Thompson, offered, "I have reason to believe that this was Muslim terrorism. Did he ever mention threats coming from that community?"

"Threats were daily. Insults and condemnations were like rain coming in waves."

"Were they written, by telephone, email, or in person?"

"All of the above." She shook her head sadly, "I told him to stop writing about them, but he refused to be intimidated. Then I told him he was barking mad. He just disregarded my concerns. I wish I wasn't the one who was correct."

"Do you have any of the records of the threats that I might see?"

"All of the documents are in storage. Emails that were received are stored on an external hard drive." She thought for a moment, then explained, "The computers are in storage but I have the hard drive." After another moment of thought she offered, "You can look at the emails—there are hundreds of them—but you can't take the hard drive."

Agent Peggy Fox found no similarity between the two assassination events. Three victims were killed with knives, one with a gun, and three with poison. Without question, these were trained professionals—most likely military. However, the poison was not something that was readily available. That pointed to more clandestine organizations, such as the CIA. It was a fact that would prove problematic. She decided the only ever-so-slim connection might be the sniper Michael O'Neal and the man who recommended him Emanuel Vegas.

Liam Beauchêne told the Satan's Shadow team what he had discovered. Kareem Reza had been a messenger for and was being coerced into cooperating with a radical Muslim organization. He had originally been recruited by a woman. However, he was now trapped because his twenty-five-year-old son, Faraz, was being held hostage in Afghanistan. He claimed to reluctantly have now become involved in a major terrorist plot against the United States of America.

"Where is Reza at this time?" General Hughes inquired.

"He is being held at a secret location on a Commandement des

Opérations Spéciale—Special Operations Command (COS) military base."

"Is he cooperating?"

"He, as they say, has no choice," Liam replied. "We are the only hope he has of ever seeing his son, once more."

"A son who will go on the targets list if the terrorist attack is successful," Ron Clew pointed out.

Liam turned to the large black man and nodded, "Yes, as will Kareem Reza." After a pause he added, "But, not if the plot is foiled."

"How can we help?" Jarvis Demoye inquired.

Liam stood and paced the room. At one point he gazed out a window at the gardens that surrounded Chateau d'Aramitz. He was in another time and another world. As a man ages it is often difficult to locate memories in one's mind. And then, there are those memories that reveal themselves unexpectedly. This was one of those sudden flashes of recollection. Ten years earlier he was on active duty with the Army Special Forces Command—Commandement des forces spéciales Terre (COM FST) based in Pau, Pyrénées-Atlantiques, France. He was on the team that investigated the August 2008 Uzbin Valley Ambush of a French patrol in Afghanistan.

It occurred during the first month French troops had taken over defense of the Surobi District, Afghanistan from Italian forces. Unaware of the fact that the Italians secret services had been bribing local Taliban groups to remain inactive, the French began extensive patrols of the region. They were concerned about the possibility of militants attacking three dams that operate in the region. Given the relative peace enjoyed in the area, French patrols ventured into areas with an overoptimistic threat assessment and insufficient equipment. Mohammed Ismayel, a Taliban commander, later stated that the more aggressive stance of the French troops motivated the guerrilla attack.

On 18 August, a French patrol was hastily dispatched to Spēr Kunday in an effort to cut off guerrilla forces from escaping into Pakistan. It was composed of 100 soldiers in 20 vehicles. Taliban insurgents who were informed of the patrol gathered approximately 140 local fighters who took up positions around the pass leading into the Uzbin Valley in order to ambush the French force. A battle ensued which lasted over eight hours. Ten French soldiers were killed and twenty-one wounded.

What Liam and his fellow investigators concluded was that the French patrol was unprepared and under-equipped given the known existence of enemy fighters in the region. They had only one radio which made communications slow and often impossible. In addition, they found that the Taliban were more sophisticated than originally believed as they used modern tactical techniques, executing a well-prepared ambush that pinned French troops in a C-shaped pincer. Highly trained Taliban snipers kept the French contingent from using some of their heavy weapons and strategic placement of fighters kept air-power at bay. Sadly, when four Afghan National Army soldiers were wounded and their interpreter killed —they fled the scene. Finally, captured French soldiers were executed and all allied bodies looted. All of these facts from years ago were now important to Liam at the present time.

Liam looked at Jarvis Demoye, retired Navy Captain, and stated, "It will be necessary to rescue le garçon from those who hold him in Afghanistan for us to enlist the full cooperation of Kareem Reza."

"Are plans in the works?" General Hughes asked.

"Action Division of the Directorate-General for External Security (DGSE) is responsible for planning and performing clandestine and covert operations including black operations. Select members of this group have been informed of the objective and are gathering intelligence."

"You will, of course, let us know the outcome of the operation," Maxwell Hughes stated rather than asked.

"The Action Division specializes in sabotage, explosives, assassination, kidnapping, and infiltration/exfiltration of persons into or from hostile territory," Liam explained.

General Hughes immediately recognized a setup that would ultimately end with a request for their involvement.

"The entire Special Operations Command (COS) is comprised of 3,746 personnel—307 general staff and 3,439 operatives." Liam shrugged, "Given conditions mondiales, all operatives have been deployed with the exception of seven 2nd Circle members." He glanced at the room and realized more explanation was needed. "Second Circle, or Tier 2 units, don't exist . . ."

"There's a lot of that going around," Adam Hayes interjected.

Liam smiled, nodded, and continued, "It is an elite group with special training and latitude in operations. They are given the best equipment, including the FN SCAR (Fabrique Nationale Special Operations Forces Combat Assault Rifle)."

"Nice weapon. It's called the MK 17 in the U.S. military," Ron Clew observed.

"It is believed," Liam continued, "that a rescue mission will involve fewer, rather than more participants. However, seven is not considered sufficient."

Once again Adam Hayes interrupted, "Do I hear a call for volunteers?"

"I think I hear my mother calling," retired Navy Seal Ron Clew added.

General Hughes smiled. He turned to Liam and said, "Without a final situation assessment you have no idea how many combatants will be required."

"Correct. However, what we do know is our operatives in-country are investigating and evaluating the situation. Once they develop a clear picture of the objective we can utilize general assets already there, but the actual extraction will require specialized skills."

"Looks like we're going to freakin' Afghanistan," Adam concluded.

"J'apprécie votre bénévolat, mon ami, I appreciate you volunteering," Liam said with a smile. He looked in the direction of Ron Clew and said, "I believe your mother would want you to do this."

"You don't know my mother," Ron retorted, then said, "However, I can't let this little guy go by himself. He might get lost, or hurt, or frightened."

"My hero," Adam swooned.

"Before we commit to anything," General Hughes spoke up, "We cannot put the anonymity of members of Satan's Shadow at risk."

"If they participate, it will be as unnamed paid mercenaries recruited through the DGSE," Liam reassured him. "Remember, the other team members are Tier Two who must also remain unidentified. Therefore, all will be given operational aliases. Identifications, such as Blue 11 or Green 6 will be used."

"As long as I'm not Black 1," Ron Clew commented.

"There is one more thing," Liam said. "From all indications, it appears that the services of a highly-skilled sniper might be warranted." He shook his head, "Sadly, that is an area where our resources are over-extended and no tireur d'élite is available." He looked at Adam Hayes.

CHAPTER 49

FBI Special Agent Peggy Fox was unassigned pending the investigation of the misfortune in Wilkes-Barre. She considered how the Bureau found the most palatable words to describe their failure for the public and media while behind closed doors she was soundly condemned for the catastrophe in that Pennsylvania city.

While unassigned Agent Fox decided to pursue her own leads, or longshots, pertaining to Satan's Shadow. She sat in the den of a farmhouse at FFP Ranch in western Virginia. To her right, sitting at a right angle in a leather chair, Michael O'Neal pondered her question.

"I don't know an Emanuel Vegas with the Secret Service. In fact, I don't know why he would know me, or for that matter recommend me."

"You've never spoken with him, emailed, or had any correspondence with him?"

"None."

"Well, he obviously knew enough about you to make the recommendation."

"After I left the Army, I did various assignments for foreign governments, our government, and for organizations that—you understand—can't be named," Michael explained. He added, "I'm sure my name is known to many people in our government and my Army record is readily available."

"What is your opinion of what happened in Wilkes-Barre?"

"I was sorry to read about that," Michael said with sincerity which was noted by Agent Fox.

"Do you have any thoughts on who might have done it?"

For a fleeting moment, Michael O'Neal envisioned Adam Hayes. Owl stood and looked out the window at the green pastures of the ranch. Finally, he answered Agent Fox's question, "From the little I've read it appears to be professionals—well-trained seasoned assassins directed by skilled and experienced leaders—most likely military." Michael turned back to look at Peggy Fox, "The use of poison is perplexing. Military don't generally use poison. That's more of the clandestine agency approach."

"Have you worked with the CIA?"

"You know I can't answer that question."

Agent Fox smiled. She knew he wouldn't answer but still took a shot. In the back of her mind she suspected the CIA, however, the Secret Service connection was odd enough to warrant further scrutiny. The challenge would be, how to approach a senior member of the Secret Service without bringing far too much unwanted attention to herself? She continued her interview of Michael O'Neal, "When you were in Wilkes-Barre did you see any individuals who might have been out-of-place?"

"They all seemed out-of-place," Michael quipped.

"Yes," the obligatory smile, "Did any persons appear to be strangers, from another place, military, or otherwise suspicious?"

"There's room for a joke there, but this is a serious subject," Michael replied. "I regret that I didn't see anyone that stood out. Due to the reason for my visit, I was operating with an elevated sense of awareness. Unfortunately, nothing presented itself."

"What do you know about Satan's Shadow?" Agent Fox inserted a surprise question to see O'Neal's reaction. He disappointed her by not having an overt reaction.

Retired Master Sergeant Michael "Owl" O'Neal was caught off-guard but didn't show it. To buy time in order to formulate a better response he replied appropriately, "Who?"

"I know you've heard of them. My question is how much do you know about them?"

"Only what I've read in the papers, seen on TV and the internet, and what you've told me—nothing more."

"So, they never tried to recruit you?"

"Hell no! Why would they? I'm retired."

"I can see that a man with your skills would be very valuable to a group like Satan's Shadow."

"Not interested."

"That wasn't the question," Fox pressed on. "Have they ever tried to recruit you?"

"I told you no," Michael O'Neal became angry being asked twice which inferred that he might be lying. He pointed out, "Tell me this, were any of the innocent victims of this group killed by a sniper?"

"No," was her only response.

Ken Farmingdale concluded that Bridget Constantine was correct, threats and insults were a daily occurrence at *London Voice.* There was a constant barrage of hate. It's a wonder that they didn't have armed guards at the doors. He had leafed through stacks of letters and began reviewing emails. They seemed to be endless and stated the most vile, threatening, hate-filled things. It gave Ken pause to wonder if what Satan's Shadow was doing would have any effect what-so-ever. The depth of hate that was expressed was done at a level of emotion that would most definitely cloud judgment. Could any of them manage to preserve enough humanity to care about anyone or anything? One had to wonder how many fiends were out there who would give up everything they love to quench their unbridled hate? Had the human race somehow regressed to that of a desperate mindless mob? The whole experience turned his stomach.

On and on he read being struck by venomous words that could only come from deranged minds. He began to wonder if there really were any "innocent" people out there. Sitting under a deluge of sewage its very difficult to believe there are fragrant flowers in the world that may be enjoyed.

Then, much like a photo appearing in a solution of developer, a picture formed in Ken Farmingdale's mind. He had read a number of complaints, insults, and threats from the same entity—OJ. At first, it was lost among the voluminous array of emails. However, repetition had its effect. This OJ was angry and caustic, and dangerous. Again and again, the initials appeared on hate-filled emails. Then, in a flash, Ken made the connection. The last visitor listed on the *London Voice* log was Omar Jahandar—OJ!

"It's not gonna happen," Adam Hayes insisted.

"With a persuasive eloquent individual like you pleading the case?" General Hughes remarked.

"He's retired, happy," Adam paused, then added, "and safe."

"We're not asking him to join the Shadow," General Hughes pointed out. "This is a coordinated operation with the French military to rescue a French citizen's son. Nothing more."

"In fucking Afghanistan."

"Not the most pleasant place, I'll admit, but you two have been in far worse."

"True, but that was when he was active—not retired."

"Maybe he's getting itchy feet."

"Not the last time I saw him."

"Give it a shot."

"Have you ever been foal watching?" Adam asked Maxwell Hughes.

"Falls watching?"

"Not falls—foal, you know horse puppies."

"No, can't say that I've had the pleasure."

"It is a pleasure of sorts. The arrival of life—pure, truly innocent life. Michael O'Neal has found his Shangri-la. Maybe, his redemption."

"I envy him that," General Hughes admitted. "I wish every man on this team could receive such a reward. But this world depends on us and warriors with his skills to provide the protection needed to defend an environment that offers such peace of mind."

"Why didn't you give Owl a coin?" Adam surprised General Hughes with his question.

Undaunted, General Hughes explained, "If you recall, I gave you the coin after you successfully executed an operation that I directed. You followed orders, initiated precise actions, adapted, innovated when needed, and showed loyalty. I never had the chance to evaluate Master Sergeant O'Neal."

"He was included in a number of operations under your command."

"In his capacity most of what he did was unseen. I never had one-on-one contact with him."

"He's a good man," Adam offered.

"No doubt about that. I just don't know what's in his mind or heart." General Hughes reached into his pocket, withdrew a challenge coin, and tossed it over to Adam Hayes. "I trust your judgment, Hayes. If you believe Michael O'Neal earned that, you give it to him with my compliments. However, along with that hunk of bronze goes the knowledge of who we are and what we have done and what we will do."

Adam tossed the coin back to General Hughes, "He's not ready. And, I won't put that kind of pressure on him."

"And the mercenary assignment with the French military?"

"I guess I'm catching a flight back to the states."

CHAPTER 50

Darius Holiday learned of his family being murdered through the prison grapevine. Even in solitary confinement word had gotten to him. He sat on his bed and stared at the grey wall. Guilt flowed over him. Through his actions, he caused what had happened. Even though all of the plans, events, moves, and counter-moves had been carefully calculated. After-the-fact, it was so easy to look back and second guess every decision he had made. While it was unforeseen forces that changed the direction he had chosen, in the end, it had all brought him to this time and place.

Guilt curled and twisted within him. He knew he shouldn't have done what he had. Poor judgment, misplaced emotion, and unanticipated weakness had momentarily blinded him. He was an empty shell. Aimless and without hope he sat silently. Dark clouds parted and the truth stared back at him from the cold grey wall. There was no denying or changing what he had done and he choked on remorse.

Why did he do it?

His intent was honorable. It was his destiny to serve Allah. Regardless of what Haji Ejder Jahandar called him, he was indeed Ihtsham Azlan—Strong Lion. He brought terror to Philadelphia and New York City. That cannot be denied. He was mujahid. Only he failed a critical test for which he became burdened with guilt.

> "O you who believe! Choose not your fathers nor your brethren for protectors if they love disbelief over belief; whoever of you takes them for protectors, such are wrong-doers. Say: if your fathers, and your children, and your brethren, and your spouses, and your tribe, and the wealth you have acquired, and business for which you fear shrinkage, and houses you are pleased with are dearer to you than Allah and His Messenger and STRIVING in His way: then wait till Allah brings His command to pass. Allah does not guide disobedient folk." [Quran 9:23, 24]

If he had truly been mujahid he would have embraced "Sword of

Truth" and the plans of Haji Ejder Jahandar and Rashid Teymouri. The FBI agent would lay dead as would additional examples of what is the fate of disbelievers. A powerful message would have been delivered. And, he would have been a part of history. He should have been strong and exposed Toufan Ghorbani Mashti's weakness. Instead, his resolve escaped him and he chose a man and his desire to protect his family over the will of Allah. By his own actions Darius revealed that he was shabal—little lion.

It all began with a fire that drove him to become a force in the pursuit of spreading the truth. And, yet here he was a caged animal held by the infidels.

Watch Dog and Owl, aka Adam Hayes and Michael O'Neal, rode along a stream on horseback. Midday sunlight filtered through trees creating sparkling reflections off the lazily moving water. The effect was mesmerizing to Adam who was fatigued from an overnight flight from Bayonne, France to Washington, D.C., followed by a long drive to FFP Ranch in western Virginia.

After the usual off-beat pleasantries Adam had requested that they get away where they could talk in private. Henceforth, the horseback ride in the countryside.

"What the hell is that smell?" Adam asked with a smile.

"Fresh air, nature, freedom, God," Michael O'Neal replied.

"It frightens me."

"No, Alice frightens you, or else we wouldn't be way out here beyond visual or listening range of the ranch house," Owl stated.

"You got me there."

"No, you got me here. What's on your mind? And, no matter what the question is, the answer is no."

"That's a pretty closed-minded unfriendly attitude, if you ask me," Watch Dog pointed out.

"No, you're about to ask me."

"You're a pain-in-the-ask. I don't know why I even talk to you."

"Would you rather talk with Alice?"

"Uh, on second thought, you'll do."

"So, what's on your mind?"

"A rescue."

"No."

"The son of a French government official is being held hostage in

Afghanistan. A radical Muslim organization is holding him in order to get cooperation from the French official."

"No."

"French commandos are planning a mission to extract the young man."

"No."

"Unfortunately, French COS forces are spread so thin around the world they need to recruit a few mercenaries to bolster the team."

"No."

"They're short on sharpshooters."

"No."

"I've already signed on," Adam revealed.

"No shit."

"At least you didn't just say no."

"I'm about to."

"They need you—I need you."

"No."

"I wouldn't ask if this wasn't an emergency."

"Yeah, you would."

"OK, you're right," Adam admitted. "I just don't like going into a hot zone with a team I'm unfamiliar with and an untried sniper backup. You I can count on to watch my back. OK, I'm a greedy self-centered son-of-a-bitch." He looked directly at Michael but said nothing else.

Michael O'Neal climbed down off his mount. Adam followed suit. The two men led their horses over to the stream. Calming sounds emanated from the running water, crickets and other sounds of nature surrounded them, and a slight breeze completed the peaceful effect. It was the idyllic kind of setting that allowed one to escape the travails of a world spinning out-of-control. Two warriors, who had seen more of the brutal, inhuman, coarse side of life than most, drifted silently among their own feelings of tranquility.

After a long interlude, Adam was the first to speak, "Forget about it. You earned this. Not every man has a vision or the ability to make it happen. I don't have any goddamned right to ask you to step back into the sewer." He turned to leave.

"I need a few honest answers, first," Michael O'Neal said still staring at the stream.

"Seriously, I changed my mind," Adam stated.

"It's my mind you need to be concerned with."

"No, forget it."

"Tell me more about the mission."

"No."

"Did you already volunteer me?"

"No."

"Were you counting on me?"

"No."

Michael turned and looked at his friend. The two of them had faced death together so many times it permanently attached them to each other in life. If Adam were to be at risk if he didn't join the operation there was little doubt that he would refuse. Brothers are of the same blood, soldiers connect on a different deeper plane. That said, Michael would walk into hell to save or protect Adam. It was that simple. He just didn't know that his comrade was teetering on the edge of the lake of fire.

A bird took flight from a stand of trees catching the attention of both men. They watched it circle and gain altitude. Adam began to climb back into the saddle when a hand on his shoulder stopped him.

Michael O'Neal asked, "Does this have anything to do with Satan's Shadow?"

Adam didn't know how to answer. It was precipitated by Satan's Shadow contacts, but was not exactly a Satan's Shadow operation. In truth, it was a French Special Operations Command undertaking. How much he needed to tell Michael he wasn't sure. Yet, he wouldn't mislead his friend. Finally, he decided full disclosure was the only honorable approach. "Michael, you and I both know that I am a part of that insanity. I won't spend time telling you how or why or in justifying what I've done. Hell is waiting for me. We all know and accept that fact." Adam turned back to gaze at the stream. "I'm sorry that I came here. The mission is indeed a rescue mission. A contact that the team works with brought the information to us. The French official has been cooperating with terrorist communications requests due to his son being held hostage. I volunteered to help." He turned back toward his friend, "It's not your fight."

"But, unfortunately, you're my friend."

"A true friend wouldn't have come here."

"I didn't say a good, or smart, or reasonable friend," Michael smiled. "You're a headstrong, pain-in-the-ass with a sick sense of humor. . ."

"Don't sugarcoat it."

"I figure, in this life we cross paths with all sorts of individuals. The ones we choose to stick to take us in directions that impact our lives.

In every case, it is a matter of choice. With you, I just made a ridiculously bad choice—so I'm stuck with the consequences."

"You're not stuck, pal," Adam responded. "As I said, I changed my mind. Let's finish our ride, shake hands, and get back to our chosen lives."

"Tell me about the mission."

"I'll tell you when I get back."

"Listen, I'm getting bored. I need some action. You know, someone who has been in the cement mixer as many times as I have can't get it completely out of his system in such a short period of time. A little challenge will do me good."

"Liar."

"So, you came here to insult me?"

"I came here to recruit you. However, now I realize it was a bad idea. I'd feel a whole lot better knowing you are here enjoying your reward."

"If I don't participate you may be going to your reward."

"In truth, that might be a welcome relief."

CHAPTER 51

A week later Ken Farmingdale rejoined General Hughes and Jarvis Demoye. He immediately inquired as to the disposition of Adam Hayes and Ronald Clew. General Hughes explained that they were on a mission with the French Special Operations Command. The rescue effort was described in broad terms as none of them knew the specific details or tactics that were being employed. Then the subject turned to London.

"I have some info and a lot of dead ends," Ken stated. He went on to describe his visits with the police, the crime scene, and the sister of one of the owners of *London Voice*. Then he shared his discovery of the venomous emails from someone called OJ and the fact that the last visitor to *London Voice* was an Omar Jahandar. The source of the emails was a Gmail account with a fictitious profile. Ken concluded by saying, "I don't believe Omar Jahandar is the culprit's real name, so it's a dead end."

"Maybe not as dead as you think," Jarvis Demoye said.

"How so?" Ken Farmingdale asked.

"What we can safely assume is Omar Jahandar is the terrorist. He is also the same person who sent the emails. Indeed, Omar Jahandar is definitely an alias." Jarvis stood, walked over to the bar, and fixed a drink. He turned back and said, "All we have to do is use what we know to find out what we don't know."

"And, you have an idea," Ken stated rather than asked.

"I do."

Sergent-chef Pierre Dumont of the French Special Operations Command (COS) addressed the assembled team in English, "Mes amies, I will speak only in English as that is the common language among us."

The nine other men in the room nodded as they waited to be briefed about the rescue mission they were about to embark upon.

"Our intelligence is scarce and its reliability unknown. We have an operative attempting to confirm information and gather additional facts. He is in a very dangerous place."

Pierre Dumont flipped a switch and a map of Afghanistan appeared on the large monitor mounted on the wall. "Our package is in Afghanistan. Of that, we are confident." He removed a pipe from his shirt pocket and lit it, "A small amount of background is required."

A light blue wisp of smoke drifted into the air as the leader of the team continued, "Eight of the ten largest cities in Afghanistan are located in the northeast third of the country. There are roads, airports, trains, and security forces serving these cities. Of the remaining two of the ten largest cities, Herat is in the northwest and Kandahar the southeast. The remaining tribal areas are essentially inaccessible and dangerous. Here," he pointed at the southwest corner of Afghanistan where the borders of Afghanistan, Pakistan, and Iran meet, "is one of the most dangerous places in the world." He looked directly at the team, "And we, mes amies, will have the pleasure of vacationing there."

"So, Disney World is out?" Adam Hayes questioned.

"Mes excuses. However, I can assure you there will be plenty of amusements to keep you occupied." He returned to his presentation, "This area of Afghanistan, Nimruz Province is essentially lawless. There are no coalition troops, or Afghan soldiers, or foreign NGO workers to be found. While neighboring Helmand Province has been the focus of counterinsurgency efforts, Nimruz Province has been ignored. Zaranj with a population of about 160,000 is the capital of Nimruz Province. It sits right on the border with Iran. In fact, it is approximately only 25 miles from the Iranian city of Zabol. I tell you all this because there is a unique dynamic that takes place in this area."

"Watch where you step," one of the French commandoes warned, "you don't want to step on the wrong side of the line in the sand and get arrested in Iran." This brought a few chuckles from the other team members.

Dumont pressed on, "A small ethnic group known as Baluchis have their own language and culture. It seems their homeland is divided among three not-so-friendly nations, however, they have remained united. Baluchis have made quite a living out of being smugglers. They transport various goods, drugs, fuel, weapons, and people from country to country. Not long ago, many in Zaranj profited enormously from the tens of thousands of Afghans, displaced by war, who emigrated west each year. It was a ten-minute drive to the border, walk up to a checkpoint, pay a bribe, and welcome to Iran."

"Unfortunately, Nimruz Province has been designated as a "No Go" zone by the Iranian government. A 15-foot-high concrete wall was erected along 70 miles of the border, guard towers were built, and rumor has it they began shooting Afghans trying to cross. However, all this didn't stop the Baluchis. They simply changed their means of getting there. In the end, it transformed a ten-minute drive into a ten-hour trek. Afghan-Baluchi smugglers take travelers south to the Pakistan border, Pakistani-Baluchi smugglers bring them west to the border with Iran, and Iranian-Baluchi smugglers take them to their final destination."

"I take it these Baluchis aren't very trusting of strangers," Ron Clew observed.

Sergent Dumont looked at the Navy Seal and replied, "No one in Nimruz Province trusts strangers. And, we would stand out like red wine with Chicken Cordon Bleu." He smiled and continued, "There is an additional dynamic at work in this province. The Kamal Khan Dam has been built on the Helmand River in Chaharbarak district of Nimroz Province. It was aggressively opposed by Iran. According to the Iranian foreign minister there has been reduction in the water flow from the Helmand River to Iran, which has adversely affected the Hamoon River and Sistan areas of Iran. Of course, various officials from Afghanistan claim the Iranian concerns are baseless. Locals believe all of the violence in the district have been caused by Iran due to the dam. In addition, Iranian weapons have been found on Taliban fighters."

"This is looking better and better," Adam Hayes commented.

"Wait, there is more."

"Why not?" Adam said as he fell back into his chair.

"Afghanistan, without question, is the world's largest producer of opiates. Where water may be precious, the drug trade is so profitable every group, organization, and government official is involved to some extent. Networks of production and transport blur the lines of responsibility." A puff of smoke from Dumont's pipe punctuated his statement. "They all work together and if Iranian forces attempt to intercede, they are always out-gunned."

One of the French commandoes whispered something in French and those who heard and understood laughed.

Pierre Dumont expanded his talk, "Most of the drugs that enter Iran go on to Turkey and eventually Europe. Yet, plenty remain in Iran. Despite the threat of capital punishment for narcotics offenses, Iran has one of the highest per capita rates of opiate use in the world."

Adam Hayes turned in his chair and said to Michael "Owl" O'Neal, "I think I'd rather be foal watching."

O'Neal replied, "You and me both."

"Then why did you bring me here?" Adam asked.

"Fuck you!"

"I never met the man," Emanuel Vegas stated into his telephone receiver. He had responded to a question posed by Special Agent Peggy Fox pertaining to sniper Michael O'Neal.

"Given the outcome of our operation in Wilkes-Barre we have to follow every thread of evidence no matter how thin," Fox stated in an official voice.

By contrast, in a friendly yet somewhat condescending tone Vegas replied, "I fully understand. My only reason for recommending the man was to offer assistance."

"I appreciate your proactive involvement. He was helpful—to an extent. But, I must ask, why Michael O'Neal?"

"O'Neal? When I made the decision to offer assistance, I checked our database and this O'Neal was both unassigned and in the general geographic vicinity of the operation. You weren't going to fly someone in from Germany or Okinawa. His credentials were solid," Vegas paused, then added, "You know we have our own sharpshooters and snipers who are used frequently to protect motorcade routes, outdoor events, and other venues. Even though I'm a senior officer, I was not in a position to authorize their assignment to a consultancy role. Our assets are spread relatively thin, as it is." His tone changed as he added, "I'm sure you know how that is."

"Yes," was her response even though she didn't have first-hand experience with personnel allocation.

In an attempt to put the subject at rest Secret Service Agent Emanuel Vegas stated, "There has always been cooperation between our agencies. I was simply promoting good will."

The FBI Pitbull did not let go, "Do you have any reason to believe that there might, even remotely, be some connection between Michael O'Neal and the group known as Satan's Shadow?"

"Why would I?" was Vegas response. "That would be one unbelievable coincidence, wouldn't you say?"

"I admit it is extremely far-fetched," Peggy Fox said. "However, I'm dealing with a ghost. Somehow, they defeated all our defensive tactics and executed their nefarious acts without detection. It reflects either extraordinary strategic thinking or an inside job. They knew what we had in place and took advantage of the gaps."

Emanuel asked, "I assume you know and trust all the members of your team?"

"I do. The only outsider was Michael O'Neal who I foolishly told what we had in place."

"Still very thin."

"When one is drowning, you grab at any vine no matter how thin."

"Agreed. Have you interviewed him?"

"I have. Nothing stood out." Peggy Fox thought for a moment and then offered, "The only peculiarity is the connection/nonconnection between you and he."

After a long day driving a taxi around London, Reginald Howard looked forward to a pint at the local pub. It was a relatively long walk from the garage but felt good after sitting for so long. He never reached his destination. On his body was the note, "This person died as revenge for the acts of the criminal group known as Satan's Shadow. Find me before more die."

CHAPTER 52

"Maybe, it's time for us to use the same tactic against this monster," Jarvis Demoye said as he reflected on what Ken Farmingdale had reported from his investigation in London.

"He's taunting us to bring us out into the open," General Maxwell Hughes agreed.

"So, we let him think he was successful and bring him to us," Demoye concluded.

"What's your plan?" Ken asked.

Jarvis ran his hand through the close-cropped beard on his chin as he pondered his idea. "He's obsessed with Satan's Shadow. That is his Achilles' Heel. It will make him bold and careless. We dangle the opportunity to get to us to get to him." He looked directly at Ken Farmingdale, "What is your take on this sister—Bridget Constantine?"

"From the time I spent with her, she seems to be level-headed, calm, intelligent, and hurting."

"Do you think she would be willing to help?"

"It would depend on what kind of help we seek."

"It would be an active role and may have a degree of danger."

"She might be convinced."

"Does she have the necessary courage?"

"Her courage is unknown, but she does have the hate."

"For my plan to work Bridget Constantine has to be an integral part," Jarvis stated.

Ken Farmingdale considered the woman he had dealt with for a very short time. She was forthcoming, telling him of her conversations with her brother and fear of what could, and ultimately did, happen. To bring the murderer, or murderers, to justice she might be open to taking a calculated risk. However, that was an unknown. He announced, "All I can do is use my irresistible charm on her."

"Where's Hayes when we need a smartass remark?" General Hughes commented. He turned to Jarvis Demoye and warned, "Whatever we do we cannot reveal who we are or our connection with the group known as Satan's Shadow."

"Only Ken will be directly involved using his State Department cover," Jarvis looked at Farmingdale and asked, "What was the name?"

"Arthur Thompson."

"Well, Artie . . ."

"Arthur."

"Have it your way, Arthur. Here's the plan. Bridget Constantine will inform the media that she has uncovered an internet connection and video file from a surveillance camera in the office that will identify the murderer of the staff at *London Voice*." He paused and made a note on a legal pad. "We better put up a camera at the location before the announcement. This guy is no fool and will most likely check to see if one ever existed." Jarvis continued, "She will finish her statement by explaining that she has two more boxes of materials to go through before bringing everything to Scotland Yard. Finally, because she fears for her life she will relocate to an undisclosed location until she goes to the police."

"And, we will make it difficult but possible for our target to find out where Bridget Constantine is hiding," General Hughes stated rhetorically.

"Exactly," Jarvis said. "Now, we will have to reconnoiter Brighton, England to find a location where we control the situation."

"As long as we guarantee Ms. Constantine's safety," Ken Farmingdale insisted.

"That's easy—how do you look in a dress," Jarvis replied.

"Forget it. She's on her own."

"I like it," General Hughes concluded. "We should make plans to go to England."

Special Agent Peggy Fox looked in the mirror. Her face had taken on a hard, cold, distant, unwelcoming appearance. The only word that came to mind was shrew. Events of the past few weeks had unquestionably taken their toll. Anger mixed with frustration. From the very beginning she had loved the Federal Bureau of Investigation. She accepted humiliation that came with being a newbie and menial tasks assigned to junior staffers. But, that was in the past—long past. Since those days, Special Agent Fox proved herself capable over and over without receiving the recognition she rightfully deserved. Why her immediate superiors looked right through her she couldn't understand. It was she who broke up a truly sinister terrorist plot that promised to have far-reaching impact, she who located and arrested the Philadelphia and New York bomber, and she who convinced

Darius Holiday to cooperate. Only as it turned out she was the unfortunate one branded as the agent who failed to protect his family in Pennsylvania from a group known as Satan's Shadow.

The countenance that peered back at her seemed a stranger. In a way she felt pity for the poor soul. Somehow, in addition to the harsh features, it had a pleading lost appearance that desperately sought answers. If she could she would find the killers who hide in shadows and bring them to justice. But, what does that mean—justice? Was the way she had been treated just? At the present time, she was unassigned pending an investigation of events in Wilkes-Barre, Pennsylvania. As a result, she was free to quietly pursue whatever leads she could uncover without interference. Unfortunately, two interviews failed to produce anything of substance. She stared into the eyes of the image in the mirror. Deeper and deeper she sought inspiration, or at the very least, a direction to follow.

Human intelligence was useless and coroner's reports offered facts but not leads. Then in a flash she knew what to do. Batrachotoxin, the poison from South American frogs, was not something that was readily available in the corner drugstore. There had to be a limited number of sources. Find the source and she would be one step closer to her prey—Satan's Shadow.

"There are approximately 4,000 French personnel deployed in Afghanistan," Sergent Pierre Dumont stated. A map of Afghanistan remained on the screen. He pointed at an area northeast of Kabul in Northeastern Afghanistan. "They are all stationed here in Surobi. Not much value to us. For this reason," he looked in the direction of Adam Hayes, Ron Clew, and Michael O'Neal, "we have called upon the aid of the United States Military."

One of the French team members said softly, "I was there on the night of Monday, 18 August 08. It was in the Uzbin Valley, a narrow mountain pass. We were part of a reconnaissance patrol with Afghan troops. I was among the advance party on foot that left our armored vehicles to inspect the pass. We got ambushed by over 100 Taliban fighters armed with IEDs, assault rifles, and rocket-propelled grenades. They came from everywhere. We fought through the night. At dawn, American fighter jets and helicopter gunships arrived." He looked at the three American members of the team, "I never saw a prettier sight." He looked at Sergent Dumont, "Nine brave men died and twenty-one were wounded in that loathsome valley."

A number of the team said softly, "Vive la France."

Pierre Dumont nodded and continued, "We will fly into Farah Airport on an American military transport. He pointed at a dot on the map in southwest Afghanistan. Keep in mind, less than a year ago, the Taliban captured this city and it required two days of fighting by Afghan Armed Forces, backed by the United States Air Force, to force them out. This is by no means a safe zone." He relit his pipe. "We now have confirmation that our package is located in Zaranj. It is approximately 150 clicks south of Farah by a dangerous hardpacked dirt road along the Iranian border. As I said earlier, there are no friendlies there. Once we leave Farah we are on our own. The Americans have allocated three unmarked vehicles for our use. Without question, we will encounter all kinds of shit along the way. We'll travel by day at a visual interval." He stopped and relit his pipe once more. "If we get to Zaranj we will stop at a supposed 'safe house' outside the city. It is there where we will make contact with one of our operatives who will hopefully have better intel. Final details of the operation will then be developed."

"What if we don't get there?" Adam Hayes asked sarcastically.

"Then I blame you."

"Why don't you blame 'Black One'," Adam asked as he pointed at Ron Clew.

"I know you had something to do with that, Pink One," Ron stated with faux venom and a smile.

Adam Hayes also smiled.

It was Michael O'Neal's turn to speak, "Once we make the rescue, if we make the rescue, things might get pretty dicey. Most likely we won't be able to return to Farah on the same road. And, we won't be able to stay where we are. What's the plan?"

"You always were the caution one," Adam commented.

"True, which is why you are still here."

Sergent Dumont described their escape, "There is a paved road that runs northeast through Kadesh, an ancient city that is still living in the twelfth century, and on up to Delaram. Route 606 is a 135-mile-long, two-lane road built by India. It changed what was a 12 to 14-hour trip into a quick 2 hours. They also built the Kandahar–Herat Highway that runs through Delaram and Route 515 to Farah making this city a transportation hub, of sorts. It's all part of the Ring Road system connecting cities in Afghanistan. India built the roads to facilitate their mining operation in

Hajigak. There has also been a signed agreement between India and Iran to build a road and rail line from Zaranj to the Port of Chabahar on the Gulf of Oman.

"Wait, there is a paved road from Farah to Delaram to Zaranj," one of the French team members observed.

"Correct."

"Then why are we planning to take a non-road road to Zaranj?"

"For secrecy. Route 606 is used by many and watched by many more. The western road is relatively ignored because it is mostly used by locals, smugglers, militants, and drug runners."

"Don't forget clandestine military operatives," Adam Hayes added.

"Noted. By sharing the road with treacherous characters that most will make every effort to avoid, we have a better chance of arriving unnoticed."

"Unnoticed is good," Ron Clew commented.

"Yeah, and if we don't get there we will really be unnoticed," Adam concluded.

Sergent Dumont continued, "Leaving, we want to get out of there as quickly as possible. Also, there is not as much scrutiny of vehicles leaving as there is of those arriving. If we get lucky there will be some small convoys traveling north."

There's a United States Marine Forward Operation Base (FOB) located in Delaram. They've built a runway that can accommodate larger aircraft. When we get to Delaram we will be flown out on a chartered French flight to an undisclosed destination."

"If we get to Delaram," Adam reminded Dumont.

"You better make sure that we do."

"Why undisclosed?" one French team member asked.

"The less you know the safer it is. Should you get captured they can cut off your pecker and you won't reveal anything."

"Ouch!" Adam Hayes exclaimed.

"Keep that in mind, Pink One" Ron Clew said as an aside.

Michael O'Neal noted the camaraderie between his friend and the retired Navy Seal. It was a welcome sight. He mentally concluded that just maybe he wouldn't have to babysit any longer.

Even though Alice, his wife, gave him an extremely hard time he was glad that he had come on this mission. She had threatened him, cursed him, and made the most disparaging remarks about Master Sergeant Adam Hayes. The Michael O'Neal temper was eventually ignited. Well-aimed remarks hit their mark with lethal accuracy. Without a doubt he was an effective sniper both with bullets and words. He regretting leaving things the way he did. If it turned out that he was destined to not return, Alice would remember their last encounter with sadness and guilt. That was something he was determined to not let happen.

"Gentlemen," Sergent Dumont's voice brought Michael back to the small staging room. We move out in one hour. Any questions?" When none were posed, he ordered, "Dismissed!"

CHAPTER 53

In a monochromatic world, things appear flat. That's because perception of depth drops precipitously when tint and hue blend into a single-color wash. The effect is both subtle and dramatically obvious. What Team Libertaire encountered were varying shades of tan that stretched out on a flat surface to a distant horizon. This visual anomaly caused a dangerous drive to be all the more hazardless. In addition to hindering the judging of speed and distance, it limited their ability to determine range of incoming threats. Ten men, wearing tan nondescript military uniforms, climbed into three tan vehicles completing a surrealistic scene.

In order to remain somewhat inconspicuous, the vehicles were intentionally non-military. The lead vehicle was an old beat-up Toyota Tundra pickup. Sergent-chef Pierre Dumont and his French Special Operations driver rode point. Second in line was an armored Land Rover with bulletproof glass. It was occupied by Ron Clew and three French commandoes. At the rear of the column was a Nissan Pathfinder carrying Adam Hayes, Michael O'Neal, and two French team members. They were the attack vehicle should there be a need. A trap door on the roof of the Pathfinder allowed for immediate deployment of weapons. By design the vehicles would travel at an extended interval to avoid being seen as a convoy.

All members of Team Libertaire carried automatic weapons. The French commandoes carried Fabrique Nationale Special Operations Forces Combat Assault Rifles (FN SCAR) chambered in 5.56×45mm NATO cartridges. Ron Clew and Adam Hayes carried M16A2 rifles that fire the same 5.56×45mm NATO cartridges while Michael O'Neal had his weapon of choice, an M110 semi-automatic sniper rifle manufactured by the Knights Armament Company. His ammunition was the Federal Cartridge Company M118 Special Ball Long Range Mk316 Mod 0 .308 (7.62x51mm NATO) round. This newer cartridge had calcium carbonate added to the powder which drastically reduced muzzle flash.

As the early morning sun rose into the sky they began their 150-mile trek from Farah to Zaranj. Extra fuel and ammunition were carried in the armored Land Rover. A welcome sight were five other vehicles that began their journey in the same direction. They were welcome because their appearance did not seem to pose a threat. Most likely they were merchants, locals, or delivery personnel heading to Zaranj. In one pickup truck fruits and vegetables were in plain sight. It worked to the team's advantage to blend in with general traffic.

Temperatures were expected to reach a high of 104 degrees by midday. Therefore, an early morning start was prudent at the very least. After two Afghani vehicles departed, Sergent Dumont and his driver followed in the Toyota Tundra on what could be generously called a road. Compacted sand, crushed stone, debris, and blood paved the way south. Of interest, but understandable, no vehicles were seen traveling north. Just as those heading to Zaranj left early in the morning the same was taking place with those heading toward Farah. Very few were brave or foolish enough to travel at night. Eventually the two traffic flows would pass each other going in opposite directions.

The three French vehicles maintained radio silence but could contact each other using satellite telephones. No contact was required at that time. In fact, conversation was also absent as all members of the team were fully occupied watching for any sign of trouble. It could arrive as an improvised explosive device (IED) planted on the road, or from an innocent looking vehicle, or a shot from a sniper, or by ambush by multiple vehicles, or a dozen other sources. The first hour passed uneventfully.

Just before reaching the midpoint of the trip two motorcycles appeared from nowhere and began chasing one of the Afghani vehicles. It was an old Honda station wagon with what appeared to be a family inside. The two motorcycles ridden by young men wearing white robes and carrying AK-47 rifles lined up on both sides of the car. It sped up in a futile attempt to run. The rider on the left side of the car raised his rifle to shoot the driver. He immediately dropped to the ground with the motorcycle flying off into the desert sand, bouncing on its side, and coming to a rest. The other motorcycle rider broke off and disappeared.

"Nice shot," Adam Hayes said as Michael O'Neal sat back down and closed the trap door in the roof of the Nissan Pathfinder.

"Thanks."

"You didn't yell, stop or I'll shoot."

"That was your job."

"I didn't know that. It wasn't covered in the briefing."

"You never pay attention during briefings anyway."

"Bitch, bitch, bitch, I'm sorry I gave you this chance to hone your questionable skills."

"You're too freakin' good to me."

"I know. That's the kinda guy I am." Adam's voice changed to a serious tone, "Did you see that?"

"I caught it."

"Heads up," Adam told the driver, "We may have company."

"Roger that," the driver answered. "What's the bogey?"

"Brown station wagon that passed, eyeballed us a little too long. Two occupants, tarp in back, I think it moved. If they turn around it's game on."

"It's game on," the driver said as he looked in the rearview mirror.

The Uniform Crime Reporting (UCR) system showed that over the past 5 years only 42 homicides using poison were reported. Of those none used Batrachotoxin from the South American Dendrobatidae frog. "That's about to change," Special Agent Peggy Fox commented to herself as she scanned her computer screen. The UCR program was a good starting point as it compiled crime statistics from over 18,000 city, university, county, state, tribal, and federal law enforcement agencies. The program was conceived of in 1929 by the International Association of Chiefs of Police and taken over by the FBI in 1930. As a result, there was a plethora of crime data available to help agency put every type of criminal event in perspective.

She next turned to the National Data Exchange (N-Dex) which shares data across agency and jurisdictional boundaries. While there was information on conventional poisons such as; Strychnine, Cyanide, Sarin, Amatoxin, and Ricin, nothing was available on Batrachotoxin. Methodically, she searched other databases until she found a cache of facts about Batrachotoxin.

Batrachotoxin kills by permanently blocking nerve signal transmission to the muscles. It binds to and irreversibly opens the sodium channels of nerve cells to prevent them from closing. When the neuron can no longer send signals, the result is paralysis. Currently, no effective antidote exists for treatment. Research is limited as there is so little quantity available. There are three species of so-called "poison dart" frogs which contain batrachotoxin in Central America and South America and nine species of bird endemic to New Guinea that have the toxin in their skin and on their feathers. As an agent of biochemical warfare, it is very unlikely to be considered due to the small quantities that frogs can produce, however, the toxins are easily synthesized in a lab and have a long shelf life. For immediate effects, the toxin must be administered subcutaneously, making it an inefficient weapon. It is much more likely to be used as a tool for assassination. "Tell me about it," Peggy Fox commented when she read that part. One last tidbit struck her. Ferdinand Magellan the Portuguese explorer who organized a Spanish expedition to the East Indies from 1519 to 1522 resulting in the first circumnavigation of the Earth, was likely killed by a batrachotoxin-laced dart. It was in the Philippines where tribes were known to use the toxins produced by birds on their weapons.

After a few hours Peggy became anxious as her search was not producing any useful data. It seemed that there was no source for the poison which, of course, meant there were only secret sources. Unless it was brought in from a foreign provider. Once again, her mind flashed three bright letters CIA.

"I don't want you to think that I don't give a toss."

"On the contrary, I think you would like to bring the perpetrator or perpetrators to justice."

"That would be bang on, but there has been little movement from Scotland Yard."

"Standard investigative procedure will not prove fruitful. Further, a nontraditional approach would be outside the scope of Scotland Yard."

"I agree. Most likely they would have cloth ears to any atypical approaches," Bridget Constantine admitted.

"Let me reiterate that I am here on a fact-finding tour—nothing more. However, after reading all those threats and insults that *London Voice* received, I believe you could be in danger. There is no telling what these animals are capable of doing. For that reason, I'm compelled to help—unofficially."

"That would be as right as rain, but what can you do?"

"I had an unofficial discussion with some paramilitary associates of mine," Ken Farmingdale, aka Arthur Thompson, explained. "We believe that the perpetrators who killed your brother are one in the same as the ones who are committing murders in London."

"The ones killing people and leaving a note about that Satan's Shadow group?"

"Yes," Ken knew he had to tread lightly to avoid giving any

impression, even remotely, that he was associated with Satan's Shadow. "The last visitor to be logged in at *London Voice* was Omar Jahandar and many of the threatening emails were signed OJ. In addition, there was reference to 'the criminal group known as Satan's Shadow' in one of the emails which is the same verbiage as the note left with the murder victims."

A chime from a clock on the mantel sounded three times. Bridget Constantine stood from the couch where she had been sitting. "It is low-tea time. Would you join me?" As she headed toward the kitchen she said, "Come."

Ken Farmingdale followed as he continued, "Omar Jahandar is most likely an alias."

"Of course." She changed the subject, "Afternoon tea is called low tea because it is usually taken in a sitting room or withdrawing room where there are low tables like a coffee table or in this case a tea table." She smiled and turned to put the kettle on the stove.

"It appears that they are trying to draw out this Satan's Shadow group with the murders and notes," Ken explained. "The problem is that the Satan's Shadow group could be anywhere. They might not be in the UK or even know about the notes."

"Afternoon tea was actually started by the French in the seventeenth century when it became popular among the aristocracy." Bridget poured a small amount of boiling water into the teapot and sloshed it around before pouring it out. She then added a number of scoops of loose tea followed by boiling water. "In 1662, King Charles II, while in exile, married the Portuguese Infanta, daughter of the king, Catherine de Braganza. Due to the fact that he had grown up in the Dutch capital he and his bride were both tea drinkers. When the monarchy was re-established and they came home to England they brought tea with them. Now, the wealthier classes always did what the royals did so they enthusiastically adopted drinking tea. Eventually, it replaced ale as the national drink." She poured tea through a strainer into two cups and handed a cup and saucer to Ken Farmingdale. "Sugar? Milk?"

"It's fine this way," Ken said.

"In the 1770s and 1780s, it was fashionable to drink tea from saucers. At that time saucers were deeper and more similar to bowls like their Chinese antecedents."

They returned to the sitting room.

"I get the feeling that you would rather not talk about the terrorists," Ken finally said.

"Tommy-rot, I'm as keen as mustard to get the bloody bastards." She sipped her tea and explained, "But first, some tea, quiet reflection, take a deep breath, and then make decisions with a clear mind."

CHAPTER 54

The brown station wagon that had turned around pursued the Nissan Pathfinder carrying Adam Hayes, Michael O'Neal, and two French team members. The French driver of the Nissan slowed to allow them to catch up. Adam Hayes, Michael O'Neal, and one of the French commandoes waited, weapons ready, prepared to dispatch the attacker.

"Alerte, plus de problems," the French driver shouted, forgetting to speak English.

"Qu'Est-ce que c'est, what is it?" the other French commando asked.

"Two bogies ten o'clock and two o'clock coming quickly."

A light green pickup truck with a machine gun mounted in the bed had come from behind a sand dune and was approaching them from the front left side. On the right side in front, another vehicle came at them. This third vehicle was a white Toyota 4Runner with tinted windows. It would take less than a minute for the three vehicles to converge on the Team Libertaire vehicle.

Michael O'Neal jumped up, pushed open the trapdoor in the roof, aimed, and took out the driver of the brown station wagon that was behind them. Bullets from the machine gun in the pickup truck pinged the side of the Nissan as the driver swerved to be less of a target. Adam Hayes and the French commando fired out the window at the approaching truck. They concentrated their fire on the combatant that manned the machine gun. Given all of the evasive maneuvers of both vehicles the gunner was untouched and continued to fire. By this time another Taliban fighter took over driving the brown station wagon and it was once more approaching the team from behind.

The French commando driver swerved off the road into the desert sand and a free-wheeling dance of death began. When facing multiple attackers, a logical and effective tactic is to keep them from surrounding you by always keeping one attacker between you and the others. This reduces their ability to strike while allowing for the defender to concentrate on the closest opponent. In this case the brown station wagon. Due to its position the machine gun in the pickup truck was rendered useless. As the station wagon attempted to swerve out of the line of fire the French driver turned in a direction that allowed them to continue to use the it as a shield. AK-47 fire came from the station wagon. With two quick shots Michael "Owl" O'Neal silenced the guns. Only the driver remained in the station wagon. He stopped, but the dance continued.

No longer blocked by the other vehicle the machine gun on the pickup truck once more opened fire. Glass shattered and rained down on the team. The French driver turned and drove directly at the pickup truck. Head on they closed the gap. Adam and his French comrade finally took out the machine gunner and the pickup truck broke off the attack.

All eyes turned toward the white Toyota 4Runner. It had maneuvered to a point where its side was facing the Nissan and stopped. They were less than a hundred yards apart. Two Taliban fighters left the SUV and were aiming rocket propelled grenades at the Team Libertaire vehicle. Time stopped. The combatants jumped from the SUV but knew no rifle shot would keep those weapons from being fired.

Emanuel Vegas, senior agent with the Secret Service, sat in a safe house and spoke with General Hughes on their secure, encrypted satellite telephone. "There has been a terrorist attack in Germany," Vegas stated.

"Oh? What are the details?"

"A group of Islamic refugees attacked and raped young women at a public pool."

"Bastards."

"There were eight perpetrators. They brazenly did their attack in the middle of the day in front of horrified onlookers."

"Son-of-a-bitch!"

"When it was over they walked off grinning with their fists in the air daring anyone to stop them."

"Have they been identified?"

There was a long silence which caused General Hughes to ask his question, once more, "Have the perpetrators been identified?"

"Their bodies have."

"Bodies?"

"All eight were found in a remote forest, hands tied behind their backs, genitals mutilated, and throats cut."

"Sounds appropriate. What about family and friends."

"Unknown. There's more," Emanuel Vegas said, "along with the bodies was a note, 'Terrorism has a price. If you commit a terrorist act your family is the price you pay. We will locate and kill every member of your family, your friends, associates, and any who offered you support. Through your actions you condemn them all to death. They can hide but we will find them. Satan's Shadow is everywhere.' Sound familiar?"

"It seems we have some copycats—welcome allies, if you ask me."

"Not copycats an awakened Bavarian Lion," Vegas observed.

"The house of Wittelsbach," General Hughes observed. "The Wittelsbach dynasty ruled the German territory of Bavaria from about 1180AD. They used the now familiar lion as a heraldic symbol. The House of Wittelsbach reigned as kings of Bavaria until 1918 when Ludwig III released his soldiers and officials from their oath of loyalty to him, thereupon declaring it a republic."

"You know a lot about that history."

"During World War II, the Wittelsbachs were anti-Nazi. The family initially left Germany for Hungary, but were eventually arrested and spent time in several Nazi concentration camps including Oranienburg and Dachau. Let's hope this newly awakened lion has that same strength of character and desire for justice."

"And, what might our role be?"

"It appears they are taking their self-defense into their own hands. Let's see how it plays out."

"An unexpected consequence of our actions."

"Not completely unanticipated. If you recall we discussed the potential for citizens to fight back when the terrorists are shown to be vulnerable. All we can hope is that we start that snowball down the proverbial hill."

"Do you think the families and friends of those eight degenerates will pay the price, as well?"

"I hope so. If not, they are just eight martyrs."

There is a small cottage for rent on Freshfield Road," Bridget Constantine told Ken Farmingdale as they sat in her parlor. She continued, "It's no oil painting. Small with a fenced in backyard. A bit manky."

"How many floors?"

"All on one level."

"What about rooms?"

"There's a meeting room in front, small kitchen, two bedrooms, and a loo."

"What about the neighborhood and street?"

"Quiet street, narrow, few automobiles, a little rundown. There were a couple of moggies."

"Moggies?"

"Alley cats."

"Oh, I see." Ken Farmingdale made a few notes on a piece of paper and then suggested, "We should go there so that I can look it over and draw a floorplan. We, of course, will underwrite the rental and other expenses."

"Ta, however, I can afford it, I'm not all fur coat and no knickers." Bridget smiled.

"That fact is exceedingly clear," Ken, aka Arthur, said with a warm smile as he grew to like Bridget more and more.

"I might go all collywobbles, but I have to do this for Patrick and the others that died at *London Voice*."

"I know, and we are going to help you," Ken reassured her. "At the moment, the associates I have in mind are on a short assignment. This will give us time to develop a plan and prepare our trap."

"Whatever you need me to do, I'll do. I'm not a bottler. No matter what kind of go, I'll do my part."

Ken Farmingdale saw the emotion in her blue eyes and the strength behind them. She was determined to find justice for those who were lost. Inside, he wanted to tell her that he was, indeed, Satan's Shadow and these culprits would not be alive very much longer. Of course, he knew he couldn't make such a confession. Instead, he reached out and took her hand and said, "I can assure you the people I have enlisted to identify and punish these murderers are professional in every sense of the word. They will apprehend or eliminate these criminals."

Bridget Constantine sat motionless. Silence draped the room like a shroud. Two strangers confronted their own feelings and goals and expectations. At that moment no more needed to be said. A clock on the mantel ticked along with silent heartbeats. Even light from outside seemed subdued in the stillness. Moments passed.

Finally, Bridget Constantine spoke softly, "Dispatched is the preferred outcome."

"Special Agent Fox, until further notice you will not be assigned any field interviews or be the lead on any investigations," the FBI Executive

Assistant Director for National Security Branch stated flatly.

A cold chill ran through her body as she attempted to conceal her anger. She felt light-headed and a slight sense of nausea made standing in front of his desk difficult. After a second, she composed herself and asked, "What will I be doing?"

"You will be assigned to the Record/Information Dissemination Section (RIDS) in the Information Management Division responsible for the release of records under the Freedom of Information Act (FOIA) and the Privacy Act."

"That's a goddamned clerical position!" Peggy Fox blurted out in anger.

Unaffected, the Executive Assistant Director for National Security Branch replied, "Until the dust settles on the unfortunate occurrence in Pennsylvania and we can review your record and capabilities that is where you will remain."

"You forget that I'm the one who caught Holiday and broke up a serious terrorist plot."

"Your country thanks you," he answered sarcastically.

"I was against using the Holiday family as bait. Or have you forgotten that?"

"It's in your jacket."

"Along with the Wilkes-Barre fiasco that I opposed, I presume."

"Maybe, if you spent less time being against the assignment and more time executing it we would not have three dead bodies."

"That's not fair and you know it."

"All I know are the facts."

"All the facts or just the ones you want to remember?"

"You're dismissed, Agent Fox," the Executive Assistant Director for National Security Branch picked up his telephone receiver to purportedly make a call.

Special Agent Peggy Fox didn't know who she hated more the Executive Assistant Director for National Security Branch or Satan's Shadow.

CHAPTER 55

A Rocket propelled Grenade (RPG) is an inexpensive way of delivering an explosive payload over a distance with moderate accuracy. It became a weapon of choice in Afghanistan when available. One limitation is that RPG rockets cannot be controlled in flight after being aimed and launched. For this reason, a common tactic is to have two, three, or four rockets launched at the same time. Mujahideen guerrillas used captured Russian RPG-7s to destroy Soviet vehicles when they were invaders.

When an RPG operator pulls the trigger, the rocket is launched by a gunpowder booster charge which forces built-up gases out of the tube launching the grenade at 384 feet-per-second. This rapid acceleration of the grenade leaving the launcher triggers a piezoelectric fuse which ignites a primer that activates the rocket propulsion system. The most commonly launched grenades are High Explosive (HE) or High Explosive Anti-tank (HEAT) rounds. While most are impact grenades, a backup time-delay system of approximately four and a half seconds will cause the grenade to self-destruct.

Michael "Owl" O'Neal, Adam "Watch Dog" Hayes, and two French Special Operations soldiers stared at the front end of two RPGs aimed directly at them. Each man knew there was not enough time to aim and fire, run, or even duck. In an instant, heat from the explosion knocked them backwards, debris and sand pelted them, an ear-shattering boom left them temporarily deafened, and a flash of white-hot light bleached their retinas. All four warriors fell to the sand.

"Holy, fucken crap! What the hell happened?" Adam Hayes barked while lying on his back.

"Drone," Michael O'Neal said as he slowly sat up, dusted sand from his clothes, wiped it from his eyes, and spit it out of his mouth.

"Oh, mon Dieu," one of the French members of the team said.

"Drone? Whose drone?" Adam asked.

"Who cares," Michael answered.

"I care. I want to send the operator a box of cigars." He looked over at the crater where the white Toyota 4Runner had been. Twisted metal, broken glass, shreds of rubber, unidentifiable debris, and a single leather sandal lay around the point of impact.

Michael O'Neal stood and looked at the wreckage. "I would guess it was one of ours. Why they were tracking us I haven't got the foggiest idea, but I'm glad they were."

"Maybe they were following them and we just got in the way," Adam offered.

"We were toast, you know that?"

"My whole life flashed in front of me," Adam joked. "It wasn't a pretty sight."

"I'm sure."

"We best get back on the road," the French commando driver said as he motioned toward the Nissan Pathfinder.

With the entertainment over the remainder of the journey was completed without incident.

Shahin Pouran sipped tea from a small cup as he pondered his effort to draw out the infidel group known as Satan's Shadow. His efforts had not produced any results. In addition, all attempts to recruit supporters to his cause had fallen on deaf ears. As a result, he grew more and more impatient. Not long ago they were all motivated and driven to spread their message through fear and suffering. Now, they seemed complacent. He felt as though he stood alone. This could not be tolerated.

A conversation he had that morning angered him. A trusted friend and jihadist spoke of concern for his family, his sons, and his daughters. He spoke of this Satan's Shadow as something to be feared. To Shahin, they were something to be hated and hunted down and executed. The other man simply stared at him. He no longer exhibited the confidence, strength, or hunger of a mujahideen. Instead, a merchant, or farmer, or common laborer sat opposite him. It sickened him. With an angry voice he told the man to go, get out of his sight.

One thing became clear to Shahin Pouran. He would have to increase the incidence and severity of his attacks. Or, it would be necessary to include high profile persons. Further contemplation brought forth a number of names that would serve his purpose.

FBI Special Agent Peggy Fox reread her letter requesting a leave of absence. After a sleepless night, she concluded that there was nothing to lose. If she accepted a transfer into the Record/Information Dissemination Section she would be lost among the millions of files until retirement. That was unacceptable. A combination of accrued vacation time and her savings would allow for a minimum of six months to pursue whatever she wished.

The decision made, citizen Peggy Fox would use her training and skills to seek and identify those who called themselves Satan's Shadow. As it was only a leave of absence she would retain her identification as an FBI agent which would open many doors. Unhindered by Bureau regulations and legal constraints she could use whatever means available to pursue her objective.

Unfortunately, there was little with which to start. No evidence had been found at the three locations where the murders of the Holiday family had taken place. She would review the files on the murders of the Hillsman family members after Ralph Hillsman, a seventeen-year-old senior at Torrey Pines High School, killed five and wounded three on a Friday afternoon. His brother, Michael, had been killed in his dorm room at Auburn University, mother and father killed at their home, and aunt, Michelle Gillespie, shot in the head. Peggy Fox made notes on a yellow pad as she prepared her plan-of-action.

Even though disappointed, angered, and frustrated by her treatment by those in power at the FBI, Peggy Fox was energized. It was the hunt that offered a welcome feeling. She loved a challenge and through the years proved to be up to the task far more often than not. A thought drifted through her mind, "Maybe, that's why her supervisors disliked her and worked against her—they were jealous and threatened by her." It was a random thought but added significant fuel to her fire. Alone in her apartment, in a near whisper, Peggy Fox declared, "I will bring down Satan's Shadow and let them choke on it."

With one page full she lifted the yellow paper to fold it over the top of the pad. It made a familiar crinkling sound. It was a sound that echoed in her ears. A mind alive and ravenous for something to digest delivered idea after idea. The notes! A common thread at all the crime scenes. Without question the paper and ink would have been analyzed by the Bureau and a scan made for any latent prints. But, what about non-evidential characteristics? The way the paper was folded. Each note had to be carried to the crime scene—most likely in a pocket. Were there any indentations that might indicate what else was in that pocket? Any substances on the paper would have been noted in a lab report. Most likely common expected traces would have been ignored. Yet, they could tell an incriminating story. Agent Fox considered the verbiage. Did the construction of sentences, words used, or style indicate any type of education or professional background? What about the actual message? Does it indicate a certain philosophy, ideology, or moral position? Does it reveal more than the authors wished to be known? At that moment, Peggy Fox decided the Satan's Shadow notes were her starting point.

The small cottage on Freshfield Road had been empty for a while. Inside it had a damp mildew smell. It was dark and the floor creaked as they walked through the meeting room toward the kitchen in the rear of the house. Ken Farmingdale opened the back door and looked out at the privacy fenced backyard. It was small with a cement patio. He heard water run behind him, turned, and saw Bridget Constantine testing the kitchen faucet. A small hall led off to the right. On either side of the hall was a small bedroom. At the end the bathroom.

"All the comforts of . . ." Ken looked around, "uh, a dump."

"Quite."

"After we clean it up, we'll go out and buy some furniture," he stated. "Once more, we will pay for it, however, I want you to make the purchase and have the furniture delivered to this address using your real name."

"Tracks in the snow."

"Exactly."

Bridget opened a few cupboards which were empty, closed them, turned, and asked, "So, Mr. Action Man, what is the plan?"

Ken Farmingdale smiled, "How the hell should I know? I'm just a liaison from the State Department. The strategic thinkers will develop a plan and let us know." After a pause he added, "Let me remind you, this whole affair is unofficial. We have no legal jurisdiction and quite honestly would create an international incident if the authorities found us operating a sting clandestinely."

"You are a cheeky monkey, that's for sure." Bridget walked over to the hallway then spun around and stated, "I'm not backward at coming forward so I'll tell you what I think."

Ken remained silent and waited.

"I think your State Department story is tommy-rot. But, you're not a blag artist. If I thought you were, you'd be in the bin bag by now. I'd bet a bar you have some connection to that Satan's Shadow organization. I don't give a toss. In fact, it would be a bit of alright. This is no piddling matter. To put it plainly, I want justice. More than that I want revenge. When they murdered my brother, they killed a part of me. He and I had a hard life, but we also had each other. He was my strength and I was his moral compass."

Ken felt vulnerable but remained silent to hear what else she had to say.

"The police aren't going to do anything. In fact, I'd prefer that they let the dog see the rabbit. When you arrived at my door you were my angel. Remember, Satan is a fallen angel. Where you came from, who you are, why you wish to help doesn't matter one bob. I'm just jarred-off enough to make a deal with the devil. So, don't play the innocent game with me. I'm not Doris. We are co-conspirators. Now, what is the plan?"

"In truth, I don't know what the professionals will decide to be the best tactic. What I do know is we will attract your brother's killer or killers to this place using you as bait. When they make an attempt on your life our team will neutralize them."

"I know it's no one's cup of tea, but I'll do my part," Bridget said, adding, "I might need a stiffener, but I'll jog on."

Ken Farmingdale smiled. He neither denied nor addressed her comments about Satan's Shadow.

CHAPTER 56

A moonless night in Afghanistan is dark—completely dark—ominously dark. Few venture out even with the aid of lanterns, or flashlights, or vehicle lights. To begin, very little reflects back which significantly limits range of view. In addition, using any form of illumination makes one an easy target. Finally, in the outskirts of villages, there is little reason to travel. If you didn't accomplish what you wanted during daylight hours it could wait until the next day when it is safer.

On this moonless night three nondescript vehicles were hidden behind the rubble of a once-proud residence. Team Libertaire had snaked through narrow streets and wide-open desert after dark using night-vision technology. It was a slow and methodical process. Once in place, ten warriors began Operation Dégager which means extricate. Three commandoes stood guard over the vehicles along with the team commander, Sergent-chef Pierre Dumont. The other six commandoes began their two-click trek in darkness.

Earlier when they arrived in Zaranj before noon, they had proceeded directly to a predetermined location on the outskirts of the city. A tall adobe ruins, which now stood as a deteriorating skeleton of a long-passed culture, offered privacy and cover. When they arrived the three tan vehicles circled the structure and entered what appeared to be a courtyard. There they waited.

Their contact was a local merchant who quietly supported the Afghanistan government by providing intelligence and material support. He hated the Taliban. He had lived through their oppressive and brutal dominance over the country. His business suffered greatly, many of his friends disappeared, they took much of his wealth, and one of his sons was executed before his eyes. His hatred ran deep.

Known only by his nickname Sheragha, master of the lion, he agreed to assist the rescue effort. As a merchant he was able to overhear conversations, tactfully gather additional information, and make valuable observations. There was nothing suspicious about his driving his old Nissan Maximum into any neighborhood which he did quite often. As he did so, a small action cam cleverly camouflaged under an old straw fedora in his back window recorded every inch of the location where Kareem Reza's twenty-five-year-old son, Faraz, was believed being held. His efforts gave Team Libertaire a detailed description of the location and the many challenges they faced.

A chill greeted the team as they proceeded to the target dubbed Waterloo. At an agreed upon point, Michael O'Neal left the team and proceeded silently to a large sand dune that overlooked the compound. He would act as security for the team, as well as backup. All ten combatants were connected by Motorola RMU2040 Two-Way Radios with C-shaped earpieces. These mil-spec radios offer 89 exclusive frequencies with codes, voice scrambling, and extended range. They would remain radio silent unless someone screwed the pooch.

Owl O'Neal settled in at his FFP and scanned the area with an ATN ThOR 4 1.25-5x Thermal Vision Smart HD Riflescope. High definition images gave him a clear view of the target area. The 5x zoom allowed for close inspection. All was quiet. Waterloo was a three-story adobe building surrounded by a six-foot-high adobe wall. The main entrance was protected with a Madrid style, six-foot-high, single swing, steel gate. The building structure had pens on the first level for goats, camels, and other animals, as well as a garage for a non-running automobile. Stone stairs led to the second level where a rooftop patio was located and the front door to the living quarters. The top floor was used for storage and housed the kitchen. It was the second floor that was the objective of the commandoes. Sheragha estimated that there were four men and three women in the home, but couldn't be sure. There also were guards in the courtyard.

The assault team comprised of Adam Hayes, Ron Clew, and three French commandoes approached the compound in the dark. U.S. Army ATN PVS72 Tactical Night Vision Goggles allowed them to move with ease. The five rescuers reached the wall quickly and silently. One of the French commandoes was lifted by the others to peer over the six-foot wall. Inside he saw that candles had been placed into cubbyholes in the walls to provide adequate light for two guards who sat at opposite ends of the courtyard. From their positions they were able to see the entire courtyard and each other. The low glow from the candles also would allow anyone inside the structure to see shadows of any intruders.

The two guards sat staring into darkness. They were staring, eyes open, but their minds drifted in other directions. Each man was lost in a world of the id unaware of their actual surroundings. This is the inevitable result of weeks upon weeks of the tedium of watching for something that never comes. On this night it came. Two French commandoes lifted to the top of the wall simultaneously dropped in unison next to the guards who, before they could react, were neutralized.

In but a few moments the front gate was opened to allow the other rescuers to join the team. Using hand signals, they moved silently toward the adobe building. A quick search confirmed that no other guards were on the ground floor level. In fact, the entire compound remained silent. Team Libertaire scaled the stone stairs to the rooftop patio. Once again, using hand signals they established the order of entry. Michael O'Neal watched the progress of the team through his rifle night vision scope.

Five invaders entered the second floor in a silent rush. The element of surprise, darkness, and night vision goggles it gave the rescue team a distinct advantage. Two guards were quickly dispatched and a second was shot as he reached for an AK-47. In a side room they found twenty-five-year-old Faraz. He seemed dazed and confused. One of the French commandoes said in French, "Nous sommes ici pour vous libérer, we are here to free you." He led the young man to the door and handed him off to Adam Hayes. Two women entered from the third floor and were detained.

From his vantage point on the sand dune, Michael O'Neal watched as Adam Hayes led the rescued Frenchman out of the building onto the rooftop patio. In the dark it was necessary for Adam to hold the man's arm to guide him. He turned to lead the way down the stone stairs. At that moment, Faraz Reza plunged a knife into Adam Hayes' back. The American retired Green Beret spun around to see the green night vision face of a smiling attacker. He also saw the man's head explode from a sniper's bullet. For a brief second Adam looked in the direction of where Michael O'Neal was positioned and gave a thumbs up. He dropped slowly to the ground.

"Man down, location secure, extricate team," Michael said into his radio.

Upon hearing the message Sergent-chef Pierre Dumont ordered the drivers to proceed to the compound designated as Waterloo. Michael O'Neal left his position and ran full speed in the direction of his fallen friend.

All fighters inside the building had been eliminated. The French commandoes then led the two women they had captured out onto the rooftop patio. In the dark one of the women stumbled over the body of Faraz Reza. With no longer any reason for secrecy Ron Clew lit a flashlight revealing the scene.

The woman yelled, "Faraz!" She turned toward Clew and bellowed, "You killed my husband."

Ron Clew handed off the woman to another commando and went to aid Adam Hayes. He found his friend near death. As he tried to put pressure on the wound Adam Hayes whispered, "Tell Owl, I'm sorry." He died in the arms of the Navy Seal.

Upon questioning, Faraz wife revealed that her husband was one of the insurgents and the kidnapping story was a ruse to get the cooperation of Kareem Reza. She defiantly spat insults at the commandoes.

Two body bags were loaded into the bed of the Toyota Tundra pickup. The three-vehicle caravan then sped north on a two-lane paved road called Route 606, also known as the Delaram-Zaranj Highway. The 135-mile-long road was financed by development grants from the Government of India. It was designed and constructed by the Border Roads Organization (BRO) of India and became one of the busiest roads in Afghanistan. That was during daylight hours. Route 606 reduced travel time between Zaranj and Delaram from 12–14 hours to just 2 hours. It was opened in 2009.

Team Libertaire was alone on the dark deserted highway. In the third vehicle, a tan Nissan Pathfinder Michael O'Neal sat silently in the dark. He was in a dark place that was darker than the Afghan sky.

The London Symphony finished a gala performance playing various pieces by Tchaikovsky, Bach, Mendelsohn, and Beethoven. A packed house applauded enthusiastically and called for more. After playing a preplanned short encore the evening was over. A packed-house audience shuffled out of the Barbican Centre. Various musicians left the stage, packed their instruments, and headed home.

Trevor Bernard Howard played first violin. He had done so for thirty years. Music lived in his heart and his soul. On this evening he was delayed by a telephone call from his daughter. She announced that she was engaged to be married. Trevor was overjoyed as he knew and liked the young man. He also knew the call was ultimately coming as his future son-in-law was old-school enough to ask for his permission before proposing. On the call with his daughter a lengthy conversation and lots of smiles followed. Due to the delay, he was alone when he left the concert hall and entered the car park garage on Silk Street.

Music played in Trevor Bernard Howard's mind as he walked slowly to his automobile. The garage was relatively empty with just a few cars remaining. His footsteps echoed in the structure as the violinist, carrying his musical instrument, approached his car.

It had been a long night for Shahin Pouran. He planned to wait in hiding until the last few stragglers from the concert entered his trap. From the beginning, he planned to strike a musician from the London Symphony as that would garner significant media attention. Then as the garage became more and more empty he became concerned that he would miss an opportunity. That was until Trevor Bernard Howard arrived.

The element of surprise and a distracted victim made the attack quick and easy. In less than a minute the music stopped.

CHAPTER 57

"It wasn't a terrorist attack—it was a military action."

"My ass!"

"We entered where he was, in force."

"Don't insult my intelligence," General Hughes spat. "He was one of them. The whole kidnapping story was a ruse and we all fell for it."

"There are extenuating circumstances."

"The hell there are. One of my men died at the hands of a terrorist. It was a mission that should never have been executed."

"I truly regret that—je m'excuse."

"Shove your apology. Where do you have Kareem Reza sequestered? And, I want a list of his relatives."

"I cannot tell you."

"Cannot or will not?"

"Take your pick, that information is unavailable."

"Terrorism has a price. If you commit a terrorist act your family is the price you pay. We will locate and kill every member of your family, your friends, associates, and any who offered you support. Through your actions you condemn them all to death. They can hide but we will find them. Satan's Shadow is everywhere."

Peggy Fox read and reread the message left by Satan's Shadow at all the murder scenes. Nothing jumped out at her. Over and over she read the words, counted the sentences, noted grammatical errors, considered words used, and finally referred to *Pamphlet 600-67; Effective Writing for Army Leaders.* As she read she compared the pamphlet's recommendations to the note. Put the main idea first. Check. Write in an active voice. Check. She then found a formula to determine the "Clarity Index." Count the number of words—57. Then count the number of sentences—6. Divide the number of words by the number of sentences—9.5. Next, count the number of words with three or more syllables—7. Divide by number of words to get percentage with 3 or more syllables—12%. Add the two outcomes 9.5 plus 12—21.5. That is the Clarity Index. The Army pamphlet states, "Use the following Rules of Thumb for the clarity index: (1) Below 20, writing is too abrupt. (2) Over 40, writing is difficult to understand. (3) Aim for an index of 30." The Satan's Shadow note definitely had an acceptable Army Clarity Index. While far from conclusive, Peggy Fox was convinced the author was military.

Agent Fox ruled out active military as it was her opinion that an operation such as this would have to be authorized at the highest level which just wouldn't happen. With the many hands involved and levels of command it would leak even if only internally at the FBI and Department of Justice. Finally, history shows that a secret operation would still be sloppy enough to leave clues at the crime scene. Those considerations directed her to retired military.

She also concluded Satan's Shadow was too sophisticated to be comprised of only enlisted men or women. It would require leadership from a strong, highly respected, persuasive, upper-level-rank individual. The operation would have to be made up of highly trained, adaptable, seasoned combat veterans, adept at stealth and willing to do what had to be done to complete a mission. She came back to the need for a charismatic leader. He would have to present a compelling argument to get ex-military to step out of their comfort zone—way out of their comfort zone—to become criminals. Slowly, she developed a mental profile of such a leader. He would be combat seasoned, well-respected, well-known, a bit of a maverick, maybe a loner, stubborn, educated, and patriotic. As hard as it was to believe, it would be his patriotism that was the driving force. Killing innocent people as a strategy to inhibit terrorism offers no personal gain or satisfaction. Instead, it only offers risk and ultimate disgrace and prosecution. He believes he is doing a very difficult thing to protect the lives of innocent Americans. Most likely he is convinced that a few innocent lives are a small price to pay to reduce the threat to hundreds maybe thousands of American lives.

Peggy Fox reviewed her notes. She was convinced that the military angle was the correct one. There was one sticking point, however. Funding had to come from somewhere. An operation like Satan's Shadow was not cheap. Once more, her mind saw three letters—CIA.

Given all of her analysis and conjecture, Agent Fox considered where to begin with her search for the military connection. She knew she would have to put in needed hours to review the records of all the high-level officers who retired from all branches of service over the past five years. The challenge didn't bother her. She just didn't want to come up empty-handed.

As Peggy thought about her next steps, a memory flashed brightly in her mind. A sniper was highly trained, experienced in stealth tactics, and accustomed to killing. Yet, none of the murders were accomplished using a sniper. That didn't mean a sniper wasn't trained in alternative assassination technique. The name Michael O'Neal presented itself. Did she overlook something? Could the very man she used as a consultant get us going in one direction only to go unnoticed in a different one. Was it possible that Michael O'Neal was able to implement a heinous poisoning scheme right under their noses using his involvement with the FBI as cover? It was possible, if not probable. She wondered how could she even investigate such a likelihood. Peggy Fox shook her head as she said to herself, "You're getting carried away chasing leprechauns."

The next obvious question was, what connection Secret Service Agent Emanuel Vegas had with the plot—if there was a plot. Why did he recommend Michael O'Neal? What connection, if any, do they have with Satan's Shadow or the CIA? Is there more there than it seems? It was a slender thread, but one that could not be ignored.

As she gathered the three notes that were in the evidence locker something unexpected happened. Her fingertip felt a slight indentation on one of the notes. Barely perceptible, she took out a magnifying glass and examined the anomaly. It was circular, much like a large coin. Unfortunately, a combination of printing on the paper and shallow depth of the indentation made it nearly impossible to determine what was on that coin. Agent Fox used her smartphone as a flashlight and backlit the note. Still not clear. She then laid the note down on the desk and used a flashlight to light it from the side. After taking a photograph and downloading it onto her computer she was able to enhance the image. Agent Peggy Fox stared at the round edge of a coin and a partial image of a dragon.

There is nothing comfortable about a military transport. In most cases you drop your gear and find a place to sit, or squat, or lay down. No comfortable seats, stewardesses, warm towels, or liquor. The Boeing C-40 Clipper is a military version of the Boeing 737-700C airline transport. It is used by both the United States Navy and the United States Air Force. Michael O'Neal found himself in the cargo section of an Air Force C-40 Clipper sitting alone on a drop seat. Along with other transport containers was one carrying the body of Adam "Watch Dog" Hayes.

The flight originated in Forward Operating Base (FOB) Delaram, Afghanistan a military expeditionary base built by the United States Marine Corps. It was originally a Soviet military compound. When the Marines arrived the initial structure of the base was only temporary and did not have a landing strip for airplanes. It became home to the 3rd Battalion of the 4th Marines and a paved runway was constructed. Accommodations were made for Michael O'Neal and the fallen Green Beret to return to the United States. It struck Michael deeply when the aircraft taxied to the runway and numerous Marines stopped what they were doing to salute as they took off.

The flight plan was to refuel at Aviano Air Base in Italy and then on to Langley Air Force Base in Hampton, Virginia. Arrangements would be made for burial in Arlington National Cemetery. Master Sergeant Adam Howard Hayes, Green Beret, recipient of a Silver Star, would take his place among the nation's honored dead.

The first soldier buried in Arlington National Cemetery was 21-year-old Private William Christman of Pennsylvania. He died of peritonitis and was buried May 13, 1864. Formerly the estate of Robert E. Lee, Arlington was seized by the government for failure to pay a tax bill of $92.07. Quartermaster General Montgomery C. Meigs proposed Arlington as the location of a new military cemetery when Washington D.C. was on the verge of running out of burial space. There are soldiers from every American war buried in this place of honor.

Michael O'Neal sat lost among memories of a lost friend. He and Watch Dog had chewed a lot of the same dirt, shivered in the cold together, fought side-by-side, made it through some hairy situations, and watched each other's backs. It was that last thought that haunted Owl. Could he have reacted faster? One second might have saved his friend. Did he see the man reach under his robe? Was there something, anything, that he missed? Guilt found a home and prepared to remain for a long time.

Surrounded by the hum of the C-40 Clipper's jet engines, Michael O'Neal stared into the cargo hold and said, "Damn you, Hayes! Why the hell did you have to bring me into this. You could have gone out and gotten yourself killed without me having to witness it. Or, be a part of it. Or, be responsible for it." Michael turned the coin he had found in his friend's pocket over and over. He recognized it as a challenge coin—not one he had seen before. On the front a dragon, sword, and a circle of thirteen stars. The reverse had the words inscribed; Est ultra de tenebris et in umbra satanas. He didn't know the translation was, "it is beyond dark in Satan's shadow" but knew enough to recognize "satanas" as meaning Satan. "Man, you stepped in it this time. I guess you believed what you were doing was for the better good. You'd never do anything that you thought would hurt your country. And, maybe this approach is logical, but you had to know it would only lead you to nowhere. I guess you knew it was a form of slow suicide. I guess that was the only end for you and you knew it." Michael O'Neal slipped the challenge coin back into his pocket.

When the jet landed at Aviano Air Base in Italy the pilot told Michael there would be approximately an hour layover. Slowly, Michael descended the stairs to the tarmac. When he reached the bottom he noticed a man wearing a tan shirt and green pants standing straight and tall apparently waiting for him. The man's short-cropped grey hair, weathered face, and stature indicated that he was a high-ranking officer of some kind. Michael O'Neal walked in his direction.

"Michael O'Neal?"

"Yes sir, I am Michael O'Neal."

"I'm Maxwell Hughes," he offered his hand. "I'm sorry to hear about Adam Hayes, he was a fine man."

"Adam Hayes was one-of-a-kind and anyone who got to know him was fortunate beyond their own understanding," Michael stated.

"I couldn't have said it better. Can I buy you a cup of coffee?" General Hughes asked.

Two men sat in a coffee shop in the terminal sizing each other up. After a few minutes General Hughes said, "I have been briefed on what happened in Afghanistan. It was a dirty business. I recommended Adam for the mission which is something that I will regret for a long time."

"We all knew what we were getting into. We just didn't know we'd get CATFUED. Nothing in the 411 even remotely indicated the possibility," Michael O'Neal paused, sipped some coffee, and added, "I only went to watch Adam's back. I really did a helluva job with that."

"You couldn't have known—none of us knew."

"Doesn't make it any easier."

"No, it doesn't." General Hughes leaned back and asked, "Did Adam ever tell you anything about our relationship?"

"The only thing he told me about was this mission."

"I see."

"He never said anything, but I got the impression he was involved with something clandestine," Michael looked directly at General Hughes, "something dangerous and quite illegal."

“What makes you say that?”

“Come’on, we both know how close partners are able to read each other. He never said anything and I can’t and won’t try to prove it, but he might have been associated with the group known as Satan’s Shadow.”

General Hughes hid his surprise as he stated, “That’s quite a leap.”

“If the loss of a few tired warriors saves countless lives it will be a welcome epitaph.”

“What’s that?”

“Something he said to me when I cautioned him about getting involved with the wrong type of operation.”

“There is still no substance to your conclusion.”

“Sir, I have no intention of sharing my speculation with anyone. Adam “Watch Dog” Hayes died trying to rescue a French citizen. He died with honor. Let him rest in peace.” Michael O’Neal rose from the table, reached into his pocket and retrieved the challenge coin, put it on the table in front of General Hughes, turned, and left.

CHAPTER 58

Aboard the Ismenios, Ronald Clew stood on the bridge with Jarvis Demoye who piloted the craft. They were headed north toward Great Britain to assist Ken Farmingdale. Ron had held Adam Hayes as he whispered, "Tell Owl, I'm sorry." He delivered the message to Master Sergeant Hayes' friend and added his own comment, "No better man ever served with me."

"It's a damn shame," Jarvis Demoye said to no one in particular.

"You know, when this dirty business is over, it would be the best way to go—on the battlefield rather than rotting in some prison cell," Ron Clew stated reflectively.

"On the battlefield is one thing, betrayal is something different."

"Unfortunately, we most likely won't be given a choice."

"When this began did you give much thought to where you would end up?" Jarvis asked.

"If you look beyond the present you lose focus and may just sacrifice the future."

Jarvis Demoye pondered, "I've wondered if we succeed in slowing or stopping the epidemic of terrorism whether or not there will be a way to sail off into obscurity."

Ron Clew looked out at the ocean. Choppy waves bounced the craft and spray washed across the windshield. His mind returned to Lexington, Kentucky where his little brother was a police officer. He remembered when he told his brother who wanted him to join the force, "Settling down isn't in my future." More than ever that was an accurate statement. He looked at Retired Navy Captain Jarvis Demoye and said, "I hope you find your way to a quiet port knowing you helped save countless innocent lives."

Jarvis replied, "I can't help thinking about Jules Verne's *Twenty Thousand Leagues Under the Sea.* Captain Nemo in his submarine Nautilus wanted to end all war. Of course, that is an impossibility. In the end, he was lost along with his submarine." Captain Demoye looked at Ron Clew and concluded, "We cannot put a stop to all terrorism, that's a fact. So, what is the end game?"

Once more thinking about his police officer brother, Ron Clew concluded, "You can't stop all crime, but you can reduce it by causing those who are considering a criminal act to think twice. Those who don't want to go to jail for ten years will not consider robbing a bank. There will always be bank robbers, but maybe fewer than if the punishment wasn't as severe." Ron smiled, "Think about it. If you went to jail for thirty days for robbing a bank there wouldn't be a safe bank anywhere." In a more serious tone he added, "We can't eliminate terrorism but we sure as hell can reduce the number of participants willing to take the risk."

In the living quarters on the Ismenios General Hughes was talking with Secret Service Agent Emanuel Vegas on the encrypted satellite telephone. He paced as he spoke, "O'Neal knows that Hayes was with Satan's Shadow. He gave me Hayes' coin."

"How much did Hayes tell him?" Vegas inquired.

"Nothing. O'Neal didn't indicate that he knew more than the coin and supposition offered. He told me he had no plan of sharing his suspicions. All he wanted was for Hayes to be buried with honors. I don't believe he would do or say anything that would keep that from happening."

"Do you think he might be a recruit?"

"Not if I read the man correctly."

There was a moment of silence as each man waited for the other to speak. Eventually, General Hughes spoke, "Our French friend is not being cooperative."

"I didn't think he would be."

"He has Kareem Reza confined somewhere. And, he's not forthcoming with where."

"At present, we need him."

"I realize that. Have you had any luck on your end?"

"That FBI agent, Fox, has been nosing around."

"Are you at risk?"

"No. And, I hate to say, with Sergeant Hayes gone there is even less potential for discovery."

"Not a price I wanted to pay."

"Agreed. On another front, those German wannabes struck friends and supporters of the eight rapists. It doesn't appear they had any family with them, however, they were associated with a militant group inside Germany. Twenty-three of their cohorts were attacked and killed in their government provided housing. You won't read about it in the press. The German government is keeping the lid on the event for fear of inciting widespread violence."

General Hughes smiled which was uncommon for the tough-as-nails military leader. He took out a cigar and lit it, then concluded, "I'd say they don't need our help."

"In addition, there has been an increase in the number of refugees who have decided to return to their native land."

"Don't let the door hit you in the ass as you leave."

"Ton fils est mort, your son is dead," Liam told Kareem Reza.

"Morte!" Kareem repeated in disbelief. "Comment? Pourquoi? Dîtes-moi, tell me."

Kareem Reza was being held as a political prisoner at France's Special Operations Command (COS) Garrison/HQ in Pau, Pyrénées-Atlantiques, France. He lived in a small guarded apartment on the base. He had provided all the information he had, which was very little, pertaining to his son. The young man had gone to Afghanistan to work on the Kamal Khan Dam on the Helmand River. Nothing seemed odd and his letters, which came occasionally, appeared positive and unconcerned. After a year and a half his letters arrived less frequently and were short and terse.

While that was happening, Kareem met Nadia Noorani in Washington, DC. More accurately, she seduced him and drew him into the terrorist's web. The final link in the chain that kept him in line was the kidnapping of his son. He cooperated fully.

"And, now, there is no reason to live, no reason to care what happens to me, no reason to do their bidding any longer," Kareem Reza lamented.

"Au contraire, you must continue to work with them and us at the same time."

"Why should I do that?"

"For justice, or revenge, because your son was killed by them. Our rescue team arrived too late. He tried to escape and was slain. Je suis désolé."

"I am sorry, as well. But, nothing will return my son to me."

"That is true." Liam changed his tone to one of consoling, "You feel the pain no man should have to experience—the loss of a child. It is pain like no other. Even time won't completely alleviate it. This is the very reason you must help us. To keep other fathers from having to endure what you must alone. Together, we can put a stop to the evil that walks among us and threatens our way of life and murders our children. Do it as a tribute to an honorable son who lived on this Earth for too short a time."

Kareem Reza looked into Liam Beauchêne's eyes. He wanted to see the depth of the man's character. They had been friends at one time. But, this was a different time, eons beyond the old days. Could he trust this man? Should he trust this man? Could he trust himself? Black mourning clouds obstructed his vision and thoughts. For all intents and purposes, he was hollow—empty—devoid of feeling. Did he care what happens in the world when his world collapsed around him leaving him alone in a cold, desolate vacuum? Would any act on his part be of any value? Is there redemption in mindless action? Does he have any choice? Kareem Reza said softly, "What do you want me to do?"

Michael O'Neal walked slowly up the steps of the farmhouse at FFP Ranch. His legs felt heavy and his gear even heavier. It was late at night and Alice, his wife, was already in bed. She didn't know he was coming home.

Upon entering the house, Michael placed his gear silently in a corner to be attended to the next day. In darkness he found his way to the den, quietly closed the door, and turned on the light. From the small bar he retrieved a bottle of Scotch and filled a glass. Then, while sitting in his desk chair, he stared out the window over darkened pastures filled with shadows. In those shadows he walked with Adam "Guard Dog" Hayes along a mountain pass. They had just finished a mission and were headed back to an LZ. Adam was his typical self, making wiseass remarks and being very animated as he did. Michael couldn't help but smile. There was always something going on in Adam's mind. Sometimes it was something that got them into trouble. And, sometimes it was something that got them out of trouble. A comment made by his irreproachable friend snuck into Michael's mind, "Someday, one of us will not return from a mission. When that happens the poor slob who has to bear the burden of the loss should fill a glass and make a toast. Something like, 'You sure as shit made it interesting. Here's to the unexpected. Thanks for being there. Now, get off my lawn.'" Once more Michael smiled and said in a whisper, "Adam Hayes, get the fuck off my lawn."

The door to the den opened and Alice walked slowly in. She was carrying a shotgun. Upon seeing Michael, she said somewhat perturbed, "You could have called."

"I wasn't sure if I would get in tonight or not."

"Why? Having too much fun with your friend the dog?"

"No."

"Was he trying to talk you into another far-off adventure?"

"No."

She looked out the window and confessed, "Every time I see that damn green Jeep drive up, my skin crawls."

"Why don't you go to bed. We'll talk in the morning."

"You are planning to go somewhere, aren't you?"

"We'll talk in the morning."

"No! We'll talk now. What has he gotten you into now?"

"Nothing."

"I don't believe you."

"I'm not planning to go on any more missions. I'm retired."

"You said that before. Then your old pal shows up and off you go." Her voice became harsh as she said, "Why don't you divorce me and marry him?"

Anger began to grow within Michael. Fatigue and a deep gnawing sense of loss fed his emotions. He barked, "Alice, we'll talk in the morning."

She wouldn't relent, "Where are you going?"

Michael sat in silence.

"Tell me! Damn it!"

Finally, Michael looked out the window and said, "Arlington National Cemetery."

In shocked silence Alice looked at her husband. It was then that she saw his drawn tired eyes and sad countenance. In an odd sort of way, he looked fragile. Her first impulse was to comfort him, but after what she had been saying it seemed out of place. She was embarrassed. Yet, her husband needed her at that moment. Finally, she said in a warm caring tone, "I'm going with you."

CHAPTER 59

While enroute, Captain Jarvis Demoye made arrangements with port authorities at Camber Quay in Portsmouth, United Kingdom to moor Ismenios at that facility. As a result, they sailed into the English Channel, around the Isle of Wight, past Southsea Castle's lighthouse, and entered the port. He then maneuvered the vessel starboard into Camber Quay. Once moored against a wall they left the boat and proceeded to Broad Street which is the end of Highway A3. Ken Farmingdale was waiting in a rented Range Rover Evoque.

"It's approximately 50 miles to Brighton," Ken stated as he headed east. "Bridget Constantine is waiting for us at an undisclosed location."

"Is she still committed to helping eliminate this threat?" General Hughes asked.

"Committed? She's hell-bent on revenge." Ken thought for a moment and then added, "I should tell you she suggested that I was associated with Satan's Shadow. Said she didn't give a damn. You might want to take that into account before meeting her."

"That does change things somewhat," General Hughes replied. He looked at Demoye and Clew, "What do you think?"

Jarvis Demoye answered, "I think we should minimize contact to reduce the risk."

"Sounds like less hands-on and more rabbit snare," Ron Clew stated, "but we'll have to see the layout."

"Roger that," Jarvis replied.

General Hughes looked at Ken Farmingdale as he drove and stated, "A snare would be more risky for the bait."

"I think we owe her an explanation and the facts," Ken responded.

"You're her contact. You can give her the facts and also the option of stepping off this one. Is she at the safe house?"

"No."

"Then we'll go there and have a look around."

Slightly more than an hour later the four members of Satan's Shadow were at the Freshfield Road cottage. They examined the grounds and the structure. Afterward, General Hughes, Jarvis Demoye, and Ron

Clew sat in a hotel room developing plans while Ken Farmingdale met with Bridget Constantine over dinner at The Beach restaurant overlooking the seafront in Brighton.

"I showed the team the cottage so that they could look it over," Ken explained. "They decided that it would be best if you didn't meet them. This way you have plausible denial of any possible crime."

"And, I won't be able to identify them."

"True."

"I can be trusted, you know," Bridget pointed out.

"I know. It has nothing to do with you. Anonymity is maintained to protect all involved which is why they work in the shadows."

"Satan's shadows?"

"Poor choice of words. What I mean is they prefer to remain covert."

"So, how will this work?"

"They are developing an operational plan and will give me the details which I will share with you."

"What if I think it hums?"

"You can back out at any time."

"You're having a bubble if you think I would do that."

"I can assure you these are professionals that leave nothing to chance. You'll be in good hands."

"Good to know."

Her neck hurt from reading file after file on her computer screen. There were so many higher-ranking military personnel who retired over the past five years that she got lost in the crowd. Generals, Admirals, Colonels, Captains, Commanders, Majors, and more from all branches of service paraded before Peggy Fox. She attempted to eliminate those who had become established in civilian life. Also made an arbitrary, but logical, decision to omit any female officers. Satan's Shadow just didn't seem like something a woman would pursue. In the end she compiled a list of retired officers who had combat experience, were not employed in a civilian occupation, had not run for political office, and did not have a criminal record. There were two hundred forty-one names on her list. General Maxwell Hughes was not on Peggy Fox's list. He retired ten years earlier. Captain Jarvis Demoye was on the list but was buried among a legion of military men.

Her list put aside, Agent Fox's mind returned to Michael O'Neal, the retired Army sniper. It was an itch she couldn't scratch. Was he involved or did he have knowledge of Satan's Shadow? After making a telephone call, she made the drive to FFP Ranch and sat with Michael O'Neal in his den.

"As I told you on the phone, I'm doing a follow-up on the Wilkes-Barre murders," Peggy Fox reiterated.

"And, as I told you, I don't know that there is any more I can add," was Michael O'Neal's response.

"Sometimes just restating facts can turn up something that was earlier missed."

"OK, give it a shot."

"You stated that you do not know Secret Service Agent Emanuel Vegas?"

"Never met the man. Never heard his name until you said it."

"I just can't seem to find the logic of arbitrarily recommending you." She stated.

"You'll have to get answers from Vegas."

"I already have."

Michael O'Neal nodded.

Agent Fox continued, "What do you know about the group known as Satan's Shadow?"

"Only what I've read, they killed the families of terrorists."

"Do you agree with what they are doing?" Fox asked a surprise question.

Michael didn't take the bait, "From a legal perspective—no. As a strategic approach, I can see the logic of it."

"So, you justify the killing of innocent persons?"

"I didn't say I agree with it. I said I could see the strategic logic of it." It was time for Michael to surprise Peggy Fox, "Tell me has there been any change in the number of terrorist incidents in the world?"

"Uh, well, I'm not really sure." Peggy made a note to check the United Nations Office on Drugs and Crime (UNODC) data base. She then continued, "Regardless of whether or not there has been a reduction of terrorist activity, it cannot justify the taking of innocent lives."

"When we fire a cruise missile into a suspected terrorist camp how many innocent lives are among the dead?"

"That's different."

"Semantics, nothing more."

"It is unintentional collateral damage, not premeditated murder," Fox insisted.

"And yet, dead is dead."

Silence entered the conversation as two individuals measured one another. Agent Peggy Fox sought any overt sign that the man before her supported the acts of Satan's Shadow. On the opposite side, Michael O'Neal wondered how much she really knew and what was she holding back to trap him. He decided a pre-emptive strike was best.

"Agent Fox, I just returned from a mission in Afghanistan helping the French Commandoes rescue a French citizen being held captive. It was a SNAFU right from the beginning. Bad intelligence, bad execution, bad luck, and a bad outcome." He paused, looked directly at the FBI agent, and said, "I lost my dearest friend in that operation. Not to enemy fire. Betrayal by the very subject we were sent to save. I took him out. The French Commandoes neutralized his wife and everyone else in the compound. Collateral damage or murder—semantics. My only regret is that I didn't talk him out of going in the first place."

"I'm sorry to hear that," Peggy Fox, human being, said in a soft sympathetic tone.

Michael nodded. He looked out the window in time to see the colt, Adam, frolicking in the paddock. In an almost whisper Michael said, "Get off the damn grass."

"Excuse me?"

"Nothing. Just saying goodbye."

Agent Fox returned to the interview. She handed Michael a paper with the enhanced image of part of a coin with a dragon on it and asked, "Have you ever seen this before?"

On this occasion, the image was enough of a surprise that Michael exhibited a momentary reaction before he caught himself. He pretended to examine the image to buy time. It is illegal to lie to the FBI. That much he knew. He also knew there was no way in hell that he was going to connect Adam Hayes to that image or Satan's Shadow if that be the case. Finally, he decided his course of action. "That's only a partial image, it's hard to be sure if I've seen the full coin or not."

"Have you seen anything resembling this?" she pressed on.

"Many in the military carry challenge coins. On occasion, I've seen different coins. What you have to understand is that I've been on numerous clandestine missions for the United States government and foreign governments. When doing so I took an oath to maintain confidentiality. You understand, lives are at risk. For that reason, you can show me a dozen challenge coins and I will refuse to tell you whether or not I've ever seen them."

"Not good enough," Agent Fox stated. "This coin image was found at a crime scene. That makes it evidence and your refusal to assist makes you at the very least guilty of obstruction of justice. On the other extreme it could make you an accessory after the fact."

"That will be up to you," Michael stood, "this interview is over."

Tariq Avesta sat in the dark back room of his brother's restaurant in Amsterdam, Netherlands. They were in the middle of a heated argument.

"Feisal, you cannot do this," Tariq pleaded.

"That church, Oude Kerk, is the center of evil, the devil's lair, it must be destroyed."

The Oude Kerk, Old Church, is Amsterdam's oldest building founded circa 1213. It is also the oldest parish church consecrated in 1306. In 1578 it became the location of the registry of marriages and the city archives. Rembrandt was a frequent visitor to the Oude Kerk and his children were all christened there. The contemporary Oude Kerk is used for both religious and cultural activities. Ironically, around the church is a square used by prostitutes who offer their services from behind brothel windows. A clash of cultures that could not be missed. In March, 2007 a bronze statue named Belle was installed in front of Oude Kerk with the inscription, "Respect sex workers all over the world."

"Think about what you are doing," Tariq implored.

"It must be done," Feisal replied. "Will you help me?"

"No. I cannot. You cannot."

"It will be done."

"If you do this," Tariq hesitated. "Those who live in the shadows will kill all of your relatives. Me, my wife, and sons will become targets of those accursed creatures of the dark."

"Your faith is weak. You are a coward."

"My wife and sons have done no one any harm."

"Leave me. I have to finish my plans."

Tariq rose from the table. As he turned to leave, he retrieved a knife from a preparation table and plunged it into the heart of Feisal.

CHAPTER 60

"So, you are convinced that our bogie is an individual?" General Hughes asked.

"Based on the fact that one individual was logged in at *London Voice* and the note he leaves says, 'This person died as revenge for the acts of the criminal group known as Satan's Shadow. Find me before more die.' 'Find me' indicates an individual," Ken Farmingdale replied.

"I agree," Jarvis Demoye added.

"Then, that's how we will play it. However, I want to prepare for the unexpected. No need to take any chances," Hughes stated.

"The location offers a degree of privacy and is small enough to allow for easy control and containment," Navy Seal Ron Clew offered.

Ken Farmingdale warned, "This guy is no fool. He's going to proceed very cautiously. If he even suspects that there is something out-of-place, he'll bolt."

"What we have going for us is the fact that he will think that he outsmarted this silly woman who is trying to hide. Of course, the very fact that she contacted the media would raise a red flag," Jarvis pointed out.

"Then she doesn't contact the media," Ron Clew said. When the team looked in his direction he added, "We let an anonymous source at Scotland Yard leak the story. The press loves leaks more than plumbers." He leaned back and said to Ken, "Right, Arthur?"

In a British accent Ken Farmingdale replied, "That would be quite all right, if you ask me."

"I like it," Jarvis exclaimed.

"OK, with that settled, let's finalize these plans," General Hughes directed.

With Liam beside him, Kareem Reza sent a message to Nadia Noorani at the United States Department of State. It read, "My son is dead. I do not know what to do. I must stop this thing." No reply was forthcoming.

As they waited, Liam described what would or could follow.

Kareem Reza was guilty of espionage which was a capital offense until February 19, 2007. On that date, the Congress of the French Parliament overwhelmingly voted in favor of Article 66-1 of the Constitution of the French Republic adding an amendment stating, "Nul ne peut être condamné à mort—No one can be sentenced to death." As a result, life imprisonment hung over Kareem's head. Based on the evidence they already had, this was the most likely outcome. With that specter in mind Liam dangled the carrot. If Kareem cooperated and helped them break up the terrorist cell, he would most likely face a short sentence or serve no time at all. Liam knew that wasn't the case but sought the traitor's cooperation using all the methods of persuasion at his disposal.

After ninety minutes a response from Nadia Noorani was received, "I am so sorry to hear of your son's death. It must be very difficult for you. I have made inquiries on your behalf. Yes, given the circumstances, you can stop this thing. There are a number of items that belonged to your son that will be returned to you. Go to the place where you left the last message and wait."

Upon reading the message shared by Kareem Reza, Liam stated, "It seems that she has done what France cannot—sentenced you to death."

"I believe you are correct. I am no longer of value to them." Kareem looked at Liam and asked, "What am I to do?"

"You will go to the place, as instructed."

"And, be assassinated?"

"No harm will come to you," Liam smiled, "I assure you."

"Just as no harm came to my son?"

"Ce sont des gens diaboliques. These are evil people. We must stop them. You must help. It is the only way for you to get free of them." He added, "And, possibly avoid a long jail term."

"I am sinking and have no way of climbing out of the abyss."

"You are wrong, my friend," Liam used an amicable term and exhibited a kind tone to draw the desperate man in. In his heart he would have been happy to let the terrorists eliminate one of their own. However, in this case, that was impossible. He needed to use this man for his own purposes. If it meant feigning friendship, so be it. "We will protect you."

Kareem Reza looked into Liam's eyes. He couldn't possibly know what the older man's thoughts or motives were, but that didn't matter as the only option was to go to the meeting place. "How do we proceed?"

"You will tell me where the meeting is to take place. Then, you and I will remain here. I will make a few telephone calls and when we are given clearance we will go to the location. Then you will arrive at the rendezvous and signal when you make contact."

"What if they kill me as soon as I arrive?"

"Is it a public place?"

"Yes, a park."

"Bien, that will make it easier," Liam concluded. "They will try to lure you to a private area and there they will assassinate you."

Kareem stared at Liam.

"Don't worry. We will intercede before they have a chance."

"It might be better if you intercede, after they act," Kareem Reza said sadly.

Special Agent Peggy Fox scrolled through the International Terrorist Activity database (InTerAct). Michael O'Neal's question about the relative level of activity prior to the introduction of Satan's Shadow compared with activity after the group's arrival intrigued her. Incidents in the report were grouped by geographic area. As would be expected, the highest number of terrorist acts were in the Middle East, followed by Central Africa. The areas Agent Fox was most interested in were the United States, Europe, and Great Britain. These three geographic areas were where Satan's Shadow concentrated their activity and were most well-known. Information was stratified by number of incidents, fatalities, casualties, and method of attack. The trend was definitely downward in the United States and Europe, while it remained steady in Great Britain. What struck her most was the significant drop in number of fatalities month-to-month. Her mind drifted into a philosophical state where she wondered if the murder of a few innocent persons could ever be justified when the result was the saving of far more innocent lives.

Kareem Reza entered the Parc de Bercy, located along the right bank of the Seine in the 12th arrondissement of Paris. It is the tenth largest park in the city. Parc de Bercy is actually made up of three different gardens connected by foot bridges. The Romantic Garden includes fishponds and dunes, the Flowerbeds is dedicated to plant life, and the Meadows boast open fields and tall trees. The park is linked directly to the National Library of France by the Simone de Beauvoir footbridge over the Seine. Reza proceeded to the Flowerbeds where he had made his last message delivery.

Upon arrival Kareem found himself alone, very alone, in a large park. In front of him to his left was the large building that housed the Cinémathèque Française, a French film organization that holds one of the largest archives of film documents and film-related objects in the world. Everywhere else were gardens, trees, meadows, sculptures, and paths. The park was essentially empty—devoid of visitors. A slight breeze blew his hair. Along with it came an aroma from a distant restaurant. He waited.

Sounds from the Seine reached his ears. A car horn echoed. Dogs barked. Then silence. He looked around only to confirm that he was a lone figure in a vast green tapestry vulnerable to forces unseen. A vision of his son, Faraz, unfolded in his mind. It was how he remembered the young man as he appeared three years earlier. He was so full of life, happy, and looking forward to an adventure in Afghanistan. Black clouds of the id slowly descended from above obscuring his view. He tried to will the vision to return but to no avail.

"Don't turn around," a voice startled him from behind.

Ken Farmingdale once again sat in the parlor of Bridget Constantine's house. It was time to put their plan into action. She ordered furniture and had it delivered to the entrapment house, asked the postal service to hold her mail for pickup, and arranged for utilities at the house using her own name but using her actual address as the billing address. The desired impression was that she did all she could to remain hidden. They proceeded to the cottage on Freshfield Road. Everything appeared normal. Bridget unpacked the clothes she brought and set up housekeeping.

While she finished moving in, Ken Farmingdale, aka Arthur Thompson, explained what was to take place. "When I leave here, I'm going to pose as an anonymous leaker from the London Metropolitan Police. I will contact a news radio station with an exclusive scoop. 'The sister of Patrick Constantine, co-owner of *London Voice*, who was murdered along with six colleagues has discovered video of the offices that identifies the perpetrator of those heinous murders. Because she hasn't finished going through all of the other materials and additional videos she has moved to an undisclosed location. Once she collects all of the evidence, she will turn it all over to the police. That should be in the next few days.' By indicating that you will be giving the evidence to the police shortly it forces our prey to act quickly."

"I know this won't be a doodle to do, but I'm keen as mustard to get on with it," Bridget said in good humor but with a hint of nervousness in her voice.

"Good. Remember, act like you are trying to remain incognito."

"I must be balmy to do this."

"You're brave."

"No, I'm barking mad, but don't worry I'll be cooking with gas."

"Just follow the instructions on this paper and let the team do the rest."

Kareem Reza stood as still as the 21 sculptures of Rachid Khimoune's "Children of the World" exhibit put up in Parc de Bercy in 2001 to honor children's rights.

The voice from behind spoke into his ear, "French commandoes killed your son. We meant him no harm. He was with us. You have been misled. I have proof. Come with me."

Reza's mind spun as the words reached both his intellect and emotions. The world, his world, was becoming a hall of mirrors reflecting conflicting realities. Truth didn't exit. It couldn't survive amid so many well-tailored deceptions. No source could confirm or deny fluid facts that fluctuated with the shifting breeze. A monologue from William Shakespeare's *As You Like It* rose from his memory, "All the world's a stage, and all the men and women merely players: they have their exits and their entrances; and one man in his time plays many parts, his acts being seven ages." Seven ages of man: infant, schoolboy, lover, soldier, justice, Pantalone, and old age. Faraz, his twenty-five-year-old son, was denied the full breadth of his life. That was the only fact Kareem Reza knew to be true.

A dull thud, slight groan, and numerous voices caused Kareem to turn. He stared through blurred vision at French commandoes taking the voice into custody.

CHAPTER 61

Blood dripped onto the stone floor. It formed a small puddle which grew along with the moans of the tortured soul whose body lay upon an old soiled oak table. The room was dark and dank and smelled of death. Stone walls reflected the scant amount of light as sounds echoed off the flat gleaming surface. It had all the appearance of being a medieval dungeon because in fact it was. Another moan indicated that the subject had regained consciousness. It brought forth two dark figures who had waited in the shadows.

"Tell us about Hidden Cobra," a deep threatening harsh voice commanded once more.

"There is nothing to tell."

"Who is involved?"

"I don't know."

"You will tell—that much you do know."

Silence was the man's answer. As a result, the interrogation resumed. With a pair of side-cutters another half inch of the man's pinky on his left hand was cut off. His screams rang out as he pulled at the shackles that held him on the table.

The dark figure once again ordered, "Tell us about Hidden Cobra."

Almost breathless the captive's weak response was, "I cannot tell you what I do not know."

"Ah, but you do know." The interrogator responded, "And, you have many fingers."

"I can count on the fingers of one hand the number of times that I've given a scoop to the media," Ken Farmingdale said in his best British accent.

"I can appreciate that, gov'nor, but why now?" the reporter at London's LBC news radio replied. He quickly added, "Mind you, I wish to have the briefing, it's just curiosity."

"I believe in the public's right to know. And, from what I have been led to believe, senior government officials are planning to suppress the story as it develops."

"May I ask who you are?"

"You know better than that. Suffice it to say that I am associated with law enforcement in a capacity that gives me access to, ah, sensitive information. I also have been in a position to, uh, overhear conversations that I find distressing."

"I understand."

"Do you remember the *London Voice* murders?"

"Absolutely, a bad go that was."

"Quite. Herein is the story. The sister of a co-owner of *London Voice* has been going through all of the materials from that organization. Apparently, she has come across a video from a well-hidden security camera that clearly shows the murderer. This, as you may understand, is embarrassing to the Metropolitan Police Service for having missed the camera not to mention the video. She informed the Yard, but has moved to an undisclosed location to finish reviewing all the materials and videos before turning them over to us. She plans on copying them as there is a hint of concern that the videos might, uh, somehow be lost."

"What is her name?"

"You can find that out for yourself."

"True."

"I'm sharing this information to protect the lady. If you have her story and make it public, they can't hide it under the porch. We will have to arrest the culprit and bring him to justice. If we don't—she's at risk."

"Where is she, now?"

"As I said an undisclosed location. I don't know where she is only that she plans to provide all the evidence within the week." After a pause, Ken added, "If you find her, don't reveal her location."

"You can count on me."

Ken Farmingdale hung up the telephone and said to himself, "I hope so."

Peggy Fox stared at the computer screen. The partial image of the challenge coin and its depiction of a dragon was the key to the puzzle she desperately wished to solve. Michael O'Neal recognized it—that she knew. In fact, he could be carrying one. That she couldn't prove. Another conversation with Secret Service Agent Emanuel Vegas wasn't warranted as it would turn up nothing. No, her next step would be to interview the ex-wife of Master Sergeant Adam Hayes, the close friend of Michael O'Neal killed in Afghanistan. O'Neal reluctantly gave up the fallen Green Beret's name knowing well that she could find out through other channels.

Evelyn Glassman, the former Mrs. Adam Hayes, lived in Rochester, New York with her fifteen-year-old daughter Marcia. Michael O'Neal had been the one who had to deliver the bad news. He felt it was important that he do it in person rather than with an impersonal telephone call. The experience was one of the most traumatic events in the life of the seasoned veteran.

When Evelyn Glassman opened the door and saw Michael O'Neal she exclaimed, "Oh!" Her hands went up to her mouth and she turned away. From behind Michael heard her say, "Adam is dead, isn't he?"

All Michael could do was nod which she couldn't see so he put his hand on her shoulder and whispered, "Yes.".

Evelyn Glassman turned back to face Michael O'Neal and confessed, "Every time the doorbell rang, I was prepared for the worst. For years it was always the same. Upon hearing the bell my mind would go into fear mode, then preparation, and finally relief when it was a delivery, or school student selling something, or neighbor wanting to borrow something. This is the first time I didn't expect bad news."

"I'm sorry," Michael began.

"So am I," she interrupted.

"I felt that I should tell you in person so that I can answer any questions you might have."

"Were you with him?"

"We were on the same mission. I was acting as backup."

"I'm glad you were with him," she said. "I wouldn't want my Adam to have died alone. There was too much 'alone' in his life. He was like a little boy hiding behind a warrior façade. Sadly, over time, less and less innocence remained until all he had left was the outward warrior persona. His strength was also his prison." Evelyn looked at Michael O'Neal and stated, "You knew you could trust him implicitly. I am certain that he never let you down. Adam Hayes never let anyone down, you, me, his family, the team, his government, the Man-in-the-Moon—you name it—Adam never let them down. The only one who was let down was Adam Hayes." Tears welled-up in her eyes, "In the beginning we really had something. I got to peek behind the stone wall to see the poet, the romantic, the clown, the vulnerable, the lost soul. But, over time that wall became a mountain that even I couldn't scale. We lost sight of each other as we drifted on unseen currents that spirited us apart until the only solution was to let go." As tears washed over frown lines, Mrs. Hayes confessed, "I never let go of my lost soul, Adam. I gave him his freedom with the hope that someday . . ." Almost breathless she concluded, "Now, that day will never come."

Michael and Evelyn discussed the steps needed for an Arlington Cemetery burial. She would contact a local funeral director who would call Arlington National Cemetery to make arrangements. A form DD214 would be required to document active duty service and an honorable discharge along with the death certificate. The cemetery staff would arrange for honors and a chaplain, as well as schedule the burial. It could be weeks before the event could take place. Michael told Evelyn to contact him if she needed anything and he left for a very long silent introspective drive home.

A few days later, FBI Special Agent Peggy Fox arrived at the home of Evelyn Glassman. She introduced herself, gave her condolences, and explained that she was doing a background check on a high-level military officer being considered for a post that required top security clearance. Adam Hayes had at one time served with the officer on special assignment.

"I'm afraid I won't be much help," Evelyn explained. "We've been separated for over three years and even when we were together, he never talked about what he was doing."

"I understand. Most military who see action are pretty closed-lipped about it," Peggy said with a smile attempting to remain casual. Almost as a second thought, she showed the partial image of a challenge coin for a group that she couldn't identify and asked, "Have you seen anything like this among Sergeant Hayes' belongings?"

Evelyn looked at the paper, "No, I don't recall seeing anything that looks like that. Wait. I may have seen a coin with a dragon on it, but I really can't be sure. It was years ago when he came for a visit after some volunteer mission with the Army. He went in to take a shower and put his keys and other things on the dresser. I vaguely remember a coin. It was bronze with a dragon that looked something like that. There was also a sword and ring of stars if I recall."

"Could you draw a picture of what it looked like," Peggy asked trying not to show her excitement.

"I'm not sure that I remember it that clearly."

"Give it a try. It doesn't have to be perfect."

With a rough drawing in hand, Peggy Fox once more offered her sympathy, gave Evelyn Glassman her card, and asked her to let her know when the burial ceremony would be held at Arlington. She indicated that she wished to attend to pay her respects to a brave man. What she didn't reveal was that she wanted to see who else attended.

The story came out on LBC news radio and was quickly picked up by print, broadcast, and online media. The reporter identified Bridget Constantine, sister of Patrick Constantine co-owner of *London Voice* who was brutally murdered, as having important evidence in the case. Reliable sources at Scotland Yard indicated she had video of the assailant that she was going to share with the authorities once she finished reviewing all of the security footage from well-hidden cameras. It was reported that while she lived in Brighton she had gone to an undisclosed location for her safety. The information is expected to be given to Scotland Yard within a week.

The story spread across various media until it reached the primary target of Satan's Shadow—Shahin Pouran. When he saw the story on television he bolted upright and listened intently. Security cameras? He didn't see any cameras. Well-hidden? That presented a problem. Immediately, he knew what he had to do.

CHAPTER 62

Liam had listened intently to what the interrogator extracted from their guest in the unofficial prison cell. What he heard ran chills done his spine. The plan was as sinister and evil as one could ever imagine. Hidden Cobra was a scheme to infect as many members of the United States Congress, Senate, and Executive branch as possible with the Ebola virus. The prisoner only knew of the plan, not the details of how it would be achieved. He did indicate that Islamic terrorists associated with the Taliban had perfected a mode of transmittal that would go undetected until it was too late. During a brief moment of clarity, he smiled and yelled, "Allahu Akbar."

After the briefing, Liam contacted Doctor Martel Chavarin a French government physician who was considered expert in the field of hemorrhagic diseases. The doctor provided a history of Ebola Virus Disease (EVD). The first recorded breakout of the deadly virus occurred in 1976 in a village named Yambuku in Zaire, Africa, today known as the Democratic Republic of Congo. It was located along the Ebola River hence the name of the dreaded disease.

Years of research produced what scientists believe were the events that precipitated the original Ebola outbreak. It was determined that a single adult male who worked at a cotton factory was the index case of the outbreak. He had received an injection of chloroquine for presumptive malaria at the Yambuku Mission Hospital outpatient clinic. Unknown to the clinic personnel at the time was the fact that he had become infected with the virus a few days earlier. Five days after receiving the injection, September, 1 1976, he was hospitalized at Yambuku Mission Hospital as the first Ebola patient. Within a week several other patients who had received injections at the clinic suffered from Ebola Virus Disease. It was later found that the hospital had a policy to use only five syringes a day to treat all patients. Over a four-week period contaminated needles created an epidemic. After that those who had close contact with infected patients or relatives fell ill. The hospital was closed after 11 of the 17 staff died from the disease. In the end there were 318 cases of Ebola Virus Disease resulting in 280 deaths.

Dr. Chavarin observed, "Sadly, the ones most affected were women between the ages of 15 and 29. It seems they visited the prenatal care unit and outpatient clinics at the hospital and often received injections."

"Tell me about the disease," Liam requested.

"It's a nasty little bug. Symptoms of EVD may appear anytime between two and twenty-one days after exposure. Although, it most commonly occurs between the eighth and tenth day. The patient might think they are coming down with the flu. Fatigue, weakness, headache, muscle pain, and nausea. But after three or four days, headaches become intense, progressively severe sore throat, high fever, intractable abdominal pain, diarrhea, vomiting, bruising, bleeding from multiple sites, principally the gastrointestinal tract, and development of a maculopapular rash."

"What kind of rash?"

"Oh, excuse me, maculopapular. It is a type of rash characterized by flat red areas that are covered with small confluent bumps. It is a symptom of many diseases—scarlet fever, measles, rubella, syphilis, or simple heat rash."

"What are the fatality rates," Liam asked fearing the answer.

"In the 1976 Yambuku Mission Hospital event it was 88%. Most died within a week, but it wasn't a very pleasant way to go. The fatality rate has declined to average just over fifty percent. However, those who survive have a long recovery period and may suffer chronic side effects." Dr. Chavarin leaned forward and added, "The original outbreak lasted about eleven weeks in 1976. A more recent outbreak in Liberia, Guinea, and Sierra Leone has lasted over two years with 29,000 confirmed cases and 11,310 deaths. When this pathogen gets a foothold, it can be a significant threat if not contained."

"How does it spread?" Liam inquired.

"Ebola is transmitted from human to human through direct contact with bodily fluids of infected persons. You understand, blood, saliva, sweat, secretions, urine, feces, any moist medium. It also can be spread through contact with surfaces and objects that have been contaminated. On dry surfaces, Ebola can survive for several hours. In external bodily fluids the virus can survive for several days at room temperature. The virus enters the body through broken skin, sexual contact, or mucous membranes in the eyes, nose, or mouth." Dr. Chavarin added, "People with Ebola are not contagious until after they begin showing signs and symptoms of the disease. If a person shows early signs of Ebola and may have had exposure to the disease, they must be quarantined. It can spread quickly once it infects human beings."

Liam had been taking notes. He reviewed what he had written and then asked, "If it first appears to be flu how is it diagnosed?"

"Quick diagnosis of Ebola Virus Disease is critical to avoid widespread outbreak. Unfortunately, early symptoms are not disease specific. This makes it difficult to distinguish from other diseases like malaria, leptospirosis, influenza, yellow fever, dengue, or even typhoid fever. It can be diagnosed through blood samples, but only after symptoms have begun. An interesting thing, though, outbreaks in other primates and antelope often precede, or are concurrent with human cases of Ebola Virus Disease in the same or nearby areas. In 1994 before the Taï National Forest outbreak half the chimpanzee population in the area perished. Before an outbreak in 2001, 64 dead gorillas, chimpanzees, and antelope were discovered."

Liam spoke slowly as he gathered his thoughts, "So, if there is an outbreak in a populated area it wouldn't really be known until a patient is correctly diagnosed. At that point there may have been multiple contacts with other potential victims. How can a large-scale epidemic ever be avoided?"

Doctor Martel Chavarin removed his glasses and wiped them with a handkerchief. "I fear in a densely populated city the potential for widespread infection is far greater than the chances for quick identification and isolation of the disease." He stood from his desk and walked around to where Liam sat, sat next to him, and said, "Consider a man gets exposed to the Ebola Virus. He then travels to a large city. Nine days after exposure he feels fatigue and muscle pain and nausea. He believes he may have the flu. His wife feels his forehead and he is sweating. She tells him he might have a fever. Then she rubs her eyes. She now has been exposed. The infected man tries to go to work. He takes mass transit. Along the way he coughs into his hand then unknowingly leaves sputum on handrails, doorknobs, elevator buttons, and more. After that he begins to get worse and vomits in the office bathroom, leaves sweat and other bodily fluids on multiple surfaces, then heads home. By the time he reaches home he has left the virus in so many places that it would be impossible to track. Say a dozen people become infected the transmittal process continues until the original victim is brought into a hospital or dies and is finally diagnosed. At that point the numbers will cascade at an ever-increasing rate until healthcare professionals can only excruciatingly slowly isolate more and more patients. There would not be an optimistic outcome." Dr. Chavarin shook his head as if witnessing what he just describes. “In a city with 600,000 population as many as a third could become infected. With a 50% fatality rate 100,000 people would perish.”

“Mon Dieu!” Liam exclaimed. His mind raced as he tried to remember what was the population of Washington, DC. Somewhere around six million, he thought. Given Dr. Chavarin’s example that would mean approximately one million people would die. The next question was obvious, “What treatment is available?”

“Each symptom is treated as it appears. If diagnosed early, intravenous fluids, balancing electrolytes with body salts, maintaining oxygen and blood pressure, and treating infections as they arise have been shown to improve the odds for recovery. Yet, sometimes there are long-term complications such as vision and joint issues. Remarkably, even after recovery it can take three to nine months for the virus to be entirely out of the body.”

“Isn’t there a vaccine available?” Liam asked.

“As of today, no. There are a number of vaccines under study. Some have proven effective but only for a short period of time.”

“What else can be done, Doctor?”

“Keep it in the jungle.”

Rain began falling as the sun set over Brighton, UK. It was just one more annoying thing to add to the others. When Jarvis Demoye positioned himself at the far end of the backyard outside the privacy fence, he discovered an active anthill with many guards just itching for a fight. With a half-dozen stinging memories he moved to a better location. Once there, he was greeted by the lovely aroma of a decomposing creature that couldn’t be identified. His third choice proved acceptable once he got an overly affectionate alley cat to go elsewhere. And, then came the rain.

Ken Farmingdale was on a laptop computer while sitting on the floor of the bedroom closet. He was connected to the desktop computer at which Bridget Constantine sat in the small living room. She had been purposely positioned with her back to the room, as well as the front door and kitchen where the back door was located—a perfect target.

General Hughes observed the front of the house from a rented Vauxhall Insignia Sports Tourer station wagon with tinted windows. It was parked around the corner but with a clear view of the cottage. He was positioned in such a way as to be hidden while able to observe through a small electronic periscope.

Ron Clew was not to be seen.

Raindrops, like the ticking of a clock, beat upon Jarvis as he watched the back of the house. A rustling sound behind him caused him to abruptly turn. The demon cat had returned.

At ten o'clock Bridget turned off the computer and prepared to go to bed. The Satan's Shadows observers remained where they were. Only one anomaly was noted that night. General Hughes observed a man walk slowly up the street. He acted casual but showed an elevated level of interest in the cottage. Also, he kept looking around to determine if anyone was watching. He continued walking up the street and never returned.

Shahin Pouran considered himself very lucky. After hearing about the woman having evidence pertaining to the honorable slaying at *London Voice* he immediately traveled to Brighton. He knew she wouldn't be at her listed address, but went there just to be sure. His next stop was the nearest post office where he found that she left no forwarding address. However, his brilliance was demonstrated when he posed as Bridget Constantine's brother and called the power company to complain that the power had not been turned on at her new address. The customer service representative checked their records and assured him that the power was on at 12627 Freshfield Road.

CHAPTER 63

Shahin Pouran knew he had to act quickly. Surely, the police would also contact the woman once they heard the news story. His only hope was that they would be typically slow moving or simply decide to wait for her to bring them the evidence—evidence he would destroy. After a surveillance walk on Freshfield Road he saw nothing that indicated that the silly woman had any guards or other security. Curse those well-hidden security cameras at *London Voice*. That was an error he would not repeat. Once he cut her throat, he would set fire to the cottage which should eliminate all evidence of the *London Voice* great victory, as well as any recording of his elimination of this gnat.

On this second night Shahin waited until dark. Given the circumstances of her brother's death he knew it was impossible to knock on the front door with some fabricated story. She might look out, see a middle-eastern man, and refuse to answer. Even worse she might call the police. This operation called for stealth to which he was no stranger. Training in Pakistan gave him many tools with which to operate. He was pleased that there were no pedestrians on the street and only a single automobile passed.

With all conditions being favorable, Shahin Pouran moved silently to the front window of the cottage and peered in. Allah blessed him once more as he observed the woman with her back to the room working at a computer. He smiled as he concluded that she mistakenly assumed that hiding at an undisclosed location would protect her. She would pay for her arrogance. First, he would force her to show him where the incriminating evidence was hidden, then he would rape her, slit her throat, and burn the cottage to the ground.

The night was dark and silent—perfect conditions for the hunter as he moved quietly through the privacy fence gate into the backyard. A quick glance around revealed no hint of any risk. He tried the back door and found it to be locked. However, it was a flimsy lock which was easily picked. With great care to avoid having an errant squeak alert his prey, Shahin moved the wooden door slowly inward. Inch by inch the portal guard gave up its line of defense. Once it was open, he knew, it would take only a few brief moments to move into the room where Bridget Constantine sat. She would not be aware of his presence until it was too late. She would not have time to react. She would not see the morning sun.

Shahin Pouran stepped into the dark kitchen. Instantly, a huge black hand covered his mouth while a 5-inch black blade on a Zero Tolerance ZT0160 Combat Knife sank deep into his back. He dropped the knife that he had been carrying. He dropped to his knees as the accurately placed thrust allowed his heart's blood to flow from his body. He heard the words of his assailant, "Consider yourself found." It was then he knew he had stepped into a trap in the darkness of Satan's Shadow. In one last desperate attempt to declare his martyrdom he tried to yell, "Allahu Akbar." The large hand over his mouth refused to yield and the voice in his ear pronounced sentence, "Satan is waiting to welcome you to hell." Shahin Pouran did not see the morning sun.

Liam Beauchêne sipped a glass of Domaine Lapeyre Rouge, from Bearn, France. The red cabernet and tannat wine from southwest France brought him back to a time when his biggest concern was passing the next day's exams. Life in its simplicity seemed boring to a youth with great aspirations and a drive to prove his worth to a highly successful father. However, it was inevitable that time would move on and leave him now sitting alone, staring into the maw of worldwide discontent and unimaginable brutality. He longed for the boredom and peace that came from a sheltered existence. At one time he believed he had indeed left his mark, but a misguided world hellbent on self-destruction washed it into obscurity. Once again, he was called upon to intercede in order to stop or, at the very least, slow the arrival of doomsday.

He considered the red wine in his glass. Vineyards in the vicinity of his childhood home are planted on the hillside at the base of the northern Pyrenees. The humid, rainy oceanic climate, and dry winds drain water away from the roots. This water stress slows growth of the vines which leads to development of concentrated high-quality grapes. In addition, annual dry spells in late summer correspond with the ripening of grapes. As a result, grapes ripen slowly and evenly creating a balance of aromatic intensity and acidity.

Liam considered the red liquid in his glass that appeared blood red. Blood seemed more and more a factor in the equation. If allowed, it would carry a deadly virus that would bring down a government which in turn would lead to greater bloodshed than the world had known for decades. Innocent blood would be spilled as ambitious tyrants vie for greater power and control as the world redefines itself. Chaos and conflict would be driven by one thing—blood.

Far below where Liam sat, a disfigured captive bled and wept and shuddered as words flowed from his mouth in a desperate attempt to avoid additional pain. The virus would be delivered by some undetectable means created by scientists somewhere in France. Who or where he did not know. It was very secretive with only a select few knowing all the facts. Additional pain failed to produce additional information.

Ken Farmingdale entered the small living room and put his hand on the shoulder of Bridget Constantine. He said softly, "It's over. Remain here until the team is finished."

"But I wish to see him, to spit on the body, to end the nightmare."

"It's better that you don't. When they are finished there will be no sign of the event and you will have had no part in its execution."

Bridget attempted to stand. A firm but gentle hand held her in her chair. She considered protesting. Then when logic overpowered emotion she understood that it was better that she has as little involvement as possible. She remained seated.

"When the police question you about the news report," Ken instructed, "tell them it was a terrible misunderstanding. Someone must have overheard you say that you wish there was video of the murders from hidden cameras. Then when you read the news story you feared that the perpetrator would believe it to be true and attempt to get the evidence or harm you. That is why you temporarily moved here. You don't have to say anything else."

Bridget put her hand on top of Ken Farmingdale's hand as she said with warm sincerity, "I know who you and your team are. Or, I believe I know. It doesn't matter to me. To me you are God's Angels who I will always keep in my prayers."

"By morning we will be a figment of your imagination. You can go on with your life knowing justice has been served. We cannot bring back your brother, however, we eliminated a threat that was keeping you from having peace and living your life. You are a brave and impressive lady. I'll long remember and be grateful to you."

"You're always welcome to visit for tea," Bridget said with a smile.

In less than an hour Satan's Shadow was gone leaving no evidence of having been at 12627 Freshfield Road.

Secret Service Agent Emanuel Vegas relayed a message that he had received from Liam while the Shadow team was incommunicado. Once back on Ismenios and safely out to sea General Hughes made contact with Vegas over a secure satellite telephone.

"Has our friend decided to give up the location of Kareem Reza?" General Hughes inquired.

"He has not."

"Then our business with him is finished."

"That may be premature."

"How so?"

"He indicated that a meeting with you is imperative for 'impending extreme consequential threat contravention'—his words. He sounded concerned. I believe there is something in the works that they have uncovered. I also believe that it is something significant, therefore, we can't walk away."

"How come I get the feeling that we are working for the French government? That possibility alone is problematic. In order to remain clandestine—and alive I might add—it is essential that we avoid too many extraneous contacts. Can you not meet with 'the man who wasn't there' and decide whether or not our intervention is necessary?"

"I suggested just that. He indicated that time was of the essence and the root of the threat lay somewhere in France. The threat, by the way, is to the United States of America."

"The ball just landed in our court."

"I'm afraid so."

A splash was heard outside the main cabin where General Hughes was sitting. That was one body that would never be found. Too bad, he thought, we don't know who the man was so no further action was possible. The *London Voice* and other murders would never be solved. Unless, he became a missing person and incriminating evidence was found on his computer or in his home.

"Where is this proposed meeting to take place?" General Hughes asked not attempting to hide his displeasure.

"Where you docked in Bayonne previously. He will be there the day after tomorrow. No need to tie up, he will board, and then you will head back out to sea."

"I don't like taking orders. Especially, when they are vague," Hughes complained.

"Yes sir," Emanuel Vegas responded using the acknowledgment of rank to assuage the situation.

In a calm, more friendly, tone Maxwell Hughes requested, "Manny, do me a favor and let me know when the services will be held for Sergeant Adam Hayes."

"Do you think it wise to attend?"

"Not for the team. It was I who sent him on a treacherous mission that should not have been executed. The responsibility is mine—mine alone. It is proper and fitting that I pay my respects to a brave man, loyal comrade, and free spirit whom I will miss."

"I'll make it happen."

"This is very important, Kareem," Liam stated as he sat across the table from the traitor held captive at a Special Operations Command military base. "The man who was taken into custody at Parc de Bercy has revealed a plot for a terrorist attack on America."

"I know nothing of an attack or a plan," Kareem Reza insisted.

"I believe you," Liam consoled the man. "However, I need your assistance." He paused to decide the best approach, "We believe that some of the messages that you delivered might have pertained to this plot."

"They were, as you know, coded messages. I don't know what was in them."

"True, but I want you to think very hard. When you delivered these messages or picked up messages to send did you see anyone who might have been suspicious?"

"I never saw anyone and was instructed not to delay. I was to drop off or pick up a message and leave immediately."

"Was there anything what-so-ever that might have stood out at the rendezvous?"

Kareem Reza sat in silence as he tried to recall what he may have seen or heard. Liam waited patiently. He knew memory is a fleeting thing, but also unpredictable. An arbitrary stimulus can trigger an unexpected memory. There was no way to predict it. Sometimes simply remaining in complete silence without trying to force one's mind to recall also brings forth surprises. This was the case with Kareem Reza.

"It may be nothing," Kareem began, "but I remember two times after I left a message where directed I saw a green automobile. The reason I remember it was there was a decal in the rear window. It had all these different colored concentric circles. In the middle were letters that overlapped each other. I don't remember all the letters but there was a U and a B, and the word Lyon was outside the circles." He looked at Liam and added, "I remember thinking they were a long way from home."

"Did you see who was driving the automobile?" Liam asked.

"One time it was parked so there was no driver. The other time it passed me and I only saw the back of the automobile and the driver. It was a woman."

CHAPTER 64

Ismenios steamed up the Adour River and landed at an industrial pier 3.7 miles west of the city of Bayonne, France. On the pier stood a Frenchman leaning on his cane. He neither waved nor called out. After Liam boarded the converted patrol boat Captain Jarvis Demoye began a slow turn to head down river back to the ocean. General Hughes was in the main cabin, while Ken Farmingdale and Ron Clew sat on the fantail.

"Good afternoon, gentlemen," Liam said in a friendly yet serious tone.

A nod was the response. Undaunted, the Frenchman entered the main cabin. Upon seeing General Hughes, he commented, "It appears I am importun—unwelcome."

"That sums it up," was General Hughes cool response.

"I regret the loss of Monsieur Hayes. We did not know."

"You had a man in that village who provided intel as to location, number of inhabitants, activities, and more and he didn't indicate that the target was one of them?" Maxwell Hughes spat holding back what he wanted to say.

"It was an unfortunate omission," Liam tried. "I assure you we will not be accepting any further intel from that source, even in the event that it was possible."

"Why are you here?"

"It is of the gravest importance." Liam sat in one of the easy chairs. As he did, he leaned heavy on his cane as a fatigued man would do. Silently, he looked out the window of the cabin at the passing shoreline. When he turned back toward Maxwell Hughes he said, "There is a plot aimed at your nation that would have devastating effect if we do not intercede."

"If you know of a plot why don't you inform your anti-terrorist folks or the United States Homeland Security department?"

"Because what we have is, as you say, uncorroborated, hearsay, and acquired by," he waved his hand palm up, "less than legal methods."

"We are not prepared to do your dirty work, at this time."

"It is your dirty work," Liam stated emphasizing the word "your."

"You have French commandoes—let them assist you."

"General, what needs to be done, they cannot do." In a plaintive tone he added, "Please, hear me out."

General Hughes sat opposite Liam and nodded.

"There is a plot to introduce Ebola Virus into the American government leadership in Washington, DC."

General Hughes stood up and stated, "Wait, the team needs to hear this firsthand."

Once Ismenios was in international waters of the Atlantic Ocean Jarvis Demoye set the craft on auto pilot and joined the others in the main cabin. They all listened intently to Liam's description of an Ebola plot against the United States of America.

"That is what we know. What we don't know is the method of delivery," Liam explained.

"That's an important bit of information, wouldn't you say?" Jarvis Demoye commented.

"The traitre we are holding did provide a small amount of information," Liam explained. "When he left messages or picked up messages at designated locations, he did see the same automobile at two of them. It was driven by a woman and had a unique sticker in the rear window. We've been able to identify the sticker as the logo of the Université Claude Bernard Lyon 1. One of three public universities of Lyon, France. The main areas of study covered by the university are science and medicine. There are both teaching hospital facilities and research facilities located there. We believe there is a connection."

"I take it that you have people investigating," General Hughes stated.

"Oui," Liam replied.

"Then, we are not needed."

"Au contraire. As you are well-aware governments move very slowly—lentement et prudemment. There are times this is of preference. Unfortunately, this is not one of those times. We must immediately define the method of delivery, determine its relative status, and prevent the execution of this nefarious plan."

"By legal and illegal means," Navy Seal Ron Clew observed.

"The authorities would talk while the flames of destruction burn down all that is around them."

"Once more, you have people who can provide what you require," General Hughes said.

"Oui, I do have those who can effectively interrogate, but quite frankly they are brutes. If I wish to have bones broken or appendages ripped from their socket, they can do it very satisfactorily. But, in this case, we need to uncover information that might not be revealed through anguished screams for mercy. A more delicate touch is required."

"We're all military, delicate is not one of our strong suits," Ron Clew interjected.

General Hughes smiled as he glanced at the large black man leaning against the counter.

"A poor choice of words. Perhaps sophisticated is more appropriate."

"What exactly are you proposing that we do?" General Hughes asked.

"At this time, all we have is a plot to deliver the virus, a green car with a sticker, and a female driver. What we don't have is time. We all must go to Lyon and the Université Claude Bernard, find the automobile, determine who is the driver, and then find out what she has been up to." Liam shrugged knowing it was most likely a futile effort.

"That's a pretty long shot, if you ask me," Ken Farmingdale observed.

"It is the frivolous action of a desperate man," Liam admitted.

"Even if we identify the lady," Jarvis said, "she's not going to tell us what clandestine experiments she has been performing on the side to support terrorist objectives."

"Unless," all eyes turned toward General Hughes, "she is informed that if she doesn't cooperate fully that her family and friends and cohorts will all be summarily neutralized by the group known as Satan's Shadow."

"That was a lot faster than I thought," Michael O'Neal said into the telephone. He was speaking with Evelyn Glassman, Adam Hayes' ex-wife. "I understand arranging for burial at Arlington can take weeks or months to schedule. Someone must have pulled a few strings. Do you need any help for you and Marcia to get there?" After a pause, "Then we'll see you there. Thank you for letting me know." Another pause, "Yes, I will spread the word."

After his conversation, Michael O'Neal told his wife when the ceremony at Arlington National Cemetery would be held. He then looked through his computer contacts to determine if any other individuals should be notified. It was then that reality struck. He and Adam had been a team for so long most of their other associates had been killed in action or moved on with their lives thus losing contact. Adam "Watch Dog" Hayes and Michael "Owl" O'Neal were more than a team, partners, allies, or friends—they were brothers. Their lives were so intertwined that one could not speak of one without including the other. They knew each other's habits and moods, likes and dislikes, interests and tastes, as well as actions they may take in any situation.

Michael didn't have any memory of his life that didn't include Adam. They did everything together. In many ways, they gave each other strength, brought out the best in each other, and defined life on their own terms. Together, they were invincible. Whether on a mission, training, enjoying R and R, or getting into trouble, Adam and Michael were together. If they were ever bored, they made their own fun. The bond they shared was something that just happened. Yet, it was based on mutual respect and unwavering trust. If Adam gave his word, Michael would always believe him because between them their word was sacred.

Michael couldn't imagine what his life would have been like or what direction it might have taken if Adam Hayes hadn't been his friend. In many ways it was frightening to think where he might have ended up had he not been blessed with that crazy, unpredictable, good natured, generous, caring dog who was always there. Watch Dog was a nickname well-earned as he pulled many out of harm's way, saw danger coming and thwarted it, made split-second life-saving decisions, and kept those around him safe.

Adam's antics were pure, innocent, and outrageously funny. His stories, sense of humor, and deep uninhibited laugh were trademarks of someone who knew how to see the funny side of life. It was a personality trait that brought comfort to many in situations where no hope or comfort seemed possible.

An irreplaceable part of Michael's past was gone. At that very moment he felt heartfelt nostalgia and overwhelming desire to simply shoot a game of pool together as they often did as young men. The banter between them as they played was always humorous, sometimes odd, irreverent, and often on a plane only they understood. Michael and Adam never had to tell each other that they appreciated what the other one did. It was the kind of friendship where nothing needed to be said.

In the quiet of his den, Michael hoped Adam's spirit could feel the love and gratitude that couldn't be put into words. "Rest in peace my friend, your life had far greater impact and value than you could have imagined."

Special Agent Peggy Fox thanked Evelyn Glassman for informing her of when Adam Hayes would be laid to rest at Arlington National Cemetery.

CHAPTER 65

With Ismenios securely docked in Bayonne the four members of team Satan's Shadow climbed into Liam's SUV to begin their seven-and-a-half-hour ride to Lyon, France. As they rode Liam provided an overview of Lyon. It was an ancient city founded by the Romans in 43BC due to its strategic location at the convergence of two navigable rivers, the Rhône and Saône. Through the centuries Lyon was part of various empires and did not come under French rule until the 14th century. During the Renaissance, the city's development was driven by the silk trade, which strengthened its ties to Italy. As a result, Italian merchants introduced fairs in the city which made Lyon the economic counting house of France. Then when international banking went to Genoa and after that Amsterdam, Lyon remained the banking center of France.

Lyon is the third-largest city (population 513,275) and second-largest urban area (population 2,265,375) in France. The city is known for its cuisine, architectural landmarks, and annual light festival. It also boasts a diverse and growing economy. Chemical, pharmaceutical, and biotech industries have flourished. Manufacture of silk continues to be an important factor and a growing software industry has led to many startups. Lyon is also the international headquarters of Interpol, the International Agency for Research on Cancer, and Euronews.

During World War II, Lyon was occupied by Nazi forces which included Klaus Barbie, the infamous "Butcher of Lyon." However, the city was also a stronghold of the French Resistance. As a result, there exist many secret passages known as traboules which enabled people to escape Gestapo raids. The city is now home to a resistance museum.

"Tell us about the university," General Hughes requested.

"The teaching and research facilities are located in Villeurbanne which is a commune in the Metropolis of Lyon. It is actually separated from Lyon by the river La Rize, a former branch of the Rhône River. Villeurbanne is a densely populated urban area. The University campus is very large. It will not be easy to find the green automobile with a university sticker in the rear window."

"What makes you think there will be only one green car with a sticker?" Ron Clew asked the obvious question.

"Well, because . . . Oh mon Dieu . . . what was I thinking?" Liam responded.

"Well, if you consider the odds, every green car has a fifty-fifty chance of being driven by a female," Ken Farmingdale observed.

"And, a sticker could be placed in the rear window of a car by a professor, student, employee, or fan," Ron Clew observed.

"Wait," General Hughes said, "Let's look at it from a different direction. Given the situation and suspected plot involving a biological attack, that is the direction we should pursue. How many female medical researchers might there be—twenty, thirty, one hundred?" The SUV hit a bump throwing all occupants briefly into the air. "We need to get a list of the research faculty and observe what color car they drive. If we get lucky, only one or two will drive a green car with a sticker in the rear window."

"We can't kidnap a half dozen women and interrogate them," Jarvis Demoye stated.

"No, but we can focus our attention on those who are suspect. Eventually, if we are lucky, we will uncover a clue that identifies the most likely conspirator," General Hughes pointed out.

"The critical word is 'eventually,'" Ron Clew pointed out. "We may not have the luxury of eventually."

Peggy Fox read the email instructing her to report to the Deputy Director of Internal Affairs at FBI headquarters in the J. Edgar Hoover Building, 935 Pennsylvania Avenue, NW, Washington, D.C. 20535. While a time for the appointment was provided no other information was included. She didn't require any further information as it was clear this was an inquest with her status at the Bureau on the line. They had all the facts pertaining to the Wilkes-Barre operation in hand. What they didn't have was a fall guy. Every effort would be made to trip her up, to get her to make an ersatz confession of negligence, or set a perjury trap. She knew the routine. The Bureau could not let three citizens under their protection get murdered and not have someone to blame, or worse, to imply collusion. Her first impulse was to resign. It was an impulse that rapidly passed. She would not give them the satisfaction. If they wanted a fight, she would give them one hell-of-a-brawl.

In order to prepare for her inquisition Peggy began gathering all of her notes and preparing for her defense. As she did, she came across a notepad with the name Michael O'Neal written on it. His unconventional manner of getting involved in the operation still bothered her. Why did an uninvolved Secret Service Agent render unsolicited assistance and recommend a retired Army sniper for professional input? Why? Why did she accept his offer so easily without asking more questions? Why? Why had her usually dependable red flag of concern not appeared? Why? Why didn't she get better answers from both men, after the fact? Why? Maybe, she should drag the two of them into her inquisition. Why not? She knew why not. The Bureau would find nothing to pursue thus adding more fuel to the incompetence fire. No, O'Neal and Vegas would remain only in her crosshairs. That was until she was certain that they were innocent. Which was something she did not expect to be the case.

The interview at FBI headquarters was cool and accusatory. Every procedure, protocol, nuance was questioned, then questioned again, then again. Peggy's perjury radar went up. One slip of the tongue, mistaken memory, time anomaly, overlooked step, or show of emotion could sink her. Even though she was a seasoned interviewer, the level of intensity and method of questioning was uncomfortable. The jackals were out for blood and she was the only lamb in the room. Then the question was asked, "Why did you bring an Army sniper into the operation?"

With the inner-strength of a boxer who is being badly beaten but fights on she maintained her composure, "I believed someone whose whole career was finding the most appropriate location to hide and take a shot at a target would provide valuable input in this case."

"So, you chose to freelance and bring unknown variables into the plan-of-action?"

"I followed all established protocols and in no way did this additional information interfere in any manner with the effort."

"Except it left you with three bodies."

"Nothing O'Neal said or did had any impact on our actions."

"In your report you state that he recommended that the family not be taken in public as a group."

"It would have made them too easy a target."

"It would appear that they were easier targets when separated. Wouldn't you agree?"

"What I believe is that they shouldn't have been used as bait," Agent Peggy Fox countered.

"That was not the question. Did you intentionally order that the subjects be kept apart?"

"Yes."

"Wouldn't it have been easier to keep them together, utilizing fewer resources, allowing for better surveillance of the many venues the victims visited each day?"

It became clear to Special Agent Peggy Fox that a case was being developed against her for both the media and government officials who wanted answers. They didn't have to be correct answers—simply feasible explanations that could be sold. Three innocent people were murdered due to the incompetence of the agent in charge who did not follow proper protocol. Special Agent Peggy Fox has been reprimanded and demoted due to her actions during the unfortunate Wilkes-Barre affair. Yes, they would tie it all up with a pink bow. If she even hinted at protesting or going public criminal charges would be considered and ultimately brought against her. The trap was set. All she had to do was step into it.

Finally, Peggy Fox spoke, "We both know what the outcome of this interview is going to be. Why not end it now? Nothing I can say will make any difference and you know it."

"I know you are getting defensive. Do you have something to hide Agent Fox?"

"You have all the facts in my report."

"It's what's not in your report that we are concerned with. You were negligent, that we know. The question is, did you do anything that warrants criminal charges against you?"

"I did my job—nothing less. It was a doomed effort right from the beginning. You can't protect three people from seasoned military assassins without taking them into protective custody. They were used as pawns without even being given the respect of being told."

"How do you know they are military?"

"I assumed it because of the discipline needed to execute such tactics while remaining completely invisible."

"And, yet you invited a military advisor to participate in your little ill-conceived plan."

"I didn't set this thing up. I was opposed to it."

"So, you made sure it failed."

"That's how you are going to depict it."

"That's how you are explaining it."

"You are very good. Without even any hesitation you fill in the blanks on a script that has already been written."

"I'm simply doing my job."

"Be careful, that's how I got here, by simply doing my job."

Connecticut Congressman Blake Kane sat at the bar in a local Bergenfield, New Jersey pub. It was an out-of-the-way place on the frontage road that ran along the railroad tracks. A few regular patrons sat at the other end of the bar conversing about this and that. He couldn't really tell about what and he didn't want to know. After a long day in New York City attending a business development conference he had driven to this specific place as requested. The Scotch tasted good and offered a warm inner glow. He was nervous.

Things had begun slowly and then over time reached a fever pitch. When Nadia called and wanted to meet, he immediately made arrangements. Without question, he ached for her. Their times together were magic. She only had eyes for him. And, she was also the key to riches and power beyond his imagination. All he had to do was betray his family and his nation. Two small steps to achieve greatness that he so undeniably desired and deserved.

The details of what was about to happen were vague and mysterious. Nadia had explained that with his help almost the entire Congress, Senate, and Executive branches of the United States government would be eliminated in one single decisive act. It was almost too monstrous to think seriously about. Yet, over time, with the help of whispers in his ear it became a logical and acceptable plan-of-action. The resulting crisis would open the door for him to assume power in order to fill the void. He then could reshape the government to assure his prolonged leadership. Power, fame, riches would be his. Adding to the temptation was the fact that it would all happen with Nadia Noorani at his side. The only obligation he had was to assist with the implementation of the plan and after assuming power pulling all American troops out of the middle east, as well as severing all ties with Israel. He would, in essence, eliminate all American influence in that region. As Congressman Blake Kane sipped his Scotch, he acknowledged to himself that he never really cared what happened in that part of the world.

History is for those who have the courage to shape it. Through the ages ambitious men stepped from obscurity to greatness by achieving the unachievable. They were visionaries who could see beyond the mundane, the commonplace, or the acceptable. Great men took the reins by whatever means necessary and changed the course of human history. In the end, they enjoyed power beyond the imagination of the masses. They ruled because they had the strength and cunning to do so. As he put down his empty glass and tapped the bar to order a refill, Blake Kane prepared to enter history. The conquest of the United States of America was considered an impossible act. That was about to change as it was his destiny.

Nadia Noorani entered the bar.

CHAPTER 66

Connecticut Congressman Blake Kane stood, rushed over to Nadia Noorani, and led her to a secluded table in the corner. He returned to the bar retrieved his Scotch and ordered a Ginger Ale for the lady. She did not drink alcohol.

"You sounded upset," Congressman Kane said, "Is there anything wrong?"

"There has been a disruption in our plans, my love."

"What kind of disruption?"

"Our means of communications have been compromised." She sipped her drink and added, "We attempted to remove the threat, but there was some type of interference. At this time, we don't know the status of the threat or of our associate."

"What does this mean for us?"

Nadia looked around the pub to make sure that no one was near enough to overhear their conversation. "Neither entity knows the details of the plan. That much I know. This unfortunate turn-of-events does require that our communications follow a different route. It also may require that you take a more active role in this most noble undertaking."

"What kind of more active role are we talking about?" Blake Kane asked with an obvious sound of concern in his voice.

"Do not worry, my love, it is of a minor nature."

"I was promised anonymity."

"And, you shall have it."

"You understand, a man in my position is under constant scrutiny. The opposition party would love nothing more than to drag me through the mud. I've been a thorn in their side, pointing out their racism, misogyny, xenophobia, greed, and dishonesty. If they thought for a minute that I was involved in anything questionable, the long knives would be out."

"You shall remain untarnished and free of false accusations until you take your rightful place as the leader of the Western World." Nadia smiled with a warmth that would melt any man's heart, "With me at your side, my love."

"Yes, we are meant to achieve greatness together. You convinced me of that."

"I am glad. It is written that men of power and great intellect will institute a new world order whereby peace will endure for a thousand years." She took his hand and predicted, "You shall be the instrument that removes the crusaders from the holy land, expels the moneylenders from foreign nations, reduces cursed American avarice, and brings equality at long last to this country."

"I will do all that, but first this Hidden Cobra thing must be implemented."

"Do not speak the name," Nadia warned. "Just knowing the name can have serious repercussions."

"You're right—I'm sorry."

"Just be patient, my love. All will be well."

"Do you know the plan? Can you share it with me?"

Nadia leaned in to speak in a low voice, "No one, except the creators of the plan, know all of the elements. For security reasons it is compartmentalized with each of us only knowing what is essential in order for us to execute our part."

"Well, at present, I'm almost totally in the dark with the exception of knowing the desired outcome."

"That, my love, is the important part for you, at this time."

Identification of the potential female terrorist collaborator turned out to be easier than anticipated. The reason was that there were very few female research practitioners at Centre hospitalier Lyon Sud. Of the dozen or so only five had automobiles, two of which were green. However, fate was on their side as only one automobile had a Claude Bernard University sticker in the rear window. They had their suspect—Antoinette Le Claire. Immediately, Liam had a complete profile and dossier prepared about the subject. She was a French citizen educated in France. As a medical doctor she chose research of communicable diseases as her area of interest and had spent time in the Middle East and Central Africa. According to a research grant she was involved in an effort to develop a vaccine for hemorrhagic diseases which include Hemorrhagic Fever, Marburg Virus, and Ebola Virus Disease. They were certain they had the right person.

The team was keenly aware that care had to be taken when apprehending Dr. Le Claire. Because it was not a law enforcement operation they were, in essence, kidnapping the lady. Therefore, it couldn't be done at the research hospital, in a crowded location, or violently. There also was the language issue. Given all these considerations, they developed a plan.

Dr. Antoinette Le Claire left her office in the late afternoon. It was chilly so she wore a dark blue double-breasted, slim, tailored coat made with an Italian woven herringbone wool blend over a casual blouse and pants. It had been a long day at the laboratory with more setbacks than advances having been made. This was the bane of medical research. Hours of experimentation and testing often lead nowhere, leaving one with a feeling of having wasted precious time. Her short-cropped dark hair shifted with the breeze. Random thoughts shifted along with the breeze as an active mind sought new directions to try in an endless search for efficacious answers. Lost in a kaleidoscope of cogitation, she was unaware of the man who followed at a discreet distance.

Once inside her green Peugeot, Dr. Le Claire began to relax. It was time to leave the lab behind and think of more enjoyable things, such as what to eat for dinner and a planned telephone call to her sister, Gabrielle. The two of them always had stories to share, reminiscences, and gossip about childhood friends. It was a welcome change from the methodical, cold, demanding activities of medical research. She drove ten minutes to her apartment building and parked in the lot. A car passed behind her space to park elsewhere in the lot.

Antoinette Le Claire lived on the ninth floor. She rode alone in the elevator. Unidentified music made feeble attempts for attention. There was no reason to be concerned or even watchful when leaving the elevator and proceeding down the hall. A delightful aroma from another apartment aroused her desire for dinner. She reached her door.

Special Agent Peggy Fox opened the door to her apartment. She was spent. Three grueling hours of biased interrogation aimed at gathering adequate evidence for proof-positive that she was the guilty party in the unfortunate occurrence in Wilks-Barre, Pennsylvania took their toll. In the end, there was no way to stop the misinterpretation and misrepresentation of every word she spoke. She could say that she liked milkshakes and it would be presented that she was having milkshakes while she should have been doing due diligence to protect an innocent family. She had very little sleep while trying to coordinate 24-hour protection of the subjects and it would be presented as gross failure to properly identify and delegate team efforts. If she pointed out that protection had to be under cover as it was, in reality, a trap to catch Satan's Shadow, the official position would be that the FBI does not use human bait—never has and never will. This breach of Bureau standards could call for dismissal or even criminal charges.

When your lover betrays you, anger and pain is tenfold more severe than when a stranger does you wrong. Peggy Fox gave up everything to be in the Federal Bureau of Investigation. She loved the Bureau. She loved being involved in a noble profession. She loved being a Special Agent. The depth of that love was deeper than she even realized, until it was exposed as being a one-sided affair. She had been played a fool. A myriad of emotions fought to be recognized. Raw nerve endings left her with an inner electrically charged feeling. Fatigue promised relief if she could close her eyes and drift into safer realms. Sleep, perchance to dream, wasn't that what Shakespeare wrote, she thought.

Through the scope of a sniper's rifle Peggy Fox lay on her couch, eyes closed, purse on the floor, keys on the coffee table, a perfect target under the glow of a single light.

Dr. Le Claire entered her apartment. Inside, she realized something was different, out-of-place, odd—but what. Before she could switch on the light, a lamp in the living room came on. Before her sat Liam Beauchêne. Instinctively, the stunned woman turned to leave the apartment.

"The door will not open, Dr. Le Claire," Liam said calmly in French. "It is being held shut by an individual I am sure you cannot over power."

With all her effort she asked in a forced calm voice, "Who are you? What do you want?"

"My name is unimportant," Liam responded. "What I want are a few simple answers."

"If you do not leave, I'm calling the police."

"Sadly, this entire building has temporarily lost access to cellphone service."

After a futile attempt to make a connection, Dr. Le Claire inquired, "What is this all about?"

"Please, have a seat," Liam offered. "I will explain everything. You are in no danger."

"That's rather hard to believe when I'm trapped in my apartment with a stranger and no access to the outside world."

"Ah, appearances," Liam indicated the couch for his guest to sit. She complied. He continued, "There is inadequate time to play cat and mouse. We know what you have been involved with and need your cooperation."

"I don't know what you are referring to."

"You do. And, I warn you my patience is extremely limited. There are means by which we will get your cooperation that I do not wish to use. Only, don't for a minute believe that I will not go to these extremes very quickly."

Dr. Le Claire stood and exclaimed, "I'm leaving."

"The large gentleman in the hall can be most persuasive in sometimes most unpleasant ways. Please sit."

Antoinette Le Claire returned to the couch, "I . . ."

"Choose you next words carefully. You have been caught, as they say, red handed. We can place you in Paris," he noted her reaction which confirmed their belief, "a contact identified you," he lied, "and you have used your expertise to support illegal activities."

"I . . . I can tell you nothing," Antoinette Le Claire said plaintively.

"Ah, but you will."

"It will put my life in jeopardy."

"That is unfortunate. You have my sympathy. But, I must insist that you tell me exactly what you have provided those for whom you have chosen to work."

"I can't."

Liam sat back in the easy chair and in a nonchalant tone asked, "Have you heard of the group known as Satan's Shadow?"

"Of course, they are in the newspaper often."

"Then you know their modus operandi?"

"I believe so."

"What is it?"

"Excuse me?"

"What do those known as Satan's Shadow do?"

"They kill people."

"Which people?"

"Relatives of terrorists."

"Magnifique! Then we understand each other." Dr. Antoinette Le Claire stared blankly at Liam. He continued, "You have a sister, Gabrielle, I believe living in Macon. And, your parents are still in Narbonne, true?"

In a whisper she replied, "Yes."

"And, you have many friends at Claude Bernard University?"

"What are you implying?"

"I am implying nothing. This, my dear, is an out-and-out threat. Time does not allow for the cat and mouse game. You will cooperate, here and now, or Satan's Shadow will descend upon those you love leaving darkness in its wake."

Through the scope of a sniper rifle Peggy Fox was a sitting target. All she had to do was pull the trigger and her troubles would be over. At least, that was the solution offered by her dream.

CHAPTER 67

After two and a half hours, Liam concluded the interview of Dr. Antoinette Le Claire. He informed her that she would be held in detention at an undisclosed location until the investigation was completed. On a satellite telephone he called for trusted Special Operations Command DGSE operatives to take the prisoner to the same military base where they held Kareem Reza. In a short period of time two large men arrived, took the doctor into custody, and left. When he was alone, Liam told General Hughes it was safe to come out. The team heard his comment through a microphone he wore and came out of their various hiding places to join him in Dr. Le Claire's apartment. Ron Clew and Jarvis Demoye entered from the hallway while Ken Farmingdale and General Hughes came out of the bedroom.

"As you heard, we have a diabolical plot and are not out-of-the-woods as yet," Liam stated as fatigue became apparent.

They reviewed what had been revealed. While in the Middle East, Dr. Le Claire had been recruited by a little-known Islamic terrorist group dedicated to destroying Western Culture. They mesmerized her with visions of divine dictates and promises of a utopian world free of the evil money hungry capitalists and American imperialists. Over time, she began to believe the condemnations and grew to hate the Evil Empire.

Armed with a research grant, she visited the Congo and gathered specimens of a Marburg-like virus that had been classified and named Ebola by the team of Dr. Patricia Webb, Dr. James Lange, and Dr. Karl Johnson, of the American Center for Disease Control's Special Pathogens Branch. Dr. Le Claire was on the team searching to find a vaccine for this deadly disease.

Research began with analysis of how the virus is transmitted. They determined that infected patients are not contagious until they show symptoms of the disease, generally between 8-10 days. Through what is called contact tracing those who have come in contact with a victim are watched for signs of illness for 21 days from the last day they came in contact with an Ebola patient. Ebola virus spreads to people through direct contact with bodily fluids of a person who is sick or has died from the disease. The virus gets in through broken skin or mucous membranes in the eyes, nose, or mouth. It can also be acquired through sexual contact.

The research team found that Ebola virus can survive in body fluids, like blood, up to several days at room temperature. On dry surfaces, like doorknobs and countertops, the virus can survive for only several hours. Ebola can be killed by using a U.S. Environmental Protection Agency (EPA) registered hospital disinfectant. It was also found that Ebola virus can remain in immunologically privileged fluids in the body after a patient has recovered. These fluids are semen, breast milk, ocular fluid, and spinal column fluid. How long it remains active is unknown.

Liam stated, "One thing is clear, the plot cannot involve introducing infected individuals into the Washington, DC area to spread the disease. They are only contagious when symptoms appear and within a few days they are either dead or severely infirmed. The disease might spread, but most likely will not touch their intended target—the leaders of the United States government." He tapped his notes and added, "That is where the doctor of death comes in."

With the threat to her family hanging over her head, Dr. Antoinette Le Claire was forthcoming and cooperative. She confessed to doing supplemental research to see what medium was needed to keep the virus alive outside the body for longer periods of time. A number of substances offered promise, however, they did not ensure infection in a majority of cases and were too easily detected. She explained that quite by accident she found the ideal medium. A friend had been hand-processing cashew nuts and broke out in a severe rash. Dr. Le Claire visited the friend and upon seeing her red, oozing, skin prescribed Prednisone. Afterward she researched cashew nuts to determine why her friend had such a reaction.

The fruit of the cashew tree is called a pseudocarp or false fruit. What appears to be a fruit, called a cashew apple, is a pear-shaped growth that ripens into a yellow or red structure 2 to 4 inches long. It is edible and has a strong sweet smell and taste. At the end of the cashew apple is a kidney shaped fruit within which is a single seed considered a nut. The seed has a double shell which contains anacardic acid, a potent skin irritant. Upon further study she found the allergen is chemically related to the oil urushiol which is a toxin found in poison ivy. Dr. Le Claire's attention turned to analysis of urushiol. The oily resin has been shown to lead to development of a rash, Toxicodendron dermatitis, in 80%-90% of individuals. It appears as red, itchy bumps and small blisters which rupture with associated weeping and oozing. A perfect way for a virus to enter the body. Further secret experimentation allowed her to develop a clear formulation of urushiol oil with embedded Ebola virus.

The terrorist group did field trials with the lethal concoction. Kidnapped victims were exposed to the oil. Two weeks later they were all dead. It was when she was describing this step that Antoinette Le Claire's countenance reflected pride in what she had accomplished. The ultimate weapon of mass destruction. Victims would unknowingly be exposed to the virus that would gain entry into their body through the rash. Their focus would be on the extreme discomfort and itching of the rash until a week later when they would begin to show symptoms of Ebola Virus Disease. By then it would be too late.

As a weapon, if a large number of individuals are exposed at the same time hundreds of contagious Ebola Virus Disease victims would flood hospitals, infect first responders, leave poisonous bodily fluids everywhere, or be found dead.

"The possibilities are horrifying," Ken Farmingdale admitted. He provided a projection of what could happen, "By the time it is discovered to be Ebola, there would be a new wave of victims every week with no way of tracing the sources."

"It is a scenario that is too terrifying to be allowed to happen," General Hughes concluded.

"The question is how can they expose a large number of persons at the same time?" Ken Farmingdale asked.

"That is the piece of the puzzle we do not have," Liam said sounding even more fatigued.

"We have the target and we know what the weapon is," General Hughes considered. "What we now have to figure out is the means of delivery. Even if you could ship a can of infected oil to the United States, you would need to have individuals make contact with it." He turned to Liam and asked, "Did she indicate how long the virus could survive in her mixture?"

"Indefinitely. There is no way of knowing."

Jarvis Demoye observed, "It's clear that the bad guys can't walk around the Capital Building wiping it on doorknobs or other public places. There is too much activity and most Congressmen and Senators don't open their own doors."

"The President definitely doesn't," Ron Clew added.

"So, how do you infect a majority of members of Congress and the Senate, as well as the President and Vice President of the United States with tainted urushiol oil?" Ken Farmingdale reiterated.

Liam spoke in a tired, weak voice, "I am sorry for mon incompetence. ça n'aurait pas dû arriver. Pour cela je serai toujours avec regret."

Jarvis interrupted, "Liam, we do not speak French."

"Oh, yes, my apologies," Liam replied. "I was expressing my regret for the operation that cost your comrade. It should not have happened. For this I shall always be regretful."

"Apology accepted," General Hughes said. "Now, let's figure out how we are going to proceed."

After hours in the back room of a small print shop on Ru Louis Calmel in Gennevilliers, a suburb of Paris, Salah el-Khazzani finished an important job. An Imam from a local mosque ordered one thousand business cards. They were, to say the least, unique. An eagle flying in front of a waving American flag was the backdrop. In gold letters the words, "Salute The American Bridge Toward Harmonious Economic Mores" created an impressive message. Under the message in white lettering was "Society for International Economic Freedom" followed by an internet address. Salah found the graphic and message to be peculiar. It was a complete contradiction of the position held by those with whom he was associated. He was unaware of the reaction of the Imam when he saw the design. The old man laughed as he focused on the first letters of the message that spelled, "STAB THEM."

Per instructions, Salah el-Khazzani worked after hours, alone, in secrecy. Even though the cards and message were confusing he did as he was told. The four-color cards were printed and allowed to dry. Then Salah donned latex gloves and a surgical mask and with a brush he covered each card with a clear varnish. The special varnish was provided by two unidentified men. He didn't ask any questions. Finished cards were packed in a standard business card box and sealed with plastic wrap.

The following day, the same two men returned, picked up the cards and remaining varnish container. They paid Salah el-Khazzani handsomely and left. Where the cards were taken the printer neither knew nor wanted to know.

Secret Service Agent Emanuel Vegas informed General Hughes of the timing of the upcoming burial ceremony at Arlington National

Cemetery for Master Sergeant Adam Hayes. Upon receiving the information, Maxwell Hughes informed the team that he would fly back to America to pay their respects. He suggested that it would be prudent if the team did not make an appearance.

"I disagree," Navy Seal Ron Clew stated emphatically. "I was on the mission where Adam died. If it hadn't been for him leading that prick out it could have been me. I need to pay my respects in person."

"That's how I feel, "Ken Farmingdale added. "I never faced combat, test flying aircraft, but I did get a taste of going on a dangerous mission with Ron and Adam. That kind of experience brings you real close together. I once said that I'm not a team player. That's all changed. It's important for me to acknowledge a brave man whose team I was honored to be a part of and whom I respect."

"It seems we all need to honor a lost friend," Captain Jarvis Demoye concluded. "I wish to salute a fallen comrade, as well.

"It's clear that I'm outvoted," General Hughes accepted. "I guess I don't need to point out that there is a degree of risk with us being seen together. If any one of us gets connected with Satan's Shadow we all would fall under suspicion."

No protests were forthcoming.

"I too will be attending the ceremony to honor a brave man," Liam stated softly.

CHAPTER 68

It was as beautiful a morning as was possible at that time of year. The sun climbed slowly into a clear sapphire blue sky. A comfortable breeze created a soothing motion to all surroundings along with a mixture of aromas from various plants and trees. While, various avian songs completed a tranquil setting.

A woman wearing a simple black dress walked slowly up the stairs of a single-story white building. Next to her was her fifteen-year-old daughter wearing a dark green blouse and black skirt. As directed, they arrived at the Administrative Building at Arlington National Cemetery 45 minutes before the scheduled burial service. Once inside, they were met by a Cemetery Representative who introduced himself as well as the NCOIC, Non-Commissioned Officer in charge.

Evelyn Glassman immediately noticed Michael O'Neal in dress uniform standing with his wife to the side. He nodded while allowing the Cemetery Representative to complete his explanation of how the service would proceed. As there are generally between 27 and 30 funeral services each weekday at the cemetery everything is run efficiently with strict adherence to time constraints. Adam Hayes wife made no request for a religious service or military honors. The burial service would be a simple gravesite ceremony.

With instructions complete there remained twenty minutes before they would proceed to the gravesite. It was then when General Maxwell Hughes in formal Marine blues approached Evelyn Glassman. As he drew near, she was stunned to see that a two-star Marine General would be at her ex-husband's funeral.

"Ms. Glassman, my condolences. Sergeant Hayes was a remarkable man with a depth of spirit we all admired. He will be greatly missed."

Somewhat confused Evelyn asked, "Did he serve with you?"

"Adam participated in a number of joint service missions."

Evelyn was struck by the fact that such a senior level officer would refer to him by his first name.

General Hughes continued, "I'm sure you enjoyed his sense of humor as much as we. Even during tough times, he broke the tension with a word or comment. He had rare courage and earned the respect of all who served with him—myself included. Again, my condolences."

"Thank you. When you speak of courage, I can't help but remember when he told me he had to leave us to protect us. He didn't say it outright but I knew he feared that he might be dangerous." Evelyn looked out the windows toward the cemetery as she recalled, "One night when I was out with friends and came home rather late I found him asleep in a chair. When I went to kiss him, he awoke with a start. Before I knew it, he was inches from striking me when he realized who it was and stopped. It frightened me. Even more frightening was the look in his eyes—cold, snakelike, focused, lethal. It frightened him. After that he became withdrawn and distant until he made his announcement. Courage? Yes, it took courage to give up what he loved in order to keep us safe."

"What we do, what we become, the hidden effect, is indeed a heavy price," General Hughes said with a slight tone of melancholy.

As General Hughes moved away Navy Captain Jarvis Demoye in dress whites approached the widow. Once more, Evelyn Glassman was bewildered by the fact that a high-level officer with a different military branch had come to honor Adam.

"I came here to show my respects for a brave man, as well as a family that shares the burden of service. No words adequately express how we feel or what you and your daughter must be going through. We can only be grateful for having spent time with a man who left an indelible impression on our lives," Captain Demoye said sincerely.

"Thank you," Evelyn looked around and saw other military branches represented and observed, "It appears Adam was involved in far more than I realized."

At first, Jarvis was taken aback and concerned about Satan's Shadow somehow having been revealed. It was the normal reaction of a guilty man to an innocent comment. Quickly, he realized his fear was unwarranted. He replied, "Adam crossed many paths during his years of service and afterward. Those who are here today are a small percentage of the many who will miss this fine man."

The next to speak with Evelyn was Air Force Major Ken Farmingdale. He was younger than the other officers and walked with a slight swagger common with test pilots. When he reached her, he offered his hand and upon taking hers said, "Every man's life ends the same way. It is only the details of how he lived and how he died that distinguish one man from another. I stole that from Ernest Hemingway. There are those who can weave words far better and more profoundly than me. This particular quote struck me because Adam Hayes distinguished himself in ways that I could never emulate. I could only admire. In a very small way I am a better man because I met, worked, and fought with a far better man."

"Your words were fine and truly welcome." She squeezed his hand as he moved aside.

A large black man in Navy dress white choker uniform approached. Immediately, Evelyn recognized the gold eagle, anchor, trident insignia of a Navy Seal. He was a Master Chief Petty Officer, but she didn't know that. All she knew was that he was an enlisted man—just like her Adam. This made her feel closer to the man who approached.

"Ma'am, my name is Ronald Clew. I was on the mission that took Sergeant Hayes' life. I want you to know we were trying to save a French citizen being held hostage in a hostile environment. Your husband acted in a brave and honorable manner. I am proud to have served with him." Ron turned to Adam Hayes' daughter, Marcia, and said, "Miss, your father was the kind of man who other brave men turned to for encouragement and inspiration. I know that doesn't help right now. In time, I hope, you find some comfort in knowing that your dad was admired by men who are very hard to impress—myself included." He turned to leave but was stopped by Evelyn.

"Did you rescue the hostage?"

Ron Clew had to think of an answer before speaking. Then he replied, "We brought the hostage home."

The final person in the room was an older gentleman in a dark suit with a cane.

"Mademoiselle, on behalf of the French government and French people I wish to express our gratitude for your husband's service to our nation and our regrets for your loss. Brave men far too often are lost keeping us safe. La liberté a souvent un coût élevé, freedom often comes at a high cost. My personal condolences and prayers for Monsieur Adam Hayes."

The Non-Commissioned Officer in charge (NCOIC) announced that it was time to proceed to Master Sergeant Adam Hayes' last resting place in Section 60. All vehicles involved should follow the hearse. Army pallbearers will be waiting at the site.

Four members of Satan's Shadow followed in separate cars. In the Administration Building they did not acknowledge that they knew each other. Michael O'Neal knew otherwise. He was certain that Ron Clew and General Hughes were familiar with each other from his experience on the failed rescue mission, as well as his meeting with the General at the airport. It wasn't a giant leap to conclude that he was in the presence of at least part of the group known as Satan's Shadow. How many there were, who was the leader, how they operated he had no idea and didn't care to learn. From those present he could understand how Adam had gotten involved.

As the procession rode slowly through narrow thoroughfares an additional vehicle joined the column at the rear. The sun pushed long shadows across the path as they wound their way to the final destination. It created a mesmerizing effect as they went from sunlight to shadow again and again. Upon arrival, mourners left their cars and waited at the curb for the pallbearers. It was then that Michael O'Neal noticed the driver of the last vehicle. A woman in her late thirties with short auburn hair wearing sunglasses exited the car. She wore a black business suit with dark blue blouse. On the jacket of the suit was a lapel pin that he couldn't make out. It was FBI Special Agent Peggy Fox.

Six Army pallbearers slid the casket out of the hearse. As it is customary to salute while the flag-draped casket is moving all military guests stood at attention and saluted. Civilians placed their hands over their hearts. Once the pallbearers made a formal five-step turn and stopped holding the remains of a fallen warrior salutes were dropped and the NCOIC issued the command, "Ready—step." He then led the processional to the grave site and indicated for the mourners to stand near a small green metal marker allowing enough room for he and the pallbearers to pass. Once again, all saluted as the flag was moving and they were stationary. The pallbearers positioned the casket on canvass straps over the grave and held the flag taut over the remains. The NCOIC did an inspection and then stepped back to allow for whatever religious or other services were planned.

At the time Evelyn was informed of the schedule for Adam Hayes' interment it was requested that any services be kept under ten minutes due to the number of funerals held each day at Arlington National Cemetery. Evelyn asked Michael O'Neal to say a few words.

"This day we part company with a friend, ally, husband, and father. He is at rest. It is our burden to continue on the path before us without his steadfast spirit to lighten the load. It will be difficult to face the future without him, while at the same time a blessing to have fond memories of him. Each of us, in our own way, found our lives enriched by a man named Adam Howard Hayes. No man can ask for any more." Michael

O'Neal stepped back to indicate that he had finished.

The NCOIC stood two paces from the casket. Two Army pallbearers folded the American flag into the familiar triangle of blue with white stars. At that point, the NCOIC saluted the flag and then accepted it with his left hand on top and right hand underneath. He proceeded to where Evelyn Glassman sat and presented the flag. As he did so he said, "On behalf of the President of the United States, the United States Army, and a grateful Nation, please accept this flag as a symbol of our appreciation for your loved one's honorable and faithful service."

An Arlington Lady then presented a card of condolence. The Arlington Ladies are a group of volunteers who attend every funeral service at Arlington National Cemetery to ensure that no military member or veteran is buried alone. The practice began in 1948 when the Chief of Staff of the Air Force, General Hoyt Vandenberg, and his wife attended a number of funeral services at the cemetery and noticed some burial services had only a military chaplain in attendance. He and his wife, Gladys, decided that a member of the Air Force family should attend all Air Force services. Mrs. Vandenberg and a number of friends then began attending Air Force burials. General Creighton Abrams' wife, Julia, formed a similar group for Army burials in 1973, followed by a Navy group in 1985 and one for the Coast Guard in 2006. The Marine Corps does not have a group as it is customary for a representative of the Marine Commandant to attend every funeral. With that the service ended.

All attendees headed for their respective vehicles. As General Hughes opened the door of his black Escalade, a female voice behind him stopped him. "May I have a word with you General?"

General Hughes turned to see a woman in a black suit. On her lapel he saw a pin with the familiar logo of the Federal Bureau of Investigation.

CHAPTER 69

General Hughes led Special Agent Peggy Fox a few blocks north of Arlington National Cemetery. They arrived at the Quarterdeck Restaurant whose address is 1200 Ft. Myer Drive even though it is actually on the bend of 12th Street N. Go figure. It was a 2-story white clapboard house surrounded by 5-story historic buildings. On one side was a covered patio with numerous tables.

The Quarterdeck is known for its Maryland Blue Crab Feast and that it offers blue crab year-round. It has been a fixture of the Fort Meyer Heights neighborhood since 1979.

They decided to sit on the patio and found a table in a corner of the building that was relatively secluded. The fact that General Hughes was in his dress blues had a distinct effect on their treatment. It wasn't often that such a high-ranking officer visited their establishment. The adage, "Rank has its privileges" was apparent as every effort was made to provide exceptional service. The two diners decided to have blue crab.

"So, Ms. Fox, what possible interest could the FBI have in the burial of a brave man?"

"What makes you think I don't have an interest in you?" Peggy Fox retorted.

"Unless you've been following me around or have a device on my car you would have had no idea where I was or that I would be there," General Hughes pointed out. "No, you came for Sergeant Hayes' funeral and saw me which led to this meeting."

"Very astute of you," Peggy complimented her interviewee.

"How can I help you?"

The waitress came with their drinks. "If there is anything else you need, General, let me know. Your order will be ready momentarily, sir." She departed.

"Do you think she knows I am here?" Peggy asked sarcastically.

"She knows," General Hughes answered. "And, she also has noted that little lapel pin, as well." He looked around, "I'm certain we are under surveillance by the staff, so watch what you say." General Hughes smiled. "Now, how can I help you?"

"How well did you know Master Sergeant Adam Hayes?"

"Well enough to come to his interment."

"Did he ever serve under you?"

"He did, however, I'm not at liberty to say when, where, or how. You do understand?"

"There seemed to be a significant number of high-ranking officers from different branches of service at his burial ceremony."

Their order arrived and the too-small table became crowded with plates, napkins, nut-crackers, glasses, and silverware. "The chef picked the best crab for you, sir."

"Thank you, Adrian," he read her nameplate.

"If there is anything else, please let me know, sir."

When the waitress left, General Hughes looked at Agent Fox and said, "The chef picked the best crab for you, ma'am."

Peggy Fox laughed. She then admitted, "I guess I'm being overly sensitive."

"It's understandable. You probably haven't dined in a restaurant with too many Generals—it's the uniform."

After tasting the food, Peggy returned to the subject, "Why do you suppose all those officers were at the ceremony?"

"I'm afraid you'd have to ask them."

"But, doesn't it seem odd for such a group to attend the funeral of an enlisted man?"

"I've attended far too many services at Arlington to consider anything as odd. It all depends on their activities in the service and what they were involved in after their discharge."

"Let's get back to Sergeant Hayes. Do you know what he did after his discharge?"

"He became a mercenary working for the military, the United States government, and foreign governments. Exact details I have no way of knowing."

"Did he work for you as a mercenary?"

"No."

"So, your experience with him was when he was on active duty?"

"Affirmative."

"And, you can't tell me any more than confirming that he did at one time report to you."

"I will tell you this. Sergeant Adam Hayes was one of the best soldiers I have ever had the honor of serving with. He was the ideal warrior—brave, obedient, innovative, loyal, and damn good at his craft. In any situation, he was the go-to guy. As you can tell I had the utmost respect for the man."

"When was the last time you saw him?"

General Hughes chose his words carefully, "Little more than three weeks ago. He was preparing for a mission for the French government. It was the mission that got him killed."

"I'm aware of that. He went with Michael O'Neal, didn't he? That would answer why the Frenchman with a cane was in attendance," Peggy Fox mused out loud. "Were you involved with that mission?"

"No."

"Then, why did you see Sergeant Hayes recently?"

"I wasn't directly involved with the mission, however, I did bring the parties together. How do you like the crab?"

"It's delicious. So, you brought together Sergeant Hayes and, what was the Frenchman's name?"

"He asked to remain anonymous."

"I could stop him and ask for his passport."

"You certainly could, but from my dealing with him, he's already on a plane." He ate a bite of blue crab and added, "You should have stopped him first."

"I can see that. How did you meet him?"

"That is another of those facts I'm not at liberty to divulge."

"You seem to have a lot of secrets, General," Peggy stated somewhat frustrated.

Unfazed, General Hughes replied, "You have access to my official files. Although you will find, without a court order and clearance from the Department of Justice, National Security Council, Department of Defense, and the Commandant of the United States Marines there will be files that are unavailable for review."

"Apparently, you've been busy."

Maxwell Hughes smiled and said, "It goes with the uniform."

A man approached the table and introduced himself as the manager of the restaurant. He inquired as to whether or not everything was to their liking. Out of courtesy, General Hughes deferred to the lady.

"Everything is delicious. Thank you." Peggy stated.

"Give my compliments to the chef," General Hughes added.

When they were once more alone, Peggy Fox took a paper out of her purse and handed it to the General as she asked, "Have you ever seen this coin before? I realize it is only a partial image."

General Hughes stared at the image of the edge of a coin and dragon printed on the paper. It was a challenge coin with which he was all too familiar. He couldn't help but wonder where she got that incomplete representation. The fact that she did have it was of great concern. He could account for all the coins carried by team members, including Adam Hayes, and the few that were with others were of little concern. If she had a coin, she would have a complete image. This came from an indentation of a coin, but where, how? Loose ends—those unexpected elements that cannot be planned on are the most dangerous manifestations of any operation. A speck of dirt in the wrong place can render a weapon useless at the worst possible time. A loose bolt can stop an advance. Debris left behind could identify who had been there thus alerting the wrong people. An indentation . . ."

"General, have you seen this before?"

"It appears to be a dragon most likely on a challenge coin," he bought time.

"Have you seen a challenge coin with a dragon on it?"

Mentally General Hughes breathed a sigh of relief. He knew he couldn't lie to an FBI agent without substantial risk. In this case, her question allowed for him to be evasive without it being obvious. He said, "I've seen numerous challenge coins through the years. A number of them had dragons. Only, I couldn't tell you where or when I saw them."

"What about this one in particular?"

"It's only a small section. What else is on the coin?"

"I don't know. Possibly a sword and ring of stars."

"That makes it very difficult."

Agent Fox could tell she wasn't going to get an answer so she changed direction when she asked, "We've established that you know the Frenchman who was at the ceremony. Do you know any of the members of the military who were there?"

"Is there anything else that I might get you, General," the very welcome waitress inquired with a broad smile.

General Hughes looked toward Peggy Fox who indicated that she didn't require anything. He answered, "Thank you Adrian. I believe we are finished. Just the check will do." He handed her his credit card and then addressed Peggy Fox, "What exactly are you investigating?"

"Have you heard of Satan's Shadow?"

"I have."

"I'm investigating three murders perpetrated by that group in Wilkes-Barre, Pennsylvania."

"And, you think Hayes knew something about it?"

"His friend, Michael O'Neal, was a consultant on our protection plans and they were together on that French rescue mission."

"And?"

"And, from all appearances this Satan's Shadow is comprised of well-trained military personnel."

"What appearances?" General Hughes asked taking over the conversation.

"All of the murders were executed with precision that I believe could only be done by someone with extensive training."

"Agent Fox, you seem like an intelligent person. Do you honestly believe that such thin evidence leads to Adam Hayes? Let an honorable man rest in peace."

Peggy Fox attempted to regain control of the interview, "Do you know the other military men who were in attendance?"

The waitress returned with General Hughes' credit card and receipt. She thanked him enthusiastically for a generous tip, turned, and scampered away.

General Hughes stood from the table. He said in conclusion, "Agent Fox, I wish you luck with your investigation. Frankly, I believe you are, forgive the pun, chasing shadows. You have nothing to lead you to members of the military. And, nothing to implicate Adam Hayes. Given that, I cannot provide any further answers. Thank you for an enjoyable lunch."

CHAPTER 70

All five members of Satan's Shadow sat around the great room of the Spanish style stucco safe house in Newport News, Virginia. Joining them was Liam, the man who wasn't there.

Emanuel Vegas spoke first, "I hope you realize why I couldn't attend the services for Adam Hayes."

"You were the only smart one," General Hughes replied. "I fear we may be in jeopardy following the paying of our respects. You all saw the FBI agent in attendance? I had lunch with her. She is investigating the Wilkes-Barre assassinations."

Jarvis Demoye leaned forward as he inquired, "Does she have anything? How did she come to be there? Did she connect Adam Hayes to Satan's Shadow?"

"She linked Adam to Michael O'Neal, the Army sniper. He . . ." General Hughes looked at Secret Service Agent Emanuel Vegas, ". . . was a consultant on the FBI protection efforts in Wilkes-Barre."

Manny shook his head, "Expand the circle slowly," he said remembering his conversation with the mysterious Dave at the CIA. "A bad move on my part. Not my finest hour." He in turn looked at Liam, "If not for the rescue mission he and Adam may never have been connected."

General Hughes added, "And, I talked Adam into including his friend. I guess there are enough SNAFUs to go around. That includes attendance at Arlington." The Marine stood, walked over to the bar, fixed a drink, and continued, "She asked me if I knew any of you."

"What did you tell her?" Ron Clew inquired.

"Evasive maneuvers, thanks to a cute waitress I didn't have to answer." He took a sip. "But, this lady, Peggy Fox, is no fool. She knew I avoided the question which opened the doors for wild speculation. For all I know, she could have concluded that she was looking at the Satan's Shadow team."

"That would be some stretch," Ken Farmingdale commented.

"She thinks Satan's Shadow is made up of highly trained military. That trident that was on your chest couldn't be missed by a blind man," General Hughes said to Ron Clew. He then turned to Liam, "She wanted to know your name but I refused to provide it."

"Merci mon ami."

"There's more," General Hughes stated, "She has a partial impression of an RMO."

When Liam looked at Ken with a confused look, Ken explained, "Round metal object—a challenge coin."

"It had a partial image of a dragon—our dragon."

"How did she get that?" Jarvis asked. "We didn't leave any notes at the points of contact. We left a note in the lobby of the Wilkes-Barre Times Leader."

"She had the notes from the other operations," Ron Clew concluded.

"The lady is thorough, I'll give her that," Jarvis offered.

"No fool, is our little Fox," General Hughes stated, he turned to Secret Service Agent Vegas and asked, "What do you think?"

"We have a fox in the henhouse," was his reply.

Two men clad in all black wearing black ski masks entered a bistro carrying AK-47s. Their objective was an establishment frequented by tourists—many from America. Outside, a third terrorist waited in a running automobile. Weeks of planning and dry runs gave them confidence that they would be able to inflict maximum carnage with minimum risk. They would be in and out in less than three minutes. The crowded pub would not require any aiming. Spray the room with 7.62x39mm rounds from a 100 round drum magazine. At 40 rounds per minute in semi-automatic mode it would allow two and a half minutes of constant fire. On this day a lesson would be taught that would long be remembered.

Once inside, the two men found themselves standing alone facing the rifle muzzles of twenty police officers. Otherwise the pub was empty. Something had gone terribly wrong. They had been betrayed. Their first impulse was to open fire. That did not happen. When they raised their weapons a massive barrage of bullets dropped them where they stood. Outside, the driver of the getaway car assumed the loud reports were from his cohorts. That was until a large police vehicle pulled up in front of his auto while a police officer smashed the side window and pointed a pistol at his head. He surrendered without resistance.

What could have been a tragedy was averted due to a number of anonymous tips received over a two-week period. Police had been informed of the terrorist plot, the target restaurant, and eventually the time of the planned assault. It was obvious the informer was an insider who knew the actors well. Without their help a disaster of enormous proportions might have occurred. The police did not attempt to identify the caller.

Agent Peggy Fox examined the list of names she compiled at the burial of Adam Hayes. Marine General Maxwell Hughes, Navy Captain Jarvis Demoye, Air Force Major Ken Farmingdale, Navy Seal Master Chief Petty Officer Ronald Clew, and the late Special Forces Master Sergeant Adam Hayes. The presence of these men fed her theory that Satan's Shadow consisted of highly trained military. "Am I looking at the perpetrators of numerous murders?" she said to herself. Immediately, her mind drifted to the future where she is the one who brings Satan's Shadow to justice. She would spit in the eye of those above her at the Bureau. More importantly, she would expose those incompetents to the media and thereby the world. It might end her career at the FBI, however, it would be on her terms not theirs and she would go out on top. A book deal, interviews, and lectures would give power to her voice and validate her professionalism.

When the lofty fantasy passed, Peggy Fox returned to her analysis. If they are the core of Satan's Shadow who else might be involved and how many of them exist? Are they simply a small cadre of vigilantes or is there a larger force hiding in the shadows? And, what if any involvement is there by Michael O'Neal? Which then begs the question, how does Secret Service Agent Emanuel Vegas fit in? He was not at the burial ceremony. Why not? Could the Michael O'Neal connection be a simple case of coincidence? How far and how deep does this conspiracy go? At that point her mind once more saw three large letters—CIA. It also saw a huge red flag. She had to move cautiously. There was no telling who and at what level government officials were involved. Could it go all the way up to the President? In an attempt to clear her runaway mind Peggy stood and walked into her kitchen. She put on a kettle of water in order to make tea.

In the back room of an apartment in a five-story brick building over a restaurant on Avenue Gabriel Peri a plastic wrapped box sat on a closet shelf. The box contained one-thousand very special business cards. They were the essential final element of Hidden Cobra. There they would sit until their lethal venom could be delivered in one glorious strike against the American government.

Six thousand miles away, United States Congressman Blake Kane read a text message on his private cellphone. "I must see u tday, futur is here." It was from Nadia Noorani.

He texted back, "That is impossible today."

"Nothing is impossible for u, my love."

"I have important meetings."

"I have ur destiny."

"Maybe later."

"Our futur cant wait."

"It must."

"Be brave, my love, take what is yours."

"Where shall we meet?"

A half-hour later Congressman Kane entered a seedy-looking consignment shop in a not-too-well-maintained building. It had a dangerous and unfriendly appearance. Inside he came upon an old shopkeeper with a grey beard wearing a thobe and kufi. The man looked at him, did not speak a word, but gestured with his head for Congressman Kane to go through a curtain into the back of the store. Apprehensive as he was Kane proceeded into the maw.

Nadia Noorani stood at the far end of the dimly lit corridor. She wore a dark green dress, sandals, and hijab. Her appearance was somewhat of a surprise as the hijab was unexpected. In fact, he had never seen her wear one before. Slowly and cautiously, he proceeded down the hall toward her. She neither spoke nor smiled. Unmoving, she waited. When he drew near, she raised her right hand to signal for him to stop. He obeyed.

"You shall have your kingdom, my love," Nadia stated in a formal voice, "but first you must declare loyalty and obedience to the coming caliphate."

Confused and alarmed, Congressman Kane asked, "What is this all about?"

"Before the Cobra strikes, you will declare fealty to Allah, the New World Order, and the true rulers of mankind. You shall have your kingdom but pay homage to the all-powerful. Your America will be our America. Under our guidance you shall rule and shape the evil empire into a vassal state. Great riches will be yours, but the souls of the people will be our domain. Sharia will prevail and there will be ever-lasting peace in the world."

"Nadia, I don't understand."

"It is simple, my love. You will sit upon the throne that we provide.

In return, you will offer loyalty and obedience."

"This is not the future we spoke of," Congressman Blake Kane protested.

"Of course it is, my love." Still Nadia Noorani showed no emotion. "Do you not understand that it would be foolish to lay the most powerful nation in the world at your feet without assurance that it would not someday be at our throats. It must be to our benefit?"

"But, I wouldn't do anything to bring harm to . . ." he stopped as he realized that he didn't really know who the conspirators were. His head was so filled with the vision of becoming the President of the United States he failed to identify with whom he was dealing. His heart was so drawn to Nadia Noorani that he trusted her motives and her words. Once in power, he would be an ally with those who made it possible. Wasn't that enough?

"Swear it!"

"This is too much, too soon."

"Swear it!"

"Why do you put me in such a position?"

"Swear it!"

"I don't know what to do."

"Obey me, my love. Swear allegiance and fealty to the new caliphate. Be guided by their words. Destroy that cursed paper called the Constitution. Rule the people with authority and bring them unto the glorious light of Allah."

"The people will not stand for it."

"At first, but sheep learn quickly. Hunger and strife are not long tolerated. They will fall in line when obedience is rewarded and disobedience severely punished."

"I'm all turned around," Blake Kane whimpered.

"Swear it!"

Slowly he relented, "I swear allegiance to the coming new order."

Nadia smiled. She took his hand and led him into a small room to detail what must be done next. Two men, hidden in shadows, put away their knives and silently disappeared.

CHAPTER 71

Air Force One touched down at Geneva International Airport on Runway 04 as wind velocity exceeded 4 knots. An interesting fact that until September 2018 this runway was designated 05 but was changed to 04 due to the North Magnetic Pole moving. The Boeing VC-25A taxied to a secure area and the President of the United States and his entourage left the aircraft. Among those who accompanied the President on the flight was Congressman Blake Kane from Connecticut who was a member of the same political party and served on the Financial Services Committee. They were in Geneva for an International Economic Forum at which the President was scheduled to speak. Three limousines waited to take them 2.5 miles to Hotel Le Richemond on the banks of Lake Geneva.

A dinner was planned for all visiting dignitaries at the International Conference Centre Geneva (ICCG). All members of the Presidential party attended with the exception of one—Congressman Blake Kane. He feigned illness from the long flight and wished to rest up for the planned conference the next day. However, once all members of the party had gone Kane also left through the door on Quai du Mont Blanc. As instructed, he crossed the road and walked along the shoreline of Lake Geneva until he came to the first marina. There he stopped and waited. In but a few minutes a black SUV pulled up, the driver rolled down the passenger side window and ordered, "Get in." Blake Kane complied.

A middle-eastern man with a dark brown beard, approximately thirty-five years old, wearing a western style brown suit drove the vehicle. No words were spoken as they rode. They wound in and out of traffic and the extraordinary number of motorcycles, motor scooters, and bicycles on the road. Kane remembered reading something about the fact that most residents of Geneva lived in apartments with only about 25 percent owning a private home. Part of the reason was the large number of foreign citizens that lived and worked in the international city.

As time went on, Congressman Kane became apprehensive realizing that no one knew where he was. He could quite easily disappear and never be found. Finally, the driver turned into an industrial area and then into an old factory building. Once inside, he heard the large doors close behind them. The SUV stopped and the driver climbed out without uttering a word. Congressman Kane followed.

They proceeded up a wooden staircase to an inner office. At the door the driver paused and knocked twice. The door opened and another man with a beard in his forties, wearing a business suit, greeted them, "I see you follow instructions well. That is good." He motioned for Congressman Kane to enter. The driver remained outside. It was a small office with a metal desk, two desk chairs, a metal filing cabinet, and a shelf filled with stacks of papers. "We've a lot to accomplish in a limited amount of time, so forgive me for being brusque. Please, to sit."

Congressman Kane began to speak but a raised hand stopped him. In his mind he thought, "How dare you treat me this way. I'm a United States Congressman for chrissake."

"We must go over the final steps of Hidden Cobra," the man stated as he also sat. He had a stern, almost malevolent countenance yet spoke in an even non-threatening manner. On the desk was a box containing one thousand business cards. "Here is the venom," he tapped the box. "You are the fangs." He leaned forward and asked, "You are returning to the United States on the President's plane, correct?"

"Yes."

"Then you will take this box with you, put it in your luggage, and take it back to America." He waved his hand across the desk, "They don't check your luggage, correct?"

"No, they don't."

"Good." The man stood and instructed the traitor, "Inside this box are business cards. On them is a vague message. The message is unimportant. There is a lacquer painted over the ink. It is a mixture of a substance that will cause a skin rash through which the Ebola virus will enter each victim's body."

"Ebola?" Kane said with a distinct sound of panic.

The man continued, "Anyone who touches one of these cards will fall victim. In ten days they will be ill and most likely die."

Kane remained silent as he tried to digest what he just heard.

"When you get back to America, you will send one of these cards to every member of the United States Congress and Senate. You will also send cards to the President, Vice-President and the cabinet." To demonstrate that they had done extensive research the terrorist pointed out, "By using the inside mail service provided among offices in the Capitol building, House and Senate office buildings, the White House, Library of Congress, the State Department, and Social Security Administration the mail is delivered without inspection or delay." He smiled, "Remember to include a cover letter, attach the business card to the front, and mail in a reusable blue U.S. House of Representatives Inside Mail envelope."

"That would mean that they would know it came from me," Congressman Kane protested.

"They will know nothing. A rash could come from anywhere and it will take weeks for the virus to do its noble deed. By then they will have received thousands of letters. Our Hidden Cobra will once more be hidden in trash heaps, gone from scrutiny, or discovery. And, Washington DC will bleed to death." An evil smile that surpassed any Kane had ever seen caused shivers to run down his spine.

"That will create so much suffering."

"It is the price of conquest. If you are to become the leader of the Western World you first have to remove all obstacles. You must look beyond the battlefield to a palace on the hill where you shall reign. A benevolent king." Again, that evil smile, "It is your destiny."

As warm visions of power engulfed him, Congressman Blake Kane pushed images of dying colleagues, opposition members, various leaders, and innocent victims into a dark corner of his mind. In their place he saw his own image everywhere throughout the nation as the champion of democracy delivering a stricken nation from a horrifying event. Through his Herculean efforts he will keep them safe, calm their fears, and maintain their lifestyle. After all, isn't that what they want most? If having a king keeps them safe and provides for them there will be little opposition. Any that does arise will be dealt with swiftly. It will be clear that he must make hard decisions for the people. Then a cold sobering thought hit him. "What about me? I will be exposed to this terrible disease."

That smile answered, "Do not be concerned. We have a vaccine. Others are working on experimental vaccines but they will not make it through the approval process in time." He reached into the desk and withdrew a syringe, "Roll up your sleeve." When Kane hesitated, he added, "Do not fear. If we wanted you dead you would have never walked through that door."

Congressman Blake Kane winced as the injection was administered.

"We do not know where, or how, or when this Ebola plot will unfold," Liam admitted. "I fear it may be too late to stop it."

On the other end of the encrypted satellite phone conversation General Hughes asked, “The doctor, did you get anything else from her?”

“She is cooperating, but doesn’t know any more than her part in the scheme.”

“Compartmentalized planning. We are not dealing with amateurs, here.”

“The only thing we know is that she prepared a type of clear varnish that causes a rash and is embedded with live Ebola virus. It could be painted on anything. Whomever touches it will most likely be infected.”

“How do they make sure the correct people come in contact with their poison?” General Hughes mused.

“I fear, mon ami, that the weapon has already left France.”

“Are you sure?”

“Of nothing can I be sure,” Liam admitted. “However, with the capture of Kareem Reza, the unfortunate demise of his supposed assassin, and now the capture of Dr. Antoinette Le Claire the terrorists must be aware that we are closing in on them. It is reasonable to assume that they have moved forward with their nefarious plans.”

After completing the call General Hughes discussed the situation with the other members of the Satan’s Shadow team. They sat in the main cabin of Ismenios anchored at Little Creek Cove, in Chesapeake, Virginia.

“The only way for that plan to work is as an inside job,” Jarvis Demoye concluded.

“And, the only insiders we have heard of are either Nadia Noorani with the State Department or United States Congressman Blake Kane from Connecticut,” Ken Farmingdale observed.

“If there is a third or fourth or fifth, we’re in deep shit,” Ron Clew stated.

“Maybe, it’s time to inform Homeland Security and tell what we know,” Jarvis said seeking the other’s opinions.

General Hughes was gazing out the window as he listened to the conversation. Upon hearing Jarvis comment he turned and said, “If we share what we know with Homeland Security the wheels of government will begin spinning in eighty directions and after they trip all over themselves the culprits planning the attack will go deep underground. Only, they won’t stay there. Eventually, when no one is looking, the plot will once again become operational.”

“That doesn’t leave us a lot of options,” Ron Clew said.

“It leaves one option,” General Hughes stated. He nodded as he offered, "We need our own insider."

"Emanuel Vegas?" Ken Farmingdale asked.

"He can get in places that we can't. He also can travel inconspicuously through the halls of Congress," General Hughes explained. "Unfortunately, he's not the right one for the job."

"Then who is?" Ken asked.

Air Force One landed at Joint Base Andrews in Maryland completing a three-day trip to Geneva. The Boeing VC-25A aircraft taxied to its final stopping point and mobile stairs were moved into place. After the President and cabinet members left other guests departed the aircraft. Congressman Blake Kane was exhausted from stress when he walked to a waiting limousine to take him back to Washington DC. He felt as though he was carrying an atomic bomb in his luggage. It was a correct emotion as what he did carry would have the same effect in terms of loss of life.

What added to his stress was the proposed timing of Hidden Cobra. He was instructed to send out the letter with attached poison business cards within a week. From then, it would take approximately ten days for the epidemic to begin. He looked at his watch as if it would provide a calendar for him to review. His head spun and stomach muscles ached from the tension.

Planning is one thing, but when it comes time to act a completely different mindset occurs. Actions get second-guessed. Images of the infinite number of possible failures sneak into one's consciousness. Strangely, the same instinct of fight or flight comes into play with a strong desire to run away to avoid the inevitable. Time seems to speed up until it generates a feeling of careening out-of-control. Connecticut Congressman Blake Kane experienced all these feelings. He knew one thing for sure, he needed to see Nadia Noorani.

CHAPTER 72

"You're on a leave of absence," General Maxwell Hughes stated nonchalantly.

"I am," Special Agent Peggy Fox replied as she sipped some coffee. "However, that does not preclude me from doing an investigation should I find the need."

"Unofficial investigation."

"Did you ask me here to argue the validity of my actions?" she replied lightheartedly. It was a conscious technique to keep the meeting friendly as she knew someone like the General would not request a meeting for no reason. A message had been left for her at the Bureau. She responded and they agreed to meet in an off-the-beaten track restaurant for breakfast. So, she drove west to Manassas, Virginia.

"I asked you to join me because I have something of grave importance to discuss," Maxwell Hughes stated as he tasted the eggs. "I really like this restaurant. Excellent food and incredible prices."

"You have my attention," Peggy Fox replied.

"You do understand that this is an unofficial conversation?"

"I can make no promises. It is my sworn duty to uphold the law."

"As it is mine to defend the Constitution of the United States of America. Cut the crap. We both know that in the real world the law is pliable. I remember learning that there are blue laws, black laws, and red laws. Blue laws are up to the discretion of the officer. Black laws are to be upheld unless there are extenuating circumstances. Supposedly, red laws are never to be broken. And yet, there are exceptions occurring every day."

"Your point being?"

"Take off your pointy hat and listen carefully to what I'm about to tell you. It is going to take an open, unencumbered, free mindset to fully comprehend what I am going to share."

Peggy found General Hughes' straightforward, no-nonsense approach refreshing. She couldn't help but like the man. He was genuine. He reflected the strength and courage of a Marine officer. Yet, he also very well could be a murderer. That was a fact she could not forget. "I'm listening."

"There is a terrorist plot that has become operational that threatens the leadership of this nation."

"Have you contacted Homeland Security?" was her initial response.

"No."

"Why not?"

"Because, first they would be skeptical and want concrete proof. Second, they would spend an egregious amount of time analyzing, discussing, and planning. And third, they are unable to act outside the law."

"And, you think I will be any different?"

"I am a good judge of character," General Hughes replied. "You have a rebellious streak that I am counting on. If, for a minute, I thought that you were a typical tight-ass FBI agent you wouldn't be sitting here."

"I don't know if that is a compliment or not."

"It's an opinion." General Hughes went on to outline what he knew of Hidden Cobra. He described the plot, presumed weapon, and known participants, both in France and the United States. It had an obvious impact on Special Agent Peggy Fox. Of that he was sure. He finished by saying, "I require your assistance."

"Wait, this is a whole lot to wrap my head around," she protested. "I think we need to take this information to the appropriate people."

"You feel free to do that," Hughes replied. "I'll order fifty-thousand body bags."

"You can't keep this information secret."

"This intel is unsubstantiated which means some egghead will spend precious time trying to corroborate what I have told you." The General drank some coffee, "The situation calls for quick decisive action—not bureaucratic bullshit." He put down his cup and stated, "Did I read you wrong? Are you incapable of operating on your own? Should I pay the tab and let you run to your superiors asking for permission to investigate a far-fetched terrorist plot?"

"You make it sound as though I can only follow protocol and not think for myself," Peggy replied showing her displeasure.

It was General Hughes turn to be strategically pleasant, "Peggy, I am on dangerous ground. You should be the last person with whom I have any contact. That being said, you may be the only person who can help stop this treacherous attack on our nation. I saw something in you during our lunch together. Something that I've seen in others that indicated I could not only trust them but also count on them. Face the facts—you have a nonconformist streak in you. Oh, you fight it to be a good Special Agent, but it is there—you can't deny it. I need that maverick and without sounding hokey America needs it as well."

"It sounds like you are asking me to break the law."

"In combat, there are often times when a split-second choice has to be made to either follow orders to the letter or react appropriately to a situation. If you blindly follow orders you might find yourself in Arlington saying goodbye to your team. If you follow your instincts and training you might sacrifice your career, but avert a disaster."

Special Agent Fox leaned back in her chair. Unconsciously, she ran her hand over the FBI lapel pin. A lifetime of work, endless training, physical hardship, ocean of tears, and sacrificed personal life had brought her to her goal of being a Special Agent in the Federal Bureau of Investigation. To forfeit that would be, in essence, the elimination of a human being known as Peggy Fox. This was not how her life was supposed to turn out. She heard a sound and looked over at General Hughes side of the table.

On the table in front of Maxwell Hughes was a challenge coin. On it was a familiar dragon. In addition, what was not on Peggy Fox's paper rendition was a circle of thirteen stars and a saber. Peggy Fox could do nothing but stare at the bronze object.

"When this is over," General Hughes stated in a steady unemotional voice, "you can arrest me and I will not resist. But first, there is critical work to be done."

"What if I arrest you right now?" Agent Fox asked.

"If you attempt to do so, you will not leave this table."

Silence hung over the table. In the balance was not simply what two persons might do in the next few minutes, but what might become of the United States of America. Peggy Fox considered what she had been told about an unspeakable plot against the nation she loved. If accurate, it had the potential to bring down the government. Could she ignore such a threat, imagined or otherwise?

General Hughes sat silently not taking his eye off Special Agent Fox. It was a calculated risk to invite her to breakfast. Even more of a risk to present that coin. Without showing it, he glanced past the young woman in the direction where a large black man waited in the shadows.

"We have a man with what appears to be Ebola Virus Disease in hospital," Liam said over an encrypted satellite telephone.

Senior Secret Service Agent Emanuel Vegas asked, "Is he able to communicate? Have you learned anything from him?"

"The man is a printer from Gennevilliers. He told us an imam from a local mosque ordered one thousand very special business cards. As instructed, he wore latex gloves and a surgical mask as he painted on a special varnish. The varnish was provided by two unidentified men. When the job was complete he packed the cards in a standard box and sealed it with plastic wrap. The same two men picked up the box and remaining varnish." Liam coughed, then continued, "Shortly after doing that special job this, Salah el-Khazzani, developed a rash on his left wrist. He said it itched terribly and he scratched it until it bled. Not long after he fell ill with what he thought was the flu."

"What was printed on those cards?" Vegas inquired.

"An eagle flying in front of an American flag. He couldn't remember the words but they had 'American Bridge' and 'Economic' included in the statement."

"So, he is being cooperative?"

"He is afraid."

"How is he doing?"

"He will not be with us for very long. It is an aggressive variety of the disease."

"We have to find out where those cards went?" Vegas stated with obvious concern in his voice.

"We are searching for the imam. Salah provided his name, but his location is unknown at this time. We believe he might have fled."

"Do you think he fled with the box of cards?"

"As I told le general, I fear the poison has already left France. How or with whom we have no way of knowing. At least, now we know in what form the poison is being carried."

"Problem is there are an infinite number of ways those cards could enter this country."

"That is true. However, we do have one advantage. We know the target."

"And, now we have a better idea of what the weapon looks like. Thank you, my friend."

An intern brought a stack of blue envelopes into the office of Congressman Blake Kane. She had addressed over 600 of the inside mail envelopes. Along with the envelopes she delivered 600 copies of a cover letter he had written making a vague FYI reference to the attached business card. When she helpfully inquired whether or not he wished for her to stuff the envelopes he told her he would let her know. A part of him thought, "Why not, it's just one more."

CHAPTER 73

A box of death sat silently on a bookshelf in Congressman Blake Kane's office. Much like a cobra hiding in high grass it waited for the right time to inject its venom. Only, unlike the cobra this serpent would not kill and devour a single victim. When unleashed, it would bring down the most powerful nation on Earth. For once the head was destroyed it would be a relatively easy task to slowly devour the remains.

Connecticut Congressman Blake Kane had been carefully selected after months of study. The man had an exceptionally high opinion of himself. He quickly rose from local political victories to the state level and finally a national office. Ego drove him, an appealing visage sold him, and limited ability made him an obviously useful tool. It was simple for Nadia Noorani to bring the hapless Congressman under her spell, just as she had Kareem Reza.

At one time, Nadia Noorani had worked for the CIA. She was an effective operative—intelligent, adaptive, fearless, and cunning. Often her beauty and resourcefulness turned unwitting men into informants and traitors. That was a welcome outcome at the Company until she turned. Nobody saw it coming. In fact, they didn't even realize that it had happened. She left the CIA to work for the Department of State. It was assumed that she was mentally exhausted. They were wrong. At the State Department Nadia had access to sensitive data that fell into the hands of America's enemies. Given her espionage training these breaches in security remained unknown as was her involvement in a plot to overthrow the United States government.

On a rainy weekday morning Nadia Noorani met Congressman Blake Kane in a small restaurant in McLean, Virginia where she lived. "Your noble allies wish the Cobra to strike next week," she relayed the instructions.

"Everything is ready to go," Congressman Kane replied. He looked around to confirm that they could not be overheard. "Have you been vaccinated?"

"Of course, my love, we don't want anything to come between us at this illustrious time, do we?"

"I'm glad. I was concerned."

"There is no need for you to worry," she replied, then tilted her head and asked, "You seem worried. What is wrong, my love?"

"It may be nothing," he looked around once more. "An FBI agent requested a meeting. She said it pertained to a constituent of mine they were vetting and had nothing to do with any criminal activities. When I asked who it is, she said she would tell me when we meet."

"That doesn't sound too perilous, but why wouldn't she tell you who was being investigated?"

"I don't know."

"Where are the items, at present?" Nadia asked.

"On a shelf in my office."

"You must move them."

"I can't take them to my home. The risk is too great."

"Go to a hotel," Nadia suggested. "Fill the envelopes there."

"What if this FBI agent knows?" Blake Kane asked with obvious fear in his voice.

"If she knew she wouldn't ask for a meeting. She'd show up with a team and arrest you. No, my love, it is good to be careful, but not fearful. Our destiny awaits and we must seize it." Nadia smiled and took Blake's hand, kissed it, and said, "I believe in you and I believe in our future together."

"There are just so many ways things can go wrong," Congressman Kane carped.

"You are up to this, my love. You have more strength than you realize. Take what is yours. It is written that you are to rule the Western World."

Special Agent Peggy Fox told the Executive Assistant Director for National Security Branch, "I made an appointment with Congressman Blake Kane but it appears that he had a family emergency and is not going to be in his office for a few weeks."

"And, his staff doesn't know what the emergency was or where the Congressman went, I presume," her superior replied.

"You assume correctly."

"Have you tracked his credit card use?"

"It hasn't been used."

"Cellphone?"

"It was left in his office."

"Checking, debit?"

"He cashed a check for a large sum recently."

"What about his home?"

"No one home."

"And, you still believe a United States Congressman is somehow involved with a terrorist group? ‘

"Yes."

"But you don't know exactly how?"

Peggy Fox stood silently. She had withheld the possible use of Ebola virus or her contact with a member of a group she suspected to be Satan's Shadow. Both of those facts would have led to countless questions that she couldn't answer. Instead, she kept her suspicions general offering just enough to possibly get a search warrant for Congressman Kane's office."

She heard the Assistant Director say, "A United States Congressman? Damn, Fox, we can't just accuse a United States Congressman without concrete supportable evidence. You know that. What the hell's come over you. You're reading too many super hero comic books." He leaned forward and added, "Unless you have more than a suspicion or anonymous tip, you're dead in the water. Maybe, you need to get back on that leave of absence. Your seeing conspiracies in your sleep."

"He ran," she offered.

"He had a family emergency."

"Right after I made an appointment?"

"Don't flatter yourself. Your request to meet meant nothing."

Peggy left the meeting with an odd set of feelings. On the one hand she was angry. The fools at the Bureau blindly ignore a potential terrorist threat. On the other hand, she felt a strange kind of excitement. She had followed the rules, informed her superiors of her suspicions, and gotten nowhere. Her conscience was clear. General Hughes was correct the bureaucracy was incapable of operating outside the lines. Then she thought, "Am I capable of crossing the line?"

"Why did you have to reveal who you are to an FBI agent?" Ken Farmingdale asked not attempting to hide his displeasure or concern. "We may all hang, as a result."

"We may," General Hughes agreed. "In war you have to make hard decisions. There is no guarantee that they are correct or will lead to a desired outcome. You weigh the facts, use your experience and training, consider the risks, and accept the responsibility. It's that simple."

"Why? That's all I want to know," Ken insisted.

General Hughes walked over to the counter in the safe house and fixed a Scotch on the rocks. He stood with his back to the other members of Satan's Shadow. All present waited in silence. Each man had his own thoughts and fears and opinions of the General's actions. Finally, the man they followed into hell turned and spoke, "In spite of what we have done, we did it with an honorable objective in mind—reduce the threat of terrorism in the world and in America. To a degree we have been successful." He looked at the others in the room. "I have no regrets, though I can't say I am proud of the necessary steps we have taken. Difficult, harsh, brutal, but essential. History will not be kind to us and will never relate our actions to a reduction of the slaughter of innocent people. All of you are brave beyond your own understanding. You volunteered for a thankless task, risked your future, and sacrificed any hope for peace-of-mind. That unnamed child who will grow up and enjoy a full life instead of lying in a morgue after a car intentionally is driven into a crowd will neither thank you nor ever know of you. That couple sitting in a restaurant gazing into each other's eyes won't feel the sting of bullets piercing their bodies and will never realize you stared into the abyss to make that possible. Hundreds, maybe thousands, will reap the rewards of living in a slightly safer world because of the people in this room."

"We all entered this thing with our eyes open," Jarvis Demoye spoke for the group.

"So, why did I reveal who we are to an FBI agent?" General Hughes repeated the question. "Karma. As a result of our anti-terrorist efforts we have become aware of the mother of all terrorist plots. It has the potential to destroy the country we love and have sworn to protect. We are in the best position to thwart this heinous attempt to bring down America. However, we don't have all the tools we need. That FBI agent can go places that we cannot easily go. Just like with our friend in France, she has access to information that we would be hard-pressed to get our hands on. Finally, I saw something in her that I believe we need. She's a huntress. We are warriors—fighters. Great for making an assault, but less effective when it comes to stalking and capturing."

"She might just stalk and capture you," Ron Crew stated.

"Thanks, Adam."

"That was kinda an Adam Hayes remark," Ron replied with as

much of a smile as he was capable of producing. "The guy's haunting me."

General Hughes continued, "The fact remains, we need this Congressman alive. If he has those tainted cards, great. If he doesn't, he might know who does or where they are. Our sole objective has to be to get our hands on those cards before they are used. That is where our little fox can be of invaluable assistance."

Secret Service Agent Emanuel Vegas observed, "We still don't know if she will be of assistance or will take you into custody for questioning."

"That's a risk I will have to take. Should that happen you will proceed without me. Find Congressman Kane and get those cards or get him to talk. Don't forget that bitch—Nadia something at the State Department. She may be knee deep in this traitorous endeavor." He finished his Scotch on the rocks and concluded, "The future of our nation is at stake. Failure is not an option. Whatever tactic is used must be flawlessly executed. Remember, in this case we are all expendable."

General Maxwell Hughes answered his cellphone as he drove back from the clandestine meeting. It was Special Agent Peggy Fox.

"General, I would like to have dinner with you."

"When and where?"

"Why not at our place in Manassas in two hours?" she said in a playful tone.

CHAPTER 74

Dr. Antoinette Le Claire sat silently as Liam outlined her situation and possible fate. He informed her that they had identified the substance she had developed and its use as varnish on business-size cards. What was left out was the plot against America. That was by design. He had to determine what she knew, what information could be coaxed out of her, and what she might be holding back.

In French he stated, "Doctor, you have been apprehended as part of a terrorist organization and face severe penalty."

Antoinette Le Claire neither answered nor showed any reaction.

"What you decide to do in the next few minutes will have a significant impact on your future and the safety of your family and friends."

That drew a response, "I've told you what you want to know. What happens to me is inconsequential. My family had nothing to do with it. What more can I tell you?"

"I have just a few more questions. If you are honest with me it will go a whole lot better."

"I will answer your questions," Dr. Le Claire agreed.

"How potent is the virus that you mixed into the oil?"

Dr. Le Claire slipped into her scientific role, "In order to accurately test the amalgam we had to ensure that healthy virulent microorganisms were utilized. We selected the strongest samples to create a best-case scenario. Failure to subsist in the medium would prove it is incompatible with the organism. In this case all results were positive. In fact, the oil seemed to be an ideal environment promoting growth."

"If I understand you correctly," Liam said, "the virus in this oil is a strong variety."

"It most definitely is a hardy strain."

"Can it be killed using a detergent or disinfectant?"

A slight smile so evil it might have been an outright grin crossed her face, "We tested a number of chemical agents that were virucidal in effect. This included alcohols, phenols, iodine, and chlorine." She seemed to forget herself or where she was. As if teaching a medical class, she explained what they had found. "Regardless of the type of microbial cell, a disinfectant will interact with the cell surface. If the chemical penetrates the cell it most often can produce a significant effect on viability. The outermost layers of microbial cells can thus have a significant effect on their susceptibility to disinfectants." Dr. Le Claire looked directly at Liam as she stated, "The medium in which our virus was placed, due to its oily nature, either coated or sluffed-off disinfectant agents. A sort of impenetrable barrier protects the virus. Without knowing it we created a super bug."

"What can be done to kill the virus?" Liam asked in a calm voice covering his horror.

"At present, without further study, the best thing I suggest you can do is use fire."

He then asked, "Is there a vaccine for this virus?"

"There is an experimental vaccine called rVSV-ZEBOV that was found to be protective against the Ebola virus in a trial conducted by the World Health Organization (WHO) in Guinea in 2015. I don't believe it will be efficacious against this particular strain."

"Then we must conclude that there is no vaccine.

"There is no vaccine."

"You have said 'we' again and again, who else at Claude Bernard University worked with you on this, uh, questionable research?"

"No other scientist knowingly worked on my project."

Liam looked at his notes and changed the direction of his interview, "Who put you up to this endeavor?"

"No one."

"You didn't start experimenting with a deadly virus to be used by terrorists on a whim."

"In a manner-of-speaking, yes I did," Dr. Antoinette Le Claire stated. "I visited Damascus before going to the Congo. While there I was introduced to the beautiful side of Islam. I was also exposed to the awful truth about the Western World and its imperialistic activities in the Middle East. I lived among the most wonderful people." She looked at Liam with an out-of-place innocence as she shared, "It was I who suggested investigating the introduction of Ebola into the West, mon ravisseur."

General Maxwell Hughes entered the small restaurant in Manassas, Virginia where he had previously met Special Agent Peggy Fox. When he entered, he noted two "official looking" men at a corner table. Immediately, he considered turning and leaving. However, something made him reconsider. If he was to be arrested, so be it. At a table on the far side of the dining room sat a woman wearing a blue dress. From behind he couldn't tell if it was Agent Fox or not. He approached the table.

"I thought you would wish to be able to watch the door," Peggy Fox stated when she became aware of the General.

"That was considerate. May I sit?"

Peggy nodded.

Both diners read menus in silence. Because the meeting had been requested by Agent Fox, General Hughes waited for her to start the conversation. He also kept his eye on the two men at the corner table. They didn't seem interested in what was occurring across the room.

"How sure are you about this alleged plot?" Agent Fox inquired.

"I'm sure enough to have contacted you at great personal risk."

"What risk are you referring to?"

"Stick to the subject—the terrorist plot."

Special Agent Peggy Fox couldn't help but smile. She had slipped into investigative mode causing her to follow any track that presented itself. General Hughes, undaunted, steered the conversation back to the subject at hand. He was unflappable, confident, and focused. Yes, she liked this man. "I assume you have faith in the source of your information?"

"The French gentleman you saw at Arlington. He provided the intel. The mission that proved to be a failure and took Adam Hayes' life was loosely related to the plot. I believe we are working with solid info and will proceed accordingly."

"We are talking about a United States Congressman," she reminded him.

"We are talking about a potential traitor of the worst kind. If I'm wrong, I'll write him a letter of apology," General Hughes said sarcastically.

"General, I tried to meet with Congressman Kane and he has disappeared."

"Damn, that screws the pooch."

"I need to tell you that I shared your conspiracy theory with my superiors and they're not buying it."

General Hughes checked the corner table once more. "So, why did you request this meeting?"

"Because if it is even remotely possible it would have a devastating effect on our nation."

A waiter approached and they ordered their dinners.

"Agent Fox, we have to accept the fact that there are forces in the world that mean us harm. They are radical, resolute, callous, and cruel. There is nothing they wouldn't do if it would destroy our way of life. Every day they are coming up with new and more sophisticated technique for attacking us. If they could put a nuclear device in the Capital building, they would do it. In fact, that might be preferable to what they have planned. I mean to stop them."

Peggy Fox looked into the eyes of a strong, unpretentious, masculine man. He made no excuses, offered no apology, and knew what he had to do. Even more, he had courage. She couldn't help but think that if she were in a war zone this is the type of man she would want as a leader. He would be easy to follow. Her investigative mind also concluded that it was clear that he fit the profile of whom she thought might be the leader of Satan's Shadow. Seasoned warriors could follow this man, fall under his spell, and execute atrocities. But, she was also aware, without the rule of law there would be chaos. However, remarkably, by stepping outside the law of man and morality there seemed to be less chaos in the world. That doesn't justify murder—or in some warped semi-logical way could it? Peggy gazed across the table. General Hughes ate his dinner allowing her to wrestle with her thoughts, feelings, and sense-of-duty. The clink of a knife on a plate echoed in her ears penetrating her electrified mind. This was a defining moment. Everything that had occurred in her life had funneled down to this single pivotal point-in-time. Her training, values, belief systems, spiritual leanings, and experiences tugged at her conscience. The next words she spoke would forever impact on her future and her destiny. Special Agent Peggy Fox looked across the table and asked, "General, how can I help?"

The man Peggy Fox had put her trust in looked up. He wiped his mouth with a napkin and stated, "Help us find Mr. Blake Kane."

"Congressman Kane," she corrected.

"In my opinion, as of now, he doesn't deserve the title."

How shrewd, she thought. In one sentence he removed a psychological barrier. "I have already begun searching for him. He's done a good job of covering his activities."

"Time is a critical factor."

"The Frenchman, did he offer any insights as to the timing of this terror operation?"

"No. However, I have to believe that the enemy will have a concern about how long the virus can survive in the varnish. For that reason alone, they will want to execute Hidden Cobra as quickly as possible. We need to find Mr. Kane, today."

"And, when we find him, what do you propose?"

"Keep those tainted cards from their desired targets."

"And Kane, what about him?"

General Hughes did not answer. He returned to his meal.

"General, I will help you find the biological weapon, but I will not facilitate murder."

After taking a sip of water, General Hughes said in an unemotional tone, "Agent Fox, go back to your ordered life where things make sense and there aren't any grey areas or undefined rules of engagement. Leave the dirty work to those who have the stomach for it."

Peggy Fox was surprised by the General's response. "What did I say that was wrong?" she asked.

"The name of the plot is Hidden Cobra. That is appropriate. We need to find that serpent and defang it. It must be done swiftly lest we fall prey to its venom. We can't be hampered with a concern about apprehending the snake handler. If the opportunity presents itself—fine. If not, he will be neutralized. It's that simple. Keep your eye on the objective."

"You're asking me, as a member of law enforcement, to ignore or break the law."

"I'm not asking you to do anything."

"You want my help finding Congressman Kane."

"Your assistance would be appreciated and may be the difference between saving our republic or sweeping up the ashes. Your concern for the law is admirable. Yet, if they succeed, there may be little law left to uphold."

"My God, how did I get to this place?" Peggy thought out loud.

"You were born," was General Maxwell Hughes' response.

CHAPTER 75

"What drove you to become a Navy Seal?" Jarvis Demoye asked Ron Clew.

They had remained in the safe house along with Ken Farmingdale while General Hughes went to meet with the FBI agent.

Ron put down the book he had been looking at, thought for a moment, and replied, "I joined the Navy to serve my country." Smile. Pause. "Not really, truth be known, I was drifting with no direction. I couldn't see a future beyond dinner. Even though I was a green kid, it was clear that I didn't have the talent to get a football scholarship to college so I wouldn't eventually end up a rich spoiled pro. The only other way to get rich, selling drugs, just didn't appeal to me." Ron leaned forward and explained, "One thing that I did know was I needed some discipline in my life to direct all the stored-up energy inside me fighting to get out." He let out a slight laugh, "There was this Navy recruiter downtown and he lied his ass off about seeing the world, meeting fascinating people, and making life-long friends."

"I bought the same sweet nothings whispered in my ear," Jarvis confessed.

"To a young man it sounded so good," Ron said. "So, I signed the enlistment papers. This particular recruiter, Maurice Drummond, did me a big favor, though. He took a look at me and said I was a 'big fella' and should consider the Seaman to Seal Program. Told me if I signed a SEAL Challenge Contract I would qualify for certain bonuses and benefits when I enlist. I was told if I entered the program at a later date, I wouldn't get the same benefits. He was like a used car salesman, 'You can drive this baby off the lot today at this tremendous savings. But it may not be available tomorrow.' I signed."

"Did you know what you were getting into?"

"Not a clue. I figured how hard could seal training be. Those cute little creatures balancing balls on their noses. Why not?"

"Now you're hosing me," Jarvis accused his fellow warrior.

"You'll never know," Ron smiled. "Things got really hectic after that. You know the drill. Before I was sent to basic, a SEAL/SWCC mentor took control of my life. He prepared me for the Physical Screening Test (PST) and the dreaded Armed Services Vocational Aptitude Battery (ASVAB). That's when the shit hit the fan."

"Why? You're a smart guy."

"I did great on the Math, Word Knowledge, Verbal, Writing, Electronics, Science, Tools and Mechanical, and Assembling Things sections. One single section fucked me up."

"Sounds like you have them all. What section?"

"AI."

"AI? Automobile Information, you're kidding me," Jarvis began to laugh.

"Hell, man, we didn't own a car."

"OK, I can see that."

"Well, my SWCC gives me a crash, and I do mean crash, course on automobile mechanics. He had me working at a repair shop, then an auto body shop, then a used car dealer. Taught me how to drive a stick. Even got a friend to give me lessons on driving an eighteen-wheeler. I can take apart and put back together a BMW if I have to."

"Then after basic you were off to the Great Lakes."

"There's nothing great about those freezing pools of torture."

"What, doesn't freeze you nuts off makes you stronger?" Ken Farmingdale joined the conversation.

"Makes you a damn soprano," Ron complained.

"You did it, that's what counts," Ken stated. "And, now you're an anchor clanker with a trident on your chest. No simple feat. It's an honor to know you."

"Shut the fuck up. A little physical pain, psychological torment, endless training, and minor hardships don't compare with getting in an untried aircraft and pushing it until it breaks. I fall and I end up with my face in the dirt. You fall and they cover you up with six-feet of dirt."

Retired Navy Captain Jarvis Demoye changed the subject, "We need to make contingency plans should General Hughes not return."

"From what little we have our best approach has to be with Congressman Blake Kane," Ken Farmingdale concluded.

"He appears to be the key subject, but it's not like we can kidnap him in the Capital Building," Ron Clew observed.

"I think we need Vegas' help in determining the Congressman's home address," Jarvis decided.

"Once we have him how do we know we can get him to provide the location of the terrorist cards?" Ken Farmingdale asked.

"That's a problem. What if he handed them off to someone else? Or, did he already deliver them to the targets? Or, if he has hidden them how do we get him to tell us where?" Jarvis questioned.

"That part, I can assure you, we can do," Ron Clew replied. "If we have him, we'll get the information out of him." The other two men in the room looked at Ron Clew and knew he spoke the truth.

A car entered the driveway. All eyes were on the door. Ron Clew peered out and announced, "General Hughes."

People follow patterns. It is this instinctual trait that often trips them up. On the other hand, a lack of pattern is why many random crimes never get solved. Special Agent Peggy Fox knew this. Without any contemporary clues to follow she decided to track historical actions. With her FBI credentials she was able to get access to cellphone and credit card records of one Congressman Blake Kane. Unfortunately, he was a busy little beaver and the records represented a mountain of data. The man must have spent every waking hour on his phone and three credit cards were used to purchase a plethora of products, make travel arrangements, and enjoy meals in restaurants. She had three months of work before her and estimated less than three weeks to stop a cataclysmic event. The wheels of disaster were turning and one small unappreciated weak individual was being overwhelmed by the task at hand.

"If we don't find the bastard, we might have to go public with the threat and alert everyone who is at risk," Emanuel Vegas concluded after hearing General Hughes' report. Special Agent Fox agreed to assist in finding the Congressman but was questionable about any further participation.

"Let's hope that doesn't become necessary," General Hughes stated. "The government has an uncanny way of tripping all over itself. There would be meetings and discussions and panicked searching for the printed threats which might or might not be successful."

"Not to mention the inevitable leaks to the press," Ron Clew added.

Ken Farmingdale expanded on that comment, "Which would be followed by chaos as over a million people try to flee Washington, DC."

“There’s more bad news,” General Hughes stated. “Our friend who wasn’t there informs me that the Doctor who developed this abomination told him there is no vaccine for this particular strain and it may be impervious to antiseptics, as well.” He ran his hand through his greying hair and concluded, “If we get our hands on this hot potato, we will literally have a Cobra by the tail and nowhere to go with it.”

“Surgical gloves and masks are the uniform of the day,” Jarvis Demoye ordered.

“And, a flame thrower the weapon of choice,” Ron Clew added. This was followed by nervous laughter in the room.

Even though he had been vaccinated, Blake Kane wore latex gloves to protect his skin from the urushiol which he was cautioned could be a skin irritant. After consuming a glass of bourbon, he sat at the desk of his motel room, removed the plastic wrapping and opened the box of toxic business cards. There before him was Hidden Cobra. Simple 3.5-inch by 2-inch pieces of paper that would do what a thousand bombs and a million troops could not do—bring down the most powerful government in the world. There before him was his ticket to his place in history. Leader of the Western World. Let them have Europe, Great Britain, and Africa. He would eventually solidify all the Americas under his protective wing.

Six-hundred addressed inside mail service blue envelopes sat in a box next to the desk. On the desk was a stack of six-hundred cover letters from him referring to the attached business card. Slowly, he reached into the box of business cards and removed one poison pill and stapled it to the front of the cover letter. He did a serpentine fold and inserted the lethal correspondence into an envelope. He smiled as he thought about how a simple clerical function was all that was needed for him to execute his conquest of the United States of America. He wished Nadia was there with him, however, she had instructed him not to contact her until after the letters were delivered. She explained that in case there was any question about her communications with foreign entities it was safer for him to remain anonymous.

At one point, an unbent staple penetrated his latex glove and pierced his finger. Kane cursed and wiped the small drop of blood off the glove with a tissue. He was grateful to have received the Ebola vaccine and hoped the oil wouldn’t have an irritating effect. More bourbon helped him past the slight mishap. Unconsciously, he wiped sweat off his forehead with the back of a gloved hand and went on with his endeavor. Envelope after envelope was filled. At one point, he noted the name of another Connecticut Congressman who he considered a friend. A slight twinge of guilt passed through his mind. Then he thought out loud, “Conquest can be painful.”

More coffee was needed. Fatigue could not become a factor in a desperate undertaking. A clear head, sharp mind, and a lot of luck was needed. Peggy Fox had decided to ignore the telephone records and concentrated on the three credit cards. After giving it careful thought, she came to the conclusion that each card might be used for different purposes. Therefore, if she could identify the one that appeared to be his choice for personal use it might give her the best insights as to where he had gone. A long shot? All she had were long shots and the hope that she could hit the mark.

The records for the first credit card seemed to be for official business expenses. They were put aside. The second card intrigued her as all charges were travel related. Airlines, car rentals, hotels, and various minor expenses were listed. In that mass of numbers and names hid her answer. It was clear that he didn’t use his credit card for this trip or destination, but if he followed the pattern of most who wished to drop out, he most likely went someplace he had been before. One-by-one she read the expenditures. Nothing stood out. More coffee. Then like a cold slap in the face it made itself known. The Hawthorne Inn in Gaithersburg, Maryland. Why would someone who lived and worked in Washington, DC stay at a motel so nearby? A tryst! Seven times in the past two months screamed, “I’m here! Come and get me.”

Special Agent Peggy Fox came to another crossroads in her life. Does she use the telephone number given her by General Hughes or take another shot at getting the Bureau involved?

CHAPTER 76

Congressman Blake Kane finished his clerical task. He pulled the latex gloves from his hands and dropped them into the waste basket. At first, he thought he should wrap them in something as they were now contaminated, but then thought, "what the hell."

Six-hundred daggers sat in a box waiting to be thrown at all those who stood in the way of President Blake Kane. He drank another glass of bourbon. Courage in a bottle warmed him and brought out the feral homo sapien. The world would change forever when victory was his. He looked at the remaining 400 business cards. My paper army remains ready for me to unleash my wrath upon whomever gets in my way. A feeling of immortality flowed over him. With him being immune to the virus he could walk up to whomever he pleased and hand them a card—their death certificate in a manner of speaking.

With Nadia by his side he would reshape America. Solve all the lingering problems. Keep the citizens safe and promote equality by controlling their actions. He was, indeed, a fine and wonderful person.

Peggy Fox, accompanied by another FBI agent, knocked on the door of the room occupied by Congressman Blake Kane at the Hawthorne Inn in Gaithersburg, Maryland. She had argued and cajoled the Executive Assistant Director for National Security Branch into taking this critical step. He finally relented but warned, "Fox if this turns out to be an embarrassment to the Bureau your career is over."

"That's a risk I'll have to take for the security of our nation," she replied.

"Not good enough."

"What will be good enough?"

"This turns out to be unfounded, I want your badge on my desk."

"Agreed."

Congressman Blake Kane opened the door. He was dressed in a blue suit, not wearing his jacket, with his shirt sleeves rolled up. "Can I help you?"

Special Agent Peggy Fox identified herself and her cohort.

"What are you doing here? Do you know who I am?" an irritated Blake Kane asked.

"We have some questions for you Congressman Kane. May we come in?"

"I could ask if you have a search warrant and what this is all about, but I won't." He presented his best campaign trail smile and added, "Come in. I'm always cooperative with the Justice Department." In the back of his mind he noted one member of the FBI who would be a recipient of a "special" business card.

When they entered the two agents found a neat room, a few papers on the desk, the Congressman's suit jacket on the bed, a bottle of bourbon and half-filled glass, and nothing else. Peggy Fox was dismayed as there was no evidence of any business cards, tainted or otherwise. She knew she couldn't reveal the actual reason they were there. In her mind she thought, "Damn you, General Hughes! You and your conspiracy theories. I put my career on the line and you left me hanging." She decided to do a little fishing, "Congressman Kane we have reason to believe that you inadvertently have had contact with a questionable individual. It may be innocent, but you do understand that we have to be extra cautious in today's geopolitical climate."

"Who are we talking about?"

Fox tried using the name of someone she knew he had come in contact with in the past. "Kareem Reza. He has been arrested in France and confessed to plotting terrorist acts against our government."

"Kareem Reza? I don't recall the name," Blake Kane replied. "But I'm glad they caught him."

"It was a number of years ago in Pakistan. He mentioned your name while under interrogation."

"I was in Pakistan a number of years ago. I believe it was Nawabshah, Pakistan. It was a diplomatic visit to see the opening of a natural gas line China built that ran from Asaluyeh, Iran to Nawabshah, Pakistan." Kane shook his head, "I met many people. The name, what was it?"

"Kareem Reza."

"No, that name doesn't ring a bell. If he says he was there he could have been but I had little or nothing to do with him."

"Well, maybe he was just name dropping and yours came to mind." Peggy Fox changed the subject, "If you don't mind me asking, why would you take a hotel room so close to DC?"

Congressman Blake Kane had to think quickly. Fortunately, that was a skill a good politician develops early in their career. "The Capital is a perpetual fishbowl. Great for meetings and Congressional sessions, but hell when you're trying to think and develop needed and effective legislative initiatives. I often come here to get away," he looked directly at Agent Fox, "but not too far away."

"I appreciate your time and cooperation," Peggy Fox said as she began to leave.

"By the way, how did you know I was here?" Kane asked.

It was Special Agent Peggy Fox's turn to have to think quickly. "I really can't answer that. I was given the assignment and this address. I'll check on that and get back to you." She couldn't get out of the room quickly enough. As she moved toward the door her eye caught the blue color of the surgical gloves in the wastepaper basket. A quick glance told her what they were.

Peggy Fox's subsequent meeting with the Executive Assistant Director for National Security Branch of the FBI was as unpleasant an experience as she could have imagined. He made no attempt at being reasonable or even polite. The Bureau was no place for unsubstantiated rumors and amateur sleuthing. It also didn't need any blemishes on its fine reputation. He fully expected a call from the Director after a call was received from the office of Congressman Blake Kane. He planned on delivering Agent Peggy Fox's head when that occurred.

It was a dark night. One of those nights when humidity or temperature or breeze or unseen forces seemed to absorb light. Streetlights didn't light as much of the road and headlights faded at far less distance from the vehicle than normal. Dark, heavy dark, was all General Hughes could think. He had driven along a route that he memorized on a previous occasion, made a call to the mysterious Dave with the CIA from the back room of a Company gas station, left a message, and traveled home.

Earlier, Special Agent Peggy Fox had contacted General Hughes after her inquisition and ultimate request for her resignation. She apologized and told General Hughes that she found that she couldn't step outside the lines. Too many years of training and experience made it second-nature to follow the rules. He told her he understood. After she described what had taken place at the hotel and her observation as to what was in the wastebasket she said sadly, "I've lost faith in the system, the Bureau, and myself." General Hughes had reassured her that it was not she who was inadequate and her observation was a critical piece of evidence.

Ten minutes after arriving home General Hughes received a telephone call. Dave's familiar voice announced, "Let's talk."

"You're at the end of my driveway, correct?"

"Nothing gets by you, sir," was the sarcastic response.

"That was quick."

"I was in the neighborhood."

General Hughes proceeded to the end of his driveway and entered the familiar dark green Cadillac Escalade. In silence they sped off.

Finally, Dave spoke, "I've heard rumors. There's a snake in the garden."

"A big lethal venomous snake," General Hughes answered, then asked, "How much do you know?"

"Only rumors from across the pond. Facts are what I need and dread."

General Hughes provided a detailed report of events that have taken place. He left nothing out. Dave was a proven ally and resource and could ultimately be a solution to a daunting issue—where are the venomous business cards.

"I'm embarrassed to admit that I didn't think Kane capable of such an enterprise. Of course, he wasn't the developer of the scheme—not smart enough. From my direct experience with Noorani, old Blake was an easy touch. She probably had him dancing to her tune within minutes of meeting. We trained her well and she could have been one of the great ones. Now, she's one of the dangerous ones. Someone in the psyche division forgot to ask her if she owned a hijab. Now, we have a capable, merciless, adaptable adversary to contend with. She is not one to underestimate if you enjoy breathing."

General Hughes, feeling left out, asked sarcastically, "Are you enjoying the conversation?"

"Not one bit. Every scenario in my head leads to the same place—chaos and death."

"I'm in the same hydraulic."

"Been on the rapids, have you?"

"I'm in one now."

"Whatever else, we have to get those fucking cards out of circulation before they do damage."

"Tell me something I don't know," was Hughes frustrated response.

"Liam Beauchêne is dying."

The surprise comment left General Hughes speechless. After a moment he replied, "I didn't know. I'm sorry to hear that."

"Emphysema and other complications. He has the heart of lion and loves his country. Age and physical abuse have taken their toll."

"I like the man."

"There are those in the French military that do not because he uncovered some traitorous activities. They might get to him before the disease."

"Either way, we lose a good man."

"Roger that," Dave agreed, then asked, "What is your plan?"

"Plan? If I were smart, I'd get the hell out of Washington, DC."

"We know that's not possible."

General Hughes outlined the situation, "There are a thousand biological bullets somewhere in DC. We know the targets are the Congress, Senate, and Executive branch. We have to find the weapon or move the target. Our little Fox tried to get the FBI to become involved but they're stuck with their heads up their ass. We know Congressman Kane did something with the cards based on surgical gloves in his hotel room. So, it seems to me getting him to talk is our only option, at this time. Only you don't walk into the Capital building and kidnap a United States Congressman that easily."

"Invite him over for a drink. Then get him to talk," was Dave's recommendation.

"I doubt he'd accept the invitation."

"I know he wouldn't. You don't appeal to him."

A light went off in General Hughes' mind, "And, how are you going to get her to cooperate?"

"I'm not exactly sure."

CHAPTER 77

There is something inside a true investigator that drives them to continue until they get results. Special Agent—for the moment—Peggy Fox was a professional. More of a dedicated and effective investigator than her superiors realized. Regardless of the consequences, she would not let the suspected plot come to fruition. It had to be stopped or proven false.

Her first stop was Congressman Blake Kane's office. As expected, the man was not there. His gatekeeper and assistant repeated what had been said before that he had a family emergency and would be away for a few weeks. She would not allow Agent Fox to enter the inner office without a search warrant.

A young intern entered the office and innocently informed the assistant, "I picked up the package and delivered it."

Peggy thanked Congressman Kane's assistant and left. However, she didn't go far. Once in the hall, she waited. In less than a half hour the young intern left the office. Rather than stop her, Peggy Fox followed the young lady. She knew she could always intercept the intern and question her but wanted first to see where she was headed. The mouse and Fox proceeded to the Capital cafeteria. It was there when Peggy Fox identified herself and stated she had a few questions. A surprised and nervous intern with wide open eyes stared at the FBI badge and mumbled that she didn't know anything.

"Relax," Peggy assured the young woman as she guided her to a semi-secluded table. "This is strictly routine."

"But, I'm just an intern. I run errands," the frightened girl insisted.

"You haven't done anything wrong."

"I hope not. It would ruin my career, my life."

"You saw me in Congressman Kane's office, did you not?"

"Uh, yes I did."

"We are investigating the loss of a package that Congressman Kane had picked up at his hotel room and delivered. Do you know anything about that?"

"Yesterday, I picked up a package from Blake," she looked panicked, "but I delivered it to the woman as instructed." She insisted, "I didn't lose it. Was that the package? Am I in trouble?"

"You're not in trouble. Where did you deliver the package?"

"Uh," she hesitated.

"Where did you deliver the package? Tell me!"

"I gave it to a woman at a Starbucks on E street and New Jersey Avenue."

"Do you know what was in the package?"

"Of course, I do. It was a box with 600 inside mail blue envelopes. I ran off the cover letters for Congressman Kane myself. I also addressed all the envelopes. They are going to every Congressperson, every Senator, the President and Vice-President of the United States and the entire cabinet." She seemed to relax slightly and added, "I offered to stuff the envelopes for Blake but he wanted to do it."

"Tell me about the woman who you gave the box to."

"She was very nice. Well dressed. A Navy-Blue suit, light tan blouse, and gold necklace. And, she wore white gloves."

"What about her physical appearance?"

"She had dark hair about shoulder length, olive-colored skin, and deep brown eyes. One thing that struck me was she wore red lipstick that I thought was too bright."

Peggy Fox smiled thinking only a female would make such an observation. She brought up a photo of Nadia Noorani on her smartphone and showed it to the intern. "Is this the woman?"

Immediately, the young woman replied, "Yes, that's her."

"And, she took the box?"

"Yes, I saw her put it in the trunk of her car." She thought for a moment, and said, "I offered to deliver the envelopes to the inside mail office for her on Monday because they don't deliver on weekends. She told me she had another document to add and she would take care of it."

"Thank you, you've been a big help. Apparently, the package was not lost after all."

"I did what I was told," the girl said softly.

"You did well."

When Peggy Fox left the cafeteria, the young intern remained at the table. Unconsciously, she began to scratch a rash on her arm.

In the safe house General Hughes ended a telephone conversation with Peggy Fox and asked the team, "Do we still have Nadia's car bugged?"

Ron Clew answered, "We never retrieved the bug. It should still be operational."

"Will it help us locate the car?"

"If you recall, we used a standalone device that has a SIM card and transmits through cell towers. By using the Silent Circle Blackphone, we can listen to the device and also access what cell tower is picking up the signal. That's as near as we can get," Ron Clew explained.

"It's a start but it won't pinpoint where the vehicle is," General Hughes observed.

Jarvis added, "We know where she lives and works."

"True," General Hughes agreed, "And, as a result of that telephone call, we now know the cards are being sent through the inside mail service of the government. The Fox in the woodpile determined that 600 letters with poison business cards attached are in inside mail blue envelopes to be delivered to government officials. Those envelopes were last seen in the trunk of Nadia Noorani's car."

"So, why don't we simply inform the mail service and have them intercept the envelopes?" Ken Farmingdale asked.

"A fair question. Three reasons. First, thousands of pieces of mail pass through that facility every day. Many simply have a name of addressee. It would be a monumental task to check every piece. And, two, they may not originate from Congressman Kane's office. Finally, the request would have to come from an official government agency. FBI Agent Peggy Fox couldn't get them to even investigate much assumed take some action," General Hughes pointed out.

"We've got to find that car and that evil bitch," Ron Clew concluded.

They started at Nadia's apartment at 8421 Broad Street in McLean, Virginia. Her silver 2015 Nissan Altima was not in the parking lot. Ron Clew remained in the parking area hidden from view as Ken Farmingdale went upstairs to apartment 21C. After knocking on the door, he assumed the apartment was empty. A failed attempt to pick the lock brought him back downstairs. With Ron left at the apartment building they proceeded to where the State Department was headquartered in the Harry S Truman Building. Nadia Noorani's car wasn't there.

Peggy Fox couldn't sit still. Nervous energy combined with a daunting feeling that there was something odd about Congressman Kane having an intern drive out to the Hawthorne Inn in Gaithersburg, Maryland to pick up the envelopes just to deliver them to Nadia Noorani. Why couldn't Nadia simply drive out there to pick them up? Unless he didn't want Nadia to know where he was. But that couldn't be right because he had numerous trysts with her at that Inn. Or did he? He must have. Why have an intern drive all the way out there? Then, like a surprise clap of thunder it hit her. She concluded it was the intern. "Yesterday, I picked up a package from Blake," Peggy Fox said out loud. "I'll be damned."

Congressman Blake Kane checked out of the Hawthorne Inn. All the pieces were now in place. Six-hundred little soldiers would be delivered Monday to those who stood in his way. Ten days later they would start dropping like flies. The first to drop would be Lacey Roper a sweet little intern who had outlived, literally, her usefulness. When he requested that she deliver the envelopes to Nadia he had carefully wiped one of the business cards on the side of the box.

There was no concern as he and Nadia had nothing to worry about because they both had been immunized. He laughed out loud when he realized Nadia might get a Poison Ivy rash from the box. "Oh well, the price of conquest," he said in the confines of his white BMW sedan. They had decided that it would be better if she placed the blue inside mail envelopes in outgoing mail at the Department of State as there generally were fewer correspondence generated and they were often semi-classified therefore not examined.

That nosy FBI agent came to mind. She knew something, but apparently not enough. It was sheer luck or good fortune that Miss. Roper had left with the envelopes an hour before Agent Fox's visit. What was clear was that she was investigating him or else wouldn't have known where to find him. That was a problem, but one that would go away after Monday. Kane realized, that if she had come prepared with a search warrant, she might have found the remaining 400 business cards in the trunk of his car under the spare tire. Another stroke of luck. He smiled as he decided that there would only be 399 cards left after Special Agent Peggy Fox opened her mail in the not-to-distant future.

CHAPTER 78

A silver 2015 Nissan Altima pulled into the parking lot at 8421 Broad Street in McLean, Virginia. Immediately, it gained Ron Clew's attention. He watched as a young woman got out and retrieved a box from the trunk. It was Nadia Noorani and she had the biological weapon. At a distance he followed her into the building. She entered the elevator followed by the retired Navy Seal. Ron pressed the 22nd floor remembering that she lived on the floor below. Nonchalantly, he asked her what floor she wanted. She told him 21 which he pressed. They then rode in silence.

When the elevator reached the 21st floor and the doors opened Nadia stepped out. It was then that Ron Clew struck. He was upon her in an instant, grabbed the box, and pulled her arm up behind her in a hammerlock. The surprised woman was subdued. Slowly, he guided her to her door at apartment 21C.

"Where are your keys?" Ron barked.

"In my purse," Nadia replied in a pained voice. She then pleaded, "Please, be careful with that box. You don't know what you have in your hand."

"Wrong. I do know," Ron stated as he slammed her down onto the rug with one arm. With his knee on her back Ron was able to remove the keys from her purse and open the door. He then pulled her inside and forced her down onto the couch. She sat without resisting.

"You move and it will be the last thing that you do," he warned. Sarcastically, he asked, "Why don't you take off your gloves." He was referring to her white gloves.

Nadia did not respond.

While watching her closely, Ron Clew called General Hughes. "General, I'm at Noorani's apartment. I have the box and the traitor. Roger that." He hung up. Then he addressed Nadia Noorani, "You just sit there and be good."

Nadia spoke in a soft voice, "You said that you know what is in the box."

"I do."

"Then you know how dangerous it is."

"That I also know."

"Then you must let me make a telephone call."

"Forget it."

"Please, understand, I work for the Company. Do you know what that is?"

"Yes, the CIA."

"Exactly. I'm an operative that was embedded in the Department of State to uncover this biological assault on America. It originated in France but we didn't have any way of knowing what it was or how it would be implemented. That is until I discovered the real traitor. It is Connecticut Congressman Blake Kane. I gained his confidence and got him to give me the poison letters to mail. He believes I am with him." Nadia paused, then told Ron, "If you let me make a call my story can be corroborated." She smiled, "We're on the same side."

"We'll wait."

"You don't understand. There are 600 letters in that box, but there were 1,000 business cards printed and treated with the toxic solution. We have to get our hands on those other 400 cards."

"And, you know where they are?"

"I know who has them. We have to get to him before he has time to hide them. One call is all I ask. You can listen in. I'll make in on speakerphone."

"Who do you wish to call?"

"The Deputy Director of the National Clandestine Service Counterterrorist Center at the Company. He will identify me and confirm my assignment." She looked directly at Ron and added, "You can make the call. Use your phone."

"What's the number?"

Nadia provided the telephone number and Ron Clew dialed it. When the connection was made the room exploded around him. Nadia, knowing what would happen, had ducked down on the couch thus avoiding being hit by a barrage of ball bearings. Ron Clew wasn't as fortunate. Steel balls penetrated his body in various places. None were lethal blows, however, a number of them struck him in the head momentarily causing him to black out. The big man dropped to the floor. It was adequate time for Nadia Narooni to jump from the couch, move to a desk, and retrieve a Kahr PM40 40 caliber pistol. As Ron Clew struggled to regain his senses Nadia fired three shots into the intruder.

When General Hughes, Jarvis Demoye, and Ken Farmingdale

arrived they found the body of retired Navy Seal Master Chief Petty Officer Ronald Clew.

"They are on to us, my love," Nadia Noorani told Congressman Blake Kane when he answered his telephone. "The plan cannot be executed. We must leave."

"What? Are you sure? Where are the letters?"

"I have them, but they cannot get delivered as planned."

"What should we do?" After a moment, Blake Kane said, "Wait, without the letters they can prove nothing. If we hide them there are only rumors, hearsay. When the dust settles, they can be mailed."

"I must leave."

"You can't be implicated."

"A man entered my apartment. He knew of the plan. I shot him. I must leave the country."

"If he was an intruder it was self-defense."

"Don't you understand, he knew about the plan. That means others know, as well. No, my love, the only answer is for me to disappear."

"Where are you?"

"I left as quickly as possible. At first, I feared there were others around. I didn't see anyone and was careful to not be followed. I drove to Falls Church and pulled into this strip mall."

"We need to meet," Blake Kane stated. "I'll take the letters and hide them. Then I'll find a way to get you out of the country."

Peggy Fox saw the caller ID and answered her phone, "General, to what do I owe this honor?"

General Hughes provided a quick rundown of events and the fact that the letters were once more unaccounted for. He also told of the loss of Ron Clew and inquired as to whether or not she had experience with the type of bug they had placed in Nadia Noorani's car.

"I can make some calls to trusted friends to get their advice. I'm sorry to hear about your man."

"We all knew the risks when we signed on. For now, we need to find Noorani before she goes underground."

"We've got a signal," Jarvis Demoye said from the other room.

"Hold on we have Noorani's car," General Hughes said as he joined the others.

A muffled voice could be heard. It was a woman's voice. "I will meet you, my love, but you should leave the materials with me. If they suspect anything, you can't be caught with incriminating evidence." A pause while a distant voice on a telephone was detected but not understood. Then Nadia's response, "I will meet you. Yes." The call ended.

"I didn't hear where they plan to meet. Did you?" Jarvis asked.

"It was muffled, but we know she is in Falls Church," Ken Farmingdale observed.

"It might as well be Hong Kong without more accurate coordinates," General Hughes complained. A fist landed with a heavy thud on the countertop.

The crackle of interference gained their attention. Then relatively clearly Nadia Noorani's voice was heard, "Yes, my love, I am here." Distant voice. "A private airplane? Out of where?" Distant voice. "Leesburg Municipal Airport—Godfrey Field. I am not familiar with it." Distant voice. "Yes, I can find it." Distant voice. "Sunchaser Aviation, Jack Leeds, I've got it."

Ken Farmingdale, upon hearing the airport name stated, "I know Leeesburg, designation JYO. It was built in 1963 to accommodate Arthur Godfrey's private DC-3. He was a well-known radio personality. It has one asphalt paved runway designated 17/35 which measures 5,500 by 100 feet. Not much there but hangers and a few private business offices. Back in 2011 the FAA funded an ILS installation making it operational in all types of weather. There is one thing, though, it's in the Special Flight Rules Area due to its location near Washington, DC." He turned to General Hughes and said, "If she gets on an aircraft there she can go anywhere."

General Hughes returned to his phone and told Peggy Fox what they had heard. Together, they agreed that there wasn't time to attempt to get the reluctant FBI involved. In addition, local law enforcement would question why they were requested to stop a private flight without a court order. Finally, of greatest importance, was finding both the 600 letters and remaining 400 business cards. Without confirming that Nadia Noorani had them the biological threat would remain.

CHAPTER 79

The smell of jet fuel filled the air. A lone twin-engine jet aircraft, Cessna Citation CJ2, stood ready for takeoff. On its tail was the logo of Sunchaser Aviation. Below the aircraft, Jack Leeds, the captain, finished his pre-flight inspection and waited for a special anonymous passenger.

Ten minutes later a silver 2015 Nissan Altima pulled into the parking lot and a young woman hastily climbed out of the vehicle. She carried a purse and large canvas bag, no other luggage.

"Jack Leeds?" Nadia Noorani asked.

"You got him."

"Do you know who I am?"

"No, and I don't want to know," he answered as he led her onto the aircraft. "Let me assure you I've flown 'special flights' before. I ask no questions except where to. In this case I was given some latitude. Everything is ready for takeoff." He closed the door and secured it. "Feel free to sit anywhere."

Nadia looked at the six leather upholstered seats that appeared highly comfortable. She turned and asked, "Do you mind if I sit upfront?"

"Not at all. Welcome the company," the pilot replied in a friendly and welcoming tone. "You can stow your gear in there." Jack pointed at a wood cabinet in the front of the passenger cabin. Nadia placed the canvas bag in the cabinet. As she did it revealed a box with blue envelopes and another box of the size that would carry business cards. The pilot secured the cabinet.

They climbed into the cockpit seats and the pilot made a call on the radio requesting clearance for takeoff. Nadia nervously looked out the window for any sign of unwelcome persons who might be approaching.

"I should tell you the flight plan shows this as a short hop to Providence, Rhode Island."

"Providence?" Nadia asked with a hint of surprise and concern in her voice.

"Don't worry, I'm going to get you where you want to go. It will just require a little finesse. This aircraft is certified for a single pilot. However, FAA regulations require two pilots on overseas flights. We wouldn't get clearance if I told the truth. A Providence flight plan allows us to fly with a single pilot over the edge of ocean. At the appropriate time, over international waters, I'll change course for St Johns, Newfoundland."

"St. Johns?"

"This is a fine aircraft, but she's not capable of a cross-Atlantic flight without refueling. On short notice I made arrangements to refuel at St. Johns—no questions asked. Then we fly to Horta International Airport in the Azores. There we will be asked questions. Do you have your passport?"

"I have diplomatic credentials."

"Perfect."

Somewhat relieved as the aircraft taxied to the end of the runway and received clearance to take off, Nadia said, "I really appreciate your assistance on this matter."

"Don't mention it." Captain Leeds throttled up and the Cessna Citation CJ2 began a smooth run down the runway and lifted off into a late afternoon sky.

"Agent Fox, I'm getting a little tired of your harassment," Congressman Blake Kane said when he found her at his residence.

"I need the blue envelopes and remaining business cards," Peggy Fox stated in her most formal FBI voice. She knew there was no longer any time to be coy.

"Don't know what you are talking about. But, rest assured, Monday morning I'll be having a long conversation with your superiors."

Please, open your trunk," she ordered ignoring the threat.

"Do you have a search warrant?" Kane smiled, then quickly added, "Oh, what the heck, I'll humor you. After all you'll only get to play detective for a few more days." He opened the trunk of his BMW. Inside there was nothing.

As the Cessna Citation CJ2 disappeared into the clouds, General Hughes said, "He wasn't supposed to take off." He turned to Sunchaser Aviation pilot Jack Leeds and asked, "Was that plane fueled?"

"To the brim. Ready to go." The pilot who had been detained at gunpoint looked at General Hughes and Jarvis Demoye and said, "Piracy of an aircraft is a federal offense. You're looking at long jail time."

"Aiding and abetting a murderer and terrorist will get you time of your own along with us."

The pilot was taken aback. Ultimately, he said, "Well, someone stole the aircraft."

At that moment the radio crackled and Ken Farmingdale's voice said, "Sunchaser flight 211, to Providence, Rhode Island confirming visual. Some cloud cover. Should break through at 1,000 feet. All systems check. Final transmission. Out."

General Hughes looked at Jarvis Demoye and said, "He has visual confirmation of the 1,000 cards."

The flight headed northwest until clear of the Special Flight Rules Area around Washington DC then turned east. Nadia Noorani became more relaxed as she realized that not only had she escaped but did so with the biological weapon. When they met briefly, she had assured Connecticut Congressman Blake Kane that Hidden Cobra could be executed at a later date. He gave her the packages to avoid being caught with incriminating evidence and smiled when she said, "Be patient, my love, our castle on the hill still awaits."

Ken Farmingdale at the controls of the Cessna Citation CJ2 checked various gauges and the heading. The aircraft climbed to 20,000 feet and traveled at 352 knots due east. Nadia commented at how peaceful it was high in the air.

"As long as I've flown, I've never lost that feeling of absolute freedom when in the sky," Ken Farmingdale, aka Jack Leeds, stated. "I don't know if it's seeing the vastness of the universe, or the relaxing quiet, or just getting away from people. Whatever, I find myself feeling more alive when above the clouds."

Little else was said as they cruised over the Atlantic Ocean. As evening fell the Sunchaser Cessna continued its due east course over dark waves. Finally, Nadia was compelled to ask, "Shouldn't we be near St. Johns, by now?"

"Oh, we would have landed at St. Johns long ago," Ken replied.

"What do you mean?" Nadia asked both confused and alarmed.

"I decided on a different destination."

"What destination. What are you talking about?"

"It's out there," Ken pointed into the deepening dark blue sky.

"What's out there?" Nadia bellowed.

"Satan's Shadow," he looked at the fuel gauge which was near empty. "Together, Nadia Noorani, you and I are going to pass through the gates of hell."

CHAPTER 80

General Hughes looked into the mirror in his bathroom. An obviously older man returned his gaze. Beyond that visage, he saw Adam Hayes with his smartass smile, Ron Clew holding a bottle of spring water, and Ken Farmingdale wearing cowboy boots. Three souls waiting to be judged by the Almighty for deeds done in the name of Satan. Fallen angels was the only term that came to mind.

The retired Marine General couldn't help but wonder if what they did and what they achieved was worth the price. Innocent lives were sacrificed while magnificent warriors were dragged into unspeakable depths and were ultimately lost. Maxwell Hughes thoughts turned to Jacob Marley, a character in the movie a *Christmas Carol,* lamenting, "I wear the chains I forged in life . . ."

General Hughes' cellphone chimed and he answered, "Speak."

"Let's chat," Dave said.

"You're at the end of my driveway," General Hughes stated, rather than asked.

"Roger that."

Inside the familiar dark green Cadillac Escalade two men rode in silence. Neither was ready to speak, while both had an overwhelming desire to talk. When events occur in rapid succession decisions have to be made quickly. Then when the event is over a distinct feeling of fatigue is experienced by those who spent all their physical, intellectual, and emotional vigor in pursuit of a goal.

"The loss of Nadia Noorani broke an important chain," Dave complained.

"The loss of Major Kenneth Farmingdale means a great deal more to me than that little tart," General Hughes spat.

"True," Dave agreed. "It seems I have an uncanny ability to be insensitive. Don't let my comment make you think that I don't care about three admirable men. I care deeply. Yet, in my warped surrealistic world I'm very much like some obsessive-compulsive head-case who can only focus on one all-encompassing thing. My fetish is identifying, capturing, eliminating, or otherwise thwarting the efforts of those who wish to do us harm. Honestly,

General, those men mean a lot to me, but I must admit there is also a sense of loss in not having the opportunity to get my hands on Nadia Noorani. Her contacts, involvement in other events, knowledge of plots, list of sleeper cells, and more are invaluable resources that are forever gone."

"I understand," General Hughes said in a friendlier voice. "Ken shouldn't have taken off and shouldn't have taken her with him on his flight from a tortured mind." Headlights illuminated General Hughes' face as he confessed, "We all have tortured minds."

"We each fight in our own way and each handle the emotional and psychological blows in our own way. Me, I write music. Unfortunately, it's usually in a minor key which doesn't cheer one up."

"I read," Maxwell Hughes admitted. "Mainly biographies. The things people did and challenges they faced and victories they won are truly fascinating. In *Harpo Speaks* I witnessed what the world the Marx brothers grew up in was like in the beginning of the twentieth century. They had hardships and all had their own crosses to bear."

Dave remarked, "The average everyday citizen who complains because his cappuccino wasn't made correctly goes about his life thinking he has it rough. Money is tight, house needs repairs, kids want this and that, his wife nags him, and his favorite team lost. He has no concept of the toll keeping the wolves from his front door takes on those who stand guard. We are human. At least, we were human at one time. Slowly, we become machines."

What followed was a prolonged period of silence.

Dave then asked, "Is it time to conclude operations?"

"Yes. Today. Tonight," General Hughes answered. "However, when the sun rises tomorrow mad-driven hate will still be there. The fight goes on, my friend. So, oil your gears. There are countless wolves approaching."

Dave laughed.

General Hughes added, "Our numbers are depleted so we will have to recruit some new souls to damn."

"I have some names for consideration."

"Leave Michael O'Neal out. Let one warrior find peace. He earned it." Hughes then said softly, "Foal watching."

Dave then asked, "Maxwell, can I buy you a drink?"

Over dinner, General Hughes gave Special Agent Peggy Fox his final report. "Two good men died so that hundreds, maybe thousands could live. They did what had to be done because they were the sum and substance of true warriors. Without hesitation they did their job. I couldn't be more proud of those men or more remorseful at their loss. There's no evidence of what almost was inflicted upon our government and way of life. Therefore, no citations, medals, brass bands, or honors will be bestowed upon these heroes. Only one old General will stand alone at Arlington and salute two who were finer than he."

"It's like a dream," Peggy admitted. You wake up and ask yourself, 'What just happened?' I believe the threat was real but can't prove it to the Bureau or to myself." She paused and added, "I'd be proud to stand beside you at Arlington."

General Hughes nodded. They went back to their dinners in silence. Then slowly General Hughes pushed the dragon, stars, and saber challenge coin across the table until it was in front of Agent Fox, "They made no excuses for their actions and neither do I. Only never forget their motives were pure. We live in an increasingly dangerous world that in the future will require making more deals with the devil. Do with that what you may, Agent Fox."

"It's Peggy Fox, I resigned from the FBI. As far as I'm concerned that investigation is closed."

"I see," General Hughes said considering the woman across the table from him.

Peggy said, "Before I left, I looked at a number of statistics on international terrorist activity and found that it is significantly lower. In fact, there are increasing numbers of civilians who are fighting back. After a terrorist stabbed two people in Stuttgart, a crowd burned down his family's store. In London, a supposed terrorist was left beaten and tied up in front of a police station with a note about his planned attack. There are many other examples. Without question, it's becoming a lot less healthy to be a terrorist."

"You know," Maxwell Hughes said as he buttered a piece of bread, "there is more of that poison varnish somewhere in France. And, the monsters who created Hidden Cobra are still out there. It's going to take a tremendous amount of investigating to find that stuff and bring the perpetrators to justice." He looked into her eyes and added, "Or, eliminate the threat. That unseen group known as Satan's Shadow may still be out there. Knowing that, I sleep better at night."

Peggy Fox looked at General Maxwell Hughes and saw a soldier standing alone on a hill facing the onslaught of vicious hordes. He was unmoving and unafraid. In spite of what she believed he did he was indeed a man of honor. She picked up the challenge coin and slipped it into her purse.

A small article appeared in the Washington Post that covered the sad news of Congressman Blake Kane passing away. It stated that he died of complications from pneumonia.

About The Author

Kenneth J Munkens

Kenneth J Munkens is a storyteller with a remarkably creative mind that never seems to rest. There is nothing common about his work. Known for his complex stories populated with multi-dimensional characters he takes readers on an emotional and intellectual journey whose destination is unpredictable.

Enter the world that Munkens creates at your own risk. His stories will make you laugh, cry, smile, wonder, and care. Empathy serves him well as he understands the wide range of emotions involved in human relationships. His humor will sneak up on you while your heart will be stung by a depth of emotion so rare these days.

Character development is an art perfected by this author. He creates real human beings that stay with you long after you finish reading. Readers often state that they feel as though they know the characters as well as they know their friends and relatives. Many long for a sequel to continue to follow the lives of characters with whom they have become attached.

Born in the Bronx, congenital eye problems and loss of his mother at a young age shaped Munkens' character giving him the strength to face the real world head on with a non-yielding spirit. Married over forty years with two grown daughters, he values family, his enthusiasm is contagious, sense of humor notorious, and fascination with those strange creatures called human beings limitless.

Other Works by Kenneth J Munkens

Downtown Dreams

Black Ice

Rude Awakening in 1969

2076AD

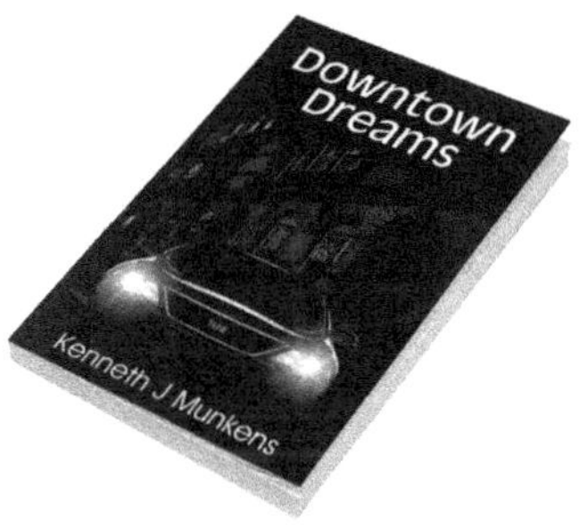

Downtown Dreams

438 pages

Downtown Dreams takes you on a remarkable journey into the world of advertising. Meet the creative minds and emotional souls of those who practice the fine art of persuasion—adpeople, contradictions wrapped up in a world of creativity, feeding on challenge, ignoring stress, reaching for the stars, and ultimately finding each other.

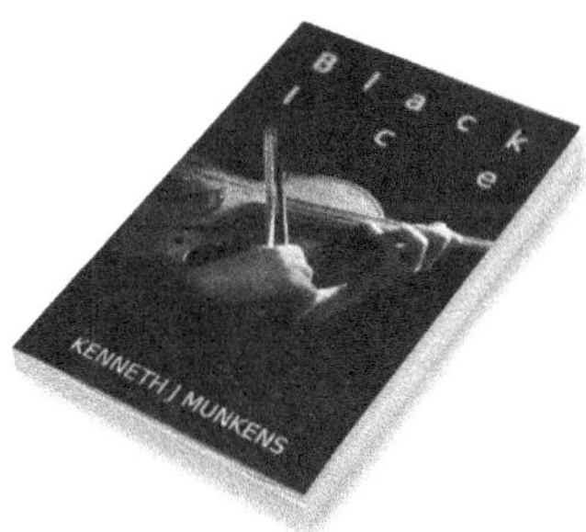

Black Ice

212 pages

A patch of black ice sets in motion life-changing events as a father and daughter search for meaning in a world turned upside down. Music, the universal language, relates the haunting story of a young girl with a violin and a secret. Sometimes as complex as a symphony or simple as a child's tune, her story is one of hope disappointment, passion, courage, and the power of the human spirit. Just as black ice can sneak up on you, words in this tale will unexpectedly touch your heart and long be remembered.

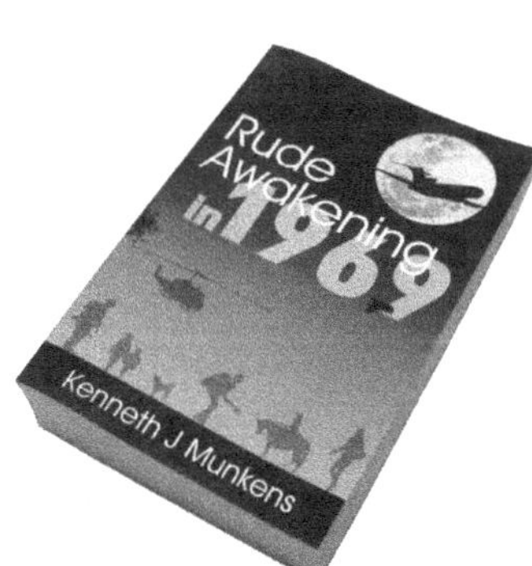

Rude Awakening in 1969

818 pages

1969 was a year unlike any other. In fact, if a writer fashioned together the events of that year into a novel it would have come across as totally unbelievable. However, what took place was real and the world changed as a result. *Rude Awakening in 1969* is an epic adventure with this remarkable year as the backdrop. The tale begins in 1963 with a disaster at sea that portends future events. As 1969 unfolds, a malicious wide-reaching peril comes into focus and the evil men, and women, are capable of demonstrated. Little by little the picture develops. Surprise, unanticipated turns of events, and misdirection are all devices used to keep the story interesting, realistic, and impactful. Much like in life, you'll find out when you get there without any hints or previews. In the end, you will have experienced 1969 as if you were there and shared the stage with characters you come to personally know and remember.

www.ingramcontent.com/pod-product-compliance
Lightning Source LLC
Chambersburg PA
CBHW070846280626
47161CB00017B/2438

* 9 7 8 0 9 6 6 3 9 5 1 5 0 *